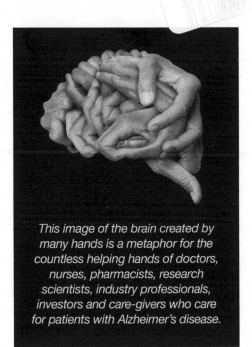

This image of the brain created by many hands is a metaphor for the countless helping hands of doctors, nurses, pharmacists, research scientists, industry professionals, investors and care-givers who care for patients with Alzheimer's disease.

Interior design by BookCreate
Seattle, Washington USA

Printed in USA

ISBN 978-0-9993811-1-3

About the Cover

*This image is a network of neurons in the brain (blue)
and beta-amyloid plaques (gold) in a patient with
Alzheimer's disease. These plaques are currently
believed to be an important cause or marker of
the disease.*

Race for the Mind

A NOVEL

Daniel Gerard Welch

DEDICATION

I dedicate *Race for the Mind* to three special women in my life.
My mother, Anna Welch, my late mother-in-law Mary Durso
and last but in no event least, my wife Marie Welch.
Each gave me lasting gifts that collectively enabled me
to write this book. I am forever grateful to them.

Acetylsalicylic acid (Aspirin)

1

Four minutes into the landing procedure flight commander Neil Armstrong tensely informed Apollo 11 Mission Control in Houston that his computer screen displayed a four-digit error code: "1202."

"Rostov, what the hell is that code?" the flight director barked, his eyes wild with urgency.

Dr. Darya Rostov led the applied mathematics department at NASA. Her job was to lead and coordinate the teams developing the mathematical solutions to an endless procession of novel problems of space flight and developing NASA's then-primitive computer capabilities. Her mission was to safely deliver astronauts to and from the moon.

"Give us a reading on that program alarm," Armstrong ordered Houston. He sounded annoyed but incredibly cool considering the life and death circumstances he faced. His landing module Eagle, a small and flimsy machine, sped just above the moon's surface 240,000 miles from earth. The on-board computer meant to guide his landing in the next few minutes had completely frozen and none of the computer technicians knew what the error code meant.

Red-faced, the flight director spewed "Damn it Rostov! What does code 1202 mean? . . . If we can't figure it out, our protocol says we abort!"

She replied like a machine gun in her unmistakably Russian accent,

"The computer is over-burdened and may want to re-boot itself. The message is intermittent so the computer isn't quitting yet."

She quickly thought. *Speed and trajectory are on plan, moon gravity readings as expected.*

"Abort or go Rostov?" hissed the flight director.

All eyes in the now deathly-quiet control room were on Rostov. She paused, took a deep breath...

"GO!" she said finally.

The flight director looked for a nanosecond into Rostov's eyes and found conviction.

"Eagle, we are go on that computer," relayed the director.

The Eagle screamed 400 feet above the surface of the moon, while Aldrin and Armstrong searched for a flat place to land.

Moments later, hearts leapt into throats as another computer error code, this one "1201" appeared simultaneously on the computer screens of Eagle and Houston. In one instant, all eyes in the control room moved to Rostov. The pressure was intense.

Darya's pulse raced. The entire mission now in her hands, she nodded and shouted as confidently as her nerves would allow . . . "GO!"

"Damn it!" the director said under his breath, praying that she was right . . . "Eagle, we are go on that alarm."

Then a heavy, sweaty, heart-pounding anticipation filled the control room. Communication with Eagle was now hit-or-miss and Houston hadn't heard from Eagle in a minute that felt like eternity.

The staff in Houston exchanged nervous, near-panicked glances all through this excruciating silence.

Minds raced: *Are the astronauts dealing with a new crisis? Too frantic to communicate? Had they crashed?*

After another 30 seconds of silent agony a weak, high-pitched "beep" crackled over the speaker system heralding a coming transmission:

"Houston, Tranquility Base here ... the Eagle has landed," Armstrong reported matter-of-factly.

Shaking visibly, Dr. Rostov sat down in her chair as Houston mission control erupted with joy, relief, pride and awe. She scanned the room and smiled as she recalled the five years she had worked with most of the people in this room. She had fought with them, laughed with them, worked all night and day with them and helped them through their biggest fears and toughest challenges.

She recalled that their biggest challenge was the time they had to solve a mind-numbingly difficult mathematical problem that had stumped mathematicians for centuries, the "three body problem." In order to determine the flight path that Apollo 11 would follow during its journey from Florida to the moon and back to earth, her team had to predict the future positions of three moving bodies: earth, moon and the spacecraft, while taking into account the influence of their gravity, speeds, weights and starting positions. Dr. Rostov and her team not only solved this centuries-old problem but then programmed the experimental IBM computers with their solution to get Apollo 11 to and from the moon.

Her late father would have been so proud of his Darya. She looked up to heaven, smiling broadly with tears in her eyes,

"We did it, Papa."

2

"I'll prove the bastards wrong!" Jack grunted through clenched teeth.

"Pardon, Monsieur?" said the cab driver, glancing into the rearview.

"Je suis désolée, Monsieur," Jack said, embarrassed by his outburst.

"Pas de problème." replied the cabbie, shrugging his shoulders and returning his focus to the streets ahead.

Jack sank an inch or two lower in the seat and stared through the steamed window. He found himself eye to eye with his own brooding reflection as the cab driver whisked him to Paris-Charles deGalle airport.

Jack Callahan had just been promoted to be the head of the European division of Covington Pharmaceuticals, the fifth-largest pharmaceutical company in the world.

His last assignment, as president of the U.K. subsidiary of Covington, had one-tenth the sales and less than a tenth of the personnel of his new assignment. He heard that some thought this job was too much for him, and was too soon. Many wanted his job.

Some said that Jack would prove the well-established Peter Principle in business, the idea that a manager rises until he reaches the position that finally exposes his incompetence at which point he is hurled brutally back down the ladder or off of it entirely.

Jack dwelled on the chatter he had heard about himself as he watched the shimmering city whiz by outside the cab's window. Jealousy, no doubt, he reassured himself, and perhaps some anti-American bias, he mused.

The cab sped along at a normal Paris city velocity, which is twice the speed of sanity and the cabbie veered, tires screeching, onto the Champs Elysees toward the Arc de Triomphe.

Jack listened to the tires moving over the old cobblestones, the sound from the tires varying in pitch with the speed of the car, humming out the sound of centuries coming together. An ardent student of history, Jack appreciated all the stories of this historic avenue.

He reflected that the cab carried him up the same thoroughfare on which Napoleon marched his troops; the same route along which the occupying Germans paraded into Paris and the liberating Allies later rode on to receive a hero's welcome.

The architecture and stores along the Champs were now a mélange of styles and nationalities, an inconvenience for Paris considering its valiant but failed attempts to preserve its wonderful culture in all things.

Napoleon, the man whose passion for architectural order in his city even dictated the maximum heights of buildings, would be insane with rage at the current disorder of the Champs Elysees, in which Fouquet's, the century-old icon of French cuisine, stood alongside such travesties as McDonald's, Hard Rock Café, pizza parlors, Belgian moules-frites shops, and multi-national specialty stores. This street, more than any in Paris spoke in one breath of France's glory years, its subsequent military defeats and the more enduring surrender to the forces of international commercial warfare and cultural dilution.

Jack could see the Arc de Triomphe looming ahead, a great white whale of a monument that seemed impervious to the gloom of this rainy morning. Jack recalled that Napoleon had erected it as a memorial to the French Grand Army and that later it became the site of the Tomb of France's Unknown Soldier of WW I. The taxi moved towards the Etoile, a star formed by the eight streets feeding into the great place on which the Arc de Triomphe stood. Jack never tired of admiring the Arc, and he decided to focus on that now – instead of the harrowing swirl of traffic through which his driver navigated.

At CDG, Jack paid the cabbie, grabbed his bag and walked into the Air France terminal. Less than two hours later he found himself on the plane that would carry him to JFK for his connecting flight to Las Vegas.

3

From the balcony of his 30th floor New York apartment, Shah finally spotted Mercury, his peregrine falcon, through the lens of his binoculars. It had been more than two hours since Shah had raised his forearm and launched the bird; now it returned on its usual post-hunt route. Shah strained his eyes to see what Mercury had in its talons, but he couldn't make it out. The raptor disappeared from sight before making his dive to Shah's arm.

As Mercury reappeared and began his descent home, Shah frowned. When the bird alighted on Shah's forearm with an impressive fanning of wings and feathers, Shah confirmed that for the third time in as many days, the falcon had returned without a kill.

"Mercury, of what use is a predator that can't kill?" he growled to the bird through clenched teeth, "To survive, we must hunt and kill. The alternative is to starve or be eaten."

Shah slowly, deliberately slipped the leather tether through the ring on his falcon's legs as usual, securing him to his gloved hand. With his free hand, he firmly grasped Mercury's muscular body, pinning its wings to its torso.

With cold, emotionless and distant eyes, Shah plunged the impotent hunter into a bucket of water he had placed there if he needed it today. After fifteen seconds of twitching and thrashing, Mercury went still. Shah took the lifeless bird from the bucket and tossed it in the trash can with as much emotion as if he were disposing a wet newspaper.

"Kill or be killed," he growled as he placed the lid on the trash can and gazed out over the city.

. . . Now standing on the balcony of a similar high-rise building, this one his Las Vegas hotel, Dr. Nathaniel Shah, Executive Vice President of Research & Development for BPL, British Pharmaceuticals Limited, the world's largest pharmaceutical company, surveyed the madness that is this city. A third-generation Anglo-Indian, whose family in Mumbai had strong and deep financial and political ties to Britain since the 1800's. Shah's position at BPL allowed him to afford the finer things in life, but they came with an annoying cost; his responsibilities to his boss and his board.

Right before leaving for Las Vegas, Shah had presented his annual budget to the BPL Board. A six billion-dollar R&D budget is a serious matter, one that BPL reviewed regularly and with excruciating detail.

He thought the presentation had gone well, but explaining his programs to a bunch of mostly non-scientists who hadn't the faintest comprehension of what they were being told, had become tiresome.

To Shah, his yearly budget presentation became a ritual akin to a prostate exam: an unpleasant, inconvenient but necessary probing. On the other hand, with his great track record for delivering innovative drugs to market, the BPL board treated him like a king. *As it should be*, Shah thought.

Shah's suite came with a personal butler service, something Shah intended to take advantage of over the next few days. The suite was appointed with a massive living room that offered a view of The Strip, which when illuminated at night, even Shah had to admit was impressive in its own garish way. But the pièce de résistance was the bathroom suite, equipped with his and her showers, a massive bathtub, an exercise room, and a room-sized closet. What a shame that Gloria couldn't join him, Shah thought . . . We could've had some wild sex in this hedonistic den.

A knock on the door interrupted his fantasy. His butler, Fitzgerald, presented himself with the bellman in tow.

"Good evening, Dr. Shah," said Fitzgerald. "I am here to unpack for you. Should I draw you a bath, Sir?"

"No thank you, Fitzgerald," replied Shah in his aristocratic English. "I'll shower and retire shortly. You can show yourself out when you've unpacked my things."

Fitzgerald nodded, bowed and went about his work efficiently and quickly, leaving after 10 minutes. Hearing the door close, Shah mused that the Americans were catching on to fine living – but oh, however slowly.

4

Jack Callahan had travelled so often over so many years that he had built up an emotional immunity from its punishment. He arrived in Las Vegas in the late afternoon and had only a faint recollection of the countless faces, brief exchanges, and small transactions he had made between Paris and his room here in Las Vegas. Jack had put himself into the semi-comatose state that protected him like an antibody from the physical and emotional pain of chronic travel.

Jack knew that there was both an art and a science to manage jet lag. Jack had learned long ago to drink as much water as he could hold to avoid dehydration, the most destructive force on the long distance traveler. That he had done. His body still functioned on Paris time, however, nine hours ahead of Las Vegas, so unless he wanted to wake up at one o'clock in the morning local time tomorrow and then fall asleep in his soup at dinner tomorrow night, he would have to remain awake until a normal local bedtime tonight.

After several hours of fighting the tide of sleep that relentlessly tried to overtake him, Jack decided to go to the casino to stay awake.

There are no clocks in Vegas casinos. Of course. Why remind people that it's late and they're losing money? Neither are there windows to break the spell with a rising or setting sun. It's just all gambling, all the time.

Jack liked blackjack but given his conservative nature he'd found a scarce $10-per-hand table and took his seat. Every blackjack table has its own personality. Some are friendly and fun loving, while others are deadly serious. One usually learned during the first hand which type of table one got.

Drawing a blackjack right off the bat, Jack exploded from his seat in excitement, his hands raised in triumph. His tablemates returned barely polite smiles that seemed to say, "Get on with it." The next few hands moved swiftly, Jack winning some, losing some. After a dozen hands he decided that he felt stifled at this table and would cruise the casino to find one with more life to it. He knew he'd likely lose his money but at least he wanted to have a little fun while losing.

Jack walked aimlessly within the casino, taking it all in. The casino attacked all of the senses without any subtlety. The slot machines hammered out an incessant xylophone-like drum roll, coins occasionally dropping into the trays of winners like a cymbal crash. Every color in the spectrum displayed itself somewhere here – on the machines, the casino chips, the various gaming tables, the cocktails, the dealers. The customers he saw came in every size, shape, color, and social class and their dress reflected it, from tuxedos to cowboy boots and jeans. The waitresses trotted around in their little outfits presenting real drinks and fake breasts to their customers. The mirrors on the walls and in the ceilings multiplied every sight many times over, intensifying the visual overload of the venue.

As he strolled through this surreal landscape, Jack thought about the gambling statistics he'd read on the web before leaving for Las Vegas. He had printed out the odds of winning at the various games – blackjack, craps, roulette, baccarat and the slots. Now, reviewing those discouraging unpromising numbers, he resolved to concentrate his efforts on blackjack, the best odds in the house. It suddenly occurred to him that as tough as the Vegas odds were, they were vastly more attractive than those he confronted every day at work. *Discovering new medicines and bringing them to market? That's REAL gambling. And we don't get free drinks from busty waitresses at the office,* he thought, amused with him-self as he made his way through the madness.

After a while he found a table with the kind of attitude he sought. He hadn't been in his seat for five seconds when self-named "Ragin' Cajun" warmly welcomed him, a neurologist from New Orleans, clearly buzzed by the Scotch in front of him and the many inside of him. The others were equally colorful and certainly friendly, if less revealing than the Cajun. "Ted" from Boston grunted hello. "I'm Lou – from Jersey," said the blond man beside Ted. "Margot from San Diego – hi!" was next. The last chair at a blackjack table is called "the anchor." This is the table's key position, because whoever sits there has to force the dealer when called for, needs to know the game and have nerves of steel. "Carlos," from Manila, occupied that seat, watching the game from behind mirrored sunglasses. Even though he was quiet, his calm and focus suited Jack just fine.

Jack placed his bet and the game continued as if he had been there all night. Cards flashed by, chips were rewarded and sacrificed. Only a card shuffle and the cutting of the cards broke the action. Jack noticed how serious a player became during the ritualistic cutting of the deck – *as if he or she were sacrificing a lamb at the holy altar of Ploutus, the god of wealth,* he thought. He sat next to the dealer in the first position right next to the "shoe," the dispenser used by the dealer to deal the several decks of cards used in the game.

As the night wore on, the fatigue took its toll on Jack's inhibitions. "Look at this new, full shoe," he said to his table mates. "It's like our life at birth. Just like with our genes, the cards are set before the game begins and they'll play a role in the outcome but they won't solely determine it. The shoe, like our lives is full of variables that we can't control...." Lou and Margot started to chuckle, in a kind way. The Cajun said, "Ah, yes, the gamble that is life...."

"That's right!" Jack said. "And the actions or inactions of virtual strangers" – he extended his arms to take in all present company – "have as much influence on the outcome as we do! A player joining or leaving the table immediately changes the cards everyone would have received had he stayed – just like a new relationship or job creates new possibilities for good or for bad! The dealer has no control and can make no decisions… like Father Time, he just keeps the game moving!"

"You gonna play or philosophize?" Carlos chirped, eyeing Jack from the other end of the table. Everyone laughed. Even Carlos allowed a slight smile. Jack looked at his watch. "Oh my God," he said, "I gotta get to bed!" The others begged him to stay – and he almost did, but he had finally regained his senses. He thanked them for the fun and tipped the dealer a few chips, and disappeared into the harlequin, buzzing crowd.

CH_3

HN O

OH

Acetaminophen (Tylenol®)

5

Despite staying up late last night at the casino, Jack awoke the next morning feeling surprisingly refreshed and greeted by a beautiful day; clear and sunny and so unlike Paris at this time of year that it made Jack eager to get outside. He dressed quickly and grabbed his convention materials to plan out his day.

The first thing he saw upon opening the meeting program was a large photograph of a handsome man being honored by the ANA at this convention for a distinguished career in neurological research – Dr. Nathaniel Shah. Jack studied the picture. He saw a man with jet black hair and golden brown skin. An aristocratic nose and the moustache beneath it was perfectly shaped and framed perfect white teeth. He reminded Jack of an Omar Sharif double but a little taller. Jack recalled that he and Shah had met, but for the life of him he couldn't say when or where. Along with his vague recollection Jack had an uncomfortable, sickening feeling about the man. It struck him as odd to have such a strong sensation provoked by a photo.

He made the short walk to the elevators and punched the down button. A moment later the elevator opened and presented Dr. Nathaniel Shah, looking just as striking in real life as he had looked in the picture in the convention brochure. Although alone, Shah's presence filled the elevator car. His olive skin seemed to glow, his exquisitely tailored Saville Row suit and expensive accessories whispered confidently of his money and taste.

Jack stepped in and immediately extended his hand. "I'm Jack Callahan, Covington Pharmaceuticals, Europe. Congratulations on the honor that the ANA will be bestowing on you at this meeting, Dr. Shah." "Oh," said Shah, caught off guard. Jack could tell that Shah enjoyed being recognized. But then who didn't. "Thank you….please tell me your name again?"

"Pompous jerk," thought Jack. *"He is playing the superiority game."* Jack repeated his name with some hidden annoyance and handed him a card while they continued some mostly one-sided small talk as the elevator made its various collections and deposits on its way to the lobby. As they exited, Shah asked Jack if he had a ride to the convention center. "No I don't." "Join me then, I have a car waiting for me." Jack couldn't know that he just been granted the equivalent of a Pope's audience; at least in Shah's eyes.

In the car, they discussed various industry issues and traded opinions on the merits, or lack thereof, of the recent business deals done between various companies. As they chatted and became more comfortable with each other, Jack expected Shah to invite him to call him Nathaniel. But that invitation never happened – it never even came close. What *did* happen was Jack's slow recollection of what disturbed him about this man when they had met for the first time; the eyes. They were coal black, with no color distinction between the iris and pupil and this blackness seemed to fill up the space of his visible eye balls. He recalled how these black onyxes locked with his own eyes with an unsettling and unrelenting intensity that seemed to penetrate into his soul, searching around in there for anything of interest – a weakness, a secret, something Shah could use to his benefit.

Shah's voice was as disarming as his eyes were unsettling, an octave higher than one would expect from his solid physical presence and it lilted as it moved through a sentence. Shah's accent was purely British; with the flawless diction and grammar that is a hallmark of a first-class education. *An impressive man*, Jack thought, as they pulled up to the convention center. *A solid businessman... for an American*, thought Shah.

Before stepping out of the car, Jack again shook Shah's hand. "Thanks for the lift, Dr. Shah, and best of luck at the meeting." Jack's playful side tempted him to call Shah "Nate," but he knew Shah may have spontaneously combusted had Jack made such a presumption. Still, the mental picture amused him; one that made Jack smile as he made his way up the escalator to the vast convention hall.

6

Looking up, Jean-Luc couldn't miss it. THE AMERICAN NEUROLOG- ICAL ASSOCIATION WELCOMES YOU TO THE ANNUAL SCIENTIF- IC CONVENTION. The massive welcome banner hung over the entrance to the cavernous convention hall.

Jean-Luc Dumas took his place in the slow, snaking line marked "Names A to E" leading to the convention Registration Desk. The registration line at the convention moved faster than Jean-Luc had expected, and soon he had checked in, received his convention program, picked up his name badge and collected his convention bag. The only thing he needed now was a big cup of hot, strong coffee. After filling the largest Styrofoam cup available, he spotted a free chair at a table where a man studied the convention program. Jean-Luc asked him if he could join him. "Of course, please," said the man. "Maybe you can help me make sense out of this schedule."

Jean-Luc put down his coffee and knapsack and extended his hand. "I'm Jean-Luc Dumas." "Jack Callahan, Covington Pharmaceuticals." "Ah, Covington Pharmaceuticals," said Jean-Luc. "I know quite a few people at that company. I have great respect for Covington." "That's good to hear," said Jack. "How do you know us?" "Well, until about a year ago I worked at the University of Laval, in Quebec as the head of Neurology. We did a lot of work with Covington in the area of neuropathic pain. In fact, in my last year there Covington was our largest grantor from industry."

"Oh yeah," said Jack, "I remember meeting your Research Fellow who coordinated all of your work with industry." Jack quickly ran through his mental files of the various projects his company had funded at Laval. "The pain program is exciting and the compound Laval is working on is particularly promising," he said. "But what *really* thrills me" – he leaned close to Jean-Luc – "is the program we collaborated on in Parkinson's." Jean-Luc's eyes lit up. "Ah yes! The team has an exciting hypothesis and is very dedicated. They hope to identify a lead experimental drug in a few years."

Jack raised his cup to Jean-Luc. "A votre santé my friend." "A *leur* santé," said Jean-Luc. "It's our Parkinson's patients who need it." Jean-Luc glanced at his watch. He had plenty of time. "How'd you get involved in the pharmaceutical industry, Jack?" "Well, I always loved the sciences and business. I couldn't decide, so I took a double major in biology and business at Loyola." "I *knew* I heard a Chicago accent!" said Jean-Luc, laughing. "I have lots of relatives in the area."

"That's really funny," said Jack. "*I* have relatives in the Montreal area – on my mother's side. We could be related!" They exchanged family names and origins for a few minutes and decided they probably weren't direct kin. "Well, anyway," Jean-Luc said, "French Canadian families were so large until very recently that we're undoubtedly related somehow, cousin." "Cousin," said Jack, raising his coffee cup.

"Anyway, I had two attractive job offers out of college; one from a laboratory supply company and the other from a small pharmaceutical company, Farmer Labs. I didn't want to sell test tubes for the rest of my life so I took the job with the drug company. I started as a sales rep in the Chicago area. A couple of years later, I was doing well in sales but tired of sitting in doctors' waiting rooms and waiting for something to happen to my career. I was just about to submit my resignation when the company promoted me and moved me to New York! My first promotion and living in the Big Apple – and I almost blew it by getting impatient!" "Impatience is not a helpful trait in our business," said Jean-Luc. "You got that right."

Jack quickly narrated the tale of his New York years and his rise through the ranks from Product Manager to Marketing Manager to Sales Director. "Then, three years ago, Covington bought Farmer Labs and offered me the U.K. general manager job in London." "Yeah, I recall that merger," said Jean-Luc. "That happened at the time I worked closely with the people at Covington. They were nervous that the merger would jeopardize the funding of their scientific project."

"That often happens, but it didn't in our case. Covington acquired Farmer to get *more* R&D projects. And after a few years in London, the company asked me to run the European business out of Paris. In fact, I just got that job." "Oh, Paris," Jean-Luc sighed. "What a city – but how can you stand those friggin' Frenchmen!" Jack chuckled. He'd heard this before. The challenges of being an American in France were well known – in fact, Jack was currently reading a hilarious book on the subject, with the wonderful title *French or Foe*. "I've just started living there," he said. "You got any advice?" Jean-Luc pretended to give it deep thought, then said, "Yes, I do. Have your scientists give you a Franco-genetic transfusion to make your DNA French." Jack chuckled. "Thanks, I'll have our gene therapy researchers at Covington start working on me right away. Maybe you can donate some of your Franco-DNA for the procedure! So how did a Quebecois like you end up in San Francisco?"

"Oh Jack, my story is far simpler than yours. I come from the area of Quebec called Trois-Rivieres, three rivers in English, where the St. Maurice River flows through three channels into the St. Lawrence. The region was a hotbed of separatists wanting Quebec to secede from Canada and I was a teenager when the separatist fever was hottest. I remember like it was yesterday, that day in July of '67 when Charles De Gaulle fueled the separatist fire by proclaiming from the balcony of his Montreal hotel, 'Vive le Quebec libre.' It still gives me goose bumps."

"The secession movement captivated me until I realized I couldn't make a living spewing propaganda. So I went back to school and decided if I couldn't make my countrymen free of English culture, I'd try to make them free of disease and pain!" "You're a romantic, Jean-Luc." "Yes, my friend, I am passionate. It's in my genes." "How'd you choose neurology?" "I didn't, it chose me. You see, along with my passion, my genes bring a lot of degenerative neurological disease to my family. Nearly all of my elderly relatives have some sort of neurological disease, and my family has been the subject of several studies concerning the contribution of genetics on degenerative neurological problems. Ironically, it's how I funded my education. My family members put in a common fund, the money that the various researchers gave them for their cooperation with their research and this funded my medical studies. My family would fund the expenses for me to become a doctor to try to prevent the next generations of the Dumas clan from getting sick."

"Wow, Jean-Luc. What an inspiring story. Mine seems so... 'mercenary' in comparison." "Yes, and I have to admit that my story works quite well with the ladies!" He gave Jack a mischievous wink and devilish smile. "So, I made my way up the academic ladder at Laval University to become the head of the department, as you know."

As Jean-Luc spoke, Jack observed him. Tall, probably about 6'3, as Jack recalled seeing him approach his table, slim but not thin. His hair had been blonde in its day but was now a mix of blonde and white with the start of some thinning at the forehead. He wore his hair combed straight back, making him look quite dashing. His chiseled features were model-like, Jack thought. His nose long and thin, mouth full and showing teeth like piano keys – thick, straight and white. His eyes were light blue and clear, looking much younger than what Jack suspected was a man in his early-50s. He dressed classically and everything about his attire was just so – shoes clean and shined, trousers crisp and well-tailored, shirt and tie impeccably matched to his suit coat. A silk handkerchief stuffed in his jacket pocket finished the elegant look.

"Then after years of scrounging around the Canadian government for research funds, a venture capitalist called me and asked me to consider joining a small team of top-notch scientists to help build a company dedicated to degenerative neurological diseases. I saw my chance to do what I lived to do. So a few months ago I agreed to move to San Francisco and become part of this start-up company. You should visit my lab the next time you're in San Francisco. We're doing some exciting things in neurological disease there. Maybe we could collaborate again."

Jean-Luc continued talking about his new company for a few more minutes before Jack looked at his watch. "Oh, Jean-Luc, I gotta catch the plenary session on multiple sclerosis – my company is working in the field." He gathered up his things and stuck out his hand. "Really great meeting you today. See you around, I hope." "Me too, Jack. It was a pleasure." They wished each other good luck and parted ways. Neither expected to lay eyes on the other ever again.

7

The Recognition Award was bestowed upon Dr. Shah at a luncheon for those who reserved in advance. Jack's secretary assumed he'd want to go, so she made the reservation. He wished she hadn't. These events were always so stage-managed and sterile. But this one turned out to be better. Shah's company, BPL made a nice donation to cater it well and the

~ 20 ~

media was well briefed. The publicity that BPL would reap from this little celebration would more than pay for the expense of the surf and turf being spun out of the convention center's kitchen.

The President of the ANA made the appropriate laudatory remarks about Dr. Shah and his contributions to neurology, then invited Shah to the podium. *He seems to be in his element there,* Jack thought. A brilliant speaker, Shah had a magnificent command of the language. But the man's keen sense of humor surprised Jack. During their time together that morning, Shah had given the impression of being as humorous and charming as a meat hook. *But oh, how he could turn it on whenever it suited him,* Jack thought. *The good doctor was as fine an actor as he was a businessman.*

Shah accepted the award and the event wrapped up shortly thereafter. Jack decided it would be nice to hang around to shake his hand and offer congratulations, a decision quite a few others seemed to have made as well. When he finally made his way through the throng, Jack said, "Well done, Dr. Shah."

Shah paused a moment as he studied Jack's face. "Jack, yes of course, my limo mate. Thank you very much indeed." But before they could go any further, a pretty reporter from a national network news channel corralled Shah. "Yes of course I can chat for a few minutes but my plane is leaving in 60 minutes. Let's be quick." Jack quickly realized he couldn't compete with that so he found his way out of the room.

After the interview, Dr. Shah felt happy that the convention was over for him. He left the hotel as he had entered it, without stopping at the desk. His expenses were automatically billed back to his company. The butler had neatly packed his bag and carefully placed it in the trunk of the hired car. All that remained was for Shah to slide into the limo's back seat and within ten minutes he would be at the private aircraft section of the airport because the company plane would fly him back to New York. The last time Shah whined to his board about burdensome commercial air travel and the onerous security measures at the world's airports, they authorized his use of one of the several company planes.

A Citation X awaited Shah. He admired it as his car approached the bird. Manufactured by Cessna, the C-Ten was one of the fastest private jet aircrafts in the sky, the Ferrari of the airways. Its eight seats, top speed of Mach 0.92, and a 3,800-mile range made it perfect for the many obligatory cross-country hops for Shah.

Joining him on the trip to New York were three BPL executives. They had a meeting at 50,000 feet and made the trip more than an hour faster than a commercial jet would have. The C-Ten made a flawless landing at Teterboro, the private airport just over the Hudson River from New York City. Just 30 minutes after touchdown Shah walked into his apartment on Central Park West overlooking the Park and was sipping a very dry martini with his girlfriend Gloria by his side.

8

Dr. Dennis Bonner, one of the top neurologists on the east coast, looked at the patient's file including the results of various tests. In the file was a print-out of an article that his physician's assistant saw on the web and printed out for him. On a yellow sticky note the PA had scribbled: "Thought you'd be interested in the bio of our new patient, Dr. Rostov."

She thought right. An amazing woman waited in the room next to him. He scanned the article and as he did he thought to himself. *OK. Immigrated with her parents from Russia in the 1930s when she was a baby....Math genius....wow...she won the Nobel Prize in physics... for mathematical insights that helped create the first computers.....well, she'll be the first laureate I'll meet...became a U.S. citizen...tons of patents for early computer hardware and software...wow!...she led the teams that created all of the essential navigation and communication systems for the NASA space program in the 60s and 70s.... professor at MIT, consulted by presidents on national security topics related to internet...Oh yeah, I remember seeing this on the news...the President awarded her the Medal of Freedom, our highest honor for a civilian.*

Bonner stroked his chin and thought about her life's work. *Yeah, no doubt ...her brain was without exaggeration among the most powerful, creative and agile that God ever put on earth.* This deeply saddened him.

9

Today Dr. Wen Lin and his wife Mei celebrated their son Gabriel's third birthday, but Mei could tell that something didn't feel right with Wen. He wasn't his usual happy self, especially when celebrating something about his pride and joy, Gabriel.

"What's wrong?" Mei asked. "You should be happy! We tried so hard to have a child, and it's his birthday today. It is a time to celebrate!" "It's nothing," he said. "I'm just tired." Mei searched Wen's eyes for something more, but they offered her no clues. She couldn't see that Wen was obsessing over something that happened three years ago at Pacific University – it seemed to him like it was yesterday....

"I am Doctor Wen Lin," he said, extending his hand to his new boss. Paul Schwartz, Chief of the Biochemistry Department at Pacific University, peered over his glasses and rose perfunctorily from his desk chair, taking Wen's hand and shaking it while continuing to read a scientific journal. Schwartz waved toward the chair across from his desk. After a confused pause, Wen took the chair. Without saying a word, Schwartz slowly and clinically, assessed Wen. He saw a thin Chinese man, about 5'5" in height, in his mid-thirties, with dark black hair framing a round face grounded by intense black eyes. Although Wen wasn't smiling, something about his eyes and mouth always made him look like one could pop out at any moment. Dr. Schwartz noted this and it softened him, ever so slightly; the faintest of smiles appeared on his own usually stoic countenance.

"Welcome to the puzzle palace, Doctor Lin." Wen looked confused, so Schwartz took the opportunity to share his favorite view of research in biochemistry. "We work on the largest, most complicated jig-saw puzzle in existence – the human puzzle. Slowly, through brain power, luck, brute force, or prayer we find another tiny piece of the puzzle and put it in its place. We only need a couple million more pieces and we'll have figured it all out." Dr. Schwartz smiled, a gesture tinted with weariness and resignation, and waited for the response from Wen Lin.

"Yes, but we're not alone, Dr. Schwartz." Now Wen truly was smiling. "We are only one of many teams here at Pacific University – a great team, of course," he added, noticing Schwartz frown. "But there are teams at universities, in the government, and in industry – all over the world – working on the puzzle with us." Schwartz just looked at Wen Lin and smiled. Many years ago, he himself had been full of optimism, so sure that Mother Nature would give up her secrets like a coy lover if only he worked hard enough to woo her. But over the long haul, Schwartz had found her to be a deceptive and stingy mother. "Yes, Dr. Lin, there are lots of us," he managed to say without laughing out loud at Lin's naïveté.

Dr. Schwartz buzzed his secretary. "Please show Dr. Lin to his cell." "He's a little tough to warm up to," she said, leading Wen Lin through a rabbit warren of corridors lined with rooms in which busy scientists focused on their work. "Well, he *is* the preeminent scientist in the field – a Nobel Laureate, mentor to two other Laureates!" Wen said. "I can't imagine the pressure on him to continue that track record." "I suppose," she said. "But he could at least make an effort to fake being human."

After turning one more corner, she abruptly stopped. "Here is your office, Dr. Lin." The tiny, but well-lit and reasonably well appointed office didn't disappoint him. Wen was accustomed to cramped quarters. Growing up in Hong Kong, he had been one of five children who lived in a very small flat in the city. His father had been a bookkeeper for a clothing shop near the Peninsula Hotel, that catered to wealthy gentlemen. From his father, Wen Lin had learned the value of hard and honest work.

Wen's mother was a tiny woman, but with a stern look or a wagging finger she could bring her much taller son into line in a heartbeat. She instilled in Wen the understanding of his obligation as the first-born male child to provide for his parents in their old age and to bring honor and respect to their family name. It was unsaid but perfectly understood that he would be the first in his family to go to college. Wen deeply appreciated his mother. He wouldn't have achieved what he had so far were it not for her constant supervision, criticism, encouragement and love. Compared to his lioness mother, Dr. Schwartz was a lamb. "This'll work out great. Thank you." "Good luck," she said, a wish sincerely shared which warmed Wen.

As melodramatic as Dr. Schwartz's puzzle metaphor seemed to Wen, it had piqued his curiosity about the rate at which important new scientific insights and new medicines were discovered. Firing up his laptop, he Googled "new drugs and success rates." Nothing promising came up on his first attempt, so he kept refining his search while he unpacked boxes and set up his office. When he powered down his laptop at the end of the day, the figures he had jotted down regarding the success rate of bringing to the market innovative, breakthrough medicines were discouraging. But then Wen remembered that adversity was no stranger to him. Before leaving, he took one last look at his new work home, a place he was certain would be the center of a long and exciting career.

His son's tugging on his shirt sleeve literally pulled Wen from obsessing over this memory of three years ago and back into the present. "Daddy, Daddy! Pay attention to me! It's time to blow out the candles!" Gabriel's birthday reminded Wen that he had been working on his current scientific theory for over three years, since just before Gabriel's birth. Sadly, the puzzle metaphor of his boss, Dr. Schwartz, had turned out to be true. Wen had made no progress at all in the advancement of his theory. No breakthrough, no major discovery; not even a promising path toward one. In more than three years he had found not a single piece to add to the massive human jigsaw puzzle.

Wen's area of scientific research was beta amyloid biochemistry, the series of chain reactions in the brain that lead to the build-up of beta amyloid plaque, believed to be the cause or at least one of the main causes of Alzheimer's disease. His objective was to discover the biochemical triggers that start the chain of chemical events that eventually lead to the creation of the troublesome plaques. If he could make a new discovery about this process, he could possibly develop a chemical compound, antibody or gene that could stop the chain of chemical events from starting. Or he could maybe break the chain reaction once it had begun or at least slow down the eventual process.

But no. So far he had nothing to show for his efforts. As he rose from the couch and took Gabriel's hand, he knew he was frustrated and depressed. He knew that something was eating away at him but he couldn't put his finger on it. "Focus on Gabriel," he scolded himself as he tousled Gabriel's hair and tickled his neck while chasing him to the kitchen table where the cake awaited them. "Let's blow out those three big candles, Gabe!"

Atorvastatin (Lipitor®)

10

Jack was glad to be back in Paris, back in the office, back to a routine. He had a million things to do and the Vegas trip had just put him further behind. Plus, he was tired.

Catching reflections of himself in the multiple mirrors on the wall opposite his desk, he sub-consciously sucked in his belly. With his whirlwind pace, he wasn't getting to the gym like he should. He moved closer for a self-assessment. He saw a man in his early 40's, about 6'2", athletically built. But stepping closer to the mirror, he could tell that the frequent flyer miles and the grueling schedule were showing up around the corners of his eyes. He still had a head full of dark black hair, but the harbingers of middle age were revealing themselves in a slight frosting at the temples. *The gray is good*, Jack thought, looking on the bright side. Maturity, gravitas. There was nothing European businessmen loathed more than a young, bouncy, Hollywood-perfect American playing on their field.

A thin scar on his chin reminded Jack of his almost forgotten ice hockey days. A badge of courage, he liked to call it. A smile slowly crept across his lips at the memory, a smile that came easily and often and that, despite his hockey days, revealed a mouthful of straight white teeth. It was a miracle, Jack thought. A testimony to his anticipation and quick reflexes.

Those traits came naturally growing up as one of seven kids in a Catholic family outside of Chicago. Jack had attended St. Bonaventure's Elementary, the school affiliated with his church – "Saint Boner's," as the boys irreverently called it. He could still vividly remember his first-grade class. In seven columns of eight desks with a couple more desks jammed in at the back sat a total of 58 kids. The nun-teachers were saints and demons at the same time, and no wonder. Who could blame them for being the latter sometimes, managing and actually teaching nearly 60 wild urchins as well as they did? Jack often thought that those nuns had dealt with a tougher management challenge than had ever been handed to him. Of course, they employed tools and techniques that were not at the disposal of modern-day business people.

In a class of 58 kids, observational skills were critical to survival. A lot happened at any given moment, especially outside the classroom. The pressure from tight in-room control exploded like a volcano upon the schoolyard at recess. This is the place where practical jokes, cruel pranks and acts of total humiliation were conceived and launched. Jack survived by developing a sort of sixth sense of the mood, direction, and intentions of his classmates. He could almost smell it when something nefarious was in the making and almost always managed to foil his would-be attackers or tip off his friends. This skill of observation and anticipation had served him well in business, too. He could read the morale and mood of his company and anticipate the moves of his competitors. This talent helped him keep his head firmly attached to his neck in the dangerously political corporate world as well.

Jack's office phone rang in a tone still unfamiliar to him. The ringtone was just one of thousands of sounds, smells, sights and textures in his new world to which he had to adjust. The transition was stressful, but fun too. Jack picked up the phone. "Monsieur Callahan, Madame Callahan is on the line," said his secretary. *Monsieur Callahan*, Jack thought. What a laugh his French-Canadian maternal grandfather would have had over that. "Bonjour, ma chérie," he cooed into the phone, exaggerating the accent for fun.

"Hi Babe. How's my ignorant, geocentric, arrogant American Executive VP today? You screw up anything big yet?" Diana always had a way of keeping Jack's feet planted firmly on the ground. He appreciated that, having seen so many of his colleagues develop egos way beyond justification. A couple of good years of business results and they started believing they had "the touch." Such ego inflation inevitably got the better of those who began to feel invincible. For about the millionth time, Jack felt so lucky to have Diana, even though she did seem to take a little more pleasure than necessary when playfully knocking him down to earth. "What mischief are you up to today?" he said. "I think I found the perfect apartment!" *She's so into this. It's so much fun sharing this new adventure with her,* he thought.

Jack first saw her in Chicago. He was on a blind date dinner arranged by a friend. They had tickets to see "A Chorus Line" after dinner. No sparks flew, no chemistry happened at dinner and they both knew they would never have a second date. The waiter was so horrendously slow that they had to make a mad dash to the theater and then sprint down the aisle to their seats. Just as they sat down the music began playing, the curtain rose… and BANG! Jack saw Diana burst onto the scene singing a song that filled the room and beaming a smile that filled his heart. He couldn't take his eyes off of her. He pined for her when she was off stage and almost leapt from his seat whenever she returned. He *had* to meet her.

The next night he returned to the theater to see the show again. This time he had arranged a backstage pass through a friend who knew the manager of the theater. All throughout the show, Jack's heart raced with anxiety. *How stupid of me to think she'd go for me! She's so spectacular and I'm so... average. She's out of my league...and I'm out of my mind. I should send an excuse and cancel the back-stage meeting.*

Despite his anxiety, Jack fought through the crowd exiting the theater and found his way backstage. The anticipation of meeting her made him dizzy as he introduced himself to the manager and explained his wishes. The manager asked Jack to wait a few minutes. "Hey, Diana," Jack heard the man shout through her dressing room door. "There's a young man here. A friend of a friend. He wants to meet you." "She said she'll be with you in a few minutes." Jack remembered recognizing that he was being irrational to hope that she'd be with him for a lifetime.

When Jack finished for the day, he headed to the address of the Paris apartment that Diana had given him to meet her and the broker. He found it in a tony part of town, the 16th Arrondissement. The apartment door stood open, and as he entered he could hear Diana talking to the rental agent. Jack heard the excitement in her voice so it would be hard to say no to her on this. In fact, Jack couldn't say no to Diana. He knew that he spoiled her and acknowledged his utter inability to do otherwise, so he had already resigned himself to the fact that he now stood in their new apartment. As he walked toward the voices, he checked out the place. It was indeed perfect.

He and Diana saw each other at the same time. Even after all these years, they couldn't help smiling whenever they saw each other after even a few hours apart. "Jack! This is Marie Ménard, our rental agent." "Enchanté, Madame Ménard," Jack said. As Jack learned his new language he always enjoyed saying "enchanté" in his best French accent. It was such a romantic word; enchanted.

Diana took him by the arm and walked him from room to room, pointing out the details of the architecture, the decoration, the views, the amenities. He took it all in, and then put on a serious face. "I don't know, Diana. It's a little expensive." She frowned. "And a little farther from the office than I'd like." She countered. "On a cost per square foot basis, it's on the low-end of the comps in this neighborhood, we are close to the *Périphérique* so that will be convenient for you to get to the office and airport, the security is state-of-the-art, it was recently renovated, the main rooms don't have any street noise ..." Jack listened to her flurry of reasons why the place was so wonderful and she nailed it.

He let her spin out her best sales pitch for a few moments, until he could no longer stifle a laugh. "It's perfect, Diana. Let's take it. But since you're mad for the place, let me do the negotiating." "Not necessary," she said. "I've already chopped fifteen percent from the asking rent." Jack would've been happy with ten percent off. "Well, at least let me try to get an extra parking space thrown in." "Already done," Diana said with a big grin.

They celebrated their excellent find the next night with dinner at Le Cinq, the Michelin-starred dining room at the Hotel George V not far from their new apartment. Diana looked amazing, and the dinner was like a beautiful dream in which Jack fell in love with her all over again.

11

Dr. Bonner called Dr. Rostov from the waiting room and showed her to the big leather couch in his office. He then sat down beside her. After meeting her they chatted and he shared with her how much he admired her work, her Nobel Prize, Medal of Freedom award and her contributions to humanity. The conversation paused and both became more serious.

"Dr. Rostov, let me get right to the point. The various tests we put you through confirm that you have Alzheimer's disease." Bonner never knew what to expect when he shared this diagnosis with a patient; he had seen it all. In this case his patient took the news calmly. The circuitry of her exquisite and powerful mind still functioned quite well despite her disease. "I've confirmed the diagnosis with my colleague at Johns Hopkins Medical Center," said Bonner. "Your disease is in the early stages." As he spoke these words to her, he sadly thought of the brutal tragedy they foretold. Her magnificent brain, a remarkable machine would eventually and inevitably be rendered useless by the relentless hammer and corrosion of her disease.

Dr. Rostov took a deep breath and leaned back into the leather couch, exhaling loudly as she sank deeper into its depth. As she processed the news, Bonner took in her features. Her face revealed the beauty that had once been there: high cheek bones, blue-green eyes, delicate nose and porcelain skin. Her snow-white hair still had traces of blonde. Physically, she had aged gracefully and well. *How ironic*, he thought, *it was her brain that was letting her down now.*

"This may explain why my son Alex now occasionally beats me in chess after 30 years of losing to me," Dr. Rostov said, with a rueful smile. Bonner again reflected on this woman's extraordinary brain and bravery. She had carried on her back the entire applied mathematics and software department of NASA, with no idea how to accomplish what her adopted country's President had asked her to do.

Wanting to get some insight into her cognitive and memory capabilities, he probed a little. "I admire what you accomplished at NASA – what an amazing contribution you made." "Well thanks, it was one of the great technological and mathematical challenges of the century – to get a ship to and from the moon in one piece. I remember President Kennedy gave us – the nation – the challenge: 'To send a man to the moon and return him safely to earth before the end of this decade.' That was the most thrilling sentence I had ever heard spoken." She then smiled and chuckled a little and then added, "I didn't know until later that my team would be tasked with leading some of the hardest parts of figuring out how to do what Kennedy demanded. That made his challenge personal!" They spent a few minutes discussing some of the challenges she faced and Dr. Bonner concluded that her long-term memory was sharp and clear.

"What keeps you busy now, Dr. Rostov?" "Well for some time I have been retired. I still get called for advice…well, not very often anymore. I spend my time now writing my memoires and staying current. Oh, and I love Jeopardy." I whip my son's ass in Jeopardy even though he's a famous journalist, world-traveler and general geek." She paused and nodded. He sensed that he saw her turn her scientific mind to the task ahead. "That will be our metric," Dr. Rostov said. "When Alex beats me in Jeopardy, we'll know this thing has really gotten hold of me."

12

Wen Lin first noticed the difference in himself a few weeks back, around the time he completed his notes on an important experiment he had been conducting for months and before he celebrated his son Gabriel's third birthday. Since then his feeling of mental disequilibrium became stronger; it distracted him by day and by night, it disturbed his sleep. During the day, he often heard a whisper that always quieted whenever he tried to find its source. He felt an abiding and strange uneasiness, like something important was about to happen. Whether that something was good or bad, he couldn't tell. This feeling burdened him like a heavy backpack that he couldn't shake off, and on some days he feared he was losing his mind.

In desperation, Wen decided to meditate, something he had practiced religiously back in graduate school to calm his nerves. Though he had not found time for it recently, the knack had not left him. As he became more effective at his meditation, a dawning slowly emerged that he may have made an important scientific error in his work... or had not quite finished something at work.

One Sunday afternoon, after a particularly successful meditation session, Wen noticed that he felt especially refreshed, as if the heavy backpack had slipped from his shoulders. With his newfound energy, he decided to drop into the lab to tidy up some things before starting on a new experiment that Monday. As he did, he came across his lab notebook from the experiment he had done several months before and felt a strange pull from it to be opened. He opened and read the notebook and reviewed the statistics, largely ignored his notes. When he saw the summary table of statistics it shocked him as if the page were electrified.

Wen prided himself on his meticulous laboratory protocol. In fact, his colleagues called him the poster boy for "Good Laboratory Practices," the standardized laboratory practices established by the government and used by universities and industry. Now he saw with a rolling of his stomach, a rare lapse in his mechanical precision. He had forgotten to plot the readings from an instrument measuring the characteristics of the neurons in various brain tissue samples. A whole column of data were absent, yet to be filled in.

This sloppiness shocked him and his professional pride compelled him to correct it immediately. Wen threw himself into the task and didn't stop until he finished entering the data from the instrument's storage into his statistical model and double-checked his other entries. When the data were entered and confirmed, he looked at his watch. Six hours had passed since he threw himself into the fix. He could now crank out the complete results of the experiment but it would take the software several minutes to crunch the data and plot the complicated figures and charts. Since he was hungry, he queued up the analysis, pressed "Enter" on his computer and left his obedient digital slave to do his number crunching.

Wen made the short walk to the area where the vending machines were. The snacks offered didn't impress him. Studying the various colorful packages of different combinations of sugar, starch, salt, and chemicals, he laughed to himself. Some of this stuff had no business in food so he decided to go with the salted peanuts. At least he knew roughly what he would get with that choice. He went to the drink machine and reviewed the choices there with the same conclusion. He chose the bottled water, opened it and took a long, satisfying drink.

Wen munched on his peanuts while reviewing the news on the bulletin board with little interest. The softball league was starting again. The university Chancellor was making his annual United Way pitch. The university was proud to announce that it had passed last year's results in the number of patents issued.

After Wen finished his peanuts and water, he figured his analysis would be finished so he made his way back down the hall. Passing Schwartz's door, Wen recalled Schwartz's often-repeated words about Mother Nature being a cold, stingy bitch who doesn't give up her secrets easily. *You've been right so far, you cynical old bastard,* thought Wen, turning the corner towards his office. He thought about next week's experiments and wondering if the instruments he needed had been calibrated by the lab technicians as he had asked. He wondered about that as he sat down at his desk and looked at his monitor. And there, waiting for him like a framed masterpiece, was the most breathtaking sight Wen had ever seen.

When the new data were plotted with the blood levels of protein and the density of beta amyloid plaque, he saw not a loose correlation between them but an exquisitely strong one! This meant that he had quite possibly uncovered an important new piece in the puzzle to stop the destructive process of Alzheimer's disease. On his screen, Wen didn't see the image of Mother Nature as a cold, mean bitch that Dr. Schwartz invoked the first time Wen met him over three years ago. Instead, he beheld a comely woman lying before him, alluring and willing, beckoning Wen to come and sample the sweetness of her charms and unwrap her elusive secrets.

13

Dr. Shah was happy to be in New York. If he had to spend time in America on behalf of BPL, New York was the only place that could accommodate his sophisticated tastes and needs and BPL's R&D world headquarters were in Northern New Jersey, a 15-minute helicopter ride from mid-town.

One of the things Shah most enjoyed about New York was the view from his 30th floor penthouse apartment overlooking Central Park. From his large terrace he could watch the changing seasons repaint the park's flora. The terrace also served his recently acquired hobby, falconry. From a breeder in Texas, Shah had purchased two peregrine falcons and a Harris hawk. The falcon, bred from champion lines was remarkably expensive; ten-thousand dollars for the little lustful raptor. The bloodier he got, the happier he seemed. Shah named him Mars, after the Roman god of war. His other falcon, lightning fast, even among falcons, was named Mercury but he was a poor hunter and Shah had drowned him for this short-coming.

The Harris hawk was a strong hunter but was from less regal bloodlines, and was less manageable than the falcons. Shah had thought an appropriate name for this unruly hawk would be "America." The breeder, a strange character whose Texas drawl Shah could barely understand, had come to New York at Shah's expense to give him private falconry lessons from his terrace. Shah took to falconry with amazing speed. According to his trainer, Shah had an unusual connection with his birds of prey. This news came as no surprise to Nathaniel Shah. Falconry was the sport of kings and noblemen, a class to which Shah felt he certainly belonged. Shah respected speed, strength and precision and these birds were most impressive in these characteristics. Mars was a particularly aggressive hunter, and Shah favored him to America for that reason.

Shah awoke at dawn to give his birds some exercise. A bird minder had been hired to take care of his birds, which entailed weighing each one each day and feeding them only as much as they needed to avoid starving. "A famished predator is an effective predator," he told Shah. He raised his gloved hand to send Mars on his morning hunt. He watched him climb, each flap of his wings pulling him higher until he was just barely within Shah's sight. Now Shah uncased his binoculars and watched Mars cruise, knowing that he was scanning the park for mice, squirrels, rabbits, pigeons; whatever looked like good sport. To Shah's delight, Mars toyed with some pigeons and terrorized them with his dives and strafed them with his talons. Shah took great pride in Mars' domination of the skies and admired how Mars enforced his mastery.

After having his sadistic fun, the falcon quickly ascended to his impressive heights and resumed his surveillance, riding the thermals that kept him aloft without moving a wing. After a few minutes of scanning the ground, Mars suddenly tucked in his wings and dropped into a power dive approaching 180 miles per hour, aimed at the edge of the wooded area near the park green. He disappeared from sight for several minutes. The next time Shah saw Mars, the falcon descended from above him, making a straight-line descent back to Shah. He turned his shoulder to Mars and raised his arm for his landing. Mars had a field mouse in its talons that made the landing clumsy which annoyed Shah for its inelegance. Shah took the mouse from the talons and noted its approximate weight, a familiar task for Shah given his early research career working with lab mice. After entering the weight into Mars' feeding record, Shah then served up the little rodent to Mars who lustily decapitated the unfortunate little creature and then devoured the rest of the package – bones, fur and all. Shah watched this spectacle with rapt attention, his eyes wide and his mouth faintly imitating that of the raptor. Something about this aroused and brought out the hunter in him and he thought of Gloria. He decided he would shower and wait for her to rise.

Gloria Segovia had been in Shah's life for approaching a year now. Born in Argentina of mixed heritage – Spanish, Swiss, and a family folklore that claimed Asian, at 38 she was a precociously successful Mergers & Acquisitions lawyer. Shah proudly introduced her as "the falcon of the banking world," an appellation Gloria pretended to dislike.

Impatient and aroused, Shah entered his bedroom to watch Gloria sleeping naked on his bed. He sat next to her and began a slow, methodical inventory of her body. She had the olive skin of her Spanish mother. Her long silky black hair, gathered exquisitely and provocatively in one of her many rare decorative combs while working, flowed over her long neck, shoulders and feminine curves. Her body was athletic but not muscular, kept in shape by her intense equestrian training. Her eyes were almond shaped, her lips full and her mouth wide. Shah found in Gloria an appealing set of contradictions. Her face and body were feminine while her voice was deep and smoky. Her skin was soft and her form, firm and taut. Her warm, voluptuous mouth wrapped ice-white teeth. Contradictory – that was Gloria. She was more woman than he had ever met and her physicality and intelligence made her more self-assured than almost every man Shah knew.

As Shah admired her languid beauty, she awoke and stretched like a cat, arching her back. She opened her eyes and saw Shah watching her. Beckoning him sleepily to her bed, and with a mischievous smile she asked why he had gotten up so early. He explained that he had hunted the peregrine falcon with great success. She purred like a feline and her eyes smiled. She asked with almost breathless urgency to hear every detail of the hunt. When he finished his narration, recounting even the tiniest detail, she begged him to tell her again how Mars had terrorized the pigeons, sending one to a spiraling death, how he had strafed the squirrels and finally, his slow, proud and triumphant consumption of his prey. She pulled Shah close to her, surprising him by her strength. The electricity in her eyes and the urgency of her breaths telegraphed her desires. Shah happily complied with her wishes.

14

Wen stared at the results on the monitor of his computer. His mouth hung open, stunned by what he saw. After he regained coherent thought, he decided to make sure he had told his computer to do the right analyses. He methodically rechecked his data array and the statistical modeling parameters of the graphics software and pushed the "Enter" button once again. It would be the cruelest of jokes if just when he thought he had her in his bed, she laughed and kicked him naked and impotent to the floor.

He held his breath while the computer chewed away at the volumes of data. After several long minutes, the results surged off the monitor and into Wen's mind and heart like a tsunami, knocking him back in his chair. The results were exactly the same! He looked around. There was nobody to share this with. After a moment of disappointment he reconsidered the situation. *Good*, he thought, and decided he'd better get the data validated and the analysis confirmed before he made a monumental ass of himself, which is what would happen if either were wrong. It had happened, Wen knew, to far greater scientists than he.

The past several months finally made some sense to him. *I wasn't going crazy; my subconscious had been hounding me. I must have made a mental note to go back and enter the missing readings and I somehow forgot to do it.* Although alone in his office, Wen now blushed at his embarrassing error.

He once again marveled at the magnificent capabilities and powers of the brain and its workings at the subconscious and conscious levels. *Dr. Schwartz's puzzle metaphor was more right than wrong,* Wen thought. *This puzzle of the human body is so complex that we have no idea even how many pieces existed. And many of the pieces we did know about, we didn't yet completely understand.*

By now it was 5:45 on Monday morning. Wen showered and changed in the staff locker room and took out his emergency clothes he kept there for times like these. He often worked through the night if he'd been lured by her seductive whisper. He pursued her shadow and the whispers of her mysteries. He chased her but had lost her every time. But this time could be different, Wen thought, remembering the computer printout of his experiment results. This time he might just have her!

Before Wen allowed himself to get more excited, he decided to have his close friend and colleague, Dr. Giancarlo Finarelli, head of Pacific University's bio-statistics department, confirm his statistics and observations. Wen had been trained by the university's patent lawyers to not label his tables when sharing his data with others outside of his lab – even though Finarelli was with the university. It was important to carefully document and fiercely protect the paternity of this idea because the time of birth and parentage of the idea could be challenged one day in patent litigation. Many great ideas were challenged.

Before sharing the data with Giancarlo, Wen updated his notebooks, time-stamped his database and saved the data to the university network database. Once he completed that, Wen was ready to share the data with Finarelli. He felt embarrassed that he couldn't tell his friend what the measurements represented, but Giancarlo knew the drill and it didn't bother him at all. "My team will be tied up meeting a damn NIH research grant proposal deadline for Schwartz's project," he said, "so it'll be a few days before I can get the results to you."

Wen heard "a few days" as if Giancarlo had said "a few hundred years." The emotions and questions that his mind wrestled with would make the three days unbearable. He worried that Finarelli would inform him of a minor, but devastating error in Wen's data or analyses. He also imagined that he had finally found a piece of the puzzle. He resigned himself to the long, three-day wait.

Levothyroxine (Synthroid®)

15

Those three days were pure torture. Wen was so distracted that he recognized his worthlessness at work, and decided to take one of his rare days off. He decided that he needed a long drive. Mounting his trusty Honda Civic, he made his way to Highway One, the magnificent 122-mile stretch of surf, sand, mountain, and sky between Monterey and Morro Bay. For the entire day Wen followed that snaking highway, his car window open to the head-clearing scent and crash of the Pacific surf.

Wen awoke early on the day he was to hear from Finarelli. But as much as he had prayed for this day to arrive, now that it was here he was strangely slow in his routine of getting to work. He didn't know why. He suspected that he simply feared bad news and wasn't rushing to receive it. When he arrived at his lab, he saw a sticky note on his computer screen. From Giancarlo, it said that Wen's results were ready. Wen's hand trembled as he punched in Giancarlo's extension on the phone.

"Finarelli here," Giancarlo shouted into the phone. "Yes, Giancarlo, this is Wen. You have my results?" "Come on over," Giancarlo said. Wen hung up and practically ran to Giancarlo's office. When he got there, Giancarlo couldn't help noticing how anxious his friend looked. "Who taught you how to do statistical analyses, Wen?" Giancarlo demanded. Before Wen could answer, Giancarlo fired another cruel insult. "Did your new research intern do his first data analysis on this project?' Wen's head went into a spin. He only half-heard the second barb because the bitch was laughing so loudly and hysterically at him from her bed.

But Giancarlo didn't have the heart to play Wen any longer. He laughed and slapped Wen on the back so hard it nearly knocked him on his face. "The data and statistics are perfect, Wen. Impeccable, just as I suspected. I wasted my time checking your spotless work." All Wen heard was "a waste of my time." Realizing that Wen hadn't snapped out of his stupor, Giancarlo took him by the shoulders and looked straight into his eyes. "Wen, the data are correct!"

Slowly, Wen grasped the message. He smiled nervously. "What does it look like?" he asked. "I don't know what these variables are, but here's the primary chart of the results." Giancarlo laid a graph on the table in front of Wen. When Wen looked at it, his heart rolled over in his chest. Staring at the graph, Wen literally forgot to breathe for a minute and then loudly vacuumed up a long stream of air as his mind raced with ideas on what to do next.

"Thanks, Giancarlo," he finally said. "Don't mention it my friend. Sorry to toy with you there, but you looked so anxious to get the results that you were like a puppy begging to be played with.

16

After weeks of pondering the puzzle of what to do next, and after reviewing his notes with the patent lawyers for the all-important eventual patent procedure, Wen and the attorneys decided he needed to further test his theory and develop more data to strengthen his patent. The most powerful data would be in humans but Wen couldn't perform a human test – Alzheimer's disease develops so slowly in humans that it would take many years to find out if his discovery were real or a biological fluke. If his discovery turned out to be valid, he could then begin to design molecules to stop the progression of this progressive disease.

Wen needed an animal model of Alzheimer's disease to speed up this timetable and test his theory. He also needed to get the permission of his superiors at Pacific University to make this project his new top priority and find the money to fund it. For two solid weeks he worked on a presentation to his superiors to convince them to allow him to work on developing his new theory. He polished the presentation until it shone.

"You have something you want to share with us, Dr. Lin?" asked

Wen's boss, Dr. Schwartz at the end of the Quarterly Research Progress Review. "Yes sir, I do," Wen said. He delivered his presentation as he had rehearsed it so many times before. As he talked, he watched their faces to get hints of their interest, but they gave him none.

At the end of the presentation, Dr. Schwartz spoke first. "Dr. Lin, what you have here is a remarkable analysis. The results are intriguing but of course, an in-vitro experiment means that, by definition, your observations may not be reproducible in an animal or in man. In short, Dr. Lin, you haven't proven that the results you observed, as tantalizing as they may be, are not just a random event; a parlor trick to be performed only with a test tube. You remember that cruel bitch Mother Nature I told you about on your first day here?

This frightened Wen, not knowing where Schwartz was going with his question. He squeaked out a "Yes, sir I do." Schwartz lunged. "She's not giving you anything here, Wen…a hint – at best – but very, very far from conclusive evidence." Wen reached inside himself for some courage and found a toehold. "Sir," he said, looking directly at Dr. Schwartz, "There is without doubt an important finding from my experiment, albeit in-vitro, and it deserves further study."

Schwartz smiled dismissively. "Perhaps, but with which funds would you conduct your experiments, Dr. Lin? And who will do your current work, from which we get valuable funding from the National Institutes of Health – keeping you and your fellow cell-mates gainfully employed?" Schwartz delivered his condescending message while he scanned every face in the room, making each person squirm. After a moment, Schwartz's lap dogs giggled as if on cue, adding to Schwartz's enjoyment of the taste of his delicious power.

"If you have no answer for those questions, Dr. Lin, I propose that you develop this work in your kitchen on your own free time, or bring it up for an NIH grant on the next round – after gaining our support – and with further evidence than what you've brought forth today."

Wen looked around the room. Everyone had ducked and covered; no eyes connected with his, feet nervously tapped, hands pretended to take notes and nothing was said. Nobody uttered a breath of support for him and there wouldn't be any, at least not in front of Schwartz. Wen thanked Dr. Schwartz, the group and excused himself, feeling humiliated. When he got back to his lab, Wen collapsed into his chair and after regarding his printed presentation slides, he stood and violently slammed them into his wastebasket.

17

Dr. Rostov shared the news of her diagnosis of Alzheimer's disease with her son Alex once they reached the privacy of his car. He felt as if he were hit by lightning. He thought she was just showing the usual signs of forgetfulness associated with aging. Hers was the most powerful brain ever – he hadn't even considered Alzheimer's disease.

He looked into his mother's eyes and saw no fear or sadness, just acceptance. He was ashamed that while she was being so strong about the news, he was paralyzed with feelings of anxiety and panic because of what he knew. As a staff science writer for The Washington Post, he had written a lot on the disease. How had he been so blind?

He slowly emerged from his emotional coma. "Mom, I'm so sorry. I'm here for you, you know that." "I know Alex, that's why I'm not afraid." She reached out and took his hand, a rare display of affection for her. Alex lost it, and sobbed into his mother's arms, ashamed at himself for weeping but unable to stop. They stayed that way, holding each other and saying nothing.

Then Dr. Rostov broke the silence. "You'd better get rolling if you want to get me home in time for dinner and Jeopardy. Are you up for an ass-kicking?" Alex managed a weak smile, incongruent with his swollen eyes and tear-soaked face. Wiping away a tear, he started the car and pointed it north toward her place.

18

From a colleague at the university Wen heard that a small company in San Francisco had success breeding mice that were genetically modified to develop Alzheimer's disease. The short lifespan of the mouse meant that the disease progressed much faster than it does in humans. "This could be the breakthrough I've been looking for!" Wen said aloud to himself. *With these lab mice I could test my theory and see results much sooner than I ever could in humans.*

He called the company and got the receptionist, a graduate student doing lots of jobs, including manning the phone. Wen explained what he wanted to discuss with someone, and the grad student knew exactly how to handle it. "Dr. Dumas is the guy you need to talk to," he told Wen.

In a few moments Wen heard another voice on the line. "Jean-Luc Dumas here, how can I help you?" Wen Lin explained that he was studying Alzheimer's disease and had made what he thought could be an important observation. But he needed to do a prospective experiment in an animal model of Alzheimer's disease and he had heard that Jean-Luc's company had such a model. Jean-Luc could hear the passion and commitment in Wen's voice. It sounded so much like what he felt for his patients.

"Do you like seafood?" Jean-Luc asked. "I am Hong Kong Chinese, Dr. Dumas," Wen said with a laugh. "The answer is obvious. If you will allow me, I will make the arrangements at a unique place I know in Chinatown. I'll email you the address."

A week later, Jan-Luc was on a sidewalk, puzzled. The address Wen Lin had e-mailed him was clear enough, but for the life of him Jean-Luc couldn't find a restaurant there. The building itself was a tired, red brick structure that seemed to have been left behind in time in this otherwise-bustling neighborhood. From across the street in a tea shop, Wen scanned the sidewalk for Jean-Luc. Finally, he spotted a tall thin man gazing quizzically at a building and looking repeatedly at a scrap of paper in his hand. It had to be Dumas. Crossing the street, Wen walked up to where Jean-Luc stood. "Dr. Dumas?" said Wen, sticking out his hand.

"How did you know it was me?" said Jean-Luc. "Dr. Dumas, you're the only Caucasian in this part of town!" Both he and Jean-Luc laughed. "But where's the restaurant?" Jean-Luc said. "Did I get the right building?" "Yes, but a very private, very special restaurant is inside. They specialize in seafood delicacies cooked in the traditional Cantonese and Szechuan styles." Wen noticed that Jean-Luc looked a little uneasy. "Trust me, Dr. Dumas, this evening will be unlike anything you've experienced. I'll guide you."

Though Jean-Luc had just met him, he looked into Wen Lin's open, smiling face and decided he would trust him – at least as far as dinner was concerned. He had already checked Wen out and found him to be a legitimate scientist from Pacific University. But still Jean-Luc couldn't help wondering: Why the unusual setting?

They entered the drab little building and ascended a flight of stairs, at the top of which, a red door stopped their ascent. The door gave no indication of what was to be found behind it. Wen picked up a phone mounted on the wall. After he spoke a few words in Chinese, the door buzzed open. "Come," said Wen Lin, motioning Jean-Luc through the door. "Let's eat. I'm hungry." They entered directly into a small dining room with about ten tables. Jean-Luc noticed that all heads turned when they walked in, specifically scrutinizing the Western guest Once seated, Jean-Luc and Wen began the usual awkward small talk – but then, without their having ordered a thing, fresh seafood cooked in the most imaginative ways began appearing at their table. "This is how it is done here," Wen said. "The chef cooks and serves whatever is freshest and he prepares it in the traditional style." Before each course, they were presented with the seafood to be eaten next; its freshness proclaimed itself by its writhing, flapping, squirming or oozing. Jean-Luc got a lesson in marine biology as Wen described each delicacy, most of which Jean-Luc had only *heard* of – if that. Before dessert arrived, Wen got to the reason for the meeting. "Dr. Dumas, I have made the following observation," he said and proceeded to explain what he had observed, leaving out some technical points that were critical to protect his pending patents. "I need an animal model of Alzheimer's disease to develop my hypothesis, and you have such a model, I hear."

Wen's observations fascinated Jean-Luc. A remarkably similar but smaller-scale experiment had been done in his lab in Montreal by a young scientist playing around with brains of deceased AD patients, but there had been no funds to pursue the idea. Still, he feared sharing his mouse model with outsiders before his company's patents on it were issued. He expected this to happen any day now.

"I'll tell you what," Jean-Luc said, leaning back in his chair. "Send me a proposal and if it's sound, I'll refer your proposal to my R&D Review Committee and I'll recommend that we collaborate. You will of course need to make sure that your proposal is endorsed by your organization and your patent counsel at Pacific University and you must be willing to sign a confidentiality and non-disclosure agreement." "Of *course*, Dr. Dumas," Wen bleated out, immediately embarrassed by the childishly high pitch of his excited response.

19

After much legal haranguing, and with Wen's promise to Dr. Schwartz that he would do the work with Jean-Luc on his own time, Wen and Jean-Luc finally got the necessary paperwork signed so that they could collaborate on a limited and prescribed basis. Wen designed an experiment that would attempt to replicate the observations in Jean-Luc's humanized mouse model of Alzheimer's that Wen had seen in the tissue samples he had harvested from human cadavers with the disease. This would provide more support that he may have indeed uncovered a key piece of the puzzle.

After many months, Wen had completed the experiment and had his results – he saw the same correlation that he had in his experiment at Pacific University. So what he saw in tissue outside of the body, he now saw in a living organism that had been designed to have the human form of Alzheimer's disease. This was reassuring news, but to make real progress, he knew he would need to take the collaboration further.

Excited by this preliminary but encouraging experiment, Wen prepared a proposal for consideration at the Pacific University department's Quarterly Research Review meeting. He wanted to take the collaboration with Jean-Luc's company further, to see how various proteins, chemical compounds, and other interventions might slow or stop the chain reaction of events leading to the development of beta-amyloid plaque, the suspected killer of neurons and the cause of Alzheimer's disease. This would be an ambitious, some would say, audacious program. Wen prepared night and day, trying to anticipate any question that Dr. Schwartz might put to him. The outcome of the last meeting with him still gave him nightmares.

When the big day came, Wen felt confident. His data were exciting and potentially ground-breaking and he had rehearsed the pitch for days. *Schwartz had to buy this one,* thought Wen. *If he didn't, Schwartz was as blind as he was brilliant.* When the moment came for him to make his presentation, Wen stood and felt the words roll effortlessly from his tongue. Even as he spoke, he remarked to himself that he was making his finest presentation ever. At the end, he confidently asked for questions. There were none. No surprise there. Schwartz's minions wanted to see what the king thought before they dared express an opinion. Resigning himself to the social order, Wen anxiously asked Dr. Schwartz for his view.

Schwartz rose slowly to make his point, removing his glasses in dramatic fashion. "Dr. Lin, as usual, your preparation, logic, and presentation are flawless. I congratulate you. Your proposal is bold and creative." Wen dared, for a moment, to feel hopeful. Then Schwartz continued. "On the scientific merits, I am willing to support your proposal. However, considering the financial aspects of your proposal, I am sorry to say that our budget this year is already over-committed. I already have to cut several ongoing programs just to meet my budget. It is the toughest financial picture I have seen and we can't look to the trustees to bail us out again as in the past. I am very sorry, Dr. Lin." He then asked for any other topics to be discussed. There being none, he adjourned the meeting. Wen remained in the meeting room after everyone left, staring at the vacant screen and unable to move.

Lisinopril (Prinivil®)

20

After Jean-Luc Dumas learned that Dr. Schwartz had shot down Wen's proposal, he got an idea. "Wen," he said, "here's what we're going to do. My company will license your patent from Pacific University and then I'll hire you to do the work you would have done in your original proposal. What do you say?"

The suddenness of the proposal put Wen off balance. His emotions had been frazzled by the ups and downs of the past several months, and now he groped for focus. "I don't know, Jean-Luc," he said. "I'm happy here at Pacific University... I've been here several years now...my work is important ...I have to think about my family – I have an almost four-year-old now."

"Bullshit, Wen," shot Jean-Luc. "How can you be happy at a place that can't or won't support you?" Before Wen could answer, Jean-Luc fired another missile. "How can you walk away from your breakthrough? You've been working on your concept for what, almost four years now? And you are *so* close to solving this Alzheimer's puzzle!"

Without knowing it, Jean-Luc had chosen exactly the right words and pushed exactly the right button. Wen wanted desperately to find a piece of the puzzle, and now he took a deep breath and ran his small trembling hands through his thick black hair. He was thinking deeply and fast. Five seconds went by. Then: "I will join you if you can negotiate the license to my patent from Pacific University." "That's fantastic Wen! I'll call you when I've done it," he said.

21

The phone rang for what seemed to be forever. Annoyed, Wen Lin picked it up. "Yes?" "Are you ready to come over to the dark side?" After three months of agony, this was the call Wen Lin had been waiting for. "Yes, boss!" he said. He then told Jean-Luc what he needed for his compensation and his laboratory. "Done," Jean-Luc said.

"I will join you on the first of next month," said Wen. He then hung up the phone and pumped his fist in the air. How fast his life was changing! Wen got out a notebook and started making a list of all he had to do. At the top of that list was to tell Schwartz he would resign. Wen put his hands behind his head and tried to think of the best way to break that news. After a few moments of coming up with nothing, he shrugged his shoulders, got up from his desk and walked down to Dr. Schwartz's office.

"The oracle is in, Wen," announced Shwartz's assistant. After two minutes, Wen Lin found himself in Schwartz's inner sanctum. For a second Wen felt a sense of déjà vu. Schwartz, sitting behind his desk, looked at Wen Lin over the tops of his glasses. Without sitting down, Wen blurted out, "Dr. Schwartz, I've decided…"

"To leave us," Schwartz finished Wen's thought. Wen was taken aback. He also felt an odd sense of calm in Schwartz's presence for the first time ever. "I am sorry for us and happy for you Wen," Schwartz said. "Did Dumas get his hooks into you?" "I join him in three weeks," said Wen. In spite of himself, he thought his words sounded slightly apologetic. "I'm so glad you're doing this, Wen," said Schwartz. "As I told you, your idea has great merit. Our financial limitations are holding you back here. Go for it, Wen. Call us if we can help."

The conversation confused Wen. His boss just told him he was great and then told him that said he was glad he was leaving and wished him well! Wen walked back to his cell thinking that this was indeed a wonderful, but strange country.

22

For some months now, Nathaniel Shah had been engaged in a clandestine activity. A headhunter had contacted Shah on behalf of a European pharmaceutical client called SNS – Societé Nationale de la Suisse, a highly profitable global pharmaceutical company headquartered in Geneva and specializing in neurological diseases. After completing an exhaustive review of qualified candidates, the search professional and SNS agreed that Dr. Nathaniel Shah fit most closely their search criteria for the ideal candidate. The position they wanted to offer him was that of the CEO of SNS.

At first, Shah was reluctant. As the number two exec at BPL, the largest pharmaceutical company in the world, he had – almost – all of the compensation, adulation and validation he or any man could use. Presidents and Prime Ministers sought him for advice on healthcare issues. When the CEO of BPL was unavailable, it was Shah who most often stood in for him. In short, although not perfect, he liked his situation. Joining a smaller, "second-tier" company – even as the CEO – would be perceived as a step down for him. And it would certainly be a step out of the limelight that he so enjoyed.

But after he thought about it for a few weeks, he found himself warming to the idea. He painfully understood that as the number two at BPL only one step separated him from the top, but it seemed like such a tall step. As much as his ego wouldn't allow him full recognition of the fact, a part of him recognized the reality that the CEO position at BPL would never be his. Shah never showed the political or diplomatic patience needed in such a high-profile position. Though he certainly had the ability, he just didn't care to play the diplomatic and political parlor games required of the job. Ego wasn't a dish for which he had developed a taste; it was something he simply couldn't swallow.

The more he thought about SNS and the more his subconscious reminded him about his limited prospects at BPL, the more he thought this move could be perfect for him. He could finally be the Number One, which he had long known was the only appropriate role for him. He could build SNS into a powerhouse and not have to put up with the crap that comes with a "big pharma" CEO job such as the one at BPL.

Once he decided to consider the opportunity at SNS, the super-secret mating game began. Shah needed to meet the four members of the "Nominating Committee," the BPL board members who had the responsibility of screening and recruiting senior executives and other board directors. These members were located all over the world, and two of them were former CEOs of major pharmaceutical companies. Once the Nominating Committee blessed Shah, he would have to meet the Chairman of the Board. Everyone knew Shah, so keeping his candidacy secret would be a challenge.

Shah didn't want BPL to fire him for an act of disloyalty, so he insisted on complete confidentiality and that documents had to refer to him only as "the candidate." He only took correspondence on his home email and, so as not to raise suspicions, refused to make significant changes to his calendar to meet the SNS Nominating Committee. Understandably, the process went slowly. But over time, Shah ultimately met and won over all four Committee members.

The final step in the search process was to meet the Chairman of the Board of SNS. This meeting would be largely a rubber stamp, since the Nominating Committee had unanimously supported Shah as CEO and they had never before agreed so enthusiastically on any other senior executive candidate. The meeting with the Chairman went as expected, and within two weeks Shah had an attractive draft employment contract in his hands. He negotiated hard on a couple of issues important to him and within two more weeks he had a deal about which he was enthusiastic.

On his next trip to London for the quarterly BPL Board meeting he would tell his boss, the CEO, of his decision. It would be perfect timing, Shah thought, imagining the directors imploring him – begging him – to stay. They would offer him wonderful things. He would pretend to reconsider, and then refuse. It would be delicious.

23

Gloria Segovia was one of the youngest partners at Denton, Patrello and Eberstein, the premier merger and acquisition law firm in the world. She trained at Harvard and then Oxford, where she met Nathaniel Shah. In legal and general knowledge, Gloria clearly belonged in the Mensa league. Her photographic memory enabled her to see an entire contract in her mind. More than that, in the way a chess master can see his moves well in advance, Gloria could see how her various ideas and solutions would play through all of the clauses and concepts of the most complex business contract. Across any negotiating table, Gloria Segovia was a formidable opponent.

On top of her intellect, she possessed undeniable physical charms, which she employed sparingly and with great skill. She knew that her mostly male opponents would be looking for her to play this card, and that they would crucify her once she did so. So she developed a series of moves that were so discreet, so apparently accidental, and so seemingly natural that they could never be interpreted as intentional. Their effects, however, were entirely the same. An open blouse button hurriedly closed, the flash of an upper thigh, an accidental brush of her long black hair over a hand, a slow lick of the lips or a micro-second flash of tongue on a fountain pen – these were the techniques she had developed over the years. But the one that took Gloria to a level without equal was her ability to blush on cue – when she was "embarrassed" by her intended target's lingering glance at her décolletage, thigh or lips.

Gloria was one of the "key issues" that Shah successfully negotiated in his employment contract with SNS. He won the right to recruit her to SNS at a magnificent salary and just short of ridiculous perqs. Gloria would be the General Counsel and Chief Administrative Officer at SNS. This was a little complicated for SNS to do because they already had a General Counsel who had been with them for 20 years, and he traditionally drew up the employment contracts. The SNS Board used an outside law firm to draft Shah's employment contract to avoid letting the current General Counsel know that he would soon become redundant.

Shah was having less success with Gloria. He hadn't yet convinced her to join him at SNS. She loved her job, loved the energy of Manhattan and loved her horses – which were stabled only an hour away in New Canaan,

Connecticut. While she loved Shah as much as she could love any man, she saw her life as more than Nathaniel Shah. If Gloria went to Geneva, it would be for Gloria, not Shah.

24

After a few months with Jean-Luc, Wen knew he had made the right choice. Things happened fast at his new company. Issues were discussed, alternatives weighed, decisions made – an exhilarating change of pace for Wen. The team around him was top shelf and collaborative, unlike in the secretive, mercenary world of academic science. He felt fortunate to be in a special place at a special time.

His experiment was running smoothly and he had an inexplicably positive feeling for the results. He had to wait for the mice to do their micely things and get the results at the planned time. Wen's cynical side, enhanced by the skepticism that the scientific community had bred into him, made him feel that things were going so well that something had to be wrong. He shrugged it off and went about his work.

Wen felt just like the expectant father he had been before his son Gabriel was born nearly five years ago. The results of his important experiment were due in six days, which passed so slowly that Wen thought he would explode from the anticipation. Under the pressure, he felt that he could hear her – the nature bitch –whispering taunts, laughing a scornful laugh at him. He got to the point that he almost cared less about the results of the experiment than just *getting* the results. For the sake of his sanity, he wanted to know the answer – whatever it would be – to stop this unbearable pressure.

He and Jean-Luc had put so much planning into this event. They had hoped it would be the start of a long program to create something meaningful for patients. They hoped what they were doing would make a lasting mark on the world long after they were gone.

A result showing some effect of the experimental drugs would be wonderful, but that might be too much to ask so early in the process. If the experiment miscarried, it would be a huge disappointment to them and their team, but they would try again – and again and again and again, if they had to. Wen didn't even want to think of that. "Six more days, six more days," he repeated to himself like a mantra. And then: "Hell, I've been working on this concept for almost five years, another six days is nothing."

And yet Wen couldn't help worrying about the consequences if the experiment failed. Had he made a mistake leaving his secure job at Pacific University? Was his theory faulty in some way? Would he be humiliated by his failure? If so, would Jean-Luc ever trust him again?

Omeprazole (Prilosec®)

25

Following a romantic and thoroughly delectable meal at La Grenouille in midtown Manhattan, Shah and Gloria returned to his apartment. Shah had put a bottle of Dom Perignon on ice waiting for them. He had also had Gloria's favorite treat prepared – plump Chilean strawberries hand-dipped in fresh Belgian chocolate from Neuhaus chocolatier in Brussels. The champagne and chocolate-dipped strawberries were the perfect end to a perfect evening.

They took their bubbles and berries with them to the terrace to enjoy the moonlit park. Once they settled into their terrace chairs, Shah launched his latest, and, he felt, his last attempt to sell Gloria on joining him at SNS. "Gloria," he said, and in his mind he quickly reviewed his key points before delivery, "how many times have you told yourself that you could run your company far better than the idiots running it now?" He didn't wait for an answer. "How many times would an M&A lawyer be asked to be a major executive at a pharmaceutical company destined to be one of the fastest growing companies in the industry? And now that you've done your twentieth deal, how different is that one from the fifth, tenth or fifteenth? You're doing exciting work, but aren't you essentially cooking the same delicious soufflé, using the same recipe, over and over again? Why not take on a new challenge?"

She pretended to be occupied with the strawberries and champagne, but she listened intensely. He continued with more passion. "Look, here's a chance to jump into the operating side of an important industry. A chance to make your mark…a chance to get a shot at being a CEO." Shah paused for effect. He knew that deep down, Gloria longed to achieve CEO status but that over the years she had reluctantly come to believe her future would be a comfortable one of law firm partnership, but not a CEO role. He watched her squirm. Her physical discomfort provided a good window on her mental state, thought Shah. If hearing this made her uncomfortable, she must now be less sure of her decision to stay in New York.

Feeling that he had successfully worn her down, he decided to go for the kill. "Just a moment," he said, and he got up from the terrace and went into the apartment. Seconds later he returned carrying his alligator-skin briefcase. He pulled out some documents. Without saying a word, he showed her pictures of the riding establishment just outside of Geneva; rated one of the finest in the world. He'd had a photo taken of stalls in the stable with her horses' names above the stalls and he had a picture brochure of his stunning apartment overlooking Lake Geneva. He flashed a copy of a lease of the new US headquarters for SNS – on Park Avenue in New York. "We would be in New York on a regular basis," he said with genuine excitement. The lease was a fake, but he would get a real one done once he convinced his Board that the company had to have a New York address.

The timing and delivery of his pitch were stellar and the one-two-three combination, impressive. Gloria stood up, gazed once more upon the park, and took a long drink from her flute of Dom Perignon. She then turned to face Shah. "I will join you at SNS, as your General Counsel and Chief Administrative Officer," she said. "I will have an office in New York. You will personally pay to have three of my horses shipped to Geneva according to my strict instructions, and you will convince the board of my strong potential to replace you." She slung her Prada bag over her shoulder. "Good night, Shah." She turned on the heels of her Manolo Blanhiks and walked straight out his door, leaving it open for Shah to close behind her.

Shah jumped to his feet, closed the door and fist-pumped the air. "I will have my muse, my soul mate and brilliant strategist with me. We'll kick ass!" Shah said, his black eyes shining with excitement.

He returned to the terrace and grasped the railing. A full moon hung over Central Park. *Now he would show them all,* Shah thought, *especially those eunuchs at BPL who never would consider him for the #1 role at BPL.* He allowed himself to fully acknowledge this painful truth that he had never acknowledged and was shocked at his harsh epiphany. Then he was pleased by it because it gave him yet another source of passion and motivation – revenge on BPL. As he drained the last splash of champagne from his glass he felt so confident and energized that he thought he could leap over the railing and fly like his beloved falcon Mars.

26

Keeping a brave face in front of her son Alex was like emotional weight lifting for Darya Rostov. After dinner that night, she was beyond tired. She sat down on her couch and within moments drifted off to sleep. Alex finished the dishes and sat next to her. He put his arm around her and stroked her white hair. Under the hair, skin and bone a series of sinister chemical reactions had long been taking place in her powerful brain.

The first chemical reaction had probably happened years before Dr. Rostov even began noticing that she was becoming more forgetful. These chemical reactions produced beta amyloid plaque, the substance that gums up the network of neurons that transmit information within the brain. This plaque is believed to turn once neatly channeled wires of the brain into tangled bunches. Dr. Rostov's brain was still trying to compensate for the relentless loss of neurons by re-routing the wiring around the tangled messes. But as the plaque built up over time, her brain had become less and less able to establish new channels. This is why she was having increasing difficulty recalling facts, figures, smells, memories and faces.

Alex laid his mother down on the couch, covered her with a blanket and decided to stay the night at her place. He would leave early the next morning to get to work.

27

On the day they were to be shown the data from the experiment, Jean-Luc and Wen decided to get two bottles of champagne. They would drink a bottle if the results were good – and two if they were bad.

The project leader was the messenger. Like a pair of Caesars awaiting news of a decisive battle, Jean-Luc and Wen craned their necks looking for a sign of her. She had been asked to come to Jean-Luc's office at 7:00 p.m., after everyone was gone, to protect the confidentiality of the data. She was late.

Finally the project manager appeared, breathless and harried. "I know how important this data set is," she said, "so I had to make sure the data were clean and straight." She took a seat without being asked and looked to her boss, Jean-Luc. "How do you want it – the full wind-up, or just the pitch?" "Give me the pitch," said Jean-Luc. "I can't wait any longer." "The results are mixed," she said. Wen felt his heart flip and then sink with a thump, but then he caught himself. *Okay,* he thought, *at least there's some good news in there.*

She continued: "Of the five drugs that you gave to the mice engineered to express the human form of Alzheimer's disease, three showed absolutely nothing – no effect whatsoever on the progression of the disease when compared to the mice that got the placebo." Wen was now less optimistic. "And the others?" he said.

She watched their eyes to see if, like the messengers of old, she would soon be executed. "Of the remaining two, one showed a trend toward an effect but did not show a statistically significant effect." She knew from their now frantic looks that she had to get out all of the news fast. "The fifth experimental drug, number 203, showed toxicity only at the very high-end of doses administered, but also showed a rapid and dramatic reduction in the development of beta amyloid plaque. I think you've smacked it out of the park, guys!"

Jean-Luc and Wen lunged for each other and danced a silly dance, doing high-fives and fist-pumps, and champagne bottles popped open. As they carried on, they knew this was a rare and precious moment in pharmaceutical research. They reveled in the warm glow of its rarity, and in the mutual respect they had for each other.

Jean-Luc stopped the merriment first. "Hold on," he said. "Who besides us knows about this?" "Nobody but our lead statistician, and she saw the results just before you did." Jean-Luc thought for a moment. "This is big. I'll call Barbara Siegel our patent attorney and have her come over first thing tomorrow morning. I'll tell her we need her help with an urgent patent issue.

28

The next morning, Jean-Luc looked up and saw her through his office widow. Barbara was New York City born, bred, and educated – Brooklyn, then Columbia and NYU. She smiled and waved to Jean-Luc as she made her way to the reception desk.

Now in her late 30s, she was very attractive, with great individual features that she seemingly made no effort to pull together. Her smile, though pleasant, appeared uncomfortable to her in some way. Her face was devoid of any makeup and her thick long hair pulled into submission by a simple pony tail. The main takeaway from a study of Barbara Siegel was that she was in fantastic shape, as befitting any marathon runner. Jean-Luc always thought her hobby mirrored both her vocation and her personality; intensely goal oriented and indefatigable.

A microbiologist turned patent lawyer, Barbara was as tough as nails. She'd made her screw-you money when her former company was acquired, so she didn't bow to anybody now. She called things exactly as she saw them, however inappropriate the place or the timing. Because of that, Barbara was close to unmanageable – but due to her many skills, extremely valuable to Jean-Luc.

Jean-Luc greeted her with the continental double kiss she always found so charming. Characteristically, she dove right in. "So, what do we have here?" she said, with a lingering trace of her native Brooklyn. Jean-Luc and Wen explained the news of their breakthrough. "Wow boys, I didn't think you had the stones to pull this off!" With that, Barbara flung off her coat and took control. "OK, this is what we gotta do, so take notes." She proceeded to blow a blizzard of details, tasks, due dates and persons responsible.

Jean-Luc leaned over and whispered to Wen, "Why is it when Barbara jumps in, I always feel that I work for her instead of the other way around?"

"Because if you don't do what I tell you, both of your asses will be fired for gross negligence," Barbara said. "Her ears are as sharp as her tongue," Jean-Luc said to Wen. And then, to Barbara: "Yes, your majesty." She was right and he knew it. He would follow her plan to the letter.

The explorers of old drew maps of newly discovered lands and they published their maps to claim the rights of their sponsors. A few hundred years later, not much had changed in the field of discovery. Modern-day pharmaceutical explorers drew chemical structures and data sets to document their scientific journeys and discoveries. Then they issued patents and scientific articles to claim their rights. The patents Barbara would take care of. The paper work had to be done by Wen. After a lengthy meeting with Barbara on how to structure the scientific documentation for future reference in any patent disputes, Wen immediately got to work.

Jean-Luc also had to call his investors. They had been so patient for three years and the call would be fun. He was happy to tell them that their investment just moved a step closer to bearing fruit.

29

The principal and founder of the leading west coast venture firm Greg Jimko, had trained as a biochemist and got into the venture capital game in the early 80's by advising a venture capital company on potential biotech investments. When he realized he had a good nose for picking winners and was making his venture capital client filthy rich, he decided to do it for himself. He approached a wealthy friend of his family for seed capital and from that little acorn twenty years ago, a mighty oak had grown.

Jean-Luc and Wen were tingling with nervous energy when they arrived for their meeting at Greg's office. Greg, ever impatient and always pressed for time, prodded Jean-Luc to start the meeting. After years of having to urge his backers to remain patient and trust in their investment, Jean-Luc had endured many moments of private doubt. Today was different. But as is the case in most scientific breakthroughs, the success he would soon describe had come to him by a completely different route than the one on which he had initially embarked. Had he not stumbled upon Wen, Jean-Luc wouldn't have made this discovery. But like in baseball, it doesn't matter how you get the runs; they all look the same on the scoreboard.

Jean-Luc smiled and began with a statement that he felt would not overstate his team's discovery, but wouldn't understate it, either. "Gentlemen," he said, slowly and deliberately, "we all know that an effect of an experimental drug in animals more often than not turns out to be unrepeatable in man, or if repeatable the experimental drug is more often than not far too toxic for humans to tolerate." Having reminded these seasoned professionals about the likely outcome of failure, Jean-Luc moved quickly to begin opening their eyes to what the discovery could mean. "That said, what I am about to show you are results from a study of various experimental drugs in a mouse model of Alzheimer's disease. You recall, gentlemen, that these mice are genetically engineered to make the same type of amyloid plaque that the human makes and by the same biochemical processes."

"Yes, yes, Jean-Luc, we know all about these mice. So what did our multi-million-dollar mice do for us?" Jean-Luc knew when enough was enough. He had several introductory slides prepared and advanced his PowerPoint presentation past them right to the punch line. "The mice treated with drug 230 develop far less beta amyloid plaque." Jean-Luc paused to get their enthusiastic response....Nothing.

Greg looked confused. "Do we care if some mice showed less plaque? What does this mean to their memory or behavior?" Having anticipated this question, Jean-Luc flipped to his next slide. "These same treated mice outperformed the untreated mice in the standard memory tests for mice that are well-recognized in Alzheimer's research." Now he waited again for his words to sink in.

Greg got it immediately. "So, we have mice that have been engineered to have human Alzheimer's disease, we've given drug 230 to some mice, and we've seen much less beta amyloid plaque in these mice. Less plaque is good. But less plaque with better memory in the same mice is the cause and effect breakthrough we've been searching for!"

Greg stood up with his eyes as large as golf balls. "Jean-Luc, this may turn out to be one of the most exciting pieces of pre-clinical data that has been seen in healthcare research since ....I can't recall when!" Greg continued standing while staring at the data, his jaw gaping from the monumental implications of what appeared on the screen. He then pivoted immediately to the economic side of the equation. "If this stuff works in humans, we have our hands on the biggest pharmaceutical product ever. This will make Lipitor® and Plavix® look like cute little products."

Finally Greg sat back down, his mind running at warp speed. "Guys, we've got to develop this concept as fast as possible without screwing it up.!" He paused a moment. "We also have to patent this stuff and everything related to it to protect our invention – we're gonna need strong IP to raise the kind of dough we'll need to develop this technology if it holds up to more testing."

Jean-Luc anticipated this. "Barbara Siegel and her firm have been working non-stop on the patent filing for weeks. They've prepared and submitted a brilliant patent file on the whole concept." "And what about publication?" asked Greg. "I am *extremely* proud to say" – Jean-Luc smiled in Wen's direction – "that Wen's article has been fast-tracked for review by *Nature* and will be published relatively soon." Greg's face was lit by his smile. "This is huge news. *Nature* is *the* journal for the publication of important research, the birthing room of great ideas. Not to jinx you guys but Nature is where eventual Nobel Prize-winning work is often first publicly unveiled." Indeed, *Nature* was where the first report on the structure of DNA had been published. For Wen and the small, privately funded team led by Jean-Luc, the *Nature* publication would be a transforming event. Wen basked in the glow of the moment.

"So much for that...we have other work to be done. What do you propose we do next to develop this concept?" Greg asked Jean-Luc. "And how much more *capital* do you need?" Jean-Luc thought he detected a bit of cynicism in Greg's question. Jean-Luc advanced to a slide entitled "Next Steps" and launched headlong into a detailed schedule of experiments, personnel, supplies, analyses, and time required to move into the next phase. "In order to get 230 into man," he said, "we must first complete the necessary animal toxicology studies in two species. If these studies show no untoward effects in the animals, we'll file an Investigational New Drug application or IND. We could start our first Phase I trial in man within 30 days of IND filing if the FDA is happy with our proposed Phase I program."

Greg barked, "So what's the answer?" Jean-Luc advanced to the last slide, on which appeared the following words:

1. $10 million to manufacture enough 230 for the first phase of development

2. $5 million to finish the animal studies needed to gain FDA approval to begin Phase I studies in humans

3. $10 million to complete the first Phase I safety trial

4. $10 million to complete the rest of the Phase 1 safety studies if the first were successful.

Greg let out a long whistle. "My God, drug development is expensive, eh?" He knew this represented only the beginning. The typical product on the market took a billion, often two billion dollars and at least a dozen years to get to the market – and that was *after* a lead compound was identified. The real gestation period from a break-through idea to a medicine in a local pharmacy was closer to 15 or more years if things moved relatively smoothly. Greg also knew that this product, for this disease would take longer and cost more than the average.

The group discussed various alternatives for raising the $35 million for the next phase of the program. In character, Greg led by summarizing the situation. "In the A Round of financing, some angels and I ponied up $15 million to see if you could make something work with the mice. We're pleased with what you've accomplished over these three plus years." Greg cleared his throat. "Given the huge sums of capital we must raise and the high risk of failure inherent in this stage of development, we'll need to widen our circle of friends and raise the fifty million dollars through a B Round of private funding." "Sorry, thirty-five million, Greg," corrected Jean-Luc.

Greg directed a fatherly smile at Jean-Luc. "Jean-Luc, I've been funding early stage research for nearly two decades and I've never met a head of R&D who *overestimated* their needs on a project. You're plying uncharted waters and remember, your drug is a biologic, which is almost always more challenging – and more expensive – to develop than a small molecule."

Metformin (Glucophage®)

30

"So, how are you liking Paris so far?' asked Jack. "I'm having a blast! Replied his wife Diana. "No regrets?" "Yeah, I miss the theatrical career I had in Chicago and London and my friends from that world, but I am meeting amazing fellow ex-pats here from all over the world. I am developing friendships with Brits, Americans, Asians, Scandinavians and Africans – it's a virtual United Nations of women." "And now they're asking you to lead them!" "Yeah, the current President of the Club asked me to serve as President next year. She told me that everyone loves me and I get things done – and she said those two traits are usually a mutually exclusive mix in our club." "So, you gonna do it?"

Diana thought a moment. "Why not? You're travelling all the blessed time, and this would help me keep busy and it'd be a good resume-builder. Not only that, I might do some good through it. We apply a lot of our budget to our Young Women's Scholarship program and a meaningful portion of it goes to women pursuing careers in the performing arts, so it serves my love." And then, with a devilish smile added, "Oh...and one more reason....I'll be a President before you!"

31

"So, Jean-Luc. You ready for the road show?" Greg exuded confidence in his element; raising capital was his power alley. He clearly couldn't wait to get at it. Jean-Luc was a total neophyte about fund-raising but he felt that with Greg, he was in exceptionally good hands. "Here's how it works," he said, rubbing his palms together in anticipation. "Venture capitalists in health care belong to an elite club. In fact, there are clubs within the club. There's the A-List of well-financed venture capitalists who've been successful for over a couple of decades, managing funds of ultra-high net worth individuals, mutual and pension funds and other elite investors. These funds have been the seed capital from which the biotech industry had been grown. Then there's the club of newcomers. There are also American and European clubs. There are East Coast clubs and West Coast clubs. There are those that focus on biotech and those that focus on diagnostic tests and still others who do healthcare services. The interesting thing is that the most successful venture capitalists belong to many clubs and call upon members of various clubs to put a financing together. Jean-Luc shook his head, as if to clear it and smiled wanly. "So what should I expect on my first financing road show?"

Greg laughed. "What you're about to do is like getting an extensive physical exam, including a close inspection of all body cavities. However, unlike your patients when you were in private practice, there isn't a curtain for privacy. Your bits and pieces will be hanging out for everyone to look at, to poke, prod and evaluate. Some you visit will be gushing with enthusiasm for your concept and then not give you a nickel when it's time to ask for commitments. Others will seem totally unimpressed by what you're selling, to the point of rudeness but then they'll come in big when we count up the willing investors. Most of the people we call on will be in between the two."

Jean-Luc looked extremely anxious. Greg grabbed him by the back of the neck – like a big brother, Jean-Luc felt. "Everybody has to lose their cherry sometime!" Greg said, laughing. "You'll be fine." And he gave him another slap on the back.

Before heading out on the road to visit the targeted VCs, Jean-Luc, Wen, and their finance director prepared the presentation they would give to the potential investors lined up by Greg. The presentation came together nicely, but it lacked one thing – they needed a better company name. Major corporations spend vast sums of money choosing a new company name and then even more money to establish it. Jean-Luc had a grand total of zero dollars to spend on the project to name the company, so he took a low-tech, communal approach. He gathered his small team together in their conference room and they began with a blank piece of paper. They worked like alchemists creating names out of root words, suffixes, prefixes, characters from mythology, names from the heavens and random thoughts. After a few hours of this linguistic chemistry the walls were plastered with dozens of pieces of paper. Then they whittled the contenders down to a list of five. A quick internet search revealed that four names were already taken. That settled it. Jean-Luc stood up and with a black magic marker wrote on the white-board: "Welcome to BioNeura."

Having worked together for several years calling themselves "AD Ventures" – the name the venture capitalists assigned it for legal purposes – the group was now struck by the symbolism of the name on the board. It meant they had passed the first hurdle, the conceptual phase and their efforts had become worthy of creating a name for their enterprise. They let the name sink in. The more they looked at it, the more they liked it. Jean-Luc thanked the team and told them he'd immediately call Barbara Siegel to get the name registered. They filed out of the room, each of them taking a last smiling look at the name on the board. Jean-Luc knew exactly what they were feeling. BioNeura, their new company name gave them a new sense of purpose and put a spring in their steps.

32

Over a period of a couple of weeks they visited Boston, New York, Philadelphia, San Francisco, San Diego and L.A. After pitching their company to more than a dozen potential investors and another two weeks of answering questions, Greg was ready to close the sale.

He clutched his telephone, the trusty tools of his trade and set about to prod, push, cajole and persuade the potential investors. At this stage, Jean-Luc and Wen could only wait like beauty pageant contestants after all the competition was done. It was now up to the judges to say if their idea were beautiful and sexy enough.

At the end of the third week of the process, Greg phoned Jean-Luc. "Can I come over now?" he asked. "Of course you can," said Jean-Luc. "Is it bad news?" "No, not at all," said Greg. "We have commitments for $50 million and could have had much more but we wanted to keep as big a piece of the company as possible for ourselves. There are some nuances concerning the terms of the financing that I need to discuss with you." Something about that made Jean-Luc feel wary, but he tried not to reveal it. "Uh, sure Greg, come over whenever you can." "I'll be right there," Greg said, hanging up without a good-bye.   He arrived at Jean-Luc's office within an hour. Jean-Luc watched him stroll up the sidewalk. *He looked happy enough,* Jean-Luc thought. *But why the dramatic visit?*

Greg bounded into the room exuding his usual energy. "Congratulations, Jean-Luc, well done! You and Wen were spectacular!" "So when do we get the money?" Jean-Luc said. "Well, Jean-Luc," Greg said, taking a seat. "As always, there are some hooks attached to this money." He looked at Jean-Luc for a split second before continuing. "First, it will be meted out in portions tied to successful attainment of several milestones in your development program." "So it's a pay-for-progress deal." "Exactly. No progress, no more money, no more company." "Sounds reasonable," Jean-Luc said.

"And another thing…my angels and I decided to take a larger piece of this investment than we had originally planned because the terms that were offered by some of the other investors were egregious. This means that my kids' future is riding even more on you – not to add any pressure, of course." Greg gave him a big mock smile.

Jean-Luc swallowed hard and met Greg's smile. He wanted to hide the anvil Greg had just tied around his neck, "Of course," replied Jean-Luc. "There's a lot riding on this for all of us."

Then Greg got up and closed the door. "I mentioned that there were some hooks attached to the financing, Jean-Luc. Specifically, we must create a Board of Directors comprised of me and a few of the new investors." *Not unreasonable*, thought Jean-Luc. "And we need to enhance the senior management of the company." Jean-Luc thought a moment. He thought of himself as a researcher and not a pharmaceutical executive. The anvil on his neck had just gotten a whole lot heavier. He suddenly felt a wave of fear. "Greg, is 'enhance the senior management team' a euphemism for I'm fired?"

Greg leaned forward in his chair and grabbed Jean-Luc's arm. "Christ no, Jean-Luc! You're absolutely essential to us! What the new investors insisted upon, and in candor, I agree with is that we recruit a seasoned pharmaceutical executive, someone who can manage the company and navigate it through Wall Street, the media, the growth we expect and ultimately commercialize the products you develop. We also need a solid Chief Financial Officer."

Jean-Luc now understood the reason for the personal visit. Jean-Luc led this team by default. He had never really asked for or expected to be the head of it forever, but he couldn't deny he was disappointed. On the other hand, he could see the merit in what Greg said. Jean-Luc quickly swallowed and digested the news. "Would I have a say in the CEO we hire?" he asked.

"You have my word," Greg said. And he stood to shake Jean-Luc's hand to seal his word like a stamp on melted wax. After that, Greg breezed out of Jean-Luc's office as briskly as he had come in. Jean-Luc took his seat and gazed out the window. *He and his little company were growing up*, he thought.

33

A couple of weeks after Greg's visit, Jean-Luc noticed the voice-mail light on his office phone flashing. He punched in his password and heard Greg's voice. "Jean-Luc, this is Greg. You recall I mentioned we needed to hire a CFO? Well, we've found him. His name is Bill Copley. Good guy. He'll be there tomorrow, so make him feel welcome and get him set up. Thanks."

Stunned at his lack of involvement in this decision, Jean-Luc deleted the message with a firm hammering of the delete key on his PC. It was unbelievable, actually; a fait accompli. He breathed deeply in and out several times and that helped to calm his anger. Eventually he remembered that Greg had promised he would be involved in the CEO selection – but he'd said nothing about the *CFO* selection. Jean-Luc decided he might as well look upon the recruitment of a good CFO as a further sign of progress, however abruptly it was handled.

Jean-Luc Googled this newest addition to BioNeura's staff. He found a bio of William A. Copley, published when he was promoted at his last company, a major public accounting firm. From the Google results, it was evident that Bill was an experienced accountant and an able navigator of the mercenary environment of partnership organizations. Jean-Luc read that Bill came from New Jersey, born and raised in Princeton Junction and graduated from Rutgers with honors. MBA from Columbia. A solid professional background, no doubt. He scrolled down and saw his photo. He laughed. Copley looked just like Billy Crystal – not now, but back when he did *City Slickers*. Jean-Luc wondered if he ought to ask Copley about the "one thing" Jack Palance talked about in that movie. *Maybe when we know each other better,* Jean-Luc thought. This amusing thought calmed Jean-Luc more. *Well, let's move on, I am sure he'll be a great addition."*

The next day Bill Copley arrived, and all such thoughts went out the window. A small man with an apparent Napoleon complex, Copley strutted like a bantam rooster and spoke in a voice that was too loud by half. From Jean-Luc's first conversation with him, he saw Bill Copley as brash, opinionated and outspoken. After two days Bill already criticized most parts of BioNeura's operation. Bill knew it all, it seemed, and proclaimed himself an expert on U.S. business history. He also bragged about his encyclopedic memory of facts, figures, and details, be they financial figures or sports statistics. *This is one self-impressed little man,* Jean-Luc thought.

What Jean-Luc didn't know was that Copley had dreamed of being a professional athlete. He had excelled on the high school playing field and was named an all-star in three different sports. But due to his size, he failed to receive an athletic scholarship to a top university. After his last rejection letter, Bill's coach sat him down and explained the facts of life: while he had overcome his small size in high school through tenacity and courage, the college recruiters had decided he couldn't do the same at the college level where size mattered so much more. It took Bill several months to accept this painful reality. When he did, he vowed to channel his energies into becoming an all-star in the business world – where his brains, work ethic and determination would matter more than his physicality.

34

Almost a year into the life of the new company, BioNeura took its first torpedo in the war of business. SNS, a European company also working in the area of Alzheimer's disease, filed a challenge on the patent BioNeura had just published on drug 230, now named BIO230. When Barbara's patent surveillance service noted the SNS objection, she called Jean-Luc and gave him a brief synopsis of the situation. Not wanting to repeat herself, she asked him to get the key managers and Wen Lin together for a teleconference so she could give them all a detailed account of the situation.

Once everyone was assembled, Jean-Luc phoned Barbara on the speakerphone. As usual, she wasted no time getting to the point. "Guys and gals, I think this is a serious threat. SNS filed a derivation proceeding, a complaint challenging our patent, claiming to have performed and presented 'prior art' in the field before we made our invention." Bill Copley shouted at her. "I thought this patent was bullet-proof!" he barked. "Not two months into this job we get a patent challenge that could kill the company?" Jean-Luc knew that what Bill was really thinking was, *I left a good job for this?* He knew that Bill always first thought about Bill.

This was the first time Barbara had spoken to, or been spoken to by Bill Copley. "If I am allowed to continue…" she said, staring coldly through him, "...I will give my assessment." Bill smiled and raised his chin slightly in defiance, but Jean-Luc noticed that he also squirmed just a little bit. "Of course, Barbara," Jean-Luc said. "Please go on." "While serious," she continued, "the threat is manageable. I see some technical and administrative weaknesses in their filing. I haven't yet had the time to fully assess the merits of their position." "How can we help?" asked Jean-Luc. "Once I dissect their complaint on a legal and administrative basis, I will need your team to help me do the same on a scientific and technical basis." "Anything else?" "Yes, one more thing. You better call your investors. Better they hear this from you."

Over the ensuing weeks Jean-Luc and Wen and others on the team worked with Barbara to prepare a response to the challenge by SNS. Everybody hoped that their response would be so strong that SNS would retreat and withdraw their challenge. Unfortunately, it could be months or years before they knew what SNS's next move would be.

Amlodipine (Norvasc®)

35

Jack's phone rang in his Paris office. "Monsieur Callahan, Madame Denise Williams est en ligne." *Denise Williams*, thought Jack. *How long has it been?* He decided the last time they spoke was when she'd tried to recruit him to a job in New Jersey. At least two years since then. He picked up the phone. "So, how's the head-hunting game these days, Denise?"

"Oh, could be better, Jack. Making a living, I guess. But if you let me place you at your next job, I might be able to buy a new pair of shoes."

Jack laughed out loud. "At a half year's salary for every senior exec you place, you've got enough shoes to certify you as pathologic!" "Yes, and I save my pointiest ones to kick jerks like you in the ass!"

Jack always enjoyed talking with Denise. He looked at his watch. "It's two AM in San Francisco. Do you ever put down your phone and sleep?" "I sleep when I can, Jack, but never without my phone." "Okay, Denise. So what's the job du jour?" "Seriously, this one is special, Jack. It has the features that you've been telling me you'd consider leaving Covington Labs for." Even though skeptical, Jack took the bait. "OK, I'll bite. Tell me more."

"My client is a Board member and major investor in a unique biotech company in San Francisco. The company is engaged in some leading-edge science in neurology and they've just published some hot results on Alzheimer's disease. On the strength of their patent and publication, they recently raised $50 million in a successful B Round of private financing. The company name is BioNeura. They're looking for a Chief Operating Officer who could grow to be their CEO."

The more Denise explained, the more interested Jack became. It had excellent and innovative science, an excellent Board and the participants in the recent financing represented a veritable "Who's Who" of A-List venture capitalists. After a few more minutes, Jack took it to the next stage. "Denise, you've piqued my interest. E-mail me at my personal address the position description and company profile. But don't pick out any new shoes yet."

Once they hung up, Jack mulled the possibility. *I wonder if that R&D guy I met in Las Vegas knows anything about BioNeura,* he thought. He buzzed his assistant. "Please pull my file from the ANA convention in Las Vegas and find the business card of a French MD, Ph.D. who works in San Francisco. "Un francais à Las Vegas ?" she asked. Such a concept would naturally strike the French mind as *impossible*. "Non, un Canadien," replied Jack. "Ah, plus logique," she replied. A French-Canadian, a lesser human than a Frenchman in the eyes of most Parisians, made more sense to her to be associated with Las Vegas.

36

Two weeks after his conversation with Denise, an Air France flight jetted him from Paris to San Francisco. On his way to interview for the COO position at BioNeura, he allowed himself to reflect on how nice it would be to live back in America. He had lived outside his native country for six years now, first in London and then in Paris, and he counted those years away as a wonderful blessing. Living outside one's home country gives a person a unique chance to see it for all its wonder and folly. For Jack, it also provided an opportunity to see America through the eyes of non-Americans. In doing so, he had developed a deeper love and appreciation for his country – a more mature love that accepted faults and shortcomings.

After nearly twelve hours of flying, Jack felt tired and dried out. He arrived at the Loews hotel in downtown San Francisco in the late afternoon and checked into his room where he admired the view over the bay and the Golden Gate Bridge. The sight never tired him. After he regained a bit of himself, he looked over the interview schedule Denise had prepared for him.

37

By 10 a.m., Jack's limo headed south to the office of BioNeura. On the way, he reviewed the biographies that he'd pulled off the web of the people he was about to meet. The happy coincidence of seeing Jean-Luc again in this circumstance made him smile and recall their first meeting in Las Vegas. *Que le monde est petit*, he thought, as he did more and more in his new language. Small world indeed.

The schedule had him starting with Jean-Luc around 10:30. At one o'clock or thereabouts he would meet the new CFO, Bill Copley, for lunch. After lunch he would meet with Dr. Wen Lin, the head of Research. Jack loathed the dinner with the investor board member. While he looked forward to meeting him a 7:00 dinner (4:00 a.m. Paris time) at the end of twelve hours of interviews with a razor-sharp and successful investor was nothing less than cruel, if not unusual, punishment.

The car pulled up to a very modest industrial park in South San Francisco. There were dozens of little businesses stacked side by side in what reminded Jack of a self-storage facility. He looked for numbers 65-67 and as they got closer to the numbers, the limo driver slowed down to look more carefully. He noted a wholesale florist, a window tinting business, a pet supply outlet. "Number 61," called out the driver like a bingo caller. "Your address should be two doors down." The driver rolled up to the second door and stopped the car with a grin that suggested that he had just found the lost city of Atlantis. "Here we are, sir. Number 65-67." A brand-new sign saying "BioNeura" indicated he had found the right place. The new sign with its crisp shiny letters made the building on which it hung appear even more tired and worn than it otherwise would have. As Jack stepped out of the car he saw Jean-Luc inside waving. Jack waved back as Jean-Luc gestured that he'd meet Jack at the front door.

"Bienvenue à San Francisco, Jack!" Jean-Luc grinned as he opened the door and stuck out his hand. "On peut parler français bien sûr. Vous êtes enfin un vrai Parisien, mon ami." Jack started to respond to Jean-Luc in French – "Oui, mais..." – but then stopped himself. "Jean-Luc," he said, "Parlons anglais, OK? Now that I'm back in the USA, let's speak English."

"Of course, Jack. I just recalled our conversation in Vegas when I suggested you become genetically Parisian in order to be accepted in Paris. I assumed you had it done and were now perfectly bilingual." Grinning and pleased with himself by his joke, he motioned Jack down the corridor towards his office.

The interview with Jean-Luc was casual and relaxed, more like a conversation than an interview. Jack wanted to know everything Jean-Luc could tell him about the concept, the data, the publication and the next steps. Jean-Luc was generous and accommodating and pleased to tell his story to someone who appreciated what had been accomplished. He narrated the events like a proud papa narrating his baby's first steps.

Jean-Luc also had a lot of questions for Jack. As much as he liked Jack as a man, he had to be sure he could rise to the huge challenges ahead. As planned by the recruiter, Greg was to assess Jack on the business aspects and his "presence" – that intangible combination of bearing, confidence, grace and control that says "I've got it together." Jean-Luc's assignment was to assess Jack's grasp of clinical development and his motivation for looking at this job opportunity.

Jean-Luc jumped in. "So, Jack, what do you figure will be the challenges we will face in developing this new medicine?" On one hand, the question was unfair. Jack didn't know the project as Jean-Luc did and he wasn't an R&D expert. On the other hand, the question was effective because if Jack had read the *Nature* article and knew enough about clinical development, he could give a decent reply. If he hadn't closely read the article, then he wasn't sufficiently motivated and shouldn't be involved in this.

Jack responded quickly and thoughtfully, pointing out where more information would help his reply, but not skirting the question. He discussed the need to refine the compound used in animals and develop a series of compounds to see if a better-tolerated, more effective one could be developed. He spoke about back-up compounds for the almost certain case that the first compound would eventually fail and another would need to take its place. He talked about the need for validated assessment tools for evaluating the effect of the compound versus placebo and standard therapy. Jean-Luc realized that Jack was not only well prepared, he had an intense interest in what BioNeura was doing.

The time with Jean-Luc flew by and then Jean-Luc escorted Jack to Bill Copley's office. "Great seeing you again," Jean-Luc said, as they shook hands. "Bill will be along shortly, I hope."

Jack surveyed Bill's office while he waited. He knew that much could be deciphered about a person by the contents of his or her office. Objects were there to say something about the occupant. Some objects said, "I am highly-educated." Others said, "I am refined and cultured." Some offices were virtual photographic altars to the person's families. Others were a trophy case that just happened to have office furniture.

Bill's office was filled with sports memorabilia, signed baseball bats, basketballs and photos of stars standing with Bill. No photos of his family. Jack thought that either Bill had no family or if he did, he was protecting their privacy. On the other hand, maybe he didn't care enough about them to have pictures.

Bill was now twenty minutes late and he had sent no word to anyone. They were scheduled to go to lunch and Jack was hungry. He also wanted to have enough time with the others on his list. After five more minutes, Jean-Luc came by. "No Bill?" he asked. "Nope." Replied Jack, struggling mightily to hide his annoyance. Jean-Luc's expression told Jack that Bill's tardiness wasn't unusual. Jean-Luc apologized again and promised to find Bill.

Ten more minutes elapsed and then Bill Copley strutted in. Jack rose to greet him. "Bill Copley. It's nice to meet you. Sorry I'm late, but the gym I go to has a pre-lunch training routine that's excellent. My trainer wanted to push me a little harder today because he thought I could handle it. I benched 250 today – a new personal best!" *What an ass*, thought Jack. *It would've been better to have lied to me than tell me his bench press was more important than meeting me.*

Bill looked disappointed that Jack didn't congratulate him. "Let's go eat," Bill said. "I'll drive." He showed Jack the way to the parking lot, where Jack was not at all surprised to see Bill's car. *A phallic-mobile*, thought Jack as he opened the door to Bill's new Corvette. The ride was short but Bill managed to maximize the number of gear shifts for the distance traveled. They were at their table in minutes.

While they ate Jack asked Bill about his background and was impressed by his track record and his excellent financial mind. He recalled from his research that Bill had done some creative deals that had been groundbreaking in their time and had gone on to become the standard templates for similar deals in the industry.

When Bill dove into Jack's background, Jack's no-brag-just-facts answers were more humble than Bill's self- aggrandizing approach, but he got his points across. He got more across than he knew. *This guy has an excellent track record*, thought Bill as he slurped his pasta. *Worked overseas, consistently delivered results and knows the business. He's young for his accomplishments. Impressive.*

They found themselves talking of sports and Bill's mental encyclopedia sprung open. Bill knew everything about everything in the major sports and even had a stunning knowledge of arcane ones like fencing and jai alai. Jack found himself wondering how Bill ever breathed since he talked constantly. But the guy was entertaining – you had to give him that. They finished their lunch and the short drive back to the office was another neck snapper. Even so, they arrived 20 minutes late for Jack's next interview: Dr. Wen Lin.

The domino effect of their tardiness put Wen Lin off his schedule so Jack sat and waited for him in his office. Wen's office space was a small square lined with shelves overflowing with scientific journals, data printouts, textbooks and correspondence. Relatively neat piles of papers presumably organized in some way waited for Wen's attention on his desk. Jack didn't need much time to make an observation on this office: Wen lived and breathed his work. He suspected that his home was the same repository of facts, figures, theories and correspondence.

A small section of one of the shelves, almost out of sight caught Jack's eye as being out of place. It contained several cookbooks. Jack pulled one off the shelf and leafed through it. The book he chose was in Chinese as far as Jack could tell, and it appeared to be ancient.

"You won't find spare ribs and General Tso's chicken in there." Jack turned to the voice which had been amused and inviting and saw a face to match. "Hi, Jack. Welcome to BioNeura. I am Wen Lin." "Wen, delighted to meet you," said Jack as he placed the book back on the shelf and extended his hand for a shake. "Congratulations on your work and that exciting article in *Nature*." Wen beamed a thousand-watt smile and bowed slightly to acknowledge the compliment.

"Thank you Jack. It's always a team effort. I played a small part." "I'm sure that's not the case, Wen, but your modesty is charming." "Do you like to cook, Jack?" "I love watching talented people cook," said Jack. "I love the output of cooking. I even enjoy reading recipes. But I don't like to cook. On the other hand, every day at work I struggle to take all of my resources and stir them together to come up with something greater than their parts. I guess I am cooking all day long."

"That makes sense," Wen said. "But I *love* to cook. I have loved it since my childhood in Hong Kong watching my mother cook. I think my love of cooking is just a creative outlet for me. In biochemistry I am constrained by physical laws. But when I cook, I can combine whatever I want. It may not taste great all of the time, but that's the discovery part that I love." Jack pointed at the book he had been looking at. "Do you cook from those books?" "Those? No. Those are family treasures. I keep them here because my house has been burglarized twice and the office is more secure. The one you opened is from the late 19th century. A novelty, since Chinese cookbooks were rare in those times. But, Jack, I'm sure you didn't fly six thousand miles to talk about cookbooks. Have a seat."

He poured them both tea and Jack asked Wen many questions about the concept, the *Nature* article, and the next steps in development. He also asked about the other programs Wen worked on, one in pain relief and another in Parkinson's disease. He found Wen's approach to both programs fascinating and innovative.

"Who's that handsome lad?" asked Jack, pointing to a framed photograph on Wen's bookcase. "Oh, that's my son, Gabriel," replied Wen, beaming with pride. He went and got the photo and handed it to Jack. "How old is he?" Jack asked. "Almost seven years old now – I can hardly believe it! Funny, he was conceived just about the same time I dreamed up the idea of what is now BIO230. Gabe and BIO230 are my two twin kids." Jack smiled. "I get it," he said. He looked at the photograph again for a long moment, then handed it back to Wen. "You're a lucky man, Wen. I envy you."

Wen had been asked by the recruiting team at BioNeura to see how much Jack understood about the research process, so he peppered Jack with questions in this area. He liked Jack's honesty when he didn't feel competent to venture an opinion and he appreciated his instincts when addressing the hypothetical cases Wen had thrown his way. From his own standpoint Wen wanted to know if Jack would be a capable student – if he had the aptitude to learn and would therefore be able to explain the science of BioNeura to future job candidates, investors and the media. At the end of the interview, he was satisfied that Jack knew what he knew, knew what he didn't know and was self-confident enough to admit the difference.

Wen glanced at his watch. "Wow, I have to get you to your car." He looked out the window and saw the limo waiting. Jack stood and stuck out his hand. "I really enjoyed meeting you. Thanks for your patience with me." "Not at all Jack, I enjoyed our discussion. You have terrific instincts for research." He tapped the books on the shelf and smiled. "I think you'd be an excellent chef." They both laughed and Jack promised to think about it. Wen walked Jack to the waiting car and waved as Jack's limo carried him away.

38

Jack had a few hours until his dinner with the founding board member. He looked at his watch: Four o'clock local time, one o'clock in the morning in Paris. He was glad he had spoken to Diana early that morning. He could let her sleep tonight. His car got on the road just ahead of rush hour and he was back at the Mandarin Oriental hotel in 40 minutes.

After a short nap Jack was ready to go again. He knew he would start to flag again around nine so he needed to avoid alcohol tonight. He got his cab at the hotel entrance and entered the restaurant just before seven. The maître d greeted him at the door and immediately seated him at what he referred to as "Mr. Jimko's table." "Mr. Callahan, Mr. Jimko called and said he would be just a few minutes late. He asked me to offer you his apologies and a glass of champagne." "Thanks, but I'll have a mineral water and lime, please."

The drink arrived just before his dinner companion did. He had just put his lips on the glass when he felt a large hand on his shoulder. "If you're not Jack Callahan, I want to know what you're doing at my table." Jack returned his glass to the table and got to his feet. "I'm Jack Callahan." "Greg Jimko. I'm a founder of BioNeura." Jack and Greg shook hands. "Welcome to San Francisco. I'm looking forward to getting to know you tonight."

"Jack, what I thought we'd do is have a drink or two on the patio, grill each other for a while and then continue our conversation over dinner. What can we get you to drink?" Jack hesitated. "Oh, I'm a little jet-lagged Greg. I'll stick with what I've got right now, thanks."

It was a beautiful evening and the fresh air felt good to Jack. Their conversation was like verbal ping-pong. It was fast-paced with volleys and serves and moved to a new topic as soon as the prior one lost speed. They talked about the developments in Washington affecting the industry, the regulatory situation in Europe, the Japanese market and its future, the role of the pharmaceutical industry in the Ebola and HIV crises in Africa and a handful of other topics.

After about a half hour on the patio, Greg extended his big arm and announced it was time to take their table. Once they were seated, Greg asked "Jack, share with me your view of the pharmaceutical industry and its role in developing medicines for diseases as prevalent and complicated as Alzheimer's?"

"Wow, what a vast question! What do you want to know?"

"Whatever you want to tell me. The floor is yours."

Jack quickly assembled his thoughts and then began his reply. "First of all, it takes the integration of myriad resources of our society to successfully develop a new medicine. A thriving university system is essential for uncovering the basic biological foundations and principles on which industry can apply its resources –BioNeura's Alzheimer's program is a great example – it began at Pacific University. Drug development is massively capital intensive so philanthropic and venture capital play a vital role getting a new idea off the ground and robust financial markets are essential for helping new companies and ideas fly higher. Our government provides the rule of law under which a patent can be issued to protect a new idea, it oversees the conduct of pre-clinical and clinical studies and is the ultimate arbiter of whether or not a new medicine will be approved for use in patients – and more and more, our government pays for new medicines. Scientific experts in myriad specialties are called upon to help develop new medicines. Diagnostic companies, advocacy groups, physicians and last but not least, the patients who volunteer to participate in clinical studies. I could go on and on...You see, the pharmaceutical industry is but one of the many essential contributors to the development of new medicines."

"What's your view of pricing of pharmaceuticals?" asked Greg.

"It's really about *value*, Greg. Alzheimer's disease, BioNeura's interest, is a perfect context for this debate. The enormity of the socio-economic impact of AD almost can't be believed – about 5.5 million Americans have AD now and by 2050, there will be over 16 million. In America alone, the current annual cost of caring for patients with AD is a quarter of a trillion dollars and is expected to reach 1.1 trillion dollars a year by 2050. Here's the thing – if a new medicine could just *delay* the onset or progression of AD let alone cure it, the savings to our economy would be measured in hundreds of billions of dollars per year – think of the *value* that a new medicine for AD would bring to our society! Think of the resources we would free-up for society to put to good use!"

"How do you factor in the *human costs* of AD, Jack – the emotional, physical and economic stress that grinds down the millions of people caring for people with the disease?"

"Exactly, Greg. Besides all of the *economic* value that a new medicine for AD would deliver, it would un-shackle from a brutal emotional and physical burden an estimated 15 million Americans who currently provide care for people with AD. Think about the cost to society of that burden and the value of what a new medicine could bring to these people? This is the *real* mission of what the broad, interdependent and interconnected eco-system of drug development is trying to do. The pharmaceutical industry is an important player but one of many in this system, working for the patients, the care-givers and their families."

"Thanks Jack," raising his glass in Jack's direction. "You presented your views pretty well for a guy whose brain is jet-lagged and working at 7 a.m. Paris time!"

39

The day after Jack's interviews, Denise the executive recruiter held a conference call among all the interviewers of the four leading candidates for the BioNeura COO job. They discussed the four candidates in the order they were interviewed. The first three candidates had some support but failed to gain a consensus among the interviewers.

"OK," said Denise, "what's the feedback on Jack?" "I think he's excellent," said Jean-Luc, and he ticked off Jack's performance in the areas that Jean-Luc had been assigned to cover in the interview. "I agree," said Wen, adding a few more points supporting his view. "He made a good impression," said Greg Jimko, the informal head of the search committee. "He's smart, confident, articulate and passionate, with a solid track record. He's worth a further look." The comments went similarly with the others, generally positive for Jack with some questions needing to be delved into further.

"Not to be a contrarian…" began Bill Copley, "…but I think Jack is a little light for the challenge. I'm not sure he has enough gravitas to instill confidence in future investors and employees. He also isn't an R&D guy and we're fundamentally an R&D company now." Bill waited to see if anyone supported his view.

"So, what do we have here?" asked Denise, the moderator. "I think we should keep looking," shot Bill. "Not a bad idea," said Greg. "Jack's good, but let's see if we can do better." "Denise, cast your net once more," said Greg. "Yes sir," replied Denise and she concluded the teleconference and thanked them all for their effort.

After he hung up, Bill Copley sat back with a contented smile. He slipped his notes on Jack and dropped them into the file folder. "So long, Jackie boy," he said, and he slid the file drawer closed.

Back in Switzerland, Dr. Shah put his feet up on his new desk, a mahogany masterpiece that he had found in an antiques shop in Geneva, not far from his office. The dealer claimed that the desk had belonged to a Prussian general. Regardless of its true lineage, it suited Shah. The desk was large, hard and strong – characteristics that he wanted to instill in SNS. Shah gazed out on Lake Geneva and admired the view, a magnificent panorama and took in not just the sparkling Alps-fed-lake but also a well-endowed marina, a range of distant mountains and a deep blue, cloudless sky.

His eye settled on the "Jet d'Eau," the fountain at the south end of the lake. This icon of Geneva blasted a 400-foot high plume of water at a rate of 500 liters of water per second and at a speed of 120 miles per hour. Shah appreciated the physical principles behind the fountain – power and focus on one converging point. They were, he thought, sound guiding principles on which to guide his actions.

Someone knocked on his door, his General Counsel. *He looks nervous*, Shah thought. *With good reason!* Without being asked, the lawyer launched into an update on the legal issues that were facing the company. Shah listened patiently, enjoying the moment. Something about it made him think of his falcon, Mars and the way he sometimes watched his prey twist and tremble in his talons before killing it.

After the lawyer had finished his report, Shah slid an envelope across his desk without a word. The man picked it up and began to open the envelope. "Don't bother to open that here," Shah said coldly. "You'll find in the envelope the terms of your severance. According to the Swiss employment law, your severance package is generous. I'll expect your office to be emptied of you and your belongings within an hour."

The man stared at Shah as if frozen solid. Then, slowly thawing, he stammered out a question but Shah cut him off. "There's nothing to say. Your services are no longer required. Good day." With that, Shah motioned through his office window for the waiting security guard to escort the GC to his office. By the time they got there, his belongings were already packaged up and waiting for him. The security guard efficiently escorted him from the building. The termination mirrored the character of the boss; cold, clinical and efficient.

Looking again at the jet d'eau, he thought...*Power and focus.* He then reached into the top drawer of his desk and pulled out a file entitled "First 100 Days." It listed the key objectives Shah had assigned himself for the first hundred days of his new job as CEO of SNS. On this, his first day, he could consider objective #1 one-half completed – "Make General Counsel Disappear and Install Gloria as New GC."

Simvastatin (Zocor®)

40

Jack opened a cryptic email from Denise, the executive recruiter. "Call me ASAP" is all it said. He checked the time and then dialed her cell phone.

"Jack," Denise said, "how are you?" "Oh, after many weeks I'm just about recovered from my depression after being rejected for the COO job at BioNeura." He tried to sound charming and nonchalant but the words couldn't hide the disappointment he felt. "Come on, Jack," said Denise. "I told you that you were still a strong candidate. They just wanted to look at some others, too." "Yeah," Jack laughed. "That's code for thanks but no thanks." Denise lowered her voice. "Jack, listen. You have strong supporters for your candidacy. Without saying too much, several board members want to speak to you again."

The thought of such a situation made Jack uneasy. "I don't know, Denise. If I'm not exactly what the board members and management are looking for, or if there's strong division at the board level, I don't want the job. It'll be hard enough given the challenges the company's facing. I don't want to go into a job with some of the board waiting for me to make a mistake so they can say 'I told you so' to their peers."

She paused; a long one that told Jack he had pegged the scenario correctly. "Jack, listen to me," Denise said, practically whispering. "As we look at other candidates, you look better and better. You're now the favored candidate by the vast majority of the search committee." What she didn't say was that Greg Jimko so strongly supported Jack that Greg had undertaken the task of quietly checking Jack out on his own. What he had learned was so impressive that he had easily convinced himself that Jack was the right man. One other thing Denise didn't say to Jack was that Bill Copley couldn't be convinced of Jack's attractiveness, but he said he could go along.

"So what do they want to do?" Jack asked. This question pleased Denise as it meant that despite his bruised ego, he was still interested. But she had to confirm it. "Jack, knowing you're the favored candidate, are you interested?" "Yes," he responded. "So what's the next step?" "They want to make you an offer, Jack." This was exciting news, but Jack didn't want to appear to be over eager. He knew he would be negotiating soon and too much interest would play against him. "I'd be happy to take a look at their offer, Denise. Send it to me at my home email whenever it's ready." "I'll have it to you in a few days, Jack." They said their good-byes and Jack hung up his phone.

41

After being at SNS for six weeks, Shah again pulled the "100 Days" list from his drawer. He had made respectable progress on objective number two, "Establish New York Office." This one required some persuasion, but not as much as he had expected. Shah had impressed and charmed the SNS Board and they wanted him to get off to a good start and feel supported. So Shah pushed this momentary advantage. He got the Board to agree on a New York office. The only issue was the location. Shah wanted a posh office location, one that fit both his personal stature and what he intended to be the future stature of SNS. He chose a magnificent location at Central Park South on the 40th floor of the Billings building. The view looking north took in all of Central Park and the upscale neighborhoods of both the Upper East Side and Upper West Side. The rent was obscene even for New York.

The Board member who chaired the audit committee balked at the expense. He said he couldn't in good conscience endorse the expenditure and wasn't comfortable with the 10-year lease. After some negotiation and some fast real estate work over a couple of weeks, Shah found an office that met his goals and one the Audit Committee Chairman could agree to.

The third objective on Shah's 100 Days list followed the strict rules of *The Prince*, the 16th-century work of Niccolo Machiavelli describing how to attain, maintain and extend power in an organization. Machiavelli's rule regarding the consolidation of control once one had seized it was to promptly kill the relatives of the last ruler. While Shah had no intention of following this rule literally, he nevertheless intended to remove those closely aligned with the previous regime. He was reasonably happy with the progress so far. Having identified four executives and managers who were closely aligned with the previous CEO, Shah had systematically moved to embarrass, discredit, discreetly threaten and generally make them feel unwelcome. So far, he had fired the General Counsel and two other executives had voluntarily resigned. He was on track with his goal of eliminating all four by the 100th day.

Having achieved his top three objectives, his fourth objective, "Recruit a New Team," now rose to the top of his list. Shah had prepared a list of new executives who would unconditionally support his regime. Now he pulled out the list and picked up the phone to call his favorite executive recruiter, a man who had worked with him for 20 years and knew exactly what Shah wanted – and didn't want – in an executive. The recruiter answered his cell phone. "This is Dr. Shah. I have an assignment for you. Call me at my Geneva office when you get to yours." "I'll call you within an hour's time," the recruiter said.

42

Preparing himself for potential disappointment, Jack nervously opened the attachment to Denise's email. He was excited about this job, maybe too excited, and he didn't want to be let down by the terms or the contract conditions. Now, as he read through it he saw that the terms were fair. The contract conditions were typical. The one point he wanted to clarify and confirm was the understanding that as Chief Operating Officer, he would be the natural choice for the eventual CEO position – provided of course, that he proved himself.

After a couple weeks of back and forth Jack had the best contract he could expect. The board wouldn't put in writing anything about Jack's ascension to the CEO role but his conversations with them made it clear – if he delivered, the CEO spot was *virtually* assured.

The decision was too important to Jack's and Diana's future not to give themselves every advantage in making the best possible call. A getaway was what they needed, Jack told Diana, let's do that long weekend Normandy trip we've been talking about!" "That's perfect Jack! You know my bags are always packed!"

They drove north from Paris on their way to the Chateau d'Audrieu, a beautiful 18th-century chateau not far from the Normandy coast. There was plenty in that part of France to keep their eyes occupied. They visited the Normandy beaches, where so many had fallen to liberate France and Europe on D-Day. They marveled at the Bayeux tapestry, the 90-meter, 11th-century woven narrative of the Battle of Hastings in 1066. They even wound throughout the Norman countryside along the "Route des Pommiers," or apple growers' road, where they stopped to sample the cider and fermented delicacies of this apple-growing region.

But wherever they went and whatever they feasted their eyes on, their brains were never far from the decision at hand. There were lots of pluses and minuses to weigh: San Francisco versus Paris, his company the established Covington Labs versus the unknown start-up BioNeura. Then the question of whether they could stand to move again had to be dealt with.

As their observations occurred to them, they dropped them into an imaginary pot that simmered over the weekend. It was the way they processed this type of decision. After almost two decades of marriage and six moves during that time, the process worked for them and they trusted it. Now they hoped it would once again help them make the right decision.

Being able to drive up to Normandy, seeing these spectacular sights, eating the delicious food, walking the grounds of this stunning chateau; the whole experience made it difficult to vote in favor of leaving their current dream assignment. On the other hand, they knew this assignment would end in a couple of years anyway and they'd then be back to Covington's New York headquarters. So from that standpoint, a move was just a question of time.

After an amazing dinner on the last night of their getaway, Jack and Diana decided to enjoy a walk in the lighted gardens. They strolled hand in hand, saying nothing, each mentally tasting the imaginary stew of thoughts they had prepared over the past few days. At the far end of the path they found an old fountain flanked by a bench, and they rested there. The gardens were fragrant and the light and warm breeze carried a hint of salt from the sea. The night was quiet and the fountain bubbled in the background.

Jack took Diana's hand. "So what do you think, babe?" Jack listened carefully as Diana spoke. He had long since come to respect her judgment and her ability to separate the chaff from the wheat of a situation. After an hour or so of talking, they came to their decision.

They walked up to chateau and entered the bar. "Une bouteille de champagne, s'il vous plaît, monsieur. Dom Pérignon, Œnothèque 1973, si vous en avez une." The sommelier raised his eyebrow at Jack's request, impressed that the American had the savoir-faire to order such a fine bottle of champagne; in French, no less. It was expensive, but the occasion called for nothing but the best and the sommelier soon presented it with the commensurate drama and flourish. Jack and Diana toasted their decision to take the job and move to San Francisco. They drank this superb champagne with some sadness, however, knowing that they would be making no more European memories like this magical weekend in Normandy.

The next morning on their two-hour drive back to Paris, Diana opened with a tone familiar to Jack. "Jack….I've been thinking…" The tone meant she had been planning something. Not only that, it meant she had made a decision she knew was right about and just needed to convince Jack of it. "What is it, babe?" Jack said. "You know Clara's in San Francisco." Clara and Diana were friends from college days, back when they were both studying performing arts in New York. Diana had been the singer, Clara the dancer. They developed an instant bond as freshmen together and went on to share four years with New York at their feet and every young man they wanted there as well. They had kept up their close friendship despite the interruptions of Clara's ballet touring schedule and Diana's travels with her flourishing theater career. The two were as close as two friends could be.

"Yeah," Jack said. "How is Clara? I haven't spoken to her the last few times you guys talked. Is she still involved in ballet?" "Well, she's teaching dance on the side, but she can't make a living at dance anymore. So she's working as an assistant to an executive in a biotech company. She lives in San Bruno, right near your new company's office." Jack now knew what would come next. "She's a fantastic assistant and is looking for something new. You should snap her up before she's hired by someone else."

Jack thought a moment. Above everything, he respected Diana's judgment of character. Whenever he went against it he inevitably wound up ruing the day. He liked Clara. She was bright, energetic and refined. "I'll tell you what I'll do. I'll interview the internal and external candidates for the job and then talk to Clara. If she's as good as you say she is, she'll naturally get the job. How 'bout that?"

"Thank you," she said. She leaned over and kissed Jack on the cheek, then turned her head and watched the scenery whiz by. She knew Clara would get the job. And she knew Clara and Jack would get along great.

43

Of all the things Shah liked about his new position as CEO of a private European company, perhaps the most immediately satisfying aspect was that he no longer had to answer to shareholders with their inane questions, nor did he have to bother with the extent of detailed financial disclosures that his American and British counterparts did. Shah had the power, perqs, and pay of an American CEO without the headaches. Of course he did have to keep satisfied the company's founding family, the Antonellis.

The Antonellis were Italian-Swiss aristocracy. Bankers, industrialists and more recently, philanthropists. They were the modern Medicis, richer than Croesus and on a first-name basis with heads of state throughout Europe and in most of the Middle East. Shah tolerated the meddling of the two Antonelli brothers whenever they poked their noses into "his" business because he knew they would lose interest as soon as the next Formula One race or sailing regatta captured their attention. So far, he was happy at SNS.

44

After his notice period at Covington ended, Jack left for San Francisco to begin his new job with BioNeura. He spent the first week assessing his staffing needs, including the position of executive assistant. After meeting five candidates being unimpressed with any, he phoned Clara.

It was great to hear her voice. After spending a few minutes catching up, Jack got to the point. "Diana tells me you might be interested in a new challenge. Is that still the case?" "Yes, I'm looking for a new gig, Jack. I heard about BioNeura from the BioCentury newsletter and I looked them up on the web. I'm impressed by what's going on over there." Her initiative impressed Jack. "Well, Clara," said Jack, "I need an assistant who wants to be challenged and is willing to work very hard. Are you interested in meeting me for a couple hours to talk about that?" "Absolutely," Clara said. "One thing I'd like to talk about is how we would make sure your friendship with Diana didn't get jeopardized if you were to take this job.

A great assistant is difficult to find, but a great friend is even harder." "I appreciate that, Jack. I'll think about it and be prepared to talk about it when we meet."

For Jack's first staff meeting, he started it as he always had, with what he called "Headlines" – a brief news update from each of his department heads. He saw no reason to abandon the practice at BioNeura, and on one of his first staff meetings he invited Jean-Luc. "OK, Jean-Luc," he said. "Give it up – what's your headline?"

Jean-Luc cleared his throat and with the dramatic little flourish of shooting his sleeves and slowly returning his pen to his jacket pocket, he began. "Our Phase I results in human volunteers confirmed, in nearly every respect, the exciting results we saw in the mice." He projected a slide on the overhead projector to show the results of the trial they had begun almost a year before. "As you can see, the beta amyloid plaques seen in the MRIs of mice genetically modified to develop the human form of AD are very similar to those seen in the MRIs in diseased humans. This makes us feel confident that the disease we have in the mice is the same disease we are trying to treat in the humans."

Wen looked on, beaming his big grin and looking like his cheeks would cramp from over exertion. "What's more," Jean-Luc continued, "after we gave the humans BIO230, the chemical by-products we collected in the blood and urine of the human volunteers is the same as that seen in the mice in roughly the same proportions and over roughly the same course in time. Furthermore, BIO230 appears to be well tolerated at the doses given. What this means, gang is that we're on the right track!" The team erupted in a burst of applause, an overt compensation for their repressed fear of failure. The unspoken fear had been that the observations seen in the mice would be specific to the mouse and not repeatable in man. This happens so often that researchers refrain from showing any enthusiasm for a new compound until they see positive animal results repeated in man.

Jack was excited, though any excitement had to be tempered by the fact that in passing from animal results to Phase I results, their odds of getting BIO230 to the market had "jumped" from a 95 percent chance of failure to an 85 percent chance of failure. *No point in bringing that up right now,* Jack thought.

Once the group settled down, he got back to business – reviewing spending, human resource issues, quality, and progress on the other compounds in the pipeline at BioNeura. Because nearly all medicines failed for one of dozens of reasons to get to the market, the accepted key to winning was to make many bets or take many "shots on goal" as the venture capitalists say. Jack knew he had to keep all of the company's compounds moving to increase their company's chances of getting at least one to market.

After the business was done and as Jack's staff left the room, Jean-Luc pulled Wen aside and gave him a big hug. "Congratulations, Wen! What an exciting time for our company – thanks to you! After work, let's go for a drink to celebrate."

Wen blushed. "Thank you for the kind words, Jean-Luc, and for the invitation. But today is my son's tenth birthday and we begin celebrating it right after work." "Gabriel is ten already?" This amazed Jean-Luc. "Where has the time gone?" He shook his head in wonder, and Wen thought he detected some deeper meaning to Jean-Luc's words. Even someone as fulfilled by his work as Jean-Luc, he sometimes wondered what he had missed by focusing solely on his passion to help "his" patients.

Jean-Luc quickly bounced out of his reflection with a big smile and a slap on the back for Wen. "You go, my friend. Have a great evening with your family. We can get that drink another time."

Hydrocodone/Acetaminophen (Lortab®)

45

Jean-Luc and Jack spent the next day together reviewing progress on BIO230 and the other programs. They were going over budget figures when Jean-Luc's gaze moved to a different kind of figure – that of a striking woman walking down the hall past his office.

"That's Clara Mitchell," said Jack. "I'm interviewing her for my assistant spot." "She's so graceful," Jean-Luc said. "She moves like she's dancing." "Good call," Jack said. "She danced professionally. She still teaches dance, in fact."

Jean-Luc craned his neck to watch her as long as he could. She had a classic ballerina's body – tall, thin, athletic and graceful in her movements. "You *must* introduce me, Jack," said Jean-Luc, rising from his chair. "Right now." "Sure, c'mon," Jack said, and as they emerged into the hallway they could see Clara being shown into Jack's office a few doors down.

Jack walked into his office and immediately gave Clara a big hug, which surprised Jean-Luc. "We've known each other many years," Jack said. "Clara and Diana were college roommates. Dr. Jean-Luc Dumas, meet Clara Mitchell." Jean-Luc shook her hand with all the Gallic charm he could muster, which was plenty. "Enchanté', Madame Mitchell," he crooned. "Mademoiselle Mitchell," she said. *Better*, thought Jean-Luc, looking her squarely in the eye while grinning charmingly.

As the three of them chatted, Jean-Luc admired Clara's long, thick, chestnut-colored hair. She had fair skin with a hint of freckles on her nose and neck and her eyes were a beguiling mix of brown, green and yellow. But Jean-Luc was seduced most of all by her laugh – soft and strong all at once, delivered by a smile that lit up her face and everyone else's. Jean-Luc excused himself and as he left, he discretely flashed a thumbs-up to Jack. *Horny Quebecois*, Jack thought. *He better not do his hiring this way.*

After a two-hour meeting, Jack decided Clara was by far the best candidate he had interviewed. In truth, part of him had been hoping she wouldn't be the best because he feared how her personal connection with Diana might influence their working relationship. Before their meeting, he found himself feeling uncomfortable with the possibility that he might have to tell Clara she didn't get the job. Who needed complications like that? He had cursed himself for potentially breaking his cardinal rule of never hiring close friends.

Clara addressed this issue head-on before Jack had to bring it up. "Jack, I thought about the issue you raised. Here's how I see it. We will *never* have an issue that will jeopardize our friendship – or mine and Diana's. If our working relationship isn't working for some reason, I'll resign. I am a superb executive assistant and I can find work in a heartbeat. All I ask is that you be completely honest with me. I promise you the same. That way, we'll tell each other if something isn't working, and if we can't fix it, I'll resign quietly once I find you a good replacement." Her strong and confident approach impressed Jack. "Good answer, Clara. Welcome aboard."

46

With the encouraging Phase I human results now in hand, Jack thought it was time to update the Board. He asked Jean-Luc to prepare a presentation, including a review of the total investment made to date, recent progress, and an update on their progress versus the objectives that were set when they raised the Series B funding. He also wanted to remind the Board of the high-level timeline and future investment needed to bring this compound through development.

A couple of days later, as Jack dealt with answering a back-log of emails, Bill Copley exploded into Jack's office without a knock on the door, a hello or any courtesy whatsoever. "Who the hell do you think you are?' he screamed as he strutted back and forth in front of Jack's desk. This shocked Jack as he'd had only generally pleasant exchanges with Bill in his months at BioNeura. He was also amused by the spectacle in front of him – a small man pacing like a caged animal, puffing up his chest, hands on hips, face as red as a ripe tomato.

As Bill ranted, Jack calmly closed down his e-mail account without even looking up. Then Jack stood and closed the door. In a friendly voice, he smiled warmly. "Good morning, Bill. Would you mind starting over again? I was so focused on my work that I missed your question." Jack knew this approach would un-do Bill.

Jack watched calmly as Bill's eyes and nostrils widened and his face reddened from the neck up like mercury rising in a thermometer. "I said, who the hell do you think you are?" "Bill, take a deep breath...and sit down." He didn't. "Jack, I'd like to know who the hell made you the head of this operation. I thought we were managing as peers." "We are, Bill," Jack said. "What has you all worked up?"

Bill placed his hands on Jack's desk leaning forward on his toes and looking up to get his face as even with Jack's as possible. "Jean-Luc told me you and he were presenting to the Board on topics including the financial aspects of the business," replied Bill. "I am the only executive the Board hears from on financial issues and I have called these meetings in the past."

Now Jack understood. Bill felt threatened and he thought Jean-Luc and Jack were marginalizing his role. "Bill, I didn't know you were the only person to call Board meetings; there's no policy on it. I believe Jean-Luc arranged such meetings before you arrived – right?"

Bill glared at him, but didn't speak. Jack continued. "We fully intended for you to present the financial material. That's why Jean-Luc approached you today." The last point seemed to soften Bill's attitude. He physically relaxed a little from his rigid posture and began to walk slowly away from Jack and toward the window in Jack's office. "Jack, we're in this together," he said. "I thought we were a team."

Jack had to admit he enjoyed Bill's little drama, the pathos in his voice, his playing hurt and betrayed. Jack knew exactly the game that Bill was playing. "We *are* a team, Bill," Jack said soothingly. "We'll make sure we develop these Board presentations together." This pleased Bill – his temper tantrum had worked exactly as planned. He knew now that Jack would think twice in the future about leaving him out of any initiatives with the Board. "Good," said Bill, as he turned and began walking out of Jack's office. "We understand each other."

Those last words hung in the air like spent gun powder and Jack wanted to slap the smirking little toad as he walked past him. But he decided to take the high road. "Next time, Bill, don't get wound-up. We need you here and we can't have you popping an aneurysm." On hearing this, Bill paused in his step but just clenched his fists and teeth and continued walking. Jack watched him as he strutted down the hall. *There's obviously more to that little display than just a finance presentation to the Board,* thought Jack, going back to his emails. *I can't worry about what mind games he's playing; we've got a lot of heavy work to get done.* But his instincts told him that he would try to keep Bill Copley under a closer eye just the same.

47

Without any warning, Jack received a registered letter from legal counsel of Societé Nationale de la Suisse, SNS He signed the return receipt and opened the letter. He scanned it quickly. "Clara, get Barbara Siegel on the line right now, please." Clara had Barbara's number on speed dial and she connected her to Jack in seconds. "Barbara, I just got a letter from SNS, informing me that they found our response to their complaint about the patent dispute between us completely unacceptable. They've decided to elevate their point of view and just filed a legal action against our patents for BIO230." "Send it over to me now, and don't mention it to anyone until my patent group studies it. I'll be back to you within two hours." "Will do, Barbara," said Jack and he made a pdf of the letter and sent it to Barbara.

Jack's heart raced. Could this handicap the company? Jack couldn't believe that SNS asserted that they had done prior work to BioNeura's in this area. This would mean Jack's team had missed this fact, which could happen if SNS operated quietly, but BioNeura knows all of the leaders in this field and they should have heard word of any interesting work going on at SNS or anywhere else. His thoughts drifted to Nathaniel Shah and their brief encounter in Las Vegas. Now Shah was the CEO at SNS. Jack remembered again with remarkable clarity Shah's piercing, cold black eyes.

48

"So, is it possible that my courageous General Counsel is a little nervous?" Shah looked up from his desk to study Gloria's face. "I told you from the beginning that we were taking a risk with this patent challenge," she said. "Our arguments are thinner than my contraceptive patch. If this goes to trial and we're proven wrong, we could suffer huge financial damages." Shah now kept his eyes on his paper, but the change in his voice reflected the annoyance rising inside him. He spoke crisply, a little condescendingly. "I know that, Gloria. We have been over this a hundred times. Our scientists worked on some experimental drugs that elicited some chemical reactions in the brain. One of the reactions related to one of the chemicals that leads to the production of beta amyloid plaques in man. I know the patents that we filed are only tangentially related to BioNeura's work and were poorly done, but maybe we can force BioNeura to license their technology to us in a settlement. If that doesn't work, we could at least extort them for a pile of cash. I think they're on the path to the real answer for Alzheimer's. Oh...and remind me to fire whoever did that sloppy patent filing of ours."

"You already did," said Gloria. "My predecessor supervised the filing of that patent." "Ah," said Shah, looking up with a harsh smile. "I *knew* there was no reason to feel bad about firing him to make room for you. He truly was an incompetent troll." "I'm shocked and disappointed, Shah," said Gloria. "Oh, come on. You know I canned him so I could put you in his place." "Not that, you idiot," she said. "I'm shocked to hear that you might've felt remorse for canning him. Are you getting soft?"

Before he could reply, she dug deeper. "You better tell your lab geeks to work up some Viagra for you before you get any softer." And she turned on her heel and walked out of his office. Shah sat back in his chair and smiled. She really knew just how to push his buttons.

49

Doctor Bonner scolded his patient as forcefully as he could scold a Nobel laureate. "Dr. Rostov," he said, "it's been too long since your last visit. While we can't yet do anything to stop the disease, we think we can slow it a little or at least make you more comfortable as it progresses. It's important that we monitor your disease closely."

Dr. Rostov reflected a moment on what her doctor had just said. "So what you're saying my dear Dr. Bonner is that you can medicate me with the outcome being that we make an incurable, destructive disease last longer and thus deliver even greater suffering for all concerned? That hardly seems like something old Hippocrates would have approved of, does it?"

He couldn't argue hard with her logic as the medicines don't modify the disease in a meaningful way. What he noted more was a change in her attitude, "Well, Dr. Rostov," he said, treading carefully, "while the medicines we have today will indeed do nothing about the eventual outcome, they may lengthen the period of time that you are lucid and functional." Dr. Rostov smiled her charming smile, her blue eyes twinkling. "Do you remember my metric of disease progression, Doctor?" "Yes, I do – your Jeopardy index. How is that going?" "Well, I beat Alex three games out of five, some weeks four out of five. The old brain hasn't gone entirely to mush yet, Dr. Bonner." He was happy to hear a hint of her old defiance and sense of humor.

"That's great, Dr. Rostov. You keep it up. In the meantime, let's do a quick physical." He helped her up to the table and she lay down on her back, her head resting comfortably on a little pillow. He took the usual vital signs, checked her reflexes, her pupil dilation, and her muscle tone. Everything looked reasonably good from the outside.

What he couldn't see was the progression the disease had made over the past two years. Darya Rostov's neurons had been under a slow but relentless attack. Like an invading army, the beta amyloid plaque had progressed significantly and captured important healthy matter from her brain. The invading forces had overcome and then destroyed little clusters of neurons there, like so many villages being sacked and burned along the way. Her brain was coping as well as it could. As the invader tore up her brain, it responded by laying down new circuitry to replace wrecked wiring, like building new roads to replace destroyed ones. This had been fairly effective – at least until recently.

"I've scheduled you for more tests to compare them to the baseline record we made a couple years ago to see how things are progressing," said Bonner. "I would also like you to think about starting some medicine." "Well, give me the names of the medicines," she said, "and I'll do my own research." "I bet you will," said Bonner, pleased to see that she intended to remain in control. "As for the physical, your vital signs are quite good. There's nothing to worry about there."

"But we aren't worried about my heart rate and blood pressure, are we, Dr. Bonner? It's the computer that worries us." She grinned and tapped her forehead. "You're of a certain age now, Dr Rostov," he said with a smile, "so we do need to monitor your overall health. But you're correct as far as the AD is concerned." He helped her down from the table. "That's why we're having more tests done. Once we have the results, you and I will meet again to discuss your 'computer.'"

He walked her out to the waiting room. Alex was there waiting for her, as usual. Several months ago, Alex had won a Pulitzer Prize for his piece on the growing incidence of HIV/AIDS in teenagers and their alarming lack of practicing safe sex. "Hello, Alex," said Bonner. "Congratulations on your Pulitzer. You two are truly amazing." As Alex helped his mother to the car, Bonner stood and watched them go. He felt fortunate to know them both. But oh, how frustrating it was that he could do nothing for her.

Metoprolol ER (Toprol XL) ®)

50

With all of the Board members in attendance, Greg called the meeting to order and Bill Copley leaped to his feet and took the podium. While Jack and Bill had agreed that the financial review would open the meeting, Jack had planned to make a few introductory comments. Now, to Jack's amazement he heard and watched Bill deliver the very opening comments that Jack had told Bill he would be making himself. So much for Bill's "I thought we were a team" charade. Jack fumed but he knew the only thing to do now was to sit there like this had always been the plan.

After the introductory comments, Bill launched into the financial review. "After many years of work done at Pacific University, work began at BioNeura on the Alzheimer's program four years ago. Since then, a total of 100 million dollars has been invested, including the Phase I trial we just finished. Jean-Luc will describe this area in more detail in a moment. To complete the work through an expected very large Phase II program, it will take about one hundred fifty million more dollars and three more years."

Another board member jumped in with a question. "At that point, what will be our probability of success?" Jack made sure he fielded this one himself. "Assuming, a relatively clean safety profile, a clear and strong efficacy result from our Phase II studies and a solid idea of the correct dosage from those trials, the industry statistics predict a thirty to forty percent chance of success for a truly breakthrough medicine."

"So," said the director in a tone of mock disgust, "it'll cost us a hundred fifty million *more...like 350 million total...* to find out if we have a thirty-five percent chance of success? I love this business" he said with a cynical smile. "It gets even more fun," Jack said, smiling at Greg. "Phase III will be long and extremely expensive because we'll have to show improvement in function – like memory, behavior or everyday activities. We'll also have to show that the therapy is safe over a long period of time because this will be a medicine taken for life. Since AD progresses slowly, in order to show a robust treatment effect in a reasonable period of time, we'll need very, very large numbers of patients – huge numbers, in fact." "So what will be the cost of Phase III?" asked one of founding venture capitalists.

"We haven't made tight forecasts," said Jack, "but we put it in the range of several hundreds of millions of dollars for all the various studies we must do, and this isn't counting the investment in the manufacturing or subsequent studies of BIO230."

The room fell silent. Greg spoke first. "Well, no bucks, no glory." Then: "And roughly what will our chance of success be of getting positive results from that part of the development program?" "I think we're getting way ahead of ourselves," said Jean-Luc. "The Phase II results will give us a lot of information that will help us assess the risks, costs and chances of the Phase III program."

Jack saw in Greg's face that he wasn't happy with the sidestep Jean-Luc had attempted, so he decided to plow ahead and answer Greg's question directly. "After we finish the huge Phase III trials, assuming we don't discontinue the program for safety reasons – which is a big "if" as we haven't yet treated large numbers of patients for a long period of time with BIO230 – we will have invested over a billion dollars. Add to that several hundred million or so we'll have to spend on the manufacturing plant – and we'll have to make that bet *before* the Phase III results are known so we'll be ready to market when the drug is approved.

"Whoa," said Greg, leaning back in his chair. "So by the time a Phase III program is done, well over a billion dollars including our manufacturing investment will be sunk? Is that the math we're working with?" "Yes, Greg. But I don't need to remind you that if BIO230 is approved and marketed, the commercial rewards will be absolutely astronomical." "Yes, yes, Jack, you're right to mention that. But what a high risk we'd take. Such a staggering amount of money and well over a decade's time." Jack had no response. They both knew these were the shockingly slim odds and harsh dimensions of the medicines industry. Huge risks, huge sums and huge amounts of time for the relatively small chance of realizing those returns. Greg summed up, "If we are lucky enough to successfully get through Phase II, it's obvious that we couldn't front that capital alone. We'll have to find a big pharma partner to help us or sell the company to someone who can afford that investment. But that bridge is years away."

Jean-Luc then reviewed the other development programs his team was working on. These were less risky than BIO230 but important because they were part of the overall portfolio of BioNeura and were much closer to the market. Jean-Luc and Jack had convinced the board some months ago to acquire the R&D assets of a small biotech company in Montreal called QuebTech Biotech. QuebTech had two programs targeted for relatively rare neurological diseases that were too small for "big Pharma" to be interested in. These two compounds were both in early Phase III development.

The Board was pleased to learn from Jean-Luc's review that the two QuebTech projects they had acquired had advanced well in BioNeura's hands. The six QuebTech employees had turned out to be stars. "I am pleased to report that both of the former QuebTech projects have been granted Orphan Drug status by the FDA and its European equivalent, the EMA. This allows us to get certain marketing exclusivity and tax benefits and helps us get a faster review by the FDA that often leads to a more rapid marketing approval in the US."

From around the table there were murmurs of "good job" and "well done." But Jean-Luc hadn't finished yet. "I am also proud to report on behalf of my small team that we plan to complete within nine months, our Phase III work on our project for Lou Gehrig's disease. This will be followed six months later by our second Phase III product, this one for myasthenia gravis, a neuromuscular disease. This means that in about two years, we could have our first two products approved on the US market, both from the QuebTech acquisition."

Bill Copley couldn't stand being left out in the cold any longer – especially with Jean-Luc and Jack being showered with praise for the success of the QuebTech operation. "Well," he said, "we're all very happy with these orphan programs, but the revenue from them won't exactly qualify them as so-called "block-busters."

Jack instantly saw Bill's game and would have none of it. "While relatively modest for big Pharma companies," Jack said, "the return on investment will be over *one thousand percent.* In addition, the payback on our investment will be made quickly and the revenue will fund the entire BioNeura staffing expense and some of the costs of the BIO230 project. QuebTech is looking like a home-run." Bill shrugged his shoulders and said, "I am not so sanguine, but I hope you're right."

Jack turned to Jean-Luc. "Jean-Luc deserves credit for acquiring these important projects, and then for efficiently advancing them at BioNeura." The board responded with polite applause for Jean-Luc and positive comments flowed to Jack. Bill sat with his arms crossed tight, looking like a man trying to keep himself from exploding. Quickly recognizing that he was the outlier, he forced a smile and offered a second or two of stingy applause for Jean-Luc and Jack.

The next item on the Board's agenda was an innocent-looking item entitled "patent matters." The Board had been briefed about the SNS challenge when it had first come up months before, but they knew nothing of the latest development. Jack realized the timing of this discussion couldn't be much worse. Just after they stunned the Board with how expensive and risky the road ahead would be with the Alzheimer's program, they now had to tell them about the patent challenge they'd just received from SNS on that program. Simply put, if BioNeura's patent proved to be as tenuous as SNS asserted, the $150 million investment that BioNeura had already made in this program might turn out to be wasted time and money – or for the benefit of a competing company.

Now Barbara Siegel took the floor. She explained the nature of the law suit filed by SNS and her view that the patent challenge had to be dealt with seriously. She explained that while she had much more work to do, she felt reasonably confident that the SNS position wasn't iron-clad, so BioNeura should be able to settle it by giving SNS some sort of a royalty payment. After twenty minutes of discussion, they agreed to create a task force to study the matter in detail for the Board.

To prepare their defense on the patent challenge, the BioNeura team spent several weeks intensely documenting the chronology of their work on BIO230. They assembled a detailed review of what they discovered and when, and with whom they shared information about it. In doing so, they created a complete history of the discovery process for BIO230. They had done this before but with the SNS challenge, it was obvious that they needed even greater precision.

This project would turn BioNeura upside-down and stall virtually all other work. Laboratory notebooks would be reviewed, catalogued, put on digital file, annotated and bookmarked. Notes from meetings with external experts would be collected and archived and copies of all material shared with advisors and investors would be assembled. Correspondence with editors and reviewers at scientific journals would be catalogued. The documentation would be a veritable diary of every thought, action and deed of the employees of BioNeura over the life of the BIO230 work. Now that the facts were at hand, the team began to formulate a battle plan – a strategy to defend against the attack by the hostile invader, SNS.

After the patent update, nobody in the board meeting seemed happy. The air hung heavy in the room and for good reason. The expense, the years, the risks, the effort, the patent challenge – all of it came rushing together with the heat of an opened blast furnace. Everyone began squirming, both physically and mentally. Sensing this, Greg called for a 15-minute break.

When the Board reconvened, they heard Jean-Luc and Wen present the exciting results of the Phase I work on BIO230. The mood in the room improved perceptibly. Everybody seemed to have cooled down, taken a deep breath and stepped back from the brink.

At the end of Jean-Luc's and Wen's presentation, the Board members had a serious talk about the path forward on BIO230. They concluded that they wouldn't begin the expensive Phase II trial until BioNeura had defined exactly what SNS wanted and how the patent issue could be resolved. In assigning that job to Jack, they gave him thirty days to meet with SNS and report back to the Board with a summary and a recommendation.

As the meeting drew to a close, Greg put things in perspective. "This is drug development, folks. Break-through medicines require big bank accounts, big hearts and big cajones. I'm certain we have the first two. This project will test the third."

51

"Dad, why're you working yourself so hard over this patent thing?" Gabriel had come to the office with Wen to use his faster computer for a school science project. Only in fourth grade, Gabriel already worked with computer software that modeled and manipulated chemical structures. Wen spotted a teaching moment and pounced on it. "Gabriel, if you're interested in science you need to know something about patents. Sit down and listen." Gabriel did as he was told, and flopped into a chair beside Wen's desk with classical pre-teen abandon. Wen took his usual seat but the situation felt too formal.

"I want to make sure you get this," he said as he rolled himself around the corner of the desk, bringing him knee to knee with his son. "Patents claim ownership of a specific discovery or technology. Patents are also referred to as intellectual property. It's like a deed to a piece of real estate – or more aptly, like a precious treasure that has to be protected from people who might want to steal it. So far so good?" Gabe nodded.

"Okay," said Wen. "Here's another way to think about it. A patent is like a fence that you put up around what you want to protect. By the time a company brings a medicine on the market, it has spent as much as fifteen or twenty years, upwards of one or two billion and vast quantities of blood, sweat and tears. If the medicine gets on the market and if it finds favor with physicians, the compound can be worth many billions of dollars in annual revenues. But a sloppy or incomplete patent defense can create an opening in that protective fence that a second company, having done little or no work or having taken no great risks, can slip through and steal the treasure. So the industry spends a lot of time, effort and money protecting their 'intellectual property.' Patents are assembled piece by piece like pickets in a picket fence and much effort goes toward filling in more and more pickets so the fence is solid and has no openings in it. A talented, aggressive and creative patent attorney is one of the most prized assets of a pharmaceutical company. "You got one of those, dad?" "Yeah, we have one of the best." "With good science training you could become a good patent lawyer Gabe. Something to think about."

"Okay," Wen said, slapping Gabriel on the knee. "Get back to work!" And he rolled his desk chair back around the desk.

52

Barbara Siegel was sometimes known around BioNeura as Patent Patton as in General George Patton. When Ike had a tough job to get done during

World War II he often handed it to Patton. Now BioNeura had a tough job to get done and Barbara – bold, aggressive, and creative – led the change. She was also as irreverent as Patton and suffered fools just as unkindly as he did. She took the patent challenge from SNS personally; SNS attacked the fort that *she* had built and she was adamant that nobody would penetrate her fort on her watch. She threw herself into the task with a totality that consumed her.

That was clear from the way she looked when she showed up at Jack's office a week after the board meeting to present her assessment of the situation to the BioNeura team. The hellish way she looked comforted Jack as it meant she took this as seriously as he did.

Barbara threw her huge battle-worn briefcase on the table. With a scowl that hadn't left her since she got from Jack the pdf of the letter from SNS about the SNS legal action. "The bastards are clever, I'll give them that. They found a pinhole of an opening in our patent defense. Their position won't hold up in court but it is legitimate enough to use it to stall you for years and scare away your investors or use it as leverage to extort a pile of money from you."

"So…" Jack said. "They have your balls in their hands," said Barbara, finishing his sentence with typical bluntness. "What are our options?" "You meet with them and find out what they want. Maybe you can work something out."

It infuriated Jack that they found themselves in this position. "Is there anything more?' he asked, looking around the table. Everyone was still awash in the wake of Barbara's report and were speechless. "Okay," said Jack through clenched teeth. "We'll go see the thieves at SNS."

53

Jack had felt guilty that Diana had put her promising stage career on hold when they were in Paris so it pleased him to see her resume her acting shortly after they moved to San Francisco. Her first roles were in several small plays in the San Francisco Fringe Festival and through a combination of talent and good fortune she got noticed by a critic at the San Francisco Chronicle. After a few bigger parts in more mainstream productions she landed the biggest role of her career, playing the good witch Glenda in the musical "Wicked."

On opening night, Jack sat in the audience waiting for the curtain to rise. He couldn't help being transported back to that time so many years before when he had first laid eyes on her in Chicago when she burst onto the stage. This moment felt very much the same. As the orchestra worked through the overture, Jack's heart raced. He couldn't wait to see her on stage again!

54

After several days of playing phone tag, Jack and Dr. Nathaniel Shah, the CEO of SNS, finally managed to set up a first meeting on the patent issue. Shah was visiting his Asian headquarters in Tokyo and he said he could stop by San Francisco on his way back to New York. He wanted his General Counsel to attend the meeting but Jack succeeded in persuading him to keep her out of it for now.

With a couple of weeks to plan, Jack committed himself to be ready for every contingency. Recalling how bright, arrogant and full of himself Shah was, Jack studied the situation and prepared various proposals for the Board to approve before he went into the meeting with Shah. For his part, Shah remembered Jack as a typical American – aggressive, smart but unrefined and rather naïve. He asked Gloria to prepare a few talking points for his meeting with Jack Callahan, but otherwise went about his regular business, not intimidated at all by Jack.

"Jack, so nice to see you," said Shah, as he extended his hand in the lobby of the San Francisco St. Regis Hotel. "How've you been?" "I've been well, Dr. Shah. And how about you?" "Well, Jack, since we first met in Las Vegas, I left BPL, joined SNS, and moved to Geneva." "Congratulations," Jack said. "We've made similar moves." Shah offered no congratulations; he just nodded as he assessed Jack. That stare that Jack remembered now drilled into his eyes with a cold, black intensity.

Then Shah changed the mood. "Let's go to my suite where we can have some privacy. We can discuss our little problem there." Jack nodded and followed Shah into the elevator, where Shah inserted his private key into the security slot and pushed the top button. They shot to the penthouse like a rocket, the elevator doors opening right into the suite itself.

After fifteen minutes of small talk, Jack had had enough foreplay and wanted to do the deed. "Dr. Shah," he said, "that lawsuit that you've filed on BioNeura's patent – we both know it won't survive the test of time." Shah smirked. "And we both know that time will be your test – as time marches on, your investors will bail out while you're fighting me."

"I have strong and long investors, Shah," Jack said, intentionally dropping the "Dr." for effect – which it definitely had as Shah's head recoiled a little at the perceived impudence. "I prefer my title be used, Jack. I've earned it, you know." Jack bowed slightly. "Of course...Dr. Shah. And I am Mr. Callahan." Shah's eyes burned into Jack's. *Arrogant American*, thought Shah. "Now, now. Let's not be silly," Shah said. "After all, we're in America where things are so...how should we call it....relaxed. Let's go to first names, shall we, Jack?" "Nathaniel it is," said Jack. Shah shuddered at being so familiar with this American, but he needed to do it to get Jack to drop his guard.

After a half hour of fencing on the strengths and weaknesses of each other's case they both sat back in their chairs and digested the situation. Eventually Shah spoke. "We either settle this on business terms," he said, "or we let it drag on in court enriching only the lawyers." "I'll win in court. I have the better side of the argument," concluded Jack. "And you'll lose your company before you'd get that chance, my dear friend." Jack heard the words "my dear friend" as they exuded from between the clenched teeth of Shah's forced smile. Jack's own words then rose from his throat as if laced with acid, and he spat them out. "Exactly what do you want?"

Shah smiled and leaned forward to Jack. "I would like you to license my patent for an up-front payment and an annual fee and pay me a percentage of any sales that come from your products that infringe upon my patent." "What range of fees and royalties are you thinking about?" asked Jack. "Oh let's not descend into the details, Jack. That's what we pay our staffs to do. I'll have my counsel send you a proposal. We'll be reasonable on the terms."

Jack refused to be sloughed off. "While we're together, Nathaniel, let's settle the terms – at least in broad strokes." This annoyed Shah, who didn't like to bother himself with what he viewed as filthy commercial details. "Very well, Jack, if you insist." Shah referred to a note he had in a file on his table. "We can agree on what is industry-standard for Phase I assets for the royalty." Jack thought, *That would be a few percent of sales...for a billion dollar product that would $30 million per year. Could be a few hundred million bucks over the life of the product...if it becomes a product.* "As for the fuck-off fee, as you Americans call it, SNS will require fifty million dollars, one-half of the expense that we incurred on our R&D program whose patents you wish to be clear of." Jack detested this guy. He wanted to throttle Shah right there in front of the million or so inhabitants of San Francisco. "Fifty million? That's ridiculous, Nathaniel!" Jack's voice had risen to just short of a shout.

Shah responded in the most superior tone he could affect; pure condescension. "Now, my dear Jack, you must know by now how the game is played. You see, I open with fifty and then you counter. We go back and forth and after great fun we agree on a number."

Shah let out a big sigh, taking no effort to conceal his annoyance and disgust. "OK, since you don't want to play along, let's omit the dickering and agree on thirty-five million." "Ten," replied Jack coolly. "Thirty or I say goodbye," replied Shah. Jack recalled his orders from his board – to settle this thing ASAP. "Twenty-five is as far as I am authorized to go by my board." "Oh your board spoiled the fun," complained Shah. With a slap on his knee he concluded, "Twenty-five it is!"

"Now the royalty on future sales?" asked Jack. "I'm bored by this game now. So just tell me – what is the maximum that your masters have allowed you to conclude with me and let's just agree on that?" "One percent" replied Jack, lying. "Oh don't take me for an idiot Jack. You have a mid-single digit ceiling now. What is it exactly?" Shah's black onyx eyes were peering into Jack's soul and Jack averted the gaze – Shah had it exactly right. "I have a little more I could do." "Jack, did I tell you how bored I am by this? I will settle for a five percent royalty, nothing less." Jack paused. This was the upper limit the board had given him. "I can only go to two." "Jack, you're killing me with this petty shit. I will agree to three to deliver me from this tortured minutiae." "Done," said Jack, feeling a pyrrhic victory in saving the two percent versus what his board gave him as his ceiling but knowing the whole deal was extortion by Shah.

Shah opened a bottle of champagne. "Let's drink to settling this little skirmish, Jack. Let's drink to…Nathaniel and Jack" He said with an over-sized laugh for the moment. He handed Jack his glass and raised his own. As Jack raised his, he thought half-seriously of waiting for Shah to drink first to see if the champagne were tainted.

The celebration was brief and anything but warm. They had a sip or two and then put down their glasses. "Jack, I have to run," said Shah, standing. My private plane is ready to go and I can't miss my slot. If I do, I'd have to wait another hour or two." "I have some things I need to do as well," said Jack. As they said their good-byes, Shah's black laser eyes locked with his own, giving him a creepy feeling like he were probing his soul. Shah never expected this patent play to stop BioNeura. He wanted to distract and extort his competition and also test the character of BioNeura and Callahan. As he probed Jack with his stare, he saw in the returned glare a formidable future rival.

Shah sat down and finished the bottle himself – he hoped that it would calm him. He'd been experiencing another of his black spells, an extended period during which the dark demon stalked him and wouldn't leave. The demon always came slowly, like a thick black fog rolling in from the sea, enveloping Shah in an overpowering aura of disgust and self-loathing. It usually took a few days for him to clear it but this time it stayed much longer. Shah knew the source of the fog and what he needed to do about it but he couldn't and didn't share this secret with anyone, not even Gloria.

One week later, the headmaster of the orphanage in Mumbai received an envelope in the mail. The envelope had no markings. Inside he found a wire confirmation from his Swiss bank account informing him that the orphanage had received $50,000 from an anonymous donor. The headmaster noticed that the mysterious deposits were getting larger – and more frequent. Beyond that, he didn't give it another thought. He thanked God for the generous contribution that would do so much for the children.

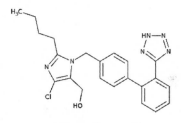

Losartan (Cozaar ®)

55

Greg called the meeting to order. Then, as if to increase the drama of the moment, he didn't say a word – he just picked up his coffee cup and took a long swig of coffee. With the patent dispute settled with SNS, Greg was taking the lead for the other Board members in exploring funding for the development of BIO230. Jack, Bill Copley, and Jean-Luc presented more specific forecasts of capital needs over the next three years.

Everyone watched Greg, who finally put down his coffee cup. "I must say, Jack," he said, looking Jack right in the eye, "you've sure got balls." Wen giggled from nervousness, then settled himself and looked down at the conference table, hoping to make himself invisible. The others remained silent, as Greg continued. "The expense figures you shared with us in the board meeting prep documents are absolutely prodigious."

One director who always obsessed and fretted about money, chimed in: "Yeah, Jack, you win the prize for the largest expense forecast ever requested by a venture-stage company in which I've had the pleasure of investing." The conference room let out a nervous laugh, glad that the important meeting had begun and the big issue was out in the open. The sums involved were indeed huge. "So let's see the details behind the numbers," directed Greg, moving the meeting into gear.

Jean-Luc and Wen presented the science first, reminding everyone of what they had accomplished and building confidence that they could deliver on the next step. Then Jean-Luc and Jack presented the goal for that next phase – not in terms of cold clinical data and methodology but in terms that described what this small team committed themselves to do for patients suffering from Alzheimer's. They painted Greg and the other board members a mental picture of just how much the science they were investing in could mean to those people suffering from AD.

Once Jack knew he had captured the minds and hearts of these money-men, he turned the meeting over to Bill Copley to begin the assault on their most vital organ – the wallet. Bill presented an abbreviated version of the team's figures, enough to give the picture without getting too bogged down in the nitty gritty. Then Jack took the floor again and brought it all together – mind, heart, *and* wallet. After which, he invited questions.

Greg leaned over to the two other directors and they whispered for a few moments. Then Greg said, "We're pleased with your presentation. We will lead the next financing round to fund this program. "However," interjected Greg – Jack hated that word at the end of a meeting. It often meant some waffling or some unreasonable conditions about to be thrown in front of them. "…the sums of money you're talking about go far beyond the capacities of our network of private capital. The equity markets are receptive to biotech right now and BioNeura has become a sexy story. The board is going to recommend that after a mezzanine round of financing we take BioNeura public." *Wow*, thought Jean-Luc, *an Initial Public Offering. I'm going to be part of an IPO!*

56

For his and Diana's 20th wedding anniversary, Jack had reserved a room at the Meadowood, an exquisite property in the Napa Valley. And he had managed to make a dinner reservation at The French Laundry, a world-class table. It was just the thing Diana needed, he thought. She hadn't been herself lately. Her offhand comments about feeling exhausted had worried Jack, who made sure she saw the doctor. Everything checked out fine. *She just needs a little rest and pampering,* he decided.

With Diana by his side, Jack felt invincible. He could take on any challenge, deal with any adversity and build great things. But if Diana felt less than perfect, Jack found himself totally distracted, as though his head had been invaded by fog. While he worked reasonably well during those periods, he lacked the creativity and boldness that marked his style. *A few days in Napa will be good for her* he said to himself, trying to will it so.

57

"Jack and Bill, meet Ben Andersen," said Greg Jimko. "Ben's a banker at Jenner Bryant, the investment bank that the Board has retained to take us public." Jack had heard about Ben Andersen, who was a veritable institution in investment banking. He had been in the game for more than 30 years, with a specialty in biotech. "Ben's been involved in more successful biotech start-ups than anyone else," said Greg. "They're my children," Ben added with a shrug. "I didn't have any kids so I raised companies." Jack liked this guy's style – smart, low key, self-deprecating. He had arrived at BioNeura's offices with a handful of young MBA types in tow, all of whom seemed to be in awe of him.

"Ben puts the 'full' in full service," Greg continued and Jack noticed a slight roll of the eyes from Ben who suddenly projected the aura of a celebrity ambushed by an effusive fan. "He does it all – informal head-hunter, business consultant, match-maker for mergers, promoter of careers...." "And, let's not forget, also a banker," said Ben. Bill couldn't help jumping into the fawn-fest: "I've watched your work with admiration, Ben. That Boston deal you did was incredibly smart." Ben had been around the block enough times to take compliments from strangers with caution – though he did seem to enjoy them. "Thanks, Bill," Ben said. "Let's hope the investors say the same about this IPO when we're done."

As they worked together, Jack saw an old-school banker in Ben. He didn't get his hands dirty. As soon as the big picture got established for the deal and the work plan was agreed to execute it, Ben stepped aside for his "teenagers" as he called his ivy-league MBAs to take over. Ben left the meeting and never returned. Jack later learned this was his modus operandi. Ben was the brain – the guy who conceptualized the deal at the front end and swooped in at the eleventh hour when final decisions needed taking. In between, he figured that since in his early days he had served as a grunt for years, it was now someone else's turn to grunt.

"We've got a mountain of work to do, Bill," said Ben. We have the SEC filing, extensive due diligence to complete on your company, audits of your financial accounts, a road show presentation to prepare and the valuation of the company." Bill shot him a look. "I know the drill," he said dryly. "I've done this a bunch of times before."

"Here's the proposed time and events schedule to get us to next January, what we believe will be the ideal moment to float the company." Ben dealt the papers around the table like a Vegas card sharp. For the rest of the meeting, the bankers and the BioNeura team reviewed and critiqued the proposed plan and Ben's associate changed it in real-time so when they finished their meeting they had an agreed-on work plan.

Over the next several weeks, Jack and Bill dedicated the vast majority of their time to fleshing out the work plan they had agreed to with the bankers. They had regular sessions with the lawyers, Greg and the Board's Financing Committee, and Greg asked them to prepare a presentation for the full Board at the next meeting. That would be in three weeks, and Jack wanted Ben Andersen involved, so he phoned him. "Ben, I'd like you to earn some of your fee," Jack said. Ben didn't miss a beat. "Oh Jack, I'm so close to retirement, I hoped I could retire without ever having done any work at all for any client – don't spoil it!" This was the banter the two of them had developed over the past several weeks. Jack found creative ways of accusing Ben of not earning his fee and Ben pretended not to mind the ribbing. Both of them knew that Ben was worth much more than his fee -for his advice, his contacts, the credibility he brought to a deal and his sense of timing.

"Ben, I'd like you and your teenagers to prepare a draft presentation for Bill and me to present to the Board and I'd like you to be at the meeting to back us up." "I'll have a draft to you Monday," Ben said. Noting that today was Friday, Jack knew the weekend plans of Ben's teenagers had just gotten trashed.

Before Ben hung up, he had one more bit of advice. "Jack, make sure you have legal representation at the board meeting. Nowadays, you need to document everything and make sure you protect yourselves." Jack recognized it as valuable advice. "Thanks again, Ben." "Just earning my paltry fee, Jack."

58

Jack had the idea of presenting to the Board as they would to prospective investors during the road show, which is exactly what it sounds like – a traveling show. Company management and their bankers take to the road in a whirlwind series of presentations to potential investors across the country.

For this draft or mock road-show Board presentation, Jack acted as master of ceremonies supplying not just introductions to the other speakers but also a strategic vision for BioNeura and an inspiring connection between the company's work and the needs of the real end-consumer, the patient. Jean-Luc presented the R&D components and Bill Copley presented the financials.

After the presentation, the Board members offered criticisms or suggestions, and the lawyers added comments for the benefit of the Board. But no big issues were identified. "Well done, Jack," Ben said. "Thanks, Ben, you too. By the end of this, you just might earn half of your egregious fee." Ben's reddening face surprised Jack and he feared that he had run this joke too far. "Seriously, Ben – you and your team are doing great." Ben suddenly became deadly serious. "This Board stuff is an important practice round, Jack. The real game is when we go for the IPO and then grow the share price thereafter." Jack saw in Ben's eyes that despite his ultra-cool demeanor, he did sweat. Success mattered to him way more than the money; it was a pride thing. That observation made Jack feel more confident that he had hired the right banker.

In an executive session of the Board without any management involved, Ben reminded them that they had to decide among them who would step up to be the CEO or conduct a search which could delay the IPO. After much debate at the Board level, Greg agreed to take on the role of Chairman *and* CEO, but he made it clear that a permanent CEO would be hired in the near future. Bill Copley was visibly relieved when he heard that the CEO position went to Greg as an interim role. To Bill's mind, this meant he still had a chance to prove to the Board that the CEO role was naturally his.

As for Jack, he knew he would be lying if he told himself he didn't feel disappointed at not being considered for the CEO. But like Bill, he was happy that the position could be his if he proved himself. That was the deal he had struck with the board when he joined the company.

59

Ben set the pace for the road show, and it was a scorcher. "Once the road show begins," he explained to the assembled team, "the idea is to get it done fast to avoid a freak internal or external event from cratering the deal. Ideally, we will try to get it done in a week but it will likely stretch to ten days or more. We'll start in Boston on Monday morning and cover the investors there. By 6 o'clock Monday evening we're on a plane to New York and by 8 o'clock we're dining with the major players in New York biotech investing. All of Tuesday and Wednesday until noon we spend in New York. Wednesday afternoon we hit Philadelphia and a group dinner in Baltimore."

Ben looked around the room for comments – none so far. "Right after dinner Wednesday evening we're on a plane flying west to San Francisco with the time zones giving back a few precious hours. Thursday and all day Friday we'll be in San Francisco and L.A."

And that's exactly how it went. By Friday night the team of Jack, Bill, Jean-Luc, Wen, Ben and Greg had presented the Road Show presentation more than thirty times to some two hundred bankers, analysts and lawyers.

In each presentation, they had laughed at one another's jokes as though they'd never heard them before and pretended to be intensely interested when they were beyond bored. By mid-week they could give each other's presentations.

The effort proved fruitful. The reception that BioNeura got from the investors was unambiguously positive. BioNeura was offering 15 million shares in a price range of $16 to $18, the hope being that this would net them around $215 million – after fees and expenses. With the cash they already had, that was just enough money to get through Phase II clinical trials on BIO230 and finish developing the two Pisces compounds to FDA approval.

Fortunately for BioNeura they were in a hot IPO market and their story was hot too. They sold 17 million shares at $17.00 per share for a total of $289 million before fees and expenses.

After a six month lock-up period, the venture capitalists could get a "liquidity event," a chance to take some of their money out of BioNeura at a handsome return in exchange for the huge risk they took years ago. The founding management – Jean-Luc, Wen, Bill, and Jack – also got a reward: the percentage ownership of the company that they accumulated since they joined was now worth a large sum of money for each of them.

"What time is it?" asked Jack. "Six twenty-five...nine twenty-five eastern time," Bill said. It was the Tuesday after their road show and the stock market was about to open. In five minutes, BioNeura stock could be traded publicly for the first time. Bill had his real-time stock quote locked on the NASDAQ symbol for BioNeura, "BNRO." "One more minute and we're trading on the floor of the NASDAQ!" shouted Bill.

Everybody crowded into Bill's office to watch the clock on the lower right-hand section of Bill's PC and the quote in the middle of his screen. At the tick of 9:30 a.m. in New York, Clara shouted "Lift-off!" "Here we go!" said Wen. But there was nothing. No trades. "What is this, Jack?" asked Jean-Luc. "Don't worry," Jack said, trying not to worry. "It'll show soon." After an agonizing minute, there was some movement. "There we go...." said Bill. "Seventeen thirty-two a share...not bad." They watched it climb to $17.58, then $17.84. Within an hour, BNRO was at $20.45 and started settling at that level. The team, fixated by the action 3,000 miles away decided not to go out to lunch but to order in Chinese food and eat together in Bill's office. They couldn't stand to tear themselves away from one of the most captivating images many of them had ever seen on a computer screen, their new share price.

When they re-convened, BNRO had lost some ground and was down to $19.34. They watched the trades like pagan priests scrutinizing chicken entrails, trying to decipher patterns and meanings in the transactions flashing before them. By 12:45 local time, fifteen minutes to market closing in New York, BNRO was now making a move back to $20.00. "Drinks on me if we hit $20.00 before the close," shouted Wen in a rare flash of emotion. As if lubricated by the promise of liquor, the BNRO share price slowly increased. It then was down, up more, down some and then just enough to finish the day at $20.12, up $3.12 on the day. "A 20 percent gain in a day!" exclaimed Wen. "Six o'clock at Milligan's – drinks on me!" He was thoroughly taken by the excitement of it all.

Everyone left Bill's office and returned to their own. Once behind their doors they all did the same thing: They tallied up what the $20.12 price meant to them today in terms of their stock options. They all felt a little richer and wondered what price BNRO shares would trade at tomorrow. Though they didn't know it, they had all been seduced by the idea of the share price and now they were married to it – whatever it happened to be. If it went up they were happy, if it went down they were sad. For that week, BNRO closed at $18.78. While that wasn't as exciting as on the first day it was nevertheless a promising start.

But the starry-eyed BioNeura team soon began to realize that as with all marriages, this one came with a certain amount of give-and-take. The "P" in IPO stood for "public," and they now had to worry about what this investing public thought of how the team was managing *their* company.

Azithromycin (Zithromax®)

60

Greg Jimko looked at his watch and it told him it was time to begin the first BioNeura Board meeting as a public company. "Let's begin, ladies and gentlemen. We have a full agenda today."

"As your Chairman and CEO," Greg began, "it's my pleasure to call to order the first Board meeting of BioNeura as a public company." These words were greeted with a small flourish of applause but Greg didn't let the self-congratulations last long. With that intro behind them, the meeting got underway. Greg moved swiftly through several routine matters and no material discussion or controversy arose. Then he turned to Jack. "The next agenda item is the BioNeura Strategic Plan and Competitive Assessment. Jack, would you please?"

Jack surprised himself at how nervous he felt as he walked to the head of the table and advanced to his first PowerPoint slide. He knew he would be closely scrutinized at this and future Board meetings and his performances would play an important role in shaping the Board's perceptions of him and his ability to step up to the CEO role one day. Still, it wasn't like him to have such butterflies. "Thank you, Greg," he said. "It's my pleasure to present the BioNeura Strategic Plan. This presentation is the work of the BioNeura executive team and I'm proud to present it on their behalf." Jack could feel himself calming down. On the other hand, Bill Copley visibly squirmed in his seat watching career sunshine fall on Jack. Bill knew Jack would be tough competition.

Jack went on to present the strategic issues facing BioNeura, the key objectives the team had identified and a series of specific strategies the team agreed would accomplish their key objectives. This Board of Directors loved big-picture topics and they engaged in the discussion with enthusiasm and insight. When Greg announced it was time for a break, Jack couldn't believe how much time had passed. They had run for two straight hours but it felt like fifteen minutes to Jack, which he knew to be a good sign.

After the break, Jack presented the competitive assessment. Many companies were identified but one stood out as the clear scientific threat to BioNeura, SNS. Jack's threat assessment of SNS touched on their CEO, Dr. Nathaniel Shah, their marketed and development projects, their strengths and weaknesses and their strategic intent as far as this could be discerned about a private company. Summing up, Greg put the SNS threat in terms that would prove prophetic. "Based on what we've seen of them in our first skirmish on the patent," he said, "we'd better sleep with one eye open and a finger on the trigger when it comes to SNS." "I don't sleep at all when it comes to SNS, Greg," said Jack.

61

They enjoyed terrific news flow over the next twelve months. TIME magazine ran an excellent series on innovations in healthcare and BioNeura got great press. The series struck a responsive chord among Baby Boomers that hit on their anxiety about various health predators that lurked just around the next birthday milestone. The boomers were growing older. Their knees and hips got sore and replaced, their hearts ached with angina, most of their body parts fell and some no longer did, with help from a little blue pill. This generation of Americans had an intense interest, some would say an obsession with their health.

After the TIME series BioNeura was hit by a deluge of calls and e-mails about BIO230, their Alzheimer's drug mentioned in the series. People wanted to get a relative into the clinical studies, wanted to invest in the company or wanted a job.

At the first anniversary of BioNeura going public, the share price stood around $30. Despite this and all the good press over the past twelve months Jack couldn't help noticing the formation of a subtle but palpable undercurrent among a segment of investors. Though the investors and the public liked the BioNeura story, the company began to take criticism for its "binary" or "all or nothing" profile. Many bankers had started advising Jack to consider acquiring marketed products to diversify BioNeura's high-risk/high-reward position. Jack couldn't disagree. Not only did he believe that BioNeura needed to diversify its risk profile, he also felt the company could use a commercial presence to market its own first two products – the ones they got from the acquisition of QuebTech – that would be ready for pharmacy shelves in the relative near future. Acquiring more marketed products could diversify risk and fast-forward the commercial skills that BioNeura would need to launch its own products.

With that in mind, Jack and Bill launched a quiet project to evaluate several small companies for a potential company acquisition. They spent a great deal of time coming to an agreement on the criteria of an attractive target company and once the criteria were agreed they started the task of screening candidates. After some weeks they had settled on Cogitate, a small, privately owned specialty company selling neurology products. While Cogitate had modest revenues from products in the largest countries around the world, it had a thin R&D pipeline. BioNeura needed a marketing infrastructure but had a good pipeline. On this basis, Jack and Bill thought that the two companies complemented each other.

When Jack called Greg to explain the project and get his feedback on the subtleties of making contact with the target company, Greg suggested they bring it up at their upcoming telephonic Board meeting. "Send me a half-dozen slides that I can send to the Board to brief them on the project," Greg said. "What do we call it?"

Jack hadn't thought of code-naming the project but saw the wisdom for reasons of confidentiality. He glanced at the sports section of the newspaper on his desk. "Let's call it Project 49 – after the 49ers."

"Sounds good. Once I get the feedback from the Board, I'll let you know."

A few days later, as Jack drove to work on 101-South he got a call from Clara on his cell phone.

"Jack, Greg's on the line. Can I pass him through?"

Jack thought about the likely reason for the call. It had been a couple of days since the Board had its telephonic call. "Tell Greg I'd rather call him back when I am in the office in 10 minutes."

"Will do," said Clara, but as she hung up the phone something about this struck her as strange. Jack had always taken a call from Greg on his cell phone before. *Wonder what he's up to*, she thought, just as Jean-Luc appeared before her desk.

"Mon Dieu!" he said with exaggerated charm, "tu es vraiment belle, Clara! Prenons l'avion pour Tahiti. Je te promets que nous y passerons des moments inoubliables!"

Clara gave him her usual exaggerated, mock-bored look. "Jean-Luc, I don't speak as much French as I'd like to, but I got the gist of your message from your leering eyes. Thanks, but no-can-do on the Tahiti, thing, Doc. I've got a company to run. Go back to your cage and find a cure for something,"

They looked at each other and smiled, both having enjoyed their regular and harmless exchange. Jean-Luc found Clara very attractive, but since she never showed any signs of encouragement he never went further than his occasional flirtations which she assured Jack were harmless, mutual fun for her and Jean-Luc. Clara wasn't physically attracted to him but she found his passion for finding cures for his patients noble and intellectually attractive.

A few minutes later, Jack arrived in his own office and immediately closed his door. He picked up the phone and punched Greg's speed-dial button.

"Hi Jack. Listen, the Board reviewed Bill's proposal and we think it's excellent. The next step is for me to call the CEO at Cogitate. Is it still Pieter Verplanken?"

Jack was stunned by Greg's characterization of the proposal as "Bill's proposal," and it took a moment to realize Greg had asked him a question "Uh…um yeah, Verplanken is the CEO."

Greg was a little surprised by Jack's pause but didn't pursue it.

"I'll call Verplanken and ask that you, Bill, and I meet with him and his CFO for an exploratory meeting. When can you be ready?"

Jack responded quickly this time. "We can be ready in a few days."

"Great, I'll have my assistant call Clara to arrange it."

"No, it'd be better if you have your assistant call me directly. The only people here who know about Project 49," said Jack, spotting his chance to set the record straight, "are the two authors of the proposal, Bill and me."

It was Greg's turn to pause. "Oh, I'm glad you clarified that."

Jack was unsure if Greg was glad that Jack clarified that only a couple staff members knew about Project 49 or that both Jack and Bill had prepared the proposal.

Jack immediately phoned Bill. "Hey, I just spoke with Greg. He liked your proposal on Cogitate."

"Oh, great, what's the next step for *our* proposal?" said Bill, adroitly avoiding Jack's bait.

Jack figured that Bill had either positioned the proposal to Greg as his own idea or allowed Greg to assume it by not describing its dual parentage. "The next step is for you, me and Greg to meet with our counterparts and Greg is setting up the first meeting."

"Terrific," said Bill. "I'm excited that the Board liked *our* project."

Jack felt Bill had over-played the "our" bit, convincing him that Bill had positioned the project as his own. "Yeah, me too. We have two days to prepare a presentation for Greg. Let's get started."

"OK, why don't you come down to my office – I have the slides on my PC now."

"Be down in a few minutes," said Jack, hanging up the phone.

Now he had a decision to make: *Do I accuse Bill of what I certainly know, or do I let it ride?* He weighed the pros and cons and decided that Bill would deny it, throw a tantrum and probably somehow turn it against him. *I'll let this dog sleep,* Jack concluded, as he headed for Bill's office.

62

Jack and Bill were waiting in the lobby of the St. Regis hotel in San Francisco. Cogitate and BioNeura had agreed that a neutral meeting point would minimize any chance observation and speculation about the reason for the companies' meeting. Greg and Pieter were having a short pre-meeting to feel each other out before the full meeting. Bill's cell phone rang. "OK, right away," Bill said. "It's Greg. We are in the Presidential Suite."

Jack made a mental note that Greg had called Bill. He checked his own phone – good signal, no message. He was sure he had told Greg he would wait for his call. Things were getting too weird. Jack decided that, when the right moment came, he needed to clarify things with Greg. Jack and Bill got into the elevator. They didn't say a word to each other.

"Welcome," said a tall, slim man in his mid-50's, "I'm Pieter Verplanken, CEO of Cogitate. Please meet my Chief Financial Officer." Having completed the introductions Pieter asked, "What can I offer you? We have coffee, tea, beer and of course, South African wine – we both come from South Africa."

"And we're shameless advertisers of our wine," added Pieter. "Help yourself to whatever you want."

Jack made a mental note. *Ten a.m. and they offer wine?* Having grown up in a family environment in which alcohol was an integral part of the culture, Jack knew the havoc it wreaked on his family. He knew that his genes gave him a more than average susceptibility to the grip of the drop and in fact, it had him by the throat when he was in college. He lost himself in drink for an entire semester and when he got his grades his dad literally knocked sense into him. Since then, Jack drank only on special occasions, cautiously with a mix of pleasure and suspicion; ever-vigilant for the feel of its hooks stealthily working their way again into his skin.

He looked at Pieter with a loathing he tried to hide. Jack hated this side of himself; the judgmental side when it came to those who enjoyed alcohol to a level he deemed excessive. He knew this attitude came from the terror and shame he felt from his knowledge that he was susceptible to the call of this dangerous mistress. *Give the guy a break*, Jack admonished himself under his breath. *He's proud of his country's wine and is sharing and enjoying some as a good host.*

Jack picked up a glass. "I have to drive but I will have just a taste of your wine, Pieter."

Bill was already ahead of him. His face contorted in ecstatic rapture, "This wine is excellent. You are justifiably proud."

The boy has no shame, thought Jack, knowing that Bill only drank wine when there was nothing else around.

"This wine," Pieter said, "is made on a piece of land my ancestors owned when they came to South Africa from Holland. Unfortunately, my ancestors sold a lot of the land to finance this or that, leaving us with a fraction of what the original family owned so long ago. If they had kept it, I'd be making wine now instead of peddling drugs." He punctuated the end of his joke with an exaggerated laugh.

As they sipped their drinks, Jack assessed the CEO of Cogitate. Pieter was neither handsome nor unattractive. Plain was the perfect word for his face. The only remarkable features of this tall, blonde plain man were his over-sized ears and his undersized hands. Jack wondered what else he could find out about him. "So, Pieter, you come from a long line of Afrikaans in South Africa. From where in Holland did your family originally come?"

Pieter loved to talk about himself and his plain face seemed a little less so as it became animated by the invitation. "My family went to South Africa from a small town near Amsterdam that no longer exists. They settled in the Stellenbosch region not far from Cape Town. My ancestors have lived there since and that is where I was born and raised."

Pieter took a sip of his wine, and then continued. "I pursued my university training in the U.S. with a Bachelor of Science degree in chemistry from Stanford. My father wanted me to get some training in American capitalism and greed, so I got my MBA from Harvard. He looked proud of himself as he surveyed the room for appreciation and respect.

He got only polite nods, which privately irked him. "After university, I worked all over Asia for various big Pharma companies. I was headquartered in Hong Kong. My, wasn't that the place to be young, horny and a little moneyed. Those China dolls are really something, huh?" Again getting no encouragement, he cleared his throat and continued more seriously. "I got a great business education in that part of the world. I found the Asians to be excellent traders – and that's a high compliment coming from a Dutchman!"

"What brought you to America?" asked Greg. "During my fifteen years of playing the imperialist in Asia, I ran across dozens of plant and herbal cures. You know, traditional medicines. My chemistry training and my passion for botany attracted me to investigate some of the traditional medicines that I thought had some scientific merit. On my own time, and with my own money, I created a small team to determine which of the couple dozen of these traditional medicines likely had real chemical activity. After a few years, I had identified half a dozen compounds that appeared to have activity in humans for diseases for which Western medicines did nothing, or next to nothing."

"When did you found Cogitate?" asked Bill. "I returned to the USA almost ten years ago. We were the first to conduct Western scientific experiments on traditional medicines. We documented activity in well-controlled clinical trials and raised the credibility of these traditional medicines."

"You've built a fine business, Pieter," said Greg. "Congratulations. You're also developing some classic Western pharmaceutical compounds. Where did you get these compounds? Some of them look interesting."

"I decided a few years ago that selling traditional medicines proven in western-style clinical studies was a good way to start a business, but what I really wanted to create was a classical pharmaceutical company. So as I developed and marketed my niche products, I licensed-in several chemical compounds from small Asian companies and universities. A Korean chemist here, a Hong Kong company there, a Taiwanese university, and so on. I had some luck along the way. A few of these compounds have shown interesting activity in the animal models and early tests in man. What I hadn't really appreciated was the size of the chemistry, manufacturing and clinical development effort I would need!"

Looking at Greg, he brought the discussion to the subject at hand. "That's why I agreed to meet Greg and his team. Perhaps we could do more working together than we can working separately." They talked for an hour or so, explaining each other's businesses and exploring ways the two companies' assets and skills could be complementary. Finally Greg asked if he could speak with Pieter in private.

"Yes, of course," said Pieter, bowing gracefully to his guests. "If you would please excuse us . . ."

After fifteen minutes, Greg and Pieter returned. Pieter opened his arms in a grand gesture. "Our companies have agreed to explore in more detail how we could work together in some way."

63

The day after BioNeura and Cogitate met, Clara poked her head into Jack's office. "Greg's on the line." Jack picked it up right away. Clara pulled the door shut, anticipating his request.

"Jack," Greg said, "I want to talk to you about Project 49." "Sure, Greg, what's up?"

"You may have noticed that one of my companies, Meridian Pharma has run into some difficulties."

"Yeah, I saw the news. Sorry the Phase II results on your lead compound were disappointing."

"Well, we believe the compound works but the trial was flawed. Anyway, what this means is that I have to dedicate a lot of my time there and I can't do that, plus do the interim CEO role for you guys and in addition take on Project 49. It's a prescription for disaster."

"How can I help, Greg?"

"I've spoken to several members of the Board and they're all happy to have you lead Project 49 under my supervision. You comfortable with that, Jack?"

"Very comfortable. Thanks for the confidence in me."

"You're welcome. Any questions?"

"Well, yeah. I have two. Will you tell Bill Copley I'll be leading this, or will I?"

"I think it would be better coming from you, Greg. Second, can I assume you've spoken with Pieter at Cogitate?"

"Yes on both, Jack. Before I ran it past the Board, I raised it with Pieter. He's fine with it. About Bill, I'll call him now."

"Great. Give me a couple of days and I'll have a game plan ready for you." "Perfect, Jack. I look forward to seeing it."

After this excitement, Jack realized the one negative in this great new opportunity would be Bill. He was sure Bill would take poorly the news of Jack's leadership. Jack decided to do his best to include Bill as a partner, and to be especially careful not to appear to overplay his authority. Now the question was this: Would Bill come to Jack's office to acknowledge Jack's role? The answer to that would be a good early sign of how the wind was about to blow.

A day and a half later, with no sign of Bill, Jack decided to drop in on him in his office. After a nearly inaudible hello from Bill, Jack opened up matter-of-factly. "Bill, I took a shot at drawing up a list of the items that we need to study closely on Project 49. It's a due diligence list. I'd appreciate your input on it."

Bill shrugged his shoulders and opened his palms – body language that said to Jack: "Whatever, you're the boss." Jack decided to ignore Bill's attitude and hope his little pout would be the end of it. "I'll send you the list by email right away. Let's use the code word Project 49 in everything we do. You never know who's listening."

As he got to the door, Jack stopped. "Oh, yeah, one more thing. Who do you think we should include in the due diligence team? We want to keep it to the bare minimum for confidentiality reasons."

Bill shot him a look laced with venom and his voice oozing in sarcasm. "Jack, you're our fearless leader on this project. You make the call."

That ripped it open for Jack. "OK, Bill. You're pissed that Greg asked me to run Project 49 for him. If you've got a problem with that, you got two options. Either you call Greg and convince him to change his mind or help me with the project. Greg and the Board are counting on your help – and so am I." Before Bill could reply, Jack continued. "One more point. Decide between these two options *today*. We're meeting with the Project 49 company next Monday. We don't have time to screw around. If you decide to work with me I'll need you a hundred percent and with zero attitude. If you can't do that, then nominate someone from your staff who can."

Bill smirked at Jack and nodded his head slowly. Behind the glare he said to himself: *You prick, you know that I can't call Greg. Besides being seen as a challenge to his decision, it would make me look like a selfish asshole who can't play on a team.* Bill squinted at Jack as if he was trying to vaporize him with his glare. Then, after a long and uncomfortable pause he said, "You'll have my answer by the end of the day." He had already decided he would cooperate, but he wanted to burn Jack's ass by not telling him so fast.

Bastard, Jack thought. *He knows as well as I do there's nobody on his staff who can do this job. And we both know he can't decline it.* Jack decided that since they were unhappy conjoined twins on this project, he'd be the bigger man and give Bill a chance to save face. "OK, Bill. I hope you'll agree to help. We can't do it without you." Jack knew Bill needed to hear that to salve his hurt pride.

When he got back to his office, Jack immediately sent the email to Bill containing the list of due diligence items for Project 49. An email from Bill the next morning pleasantly surprised Jack. "I'm with you on Project 49. Let's get started." Jack wished it were face-to-face, but given Bill's frame of mind, Jack figured the email was the best he would get. "Thanks, Bill. I'm glad you're in. Let's meet first thing tomorrow morning."

64

During breakfast Diana stopped Jack's heart with a question. "Jack, you remember when I was really sick a while ago and got better? "Yeah . . ." said Jack, as he removed the spoon from his mouth, unable to swallow until he heard the next sentence from Diana.

"Well, I didn't want to say anything because you've been so stressed out at work, but . . ." Jack felt his heart accelerate and heard the blood pump in his ears as he feared what she'd say next.

"I think I need to schedule a visit with the doctor."

Jack looked into Diana's eyes.

"I just feel lousy," she said.

Jack's head swam and his heart flipped a little, but he kept his composure for Diana's benefit.

She reached her hand out and took his, smiling. "We'll get it checked out, Jack. It'll be fine."

He got himself together and stood up to hold her. "Nothing is going to happen to you." He kissed her softly and they hugged tightly, each secretly worried that something might not be fine.

Zolpidem (Ambien®)

65

Bill and Jack were in Jack's office when they called Greg to update him on Project 49. "The diligence is checking out positively so far," began Jack. By now the project had simply become "49" among the tight little team assigned to confidentially pursue it: Jack, Bill, Jean-Luc, Wen, and Clara.

"The products 49 are marketing are growing well and the majority of physicians view their products as credibly tested medicines that have value," Jack told Greg. "Their commercial infrastructure would be perfect for us to launch our two new BioNeura compounds from QuebTech Biotech." Ever sensitive to Bill's insecurities, Jack gave Bill some airtime. "Bill, would you share with Greg the financial assessment?"

"Hi, Greg. The books are solid. From my audit days, I know I'm looking at a simply structured company that is conservatively run and from what I can tell, honestly. It's not throwing off as much cash as we hoped, but I see no accounting red flags here." Jack continued. "Jean-Luc and Wen are enthusiastic about two of their new compounds in Phase I."

They continued through a list of topics from environmental questions to legal issues to employee problems and the like. After about two hours, Greg summed things up. "Unless I've missed something, 49 is green light, right guys?"

Bill and Jack both answered affirmatively.

"Oh, and by the way, Pieter Verplanken said you guys have been great to work with and his Finance team has a lot of respect for Bill."

"Thanks, Greg," said Bill, opening like a flower. Jack smiled to himself. He had asked Greg to find an opportunity to stroke Bill and Greg found it. Manufactured or not it was effective, judging by the way Bill's little chest puffed up when he heard Greg's compliment.

"Full speed ahead, guys," concluded Greg, signing off as usual without a good-bye.

"That went well," said Bill as he walked out of the room.

Despite the good meeting that just transpired, Jack felt uneasy. During the phone call Jack had mentioned to Greg that there might be some potential people issues that required more investigation, but he decided not to go into what he had learned about Pieter. In any case, it seemed too soon to share the vague but concerning hints of issues involving women and drinking. In fact, the "evidence," if you wanted to call it that, was simply some comments from people who knew the man: "Pieter's a fox that's always trying to get into the hen house," or "He really loves his wine." In one case, the indictment appeared to be bitter ranting by someone Pieter had fired years ago. No, too soon to tell Greg. Jack decided to quietly look into it more on his own.

66

Over the next two weeks, BioNeura and Cogitate were in constant discussions as the two teams were winding up their respective assessment of each other. With the board's approval, Jack got authorization to begin the negotiations with Pieter to acquire Cogitate. He had strict and precise boundaries for negotiation within which he could commit the company.

Jack and Pieter agreed to meet at noon at the Ritz-Carlton on Nob Hill, where Pieter said they could be assured complete privacy. The suite was in the name of Ben Jensen, Pieter's pseudonym for his visit. Jack knocked and Pieter opened the door with a big smile and his broad South African accent. "Jack, welcome to my California branch office."

And what an office it was: Pieter had reserved the Presidential Suite, a massive space including two bedrooms, a huge living room, a dining room, a full bar, a master bath fit for a sultan and all of the audio-visual gadgets one could imagine.

"Jack, before we begin, let's toast to a successful negotiation. To celebrate the origins of our two companies I brought with me a bottle of a very special Chardonnay made in South Africa, bottled uniquely for a few prominent families there. It's called Family Reserve. For the California side, I brought a bottle of Colgin 1997, what I believe is one of your finest cabernet sauvignons."

Jack was impressed by the care and thought Pieter had given to the choice of wine. Pieter had already opened them before Jack arrived so he began pouring them. He lifted the Chardonnay and clinked Jack's glass. "Here's for wisdom and creativity in this important negotiation."

"And may our negotiations be as fruitful as the harvest that gave us these fine wines," added Jack.

"A poet in our midst!" returned Pieter as he brought his glass to his lips. Pieter took a large gulp, swished it around in his mouth and swallowed it, closing his eyes as if in ecstasy. He poured from the second bottle and repeated the ritual, this time taking a larger pull on his glass and taking an even longer time to swallow and recover from his near-orgasmic experience. "Pieter really enjoys his wine." The words rang in Jack's ear. *Enjoys it or is owned by it?* wondered Jack.

As they got right into the mating ritual of a corporate acquisition discussion, their first steps were made straight from the choreography book. Jack and Pieter told each other how exciting a combination could be and how great it would be for patients and shareholders. When that line ran its course, the next steps made in the dance were the "concerns." This is where each man respectfully shared the deficiencies they found with the other's company – its products, its management, what-have-you. It was a delicate part of the dance, because each wanted to tell the other that while attractive, the deal wasn't perfect and they were ready to walk away from it if the terms didn't reflect these "concerns."

Jack and Pieter were both experienced in deal-making and were able to tell another executive that his company was beautiful but not perfect in a way that didn't insult the other. Pieter looked at his watch. "My word, it's past one o'clock. I'm famished, what about you, Jack?"

"I'm feeling a little peckish myself," replied Jack.

"Great, I took the liberty of ordering lunch for us both. It should be here any minute." As if prompted to do so, a knock on the door signaled that lunch had arrived. "Pour us some wine, Jack, and I'll get lunch arranged."

A serious-faced squad of servers arrived with a small armada of serving carts. They swooped into the room and got to the business of arranging the dining table with the intensity and skill of a Formula-One pit crew. Within a couple of minutes, a sumptuous feast awaited them with linens, candles, crystal, exquisite flowers, and fine silver. The headwaiter stood with folded hands. "Sir, I am ready to serve you whenever you wish," he said.

"We will need some privacy," replied Pieter. "Please serve us and then leave us," he ordered in the tone well practiced with his servants.

"Of course, sir."

They were served as elegantly as the table was set, and within a few minutes Pieter and Jack were enjoying an outstanding lunch.

Afterwards, they got down to the real reasons they were meeting – price and terms.

"Jack, what do you figure my company is worth to BioNeura?" Pieter asked.

Not wanting to put a figure on the table, Jack responded coyly. "I was counting on you to tell me what you thought it was worth, Pieter."

Pieter grinned and took another swig of his wine, savoring its bouquet and watching its legs run down the insides of his wine glass. After a moment, he wrote a number on his business card and slid it over to Jack. On it was the barely legible scribble "$500 million – cash." Jack looked at it and gave Pieter no indication whatsoever of what he thought of it. Thanking Pieter for sharing the figure, Jack said he would think about it as they explored other topics and he moved on to the next subject. "What thoughts do you have on management, Pieter?"

"Well, I am kind of tired of the rat race, Jack. I was figuring Greg would want to run the new, combined company or the Board would name someone or recruit someone to run it . . . someone with your background and experience for example." They covered a few more topics and then came a pregnant pause. Both knew they were at the moment to talk numbers.

"OK, let's talk about the $500 million figure and the cash component separately."

They spent an hour debating the value of the various components of Cogitate, with Pieter justifying his numbers and Jack explaining why Pieter's figures were inflated. At the end of the day, Jack and Pieter summarized their progress. They had agreed on Pieter's role, or lack thereof, in the new company, the general structure of the organization and how various legal matters would be settled before the closing of the deal. They agreed they had made a lot of progress in their first day together.

"So," Pieter said, "what do you think of my offer, Jack?" Jack sat back in his chair. He decided it was wise to put his cards on the table now to avoid wasting any time.

"We can't swing a cash deal, Pieter, and the $500 million is meaningfully higher than we figure your company is worth."

Pieter looked deflated. He had obviously thought Jack's earlier lack of response to his offer was a good sign. Now he stared out the window, seeming to search for his words as he tapped his foot gently on the fine Oriental carpet.

"I am sorry we have wasted each other's time, Jack. I thought Greg was serious about this . . . evidently not."

Jack studied Pieter's eyes closely for any hint of his real thoughts. He decided Pieter was genuinely disappointed and that he was not playing the Greg card to see if Jack had something more to give him.

"We have a little room to negotiate but the gap between us is meaningful. Perhaps there's a creative solution to close the gap."

Pieter took a deep breath and let it out slowly, all the while studying Jack's face this time. "No," he said, rising to his feet, "evidently, the gap is too wide for you to make a specific counter-offer." His expression changed from serious to friendly. "Let's agree that we had a wonderful lunch and shared some special wine but failed to join our two terrific companies."

Pieter extended his hand and Jack shook it, recognizing this may be Pieter's test to see how desperate BioNeura was to buy Cogitate. Jack decided to play it cool and relaxed. "I understand, Pieter. But before we decide it's finished, let's think over the next few days about what we each said and see if we can come up with a creative solution to close the gap."

"I suppose there's no harm in that," Pieter said.

"Fine, I'll do it. Good-bye, Pieter."

Jack left Pieter in his room and made his way to the elevator.

The elevator ride to the lobby was time enough for Jack to get depressed. Cogitate was such a prize. He had to get it. Jack knew he would be the best internal candidate to run the combined new company but he told himself not to let that influence his desire for this company. "I'll figure out something," he said aloud to himself as the elevator doors opened.

Pieter thought to himself. "Well, Jack," he said as he inspected his reflection in the mirror facing him " . . . let's see how you return my serve." He then drained the last of the cabernet from his glass, polished off the last of the chardonnay and grinned broadly back at himself.

67

After dinner Jack and Diana relaxed on the couch in their high-rise apartment and enjoyed the view of San Francisco spread out below them. For a long time, neither of them said a word.

Diana broke the silence. "Jack, the doctor called with my medical test results."

Jack's heart sank and his body tensed. Diana saw his expression and reached out to take his hand. "The results are not bad, Jack. Or, at least they didn't show anything obviously wrong. The doctor wants to monitor me closely and recheck things in a few months."

"I think we should get a second opinion, Diana."

"No, Jack. It all makes sense, I'm feeling better lately and I'm over it now."

"But you'll get it checked again in a few months, right?"

"Yeah, I promise."

They held hands and watched the cityscape transition from daylight to darkness as the sun set and the buildings slowly came alive with light.

68

Jack was getting concerned. It had been two weeks since he met with Pieter at the Ritz. Jack had phoned him twice in the last three days wanting to put new terms on the table, but Pieter hadn't returned his calls. Since Jack didn't want to appear too hungry, he decided to not call again and see what happened.

A few days later, Clara poked her head into Jack's office. "Jack, Greg wants to talk to you."

"OK, get him on the line, please."

"No, Jack, he's here." That was unusual, Jack thought. But Greg did have some investments in companies in the area, so he must have decided to drop in.

"Great, show him in right away, please."

Greg chatted up a storm with Clara. He, too, was smitten by Clara's charms, and Jack thought he looked positively hypnotized as he walked into the office with her. Greg shook Clara's hand and thanked her for showing him in. Then he turned to Jack, still glowing from his brief encounter with Clara. "Hello, Jack, how are you?"

"I'm fine, Greg. What a pleasant surprise to see you here."

"Yeah, I was in the area and thought I'd pop in."

As Jack closed the door, it struck him that Greg seemed a little uncomfortable. *Probably rushed, is all*, Jack thought.

Greg began slowly, deliberately. "Jack, I need to fill you in on some rapid developments on Project 49."

Jack was excited – perhaps things had moved ahead on another channel. And he was right.

"About a week after you met Pieter, he called me. He said he was still in town and wanted to see me, so I met him. He put a proposal to me."

"So how does it look?"

"It's very interesting. The board has reviewed it and agreed to move ahead on the basis of his proposal."

The drama was killing Jack. Almost breathlessly, he asked Greg directly: "What are the terms?"

Greg took a deep breath and paused for a moment. "Pieter would agree to sell Cogitate to BioNeura for $450 million – half cash and half in BioNeura stock."

Jack nodded. "I'm not surprised he came off his ridiculous $500 million figure, but he proposed an all-cash deal before, what changed his mind?"

Greg looked Jack square in the eye. "Pieter decided to take half of the deal in BioNeura stock on one condition." Jack braced himself. Greg nervously cleared his throat. "Pieter and his investors will take our stock only if Pieter would become the CEO of the new, combined company."

The words hit Jack like an injection of pure narcotic. His head swirled, his stomach turned and he stopped breathing. Jack slowly collected himself. *Well done, Pieter*, he thought. *Drop your price to look like you've made a concession and take BioNeura stock in exchange for running the exciting combined company you wanted to run in the first place.* He thought again about his meeting with Pieter "I just want to quit the rat race. I am tired," he recalled hearing Pieter say. *It was now crystal clear that there was a lot more race left in this rat,* Jack thought.

"This is why I wanted to tell you this in person," said Greg. "Pieter says he would be thrilled if you'd agree to be the Chief Operating Officer for the combined company, reporting to him."

Jack tried hard to hide his disappointment at not getting the CEO job. He knew the deal wasn't done, but the $450 million price and the cash plus stock deal were already pre-approved by the Board. The rest was just details. The deal would be done and he'd be second fiddle . . . again. "That's very kind of Pieter to say, Greg. I'll think about it." Jack struggled to get out his words as positively as he could.

Greg knew this would be a disappointment for Jack and saw it plainly on his face. He was ready for it. "I have spoken with the Board, and we have agreed to put a counter-proposal to Pieter." Jack felt his spirits lift a little. "Pieter would agree to a succession plan that would include you as his successor within three years, provided you perform to expectations, of course." Jack nodded slowly. He recognized this as a good-faith effort by the Board to retain him. Before he responded, Greg added, "And with the added responsibility of the COO role for the combined company, there would of course be an increase in salary, bonus and stock options." He pulled an envelope from his inside coat pocket and handed it to Jack. Jack looked down at it for moment but didn't open it.

So there it is, thought Jack. *The golden K-Y Jelly. As I get shafted in the butt, they give me some lovely lubrication.*

Greg continued. "We all want you to stay, Jack, including Pieter and his investors. You'll be the operational leader of the team."

Jack tried a smile and knew his effort was weak. "Thanks for your support, Greg. I appreciate what you've done for me under the circumstances."

Greg rose from his chair. "Think about it hard. You'd be right in line to run the whole show in a couple of years or so when the company will be even bigger and more valuable."

"Yeah, I'll think about it," he replied, worrying less now about how his tone may sound to Greg.

When Greg left, the cruelty of the irony struck Jack. Ha! *Ironic . . . closing the Cogitate deal will be one of the biggest successes of my career – and my biggest disappointment.*

Jack decided to leave early to think about what had just hit him. "Clara, I'm leaving the office for the day. Please reschedule whatever I had."

Clara knew Jack wouldn't share what was bothering him. He wasn't that type of guy. "OK, Jack. I'll take care of it. Let me know if I can help in any way."

Jack looked at her, knowing she knew he had just gotten some bad news. He managed a smile. "Thanks, Clara."

A glorious autumn day was unfolding in the Bay area. As Jack slipped his car into the traffic heading for Highway One, his first thought was how to break the news to Diana. She would be supportive, he knew. They had gone through so many ups and downs that he knew she would be there for him. He was so lucky to have a wife and friend like Diana.

The embarrassment was a big part of what bothered Jack. Diana was his biggest fan and he felt humiliated at the thought of telling her that he had failed to get the prize. *No, not that*, he corrected himself. *She won't be disappointed, she'll be prodigiously pissed off that Pieter was disingenuous and played Greg to get the CEO job.* But as much as Jack might tell Diana, and himself, that all this was just part of the price to pay to buy Cogitate, he couldn't help feeling he had failed in some way, that he got out-maneuvered and that he had failed Diana. But he knew Diana wouldn't see it that way. Even so, his deep love for her and his complete dependence *on* her made him just insecure enough to worry about it.

By the time he could see the beautiful coastline along Highway One, his rational side had begun to win out. *Diana will be there for me, as always*, he thought. He suddenly felt overcome with love for her. Then he moved his mind to the question at hand: *Do I stay with the new merged company or do I leave?*

He spent an hour or more cruising along the coast, only partially perceiving the sun, surf and open road. He worked over in his mind the various options. He could leave and start over again somewhere, but that wasn't without risk; you never know what you've joined until you've been there awhile. Or he could stay and just move his expectations out a couple of years. He could go back to "Big Pharma," but his time at BioNeura had convinced him that the politics, bureaucracy and general nonsense of Big Pharma and big biotech companies were not for him.

Jack pulled into a scenic overlook and watched the sun sparkle on the deep blue ocean in front of him. The bright white clouds, like downy cruise ships, moved slowly across the horizon. He reached into his coat pocket and pulled out the envelope Greg had handed him. *Let's check the quality of this K-Y jelly,* he said to himself. The quantity and quality proved to him that Greg was serious about keeping him. The salary and bonus would be a very nice bump, but it was the number of stock options he'd get in the new, combined company that impressed him. *If we execute well and BIO230 hits, I could become wealthy*, he thought, warming up to Greg's proposal. *On the other hand, if BIO230 is a bust, these options will be worth about what this envelope is worth.*

But he had already accepted that risk. If he were to leave now, he would forfeit all the stock options he had already been granted. He watched the puffy cruise ships sail further into the distance as he integrated thoughts, facts, ideas, risks and feelings. *I think I'll make this work*, he decided. *But let's see what my wise friend and counselor has to say.* Starting his car, he turned around and began the drive home to Diana. He wanted to get there at his usual hour so she wouldn't be alarmed.

As soon as he walked in the door he could tell she knew. She walked straight to him and took his hands and asked, "Are you OK, baby?"

Jack made the connection. "Clara called you."

"She's a good friend of us both. She saw that you were upset when you left the office early and she was concerned about you."

Diana took his hand and led him to the couch. "Let's talk about whatever it is. I know we'll figure it out."

Jack looked into Diana's eyes. He smiled warmly and kissed her on her forehead, nose and lips. "I love you."

Jack was right. Diana was massively pissed at Pieter and Greg. But after a while, she accepted the reality of the situation and her protective side gave way to her problem-solving side. Through hours of talking, they came to the conclusion that Jack had come to by the ocean; they would make this work. He decided to be excited about the new opportunity and the chance to become the CEO of the new, more powerful BioNeura.

At the conclusion of their talk, Jack was overcome with love for Diana. Seeing her in the light of the setting sun, as it came through their apartment window took his breath away. He reached out for her and loved her like the first time; better than the first time. He had so much more love to give her now and he made sure that she knew it.

As they lay in each other's arms, Jack's heart flipped inside his chest when he thought about how he would cope if anything were wrong with Diana. Immediately banishing that notion from his mind, he pulled her close to him, comforted by the fact that she felt much better lately and had started jogging again, something she hadn't done in years. *Thank God*, he thought.

69

Things moved really fast. Within a few weeks, the lawyers, bankers, and managers had worked out all of the details. The BioNeura Board approved the deal and Cogitate's relatively few private investors did too. The press release announcing the deal went out at the close of the stock market and it announced a conference call with investors at 4:30 p.m. that afternoon, to provide more details. Pieter, Jack, and Bill Copley, the CFO of the new BioNeura would handle the conference call. The slides were ready, the Questions and Answers had been edited and re-edited, the presentation had been sent to the web-cast service and the three executives had their scripts in hand. Securities lawyers, bankers, executives, and more lawyers had screened everything. They were ready. Show time was in 30 minutes.

Hydrochlorothiazide (Microzide®)

70

Dr. Bonner reviewed Darya Rostov's file before he called her into his office. As he looked at her imaging test results, he could detect the telltale path of destruction of AD and imagined what her brain must look like. The damage he saw reminded him of aerial photos of Germany during the high-intensity bombing the Allies employed to break the back of Hitler's war factories. The diseased section of Dr. Rostov's brain looked like the dark sections of North Korea. There was no industry there. No commerce. No communication. No life. On the other hand, the healthy sections of her brain yet untouched by the ballistics of the disease were still bustling with life and purpose.

He imagined zooming in on just one of the millions of microscopic clusters in Dr. Rostov's brain, one holding memories of her life, another her accumulated knowledge, yet another the building blocks of her personality. He recalled from as far back as his first visit with her the joy that came to her face whenever she spoke about her father. Now Dr. Bonner imagined peering into a cluster of neurons that might contain Dr. Rostov's memories of a living room in which a scene was unfolding – a scene holding the memory of Darya's father – his voice, his possessions and the sweet aroma of his pipe tobacco. Darya loved her father for encouraging her intellect and her unorthodox pursuit of a mathematics career in an age when her peers were expected to pursue a husband. Her father was so proud of his Darya and she glowed in the pride that he shined on her.

As Dr. Bonner imagined the warmth and comfort of this scene, it suddenly went black. The disease had vaporized the microscopic living room and everything in it.

He truly hated this disease – the Grim Reaper's colder and much crueler brother, the one who takes the essence of a life well before he actually takes the life – and leaves the un-dead shell of the person behind, unable to care for himself.

71

"That lying bastard!" shouted Shah at his computer screen at home. Gloria ran into his study.

"What the hell's wrong with you? I nearly jumped out of my skin when I heard you scream."

"The damned Dutchman just sold his company to BioNeura."

Gloria instantly morphed from irritation at Shah to shared anger toward Pieter Verplanken. "What? We had a handshake on $475 million and he sells the company for $450 million?" She scanned the Press Release over Shah's shoulder. "Ah, yes," she said. "You see what makes up the difference don't you?"

"Yes, of course I see it," said Shah. "Something I would never have given that prick." He got up and stomped around the room, then stopped and looked out at the beautiful blue lake. "What can we do, Gloria?" he implored. When he spoke, he sounded and looked like a little boy who had lost his beloved dog.

"I am afraid there's *nothing* we can do," she said. "Cogitate is a private company. They sell at whatever price and terms their private investors choose. We've lost this one, Shah."

The words hit his ears like flaming arrows. He couldn't bear to lose this. Cogitate was a key plank in his platform to move SNS ahead a decisive step or two in the neurological field.

"Well, we do have one card to play, perhaps," said Gloria. "You remember Pieter said that if you weren't successful buying him now, you could perhaps buy him later? I think the door is currently closed, but we may have a key to reopen it in the future. Give Pieter a call and congratulate him. And remind him of his invitation to try to buy him, now BioNeura later." She thought a minute more. "And save that file we developed on him about his boozing and his extra-marital adventures with his employees. That might come in handy if we have trouble convincing him to play one day."

Shah pondered a moment and began to settle down. He looked up at her and surveyed what he saw. "Such a fine head on such a fine body," he said, reaching his hand inside her dressing robe until he found what he sought. She smiled and let her robe slip off her shoulders and slide slowly to the floor.

72

Time really flew now. The proposed acquisition required a review by the Federal Trade Commission to make sure the combination wouldn't create a concentration of products amounting to a monopoly. The review went swiftly. The relatively small size of both Cogitate and BioNeura making the reviewer's conclusion obvious. So after less than a month, the biggest regulatory question of the acquisition was resolved.

The last major hurdle would be the BioNeura shareholder vote to approve the deal. The vote looked like it would be close as the votes cast so far revealed about a 50-50 sentiment but only about half the shares had voted. A strong faction of stockholders already voted against the acquisition, despite the strategic rationale and financial justification that BioNeura management had put forth. Greg and several Board members agreed to help management sell the transaction to shareholders. It wasn't going to be easy.

By the day before the shareholders' meeting, the votes in favor of the deal won; the last minute selling of Jack's team and the board turned the trick. Having cleared all the hurdles, the deal closed. Jack was pleased. Running the process in his mind from his original Project 49 idea to this shareholders meeting, he had to admit the acquisition smelled very sweetly so far. Now he had to look ahead. As COO of the new BioNeura he faced the launch of BioNeura's two new products and the expansion of the current Cogitate commercial infrastructure into one that would handle the five products of the combined companies. After meeting and evaluating the leadership of the Cogitate sales and marketing group, he had decided he needed to change it. And he had the perfect person in mind.

Several weeks earlier, Jack had asked his trusted headhunter, to run a background check on Meg Wilson. Jack's head-hunter was now on the phone giving her report. "Meg checks out very strongly, Jack. There are a couple of things to consider, but overall she seems to be very strong. If you don't hire her, I'm going after her for an exciting job I'm working on at a major pharma company near where she lives."

Jack wasn't surprised at the positive report, but asked for the details nonetheless. "First give me the positives, then give me the concerns," he said.

"OK, here goes. Meg's very intelligent and extremely hard working. She is a creative problem solver and has come up with some innovative marketing tactics that are now used widely in the industry. Meg's a talented motivator and leader of sales forces. She's serious without being boring. She's well connected in the industry and has a good reputation. She has served on the sub-committees of the Pharmaceutical Association, so she plays at a national level. Meg worked overseas – she ran the commercial infrastructure for a major pharma player."

She paused a minute, and Jack jumped in. "That sounds like Meg. Now give me your concerns."

"OK, I have a few. Meg is hyper. She can't sit or keep from speaking for more than a minute." She then paused. Jack sensed her discomfort as she started again, stumbling a little as she did. "There is something that came up, Jack, and I don't know how to say it."

"So just say it."

"OK. There are rumors of a past romantic link between you and Meg."

"I'm aware of that" Jack said, disappointed for Meg that the old rumors persisted. "We had and have a genuine and deep mutual respect and friendship which people didn't understand – or didn't want to, because the rumor was more interesting."

"I've seen that a lot, Jack."

"Meg was about four or five years behind me in the company. When I advanced, I always wanted her on my team – she is *that* good. She advanced with me, in a way. She never, ever let the company or me down. Nobody can call that into question."

The head-hunter heard a hint of defensiveness coming through the line from Jack. What Jack said next explained it. "I should've been more aware of the potential for jealous and malicious minds to spin rumors about Meg and me. We like and respect each other and thought it was obvious to everyone that there was nothing more going on. Unfortunately, Meg got hurt. Despite her excellent performance her credibility at our previous company suffered and she decided to leave."

"That's another thing I've seen, Jack. I see it all the time. The woman goes, the man stays."

"Yeah, the whole thing is wrong. I still feel awful for not anticipating the way it all played out."

"Well, don't beat yourself up, Jack. Meg has done spectacularly well where she went, so she ended up fine. The only advice I'd give you on Meg is to hire her before I do. And learn from your last experience – oh, and if I were you I'd tell your board about the past speculation to make sure they are aware prospectively."

"Good advice, thanks."

"You're welcome. Bye for now." Armed with this objective report, Jack decided to try to recruit Meg to BioNeura.

During his meetings with the Cogitate employees, Jack collected some very disturbing information. A person who identified himself as a "concerned investor" sent Jack a "friendly warning," as he put it, in a voice mail. "G'day Jack," the Australian-accented message began. "We have a mutual friend who asked me to send you a heads-up on your new boss. With litigation being as it is, I'm not going to give you any specifics. Just watch yourself, Jack, and keep an eye on Pieter. He is a walking lawsuit. You'll know what I mean soon enough. Please erase this message. And best of luck."

Jack listened to the message once again and then erased it. He recalled from the due diligence he did on Cogitate the points of concern around Pieter's "extracurricular activities." *That has to be it*, he thought. He would learn very soon if he were right.

73

After a struggle to have Jack's and Meg's schedules coincide, Clara arranged for Meg to visit him in San Francisco. She was due in the office in a few minutes, so he busied himself by getting some emails done. They were like weeds, he thought. If he didn't deal with them constantly, they'd overrun him.

He had nearly emptied his inbox when he heard a sharp rap on the door. "Hey, I didn't know monkeys could type," she said.

"Or talk," Jack said, returning serve in their usual rapid-fire banter.

Apparently, they hadn't lost any steps in the years since they worked together. Meg dropped her briefcase on the table and they hugged like the old friends they were. But seeing Clara take note of the hug, Jack somewhat abruptly ended it. Best not to start the old rumors again, he thought. Pulling away so abruptly triggered some confusion that he saw in Meg's eyes.

Meg noticed the puzzled look on Clara's face as she turned to leave the two of them alone. *Oh no*, Meg thought, *I hope Jack isn't doing the horizontal with Clara.* Then she gave it more thought. *Nah, that's not Jack.*

They settled into a long conversation catching up on mutual colleagues, commenting on their triumphs and torturing each other over their "less-than-impressive" decisions. They were good friends who respected each other and complemented each other.

"So, who am I meeting today, Jack? It looks like everyone including the janitor."

"No," Jack said, "the janitor is reserved for the final meeting if you get past the rest of us!" Then he explained who each person was, what they did and their personalities. After that, Meg began the meat grinder, that ritualistic all-day procession of interview after interview. Jack knew she would shine.

After her last interview with BioNeura executives, Jack asked her how she felt about the team, the company and the opportunity. "I'm really excited about it, Jack. More so than I thought I'd be. You really have a great team here, and with the Cogitate acquisition you have the resources, scale and experience to finish what you started." Jack was thrilled that she was interested in continuing the process.

Meg got to her hotel room and picked up a message from Jack. BioNeura was prepared to make her an offer. She called him back immediately and asked him to send the offer to her home email address to avoid any chance of its being seen or noted at her company. Three weeks later, Meg was on the BioNeura payroll. The Jack and Meg team were back in action.

After a couple of weeks on the job, Meg sat down with Jack to give him her first impressions of the infrastructure, organization, and issues in her new area of responsibility. "Jack, we have a couple of problems," she began. "One of them I can fix. The other one," she paused for effect, looking sternly at Jack and pointing at him, "*you* gotta fix."

Jack liked fixing things so he was ready to get busy, but Meg's tone when she mentioned the second problem made him uneasy. "OK, tell me about the one you'll fix and then the one I have to fix."

"OK, the head of Sales and Marketing for Cogitate who now works for me is not up to the expanded role. The problem is, he thinks he should have my job and is bitter about not getting it."

"A case of self-image not matching with reality?"

"Exactly," answered Meg.

They discussed her proposal for replacing him and it was impeccable. "OK, Meg," Jack said, "just do it while preserving his dignity. And be sensitive to the impact this will have on the newly integrated team. We don't want the Cogitate people to think this is the beginning of a bigger housecleaning of their employees." Meg nodded, and Jack knew she had already thought of that.

"So, the second problem?"

Meg began slowly and deliberately. She knew she treaded on thin ice and didn't want to fall into a crevice. Jack feared that he knew the problem. *Tell me Pieter didn't hit on her*, he thought. "It's Pieter," Meg began, and Jack's heart skipped a beat.

"What about Pieter?"

"Well it's Pieter and the culture he developed or allowed to be developed in the sales and marketing part of the company."

Jack was relieved that he hadn't tried to seduce her, but was uneasily curious. "Go on," he said.

"Pieter is an issue, Jack. He's a lawsuit begging to happen." Those words rang in his ears – nearly the exact words on the voice mail he had received several weeks earlier.

"Give me specifics, Meg."

"OK Jack, here goes," and she referred to a hand-written list of points. "Pieter personally interviewed all sales reps."

"That's not a crime, Meg. Many founder-CEOs at small companies do that."

"I agree," Meg replied. "But there's more to it. I attended a sales meeting last week and after I met a few of the female sales reps, I thought I was at a beauty pageant not a sales meeting. I reserved judgment until the end of the meeting, but I am now convinced that Pieter is supporting the tactic of hiring extremely attractive and young sales reps – mostly women and some men, to sell Cogitate products."

Jack leaned back in his chair. "We better get some legal advice."

"Wait, there's more. The sales meetings at Cogitate are more like fraternity parties, with pledging, hazing, Jacuzzi jams; the works. The sales managers were all of 25 years old, supervising 22 and 23 year olds. Pieter calls these meetings the "playing hard" part of his culture of "working hard and playing hard.""

Jack was devastated. *This merger could "infect" the healthy company culture that we so carefully built at BioNeura. I gotta isolate this cancer and rip it out.* Jack leaned forward to Meg.

"So this is the thing I have to deal with Pieter about?"

"You got it, Jack. And the sooner you do it, the better off we'll all be."

Jack thanked Meg for bringing it up to him so straightforwardly. "I hope you're not regretting joining us, Meg."

"Jack," she said, "this is business . . . and typical with a new acquisition. There are different corporate cultures that have to be meshed into one. Unfortunately, the commercial part of Cogitate has a screwed up culture." She grabbed her notes and concluded. "I'll only question my decision to join BioNeura if you don't do what needs to be done with Pieter."

"I'll do the necessary, don't worry, Meg."

"I won't, Jack," she said, looking him seriously in the eyes and clearly setting her expectations of him.

So far, Jack's relationship with Pieter had been great. Pieter left Jack to run his piece of the new company and he was generally supportive of the changes that Jack wanted to make. The integration of the two companies had gone very well so far. The issue Meg had brought to him would be the first uncomfortable moment between them. If the topic were a business issue it wouldn't be so difficult. There would be a "cut and dried" debate of the issue, the alternatives and various consequences; standard business fare. This issue, on the other hand was as uncut and undried as they came; an issue that directly challenged Pieter, his personal choices and the culture he had built at Cogitate. Jack knew it would be tough and knew he couldn't shirk his responsibility to deal with it.

74

"Pieter, we have a problem we need to talk about." The serious tone of Jack's statement struck Pieter.

"That sounds ominous, Jack. What is it?"

Jack proceeded to give the details, leaving Meg out of it for now. No need for the messenger to be implicated in this. Jack outlined the issue, the legal exposure they were running, and Jack's concern about how this practice was inconsistent with the values that BioNeura lived by.

After listening carefully, Pieter began his response. "Jack, first of all, although BioNeura bought Cogitate, its CEO as you well know, is from Cogitate. Talk of values for the new combined company is premature and the old BioNeura values are not necessarily those that I will support for the new BioNeura."

Pieter continued, graciously and cunningly, "we do need to do something about the harem. It's gotten a bit out of hand, I agree." *Maybe there is hope yet*, Jack thought. "On the 'culture thing,' let's work on that together, Jack. I think it's a lot of fluff and bullshit but it seems to be all the rage in American business now."

"Pieter, I can assure you culture and values are not bullshit. A company with strong and sustaining values stands the test of time. Companies that don't have them may do very well for a period of time but eventually they crumble on their own rotten foundations. There are scores of examples. Strong research on it."

"I didn't know you were so passionate about this, Jack. I defer to your superior knowledge – and more Puritan values," he added with obvious sarcasm.

Jack knew then that the conversation had turned personal. Pieter felt that Jack had impugned his character. "Pieter," he said, "put the values point aside for a minute. The bigger issue is, you can land yourself in jail and the value of that big lump of BioNeura stock you now own from the acquisition could get crushed if you don't change things." Jack knew he hit a bulls-eye on his wallet.

"OK, OK. Why don't you and Meg put together a plan on how you'll wean us off the beauties and keep me out of jail," he said sarcastically.

Jack hated the way Pieter minimized the issue, but didn't push it. "OK, I'll have it to you in two days." That ended the very tense agenda item. They talked about a couple of other issues, but the poison gas of the last conversation still hung thickly in Pieter's office making it difficult for either of them to fully concentrate on the topics. Finally Pieter got a phone call and decided to take it, dismissing Jack with a hand signal that said he had to take the call. Jack left Pieter's office fearing that no real progress had been made.

After Pieter hung up his phone, his thoughts returned to his conversation with Jack. *Nervous American twit,* he thought. *His lawyers and his new bitch Meg have him all wound up over nothing. What they ought to be worrying about is making next quarter's sales and profit numbers. I've run my shop for nearly a decade and we never had a legal issue with our personnel. They all love the company and me. I'll be damned if I'll let that goody-goody change what made us successful.* He decided he would outwardly go along with Jack on this issue. Then he would look at Jack's proposal and decide what to do then.

Furosemide (Lasix®)

75

Bill Copley felt marginalized. Before Jack's arrival he had been the main contact with the Board. Before the acquisition of Cogitate, he was a central figure with his hands on the spigot that allowed the cash to flow to the spenders, the R&D people, who made up 90 percent of the staff. Now, Jack Callahan ran the operations, generated cash flow and led the integration of the acquisition and the creation of a bigger company. So far, the Cogitate acquisition had gone very well and the Board was very pleased with its progress. Jack was getting lots of positive feedback from the Board, and Bill hated it.

With little to do and lots of jealous energy to burn, Bill poked around "trying to be useful and fulfilling my fiscal responsibility to the shareholders," as he put it when asked why he was looking into this or that process or system. And sure enough, after several weeks Bill found something; something that made him feel very excited, better than he had felt in a long time.

In his effort to understand the new sales force that BioNeura bought, and to be able to appreciate what they did, Bill attended a regional sales meeting in New Orleans. What he learned there alarmed him . . . and it was absolutely wonderful. At the bar on the night before the meeting, he met a very attractive female sales rep from Miami. She didn't know who Bill was and at first he didn't know she was with BioNeura. She was very unhappy. "I'm dreading this sales meeting," she said. "It's such a joke. I have a PhD in biochemistry. I thought I joined a serious pharmaceutical company."

That was when Bill realized she was a Cogitate sales rep. *Perfect*, he thought. "Let's get another round here," he said to the bartender and when they had fresh drinks he turned to face her.

"I'm all ears," he said.

"Well," she continued, "after I started with Cogitate, I soon saw what the game was here. My peers in the Cogitate sales force are the hottest men and women assembled in one place. You should see it. It's ridiculous. I hate it."

Bill fought the temptation to invite her to his room to "console" her. Instead he pressed on with subtle questions while keeping full the drink in her hand. They talked for an hour and what he heard both shocked and pleased him. She wobbled a little as she finally stood up. "I've had enough to drink," she said. "I'm going to bed. Nice talking to you – what's your name?"

He scanned the bottles at the bar . . . "James Beam," he said.

"Well good night, James. Thanks for listening to my tale of woe."

"Good night yourself. It was my pleasure."

As his plan slowly germinated in his mind, Bill knew it wouldn't be good for that sales rep to find out his identity. He got way more than he hoped when he decided to attend the meeting. He left a message with the head of Sales that he needed to return to San Francisco early for some urgent business.

As his plane lifted off for San Francisco the next morning, Bill had a delicious thought: *What a chance to embarrass Jack! I wonder how the Board will feel when they find out the Cogitate sales force team isn't recruited solely on their grasp of science. And Jack wasn't even aware of this issue before the acquisition!"*

The plane reached cruising altitude and Bill accordingly developed a higher order of thinking. *This is not about Jack. This is about my responsibility as the CFO of a public company, he convinced himself. I have a fiduciary obligation to act on this.* His loftier thoughts made him feel less dirty. *Now – exactly how and when to do it?* He turned this question over in his mind for the duration of the flight.

76

"Sounds like he blew you off, boss," Meg summed up after hearing Jack's report of his confrontation with Pieter. Jack knew she was more right than wrong and felt embarrassed in front of her. "I expected as much, Jack. I have unfortunately learned more of Pieter's antics over the past couple of days. It seems he makes an annual sex trip to Thailand. It used to be that it was his own personal story. But now Pieter is telling his employees about it, female and male. It creates an uncomfortable and inappropriate work environment." Jack winced and nodded without commenting.

"And we also have another problem, Jack," Meg said.

"What *now*?"

"He has dropped his anchor in the company harbor, as they say."

"What?" Jack feared that he correctly deciphered the metaphor.

"Pieter is eating the cherries off his own fruit cart. Any clearer?"

"He's shagging his employees," Jack concluded.

"Less elegant than my approach, but you've got it, Jack," replied Meg. "And it gets even more complicated. Pieter appears to be a wine aficionado. The problem is that he drinks it so fast that nobody thinks he even tastes it. He's a lush, Jack. He drinks to excess on company time and with company funds."

"Damn!" Jack exclaimed as he sprang to his feet, running his hands anxiously over his forehead and through his hair. "I had heard some rumors about the drinking and the women but the investigation we did before this deal produced nothing concrete."

"Where there's smoke, there's usually fire, Jack."

"Yeah, I know," he said. "We had to move quickly on the acquisition. We knew, or thought we knew that Pieter was talking to other companies about selling his business to them. I figured we'd deal with it after we bought it." He looked at Meg apologetically.

"Well, you've bought it. Now deal with it – fast."

77

"Jack, can I have a word?" By now Jack knew Clara well enough to recognize her code for something important.

"Sure, Clara, come in." She did and closed the door, confirming Jack's instincts.

"I've become friendly with Bill Copley's assistant," Clara said. "She's a dancer too and we work out together."

"I'm aware of that," Jack said, anxious to deal with the matter at hand. "I had a couple of drinks with her after work on Friday. She really doesn't care much for Bill, as you may know." Jack thought of saying that she showed fine judgment, but he resisted criticizing a peer in front of Clara. "She told me how much she respected you and she told me to watch your back."

"About what....did she say?"

"She wouldn't say much more because she realized she shouldn't have said anything at all, but she told me that Bill left a document on his computer screen when he went to the men's room. She happened to catch the title: 'Major Issue in Cogitate Sales Force' and the bullet point that followed said you were ignoring or possibly supportive of some problems in the sales force. She tried but couldn't see more." She stopped talking and studied Jack's face. Then: "Do you know what this is all about?"

"I have a suspicion, Clara. Between us, I do know of something and I am not at all supportive of it. I'm working on it."

Clara smiled. "I knew that would be the case." She looked relieved as she got up to leave. "If I learn more, I'll let you know."

"Clara," Jack called after her. "Thanks for watching out for me."

She just smiled as if to say, "All in a day's work."

78

Armed with knowledge of Bill Copley's impending sabotage, Jack decided to try again with Pieter – this time more forcefully. He dropped into his office as he knocked. "Pieter, you've had our proposal for what to do to address the issue we spoke of, for over a week. What did you think of it?"

Pieter looked annoyed by the intrusion and after scanning his desk for a few seconds, picked up the document. "First of all, you shouldn't put such a report in print. I would have expected you to know better than that. I will destroy it and you and Meg will do the same, including any electronic files. Second, I found the document a little preachy, Jack."

This infuriated Jack but he held his tongue. "The content of the proposal, Pieter?"

Recognizing that Jack was growing angrier by the second, Pieter affected more seriousness. "Yes, the content. Well, it's sensible, but . . . "

"But what?" Jack pressed, more edge creeping into his voice.

"But why such a drastic shift all at once? I'll admit we can pull back a little but as you Americans say, 'If it ain't broke, don't fix it.' Right, Jack?"

"Pieter," it's broke. We either implement these changes immediately or I'll resign. And Meg will join me."

Recognizing just how seriously Jack took this, Pieter changed direction. "Jack, I realize I am a bit 'old school' as they say. Being South African and not having worked much in the USA, I am not as attuned to the legal issues as you and Meg are. I give up. You win. We will implement the changes. On one condition."

"What's that?" asked Jack, dreading what the condition would be.

"Let's implement it after the end of the year. That's only seven weeks from now. Let's not upset the apple cart and screw up our ability to deliver the year-end numbers you promised to Wall Street."

Jack noted that Pieter put emphasis on these being '*Jack's*' promises to Wall Street. In fact, Pieter had him here. It *was* Jack who made the promises.

"I'll accept it on condition that we work on the implementation plan now and on January 1, not a day later, we implement it as proposed in that document," Jack said as he pointed to the document in Pieter's hand.

"What document?" said Pieter, feigning puzzlement as he fed it into his paper-shredder. Pointing to the shredder, "You and Meg will do the same. We both recognize this as an issue and we will fix it in less than two months. No need to give the lawyers documents to screw us with one day, now is there?"

Jack responded coldly. "I have your word that we will implement this plan as proposed?"

"And I have yours that you will destroy this document?"

Jack nodded.

"Deal," said Pieter, reaching out his hand to seal it. Uncertain of the value of Pieter's word, Jack reluctantly grasped Pieter's hand and shook it. As he left Pieter's office, he saw Bill, who greeted him warmly . . . a little too warmly, Jack thought.

79

"Good news, Jack." Meg began. "Since you've spoken with Pieter he and his cronies have really calmed down. I attended a sales meeting in Chicago and there were no issues. It was a very professional meeting, you know, in spite of the fact that I was surrounded by impossibly beautiful people."

"Excellent news, Meg. Maybe his word is good after all."

"That would be nice," she said. "A CEO we can trust while we'll be in Europe. Speaking of which, the Europeans are ready to present their budgets and business plans next week."

"Great," said Jack, "and I'm ready to get the hell out of here for a while. After so long in the BioNeura pre-marketing world, I'm looking forward to talking about competitors, marketing plans and market share! Real operations!"

Meg laughed. "I never thought I'd hear you say you were pumped up about budget reviews or traveling, Jack. You used to loathe them both."

Jack laughed with her. "Well, we both know I'll loathe them soon enough. But for now let me enjoy the relative novelty."

Over the next week, Jack and Meg visited the "big five" European countries that account for more than 80 percent of pharmaceutical sales in Europe. They started in London, then hit Madrid, Paris, Berlin and finally Milan. The week was grueling, packed with hundreds of handshakes, seemingly thousands of presentation slides and tens of thousands of calories.

Anticipating a need to recuperate, they had arranged to stay over in Milan on Saturday before flying back to San Francisco the next day. For Saturday lunch, they met at a small Milanese trattoria near the 19th-century Piazza del Duomo. There they compared notes on their whirlwind trip and completed an impressive list of action items to be sent to the countries' general managers.

"I thought we had a productive week," said Jack. "How about you?"

"Yeah," Meg said, "I think we got what we wanted out of it. And I think the European team feels they can trust us. Time will tell."

With the mention of trust, an uncomfortable pause settled between them. Both Jack and Meg were thinking the same thing but dreaded taking about it. Before they left for Europe, they made a plan to discreetly bring up Pieter's name during their trip to see what comments might surface. The agreement was to not compare notes until the end of the week to avoid biasing each other on their "research."

"So," said Jack, finally, "that concludes the business review, now on to the human resource aspects." He looked at Meg and raised his eyebrows. She sighed.

"A pig, Jack. Bottom line, he's a total pig." The heat of her words pushed him back in his chair.

"Wow," he said. "I didn't get much info at all. Tell me what you got."

"It's amazing what I learned in the ladies rooms of Europe," she said. "You may have noticed I often visited the bathroom during our dinners with the staffs of the various countries. That's where I learned that Pieter is nailing anything that wears a skirt, employee or non-employee, client or non-client."

Jack rolled his eyes. "I got some vague comments along the same lines, but nothing specific or as direct as what you got."

"Well, I got my intel from the female employees and the wives of some of the employees. The guys you spoke to probably are still loyal to Pieter. Or they don't yet know your views on getting extramarital tail and want to be careful."

"Yet another reason I hired you, Meg – your ability to enter the ultimate truth chamber where I cannot . . . the ladies room."

Meg briefly smiled at Jack's attempt to lighten the mood, but her mind had already moved to the problem-solving phase. "It's your move, champ," she said. "This is serious and it's your responsibility. What are you going to do about it?"

"You don't need to tell me my responsibilities, OK Meg?" he said angrily. They remained silent for a long moment, letting the tension ease. Finally Jack spoke. "We have a long plane ride home tomorrow. I'll decide on my move before we land." Despite the tense exchange, they were able to enjoy their excellent lunch and admire the entertaining promenade of superbly dressed Milanese pass by.

Pantoprazole (Protonix®)

80

As the wheels of their 747 abruptly touched down in San Francisco, Jack realized he had forgotten the physical punishment that a Europe-California round trip inflicted. Eleven hours of flight time made for a very long passage.

On the other hand, it gave him ample time to think. Well before the wheels touched terra firma Jack decided how he would handle the "Pieter problem," as he had come to call it. He would take it to the Board. Prior to the next Board meeting he would meet with the director with whom he had the best relationship – it happened to be Greg, the Board chairman – and candidly explain the problem.

Jack didn't like going behind his boss's back, but Pieter left him no choice; twice Jack had raised the issue with Pieter and gotten no action so now he felt he had to make a higher appeal. Meg agreed with the plan. Jack would have to move fast, as the next Board meeting was in two weeks. He wanted to give Greg enough time to consider the problem before the meeting of all the directors.

Two days later, Greg's assistant showed Jack to Greg's office, a magnificent room on the 30th floor of the Transamerica building with a stunning panorama of the San Francisco Bay. "He'll be in momentarily," she said, and left him alone with the view. As Jack looked out the window and down to the street, he reflected on how very dangerous this meeting would be. *Should I just jump now?* he thought.

At that moment Greg bounded into the room in his usual super-charged way. "So, Jack, how are things on the continent?" Greg stuck out his hand for a shake in passing as he slipped around behind his desk to take his chair.

"Not bad, Greg. I think we can make some money over there."

"Great! Glad to hear it! Have you laid down the law for your new general managers over there? They're very far away. You got to decide early on whether you'll manage them with fear or trust."

"I'll start with trust and if that fails, I'll bring the fear."

"Good," said Greg, grinning. "I like it."

They talked for twenty minutes and Greg looked at his watch. "I've got about five more minutes, Jack. What else is on your mind?"

Jack would have preferred a smoother transition into the subject, but the moment had arrived and he had to seize it. "Well, I have a very delicate matter to discuss" Jack began cautiously. "It's about Pieter."

Greg frowned. He clearly didn't want to get in the middle of a squabble between his two top executives. "Have you spoken to Pieter about it?"

"Yes, twice. But he didn't take it seriously and I'm afraid it could become a serious legal issue for the company *and* the Board."

"So what exactly is it, Jack?" Greg asked.

Jack could sense his annoyance. Jack had decided to go for the most serious offense and the one that he felt would be more solid. "He is sleeping with or probably more accurately, has slept with several employees."

"Did he do this before or after we bought his company?

"I don't know of any incidents since we bought them," replied Jack.

Greg leaned back in his chair and his eyes rested on a freighter slowly making its way toward the Golden Gate Bridge, its wake a long white tail in the dark blue water of the bay. Then he looked back at Jack. "Let's give him the benefit of the doubt, Jack. Now that he's a CEO of a public company, let's hope he'll keep it zipped up when it comes to employees."

"Well, it's the attitude he fosters that I'm afraid of, Greg. He sends a message that is demoralizing to women and undermines the credibility of the leadership."

"Jack, *I said,* let's give him some time and the benefit of the doubt. You explained it to him twice. If it continues, you'll let me know, right? I have to make a meeting." Greg stood, shook Jack's hand, and bade him good-bye.

That didn't go well, thought Jack as he walked the couple of blocks to his car. He couldn't tell what impression he had made on Greg, but he didn't seem to grasp the seriousness of this situation. *But that's ridiculous,* Jack thought. *Greg's a serious businessman. He knows what havoc a situation like this can bring.* He decided to circle the block to clear his head. About halfway around he came to another conclusion: Greg had just been playing it cool and reserved in front of an employee. As soon as Jack left, he thought to himself. *Surely Greg would talk to his peers on the Board and take some action. At least I hope that's what he'll do.*

Indeed, Greg thought about Jack's visit as his audio-visual expert made the electronic connection with his next appointment, a videoconference meeting. *Pieter is smarter than that,* Greg said to himself. *Jack's being a little judgmental with his new boss. Maybe he wants to get him booted. I hope this doesn't create a problem between them. I really don't need that now.*

With that, Greg pressed the button raising the screen for his videoconference. Already on-screen was his next appointment, a fellow venture capitalist in New York. "Hey partner, how the hell are you?" said Greg and they plunged right into their meeting. Greg didn't give the Pieter problem another thought.

81

Jack and his staff had been extremely busy over the past two weeks. The next Board meeting would be held in Sea Island, Georgia and Jack's team had been preparing the main presentation. Since several of the Directors were new to both BioNeura and the pharmaceutical industry, Jack's assignment was to present an overview of the industry and then present a combined picture of the operations and futures of Cogitate and BioNeura.

His staff did an excellent job on the prep and Jack sent a draft of the presentation to Pieter, who e-mailed back saying, "looks fine by me." After all the work that had been put in on this presentation, Jack knew it was more than fine; it was excellent. But he had long since stopped expecting praise from his bosses. He had enough experience to know when he had done a good job and when he hadn't.

To prepare for his presentation, Jack reviewed the profiles of all the Directors. Most of the earlier investors and Board Directors had recently "cashed out" following the BioNeura and Cogitate merger. The depth and breadth of experience that Greg Jimko had assembled around him on his Board impressed Jack. *So that's my audience*, thought Jack. *I'd better be bullet-proof on my material.*

At the bottom of the board agenda page an asterisk caught Jack's eye. It noted that two new Board member slots had been approved. A roster of candidates would be submitted to shareholders for voting in the very near future.

82

Nathaniel Shah put his feet on his antique desk and took in the magnificent view of Lake Geneva outside his window; a natural masterpiece. The sky was a canvas of deep blue made more vivid by the bright, white clouds sailing across it. The lake itself, multiple shades of blue and green sparkled and changed texture at the whim of the wind while green forests and vineyards created a verdant frame of the entire scene. In the foreground, the marina was stocked with the most impressive collection of sleek, angular and expensive floating toys, which Shah had observed, were almost never used. *Just trophies*, he thought. *Shining trophies on a floating shelf.*

His eyes returned to his desk and to the recent *Wall Street Journal* article about him. He never tired of reading it. Approaching the two-year mark as CEO of SNS, Shah began to receive the public recognition he so desperately craved. He thought about how far he had come and his chest expanded with pride. *Look at me now! I'm an MD, a CEO of a thriving company, respected by my peers, feared by my competitors . . .* As he spoke these words, the dark thoughts began to slowly rise – but he successfully suppressed them by reading the article once more…this time aloud:

"Under the leadership of Dr. Shah, SNS increased revenues on its main products by over twenty-five percent and profits grew by 35 percent. Shah licensed from his former employer, BPL, two very promising neurological compounds now in Phase II testing. He also began a small operation in the USA, with Gloria Segovia, the General Counsel and recently appointed Chief Operating Officer, doing an excellent job establishing SNS in the profitable US marketplace."

The Jet d'Eau, Geneva's soaring and powerful signature fountain, captured Shah's mood as he tallied the pluses and minuses of his tenure at SNS. The one minus his ego would allow him to count was the painful failure to acquire Cogitate. *It would've put SNS in a new league*, he thought, watching a 50-foot Hatteras yacht cruise by. *I'll just have to hunt for another Cogitate*. With a look of firm conviction he took up his Mont Blanc Meisterstruck pen and jotted a phrase in bold capital letters and added an exclamation point at the end. He admired the words on the paper: TIME TO HUNT A COMPANY!

After that, he opened the sliding door to his terrace overlooking the harbor. "Hello, my children," he said in a tender tone disturbingly discordant with his visage. His gloved hands reached into the larger of the two cages on his terrace. America, his Harris Hawk emerged tethered to his wrist. Shah quickly and expertly removed the rawhide tether from the predator's ankle ring. "Time to hunt, America!" he announced, and watched with great relish as his deadly hawk powerfully pulled itself into the blue sky.

83

It rained steadily in Sea Island. Low, water-soaked clouds lumbered like laden fog barges over the manicured golf courses and gardens as a strong wind, heavily scented by the surrounding Atlantic blew the cold, stinging rain side-ways. Jack hoped that this dreary weather wasn't a harbinger of things to come for the meeting.

Although planes were delayed for some, all of the Board Directors arrived in time for the cocktail reception in the main salon of The Lodge, a five-star hotel with a cozy name that matched the accommodations. As the sun set, it slipped below the retreating clouds revealing a brief but spectacular sunset that put Jack's earlier anxieties to rest.

Jack liked this type of event. Personable and naturally garrulous, he genuinely enjoyed people and found this collection of personalities to be extremely interesting. He moved from Director to Director introducing himself to those he hadn't yet met and engaging them in conversation. His mission was to size up his audience. For the most part, the biographies on the website didn't do them justice. *This is a far more impressive bunch than their brief bios conveyed.* Jack felt a hint of anxiety about his presentation but he knew he had prepared well and his presentation was solid.

In a corner of the room Pieter was talking to Greg Jimko and Greg looked more composed than when Jack had met him in his high-rise downtown office a couple of weeks before. They looked very serious, so Jack decided not to cut in. But he kept his eye on them. After Greg and Pieter broke up, Jack made his way to Pieter. "Is there something I can do for the meeting tomorrow?" Jack said.

Pieter replied coldly. "No, you've done more than enough already, Jack," and Jack noticed Pieter's eyes shoot to Greg's.

"Sure. Okay," Jack said, leaving Pieter to join another group. He thought the exchange with Pieter was weird, but decided to slough it off. *He's probably distracted about the Board meeting,* he said to himself.

After a fantastic dinner served in a private room overlooking the championship golf course, Jack and the other guests enjoyed cigars and cognac on the veranda. The weather was clearing, Jack noticed. But as the skies cleared, his own mood grew gloomy as he thought more about Pieter's odd demeanor. Deciding to retire early, he bade everyone a good night. "Sleep well, Jack," said Pieter, seeming like himself again. "You're the main event tomorrow!" Pieter smiled and raised his cognac to Jack and then turned back to his guests.

84

"Welcome to Sea Island, Ladies and Gentlemen," said Greg, calling the meeting to order. "We have a lot in front of us, so let's get started." He then nimbly began leading the assembled board directors and staff through several items on the agenda. Moving to introduce the next item on the agenda, Greg nodded to Jack, his cue to take his place at the podium. "Jack Callahan has been asked to recap the operating results for BioNeura and to share with you his perspective on the outlook and major trends of the pharmaceutical industry. Jack, the floor is yours."

Jack thanked Greg for the introduction and launched into his well-rehearsed presentation. With the addition of Cogitate, BioNeura was now a serious company with operations in North America and Europe and generated a respectable operating profit. Jack compared the results to the objectives he had set when he proposed that BioNeura acquire Cogitate and he did his best to hide his pride that all objectives were met and many were exceeded. Jack asked Jean-Luc to review the R&D pipeline to round out the operational review. Jean-Luc did a great job and left the Directors very excited about the potential of their drug pipeline, particularly BIO230, the Alzheimer's program.

Jack then launched into his view of the industry. He described the general trends but focused on the increasing pressure to regulate the marketing of pharmaceuticals. Explaining to the Directors that pharmaceutical marketing is the most regulated communication in America, Jack pointed out that everything that appears in sales training materials, sales brochures, advertising in medical journals, television ads and every other form of communication must go through rigorous review within the company and is often subject to close scrutiny by the government. The goal is to make sure the communications are fair, honest and reflect the positive attributes as well as the less desirable aspects of the medicines the company promotes. He explained this is why the medicine ads on television go to great lengths to mention all of the horrendous things a medicine may do.

"In addition to the FDA, there are other checks and balances put in place. One is the 'whistle blower' legislation that awards forty percent of the fines levied against an offending company to the person who blows the whistle, or tells the government about an illegal practice. This has initiated hundreds of actions against drug companies. The pharmaceutical industry has also adopted its own code of marketing practices."

Jack went on to explain that certain discounting practices could be viewed as fraudulent if the same discounts aren't offered to government agencies. If a company promotes a medicine for a use that is not yet approved, the company can be sued for fraud and abuse of the healthcare reimbursement system. He touched on regulations of the Drug Enforcement Agency, the Environmental Protection Agency and on and on. Changes to generic laws to help them introduce "knock-off" versions of the innovator's medicines, without having to take any scientific risks or spend a penny on research and development, was another trend, "sure to increase as the government pays more and more of prescription costs." Jack highlighted the recent settlements against the pharmaceutical companies that were found to have broken one of the various laws. The financial penalties were staggering. To make his point he showed all of the rules, regulations, and laws that affect the pharmaceutical industry. He quickly advanced slide after slide after slide.

"Despite all the rules and regulations, for those companies willing to invest in innovation and promote their medicines in fair and balanced ways there is great opportunity for changing the lives of people around the world while providing an excellent return on investors' money." He closed by demonstrating why he believed BioNeura would be one of the companies that would win.

Jack knew from the connection with his audience and the questions they posed to him that he had made an effective presentation. Greg opened the floor to discussion. But before anyone could comment, Pieter launched a series of surprisingly aggressive questions. He challenged Jack on his view of the industry and said he thought Jack's views were far too negative. Jack maintained his composure and respectfully fielded Pieter's comments one by one, but inside he felt surprised and betrayed. Pieter had looked over the presentation a week before and again less than 24 hours prior to the meeting and hadn't mentioned a single one of these points.

Just when Jack relaxed a little after he finished deflecting Pieter's barrage, Bill Copley lobbed several grenades of his own in the form of challenges to Jack's views on the financial results of the company. "I think the results you've delivered are good, but don't you think you could have done better had you integrated BioNeura and Cogitate more quickly." Jack struggled to maintain his composure as he answered the question. Jack's mind swirled with multiple thoughts. *Everyone knows that criticizing a peer during a Board meeting was bad form. Wait a minute . . . Bill was involved in all of the decisions about integrating the two companies . . . and it was Bill who didn't want to go quickly to not upset the businesses.* Before Jack could answer Bill's first question, Bill lobbed in more incendiary devices in the form of questions.

Why is Pieter doing this . . . allowing this? It was too much for Jack to tolerate. He did his best to answer the questions well but he knew he failed. He seethed and felt foolish and beaten as he twisted in the wind.

The Directors became silent. "Since there are no more questions, let's move on to the next agenda item. Thank you, Jack."

Jack didn't remember returning to his seat but found himself in his chair with his head spinning. *What the hell just happened? Both Pieter and Bill saw his presentation a few days ago and made no objections or suggestions. Why did they ambush me in front of the Directors?*

The rest of the morning was a blur for Jack. The Directors moved through the agenda, at the end of which the Chairman announced there would be a closed Executive Session and asked the non-Directors to excuse themselves until it was finished. "We'll call you on your cell phones when we need you back. Thank you."

Bill and Jean-Luc left the meeting room at one end and Jack exited from the other, nearest his chair. When Jack got into the corridor he couldn't see Bill or Jean-Luc and since he didn't want to talk to Bill, he walked out toward the golf course to try to clear his head and calm his nerves.

After Jack, Bill and Jean-Luc had left the meeting room, Greg announced a report on Board composition. "As you know, I asked our head of the Board's Nominating Committee to make a comment about the Board composition." Taking the floor, she described the strengths and weaknesses of the Board. "The only weakness I see in an otherwise well-staffed and organized Board is the CEO succession planning considering Pieter's plan to move on in a couple of years or so. Further, it is our duty to prepare a successor to Pieter in case there is an unforeseen development or he decides to depart earlier. One way to provide succession planning is to bring the highest potential internal executive onto the Board of Directors to gain insight and training from the experience."

The Board debated the pluses and minuses of adding another manager to the Board. After twenty minutes, Greg interrupted the discussion. "I'm satisfied that a full and open discussion has transpired. Do we have a motion?" Someone made the motion and another seconded it. Greg called for a vote which resulted in a unanimous chirping of "aye."

"Now," Greg said, "having decided to nominate a member of management to the Board, we need to go through a careful process to select this executive. Pieter, since you know the mangers better than anyone, I will ask you to give your assessment of the top two candidates and then excuse yourself for a discussion among us." Pieter laid out his two options and listed the pros and cons of each. He then gave his recommendation. "If there are no questions for Pieter, he is excused," Greg said. "Thanks Pieter, we'll call you on your cell phone in 20 minutes or so."

Gabapentin (Neurontin®)

85

Dr. Bonner asked his assistant to show Dr. Rostov to his office. "How's Alex doing?" Bonner asked, just making small talk.

"Oh, he's fine," she said, with that twinkle in her eye. "He's up for another journalism prize. This one for a series of articles he did on Alzheimer's disease and its increasingly catastrophic impact on the economies of the developed world. No surprise he has an interest in AD, eh doc?"

As Bonner was about to comment, she cut him off. "I gotta tell you, he's getting to be a royal pain in the ass. Getting on my nerves. Moody? I've never seen such mood swings. In the last few months, I've had to talk him straight more than I did when he was a teenager!"

Bonner sympathized with Dr. Rostov and made a quick note to his file. To him it seemed likely that it was Dr. Rostov who was becoming the pain in the ass. This was a common behavioral change seen at this stage of her disease. AD causes personality changes and rarely for the better. Observing her closely over the course of their half-hour together, Bonner noted that her moods swung from pleasant to disinterested and annoyed to angry. *Sad,* he thought, *she is beginning to lose the battle.*

During his physical examination of her she uncharacteristically whined about various minor ailments and demonstrated a new level of angst. "How's the 'Jeopardy Index' you told me about?" Bonner asked.

"Are you two still playing?"

"Not as much," she said, her tone reflecting annoyance. "The questions are inane." Dr. Bonner just nodded but he suspected the real reason they weren't playing Jeopardy so much now was that she wasn't still "kicking Alex's ass" as she had bragged about before.

After the visit, Bonner walked Dr. Rostov to the waiting room where Alex was waiting for her. Bonner was shocked – Alex seemed to have aged more over these past several years than his mother had. Bonner of course knew the massive toll that AD took on the care-givers, the anxiety and anticipation of worse times to come hung over them like the sword of Damocles. *But still, Alex had really deteriorated,* he thought.

Dr. Rostov announced that she had to visit the ladies room before she left. But she didn't really have to go; she just wanted to give Bonner a chance to glean information on her progress from Alex's perspective. In her heart of hearts, Darya Rostov feared it wasn't Alex who was developing into a pain in the ass. Over the years, she had become nearly expert in AD and knew the behavioral signs that she now noticed in herself.

86

The expected 20 minute closed session of the Board meeting in Sea Island had gone on for more than an hour. Finally Jack, Pieter and Bill received calls to return to the Board meeting. When everyone was seated, Greg announced that they had one more item to cover. Based on the way Greg announced this item, Jack got an uncomfortable feeling in the pit of his stomach. Jack hoped that after his beating, his nerves were over-active and that he wasn't reading anything into this.

Greg looked to Pieter and nodded. Pieter began. "It has come to my attention that Jack has made some comments to a Board member, or possibly several, suggesting that I am having or have had inappropriate relations with employees. Given the seriousness of the allegations, Greg and I thought it best to have all Directors and our external counsel participate in a discussion to ensure transparency. He stared at Jack as he continued. "I want to clear the air and the record."

Jack wasn't prepared for this moment. After encouragement from Greg to speak up, Jack explained what he had learned and named the female sales rep who said that Pieter had groped her. He had more details about others, but his facts were less specific. Strangely, Greg turned to Bill and asked him to share his views. *What does Bill have to say about this?* Jack asked himself. He recalled the heads-up that he got from Clara through Bill's assistant, that Bill was preparing a slide deck that accused Jack of knowing about and allowing sexual abuses to occur in the commercial department but was doing nothing about it. *Good, Bill's comments will at least support the fact that Pieter created a hostile work environment for women,* he thought.

Bill was clearly very prepared. "Having heard some rumors, I felt a fiduciary responsibility to investigate them," he said. "I did so at various sales meetings. As far as I can tell, the allegations are without merit. The sales rep that Jack mentioned doesn't recall any such event." Jack had to consciously work at keeping his mouth from dropping open. He couldn't believe his ears as Bill droned on for several more damning minutes explaining how he had conducted a systematic investigation and failed despite great effort to uncover any clear evidence supporting Jack's allegations. When Bill finished, Greg stroked his chin a few seconds. Then he said, "Jack, Bill and Pieter will you excuse us for a few minutes? I want to talk some things over with the Board. We'll call your room when we need you back here."

Jack felt dizzy and nauseous. He fumbled with the buttons on his jacket as he left the room and had to concentrate to put one foot in front of the other without tripping. Somehow he found his way back to his hotel room and sat down on the end of the bed. His foot tapped like a jackhammer and his hands shook as he ran his fingers through his hair. His mind raced as it furiously tried to make sense of what just happened—*first the ambush by Pieter and Bill during my presentation and then this kangaroo hearing where Bill turned out to be a surprise witness against me. What the fuck?!*

After several minutes he began pacing the room, his nervous hands moved from his face to his hair to his pockets and back again, as they failed to find a comfortable resting place. He was so anxious he couldn't catch a full breath. Then he stopped moving as if frozen. His eyes fixed on several beautifully colored little bottles neatly arrayed behind the glass of the mini-bar. *No!* he thought.

Jack paced some more. A few paces later he looked again at the little bottles. He took a deep breath, sat on the bed and gazed out his window. Then as if on a string, his eyes were pulled again to the mini bar. On his desk lay the mini-bar key. He rose and began pacing once again. He couldn't take this stress.

"Damn it!" he shouted, grabbing the mini-bar key. He opened the bar, took out two bottles of Scotch and sat back on the bed. Jack stared at them in his hands and felt the coolness of the glass on his fingers. He rolled them on his hot face and shivered with relief. He imagined the warmth that the amber liquid inside could bring and how deliciously calming it would be. He twisted the bottle caps and they opened with a metallic click. Jack could already taste it in his mind.

The ringing phone startled him and the bottles tumbled to the carpeted floor. "Jack," Greg said, "we'd like you to come back to the meeting room now." Jack looked at the little bottles on the floor and felt disappointed and relieved at the same time. "I'll be right there, Greg," he replied. He grabbed his briefcase and left his room.

Still in shock and mortified, Jack met no one's eyes as he took his seat at the large conference table in the meeting room. Greg began, "Jack, Bill and Pieter thank you for your patience during our closed session. "Gentlemen," Greg continued, "here's how I see things. Jack, acting in the best interests of the company raised what he saw as an issue with Pieter's behavior. Pieter evidently is very gregarious and a flirt and he knows that he needs to be more circumspect as it appears that people are prone to misunderstand his intentions." Pieter nodded slightly, looking contrite. "However, there is no evidence of any indiscretion on Pieter's part. Recalling Jack's visit to his office a couple of weeks ago, he continued. "But let me say this, Pieter. If any evidence were to arise, there would be swift and firm action against it. Are we understood?" Pieter nodded and murmured "yes." Greg remarked to himself that the look on Pieter's face was not as contrite as he would have liked and he thought he saw the faint hint of stifled smirk.

Then, as he had carefully rehearsed in his mind, Pieter turned to Jack and extending his hand, graciously forgave Jack. Pieter appeared to be the ultimate gentleman, magnanimous in his forgiveness. In comparison, Jack looked like an over-zealous alarmist. "Jack, no harm done," said Pieter. "We need you here at BioNeura, and I need you with me. All's forgiven. Let's move on."

All Jack could manage was to nod and utter an incomprehensible mumble. He was in a state of total disequilibrium; his mind numb and thick.

"OK, let's wrap things up – we have one more detail," said Greg, regaining control of the meeting. During the session, we decided to add another Board Director, one from management. After considerable discussion, I am pleased to announce that Bill Copley is nominated to join the Board and he will stand for election at the next Annual Shareholders' Meeting." The Board applauded Bill. The clapping and comments were a faint murmur for Jack as he struggled to grasp the personal catastrophe that just happened to him.

87

Jack didn't know it, but his fate had been sealed before he even arrived at Sea Island. A couple of weeks earlier, Pieter and Bill had a chat and Pieter told him a secret. "Bill, a new Director will be nominated at the upcoming meeting. It will likely be a senior executive from BioNeura and I've got two logical choices, you and Jack. I haven't decided yet – a tough call. I need someone I can trust . . . someone who doesn't over-react to things . . . someone who has my back." Pieter went on to tell Bill what Jack had been saying about Pieter's dalliances with female employees and an overall inappropriate culture that Pieter fostered. "Jack is a star performer but I am struggling with trusting someone who's so willing to believe these rumors and someone who doesn't *trust me*."

Bill caught on fast. "Yeah, I heard some rumors. But after I checked them out, I found them baseless. You have my complete trust."

Pieter smiled broadly. "I knew you would see it more clearly than Jack did. Oh, and before I forget, I don't entirely agree with many of the positions Jack will be taking in his presentation to the Board but I don't want to be a lone critic. You know what I mean Bill? Bill immediately understood Pieter's meaning.

As the board meeting in Sea Island finished its business for the day, Bill Copley felt positively reborn. Being elected to the Board and seeing his rival humiliated all in the space of an hour had him bursting with excitement, not to mention intoxicated by his new power. As Bill and Pieter walked together back to Pieter's room, Bill said "I think you should take this opportunity to fire Jack. He's weak and untrustworthy." Bill struggled to keep up with Pieter's long strides as he waited for a response.

"No, no, Bill. Jack's a good guy and we need him," Pieter said, continuing the magnanimous act. "He just got carried away." Pieter knew Jack still had champions on the Board, despite this setback. And Pieter's own position wasn't yet strong enough to risk a show-down. Pieter had already decided how and when he would finish Jack and it would be far easier now that Pieter had a grateful and eager henchman. He patted Bill on the back. "Come, my fellow Board Director," he said. "Let's go get a celebratory drink!"

88

In the weeks since Sea Island, Jack replayed his disaster hundreds of times in his head. The pain was excruciating. Each time he went over it he searched for something he could've seen coming, something he could've done to dodge the train that rolled over him. Since Sea Island he avoided his staff, cancelled staff meetings without reason, took long lunches and in general was a shadow of himself.

Jean-Luc had had enough and his French blood boiled. He barged into Jack's office and slammed the door shut. "Jack, look!" he said, speaking just short of a full shout. "Yes, you screwed up! Yes, you embarrassed yourself in front of the Board!" Jack looked at Jean-Luc with his mouth agape, his eyes wide and arched. Jack was getting angry and began to rise to defend himself.

"I was . . ."

"Sit down and shut up. Let me finish." Interrupted Jean-Luc. "On the bright side, you weren't fired."

"Not yet," replied Jack dejectedly.

Jean-Luc swept his hand angrily, physically wiping away any thought of Jack getting fired. "Jack, if you were going to get the axe, it would've fallen by now. So you obviously have friends on the Board. Pick yourself up, Jack. Worse than what happened in Sea Island is how you're acting now. You're like a whipped dog, slinking around here with your tail between your legs. We're not used to seeing this Jack- and it's scaring the hell out of us. In fact, it's starting to undermine how some of your team thinks about you." Jean-Luc paused to see if his words hit their mark.

Jack folded his hands on his desk and with a deep exhale let his chin drop to his chest. After a long few moments, he spoke. "Jean-Luc, I have never in my life been as humiliated as I was in Sea Island."

"I know that. This is hard for you because you've never stepped in a pile of shit as deep as you stepped in there. But you're perpetuating the humiliation now with your public self-flagellation. It's pathetic, Jack – I gotta tell you as a friend and as someone who admires you."

Jack's head remained bowed. After a few moments he looked up. "Thanks," he said, standing and putting some things in his briefcase. "You're a true friend. I'm not sure I have many anymore. I need to get outta here. I'll see you Monday." But Jean-Luc didn't know if Jack would return.

89

"Jack, can I speak with you?" Clara's tone was anxious. She looked up and down the hallway, then stepped into his office and closed the door. "Jack, there's a rumor running about you and Meg."

"What is it?"

"That you and Meg have been involved for a number of years and your recent trip to Europe together was a well-disguised love junket."

"How active is this rumor?"

"I don't know, but Bill's assistant, was asking me about some receipts from Europe – very specific questions. Bill's department never asked for info like this before. I found it odd."

"Me too. Thanks for the heads-up."

Clara looked closely at Jack as she stood up to leave. Jack saw the question mark in her eyes. "No, Clara, there's nothing there. Meg and I are colleagues and good friends. That's all." Clara knew it but still wanted to hear it. She left feeling relieved at having told Jack and for his assurance that it was all rumor-mongering.

When Clara left his office, Jack integrated this latest news. "Damn it," he said aloud. "So this was how Pieter was going to get rid of me." With Bill's help, Pieter would deflect scrutiny from his own affairs by pointing fingers at Jack and Meg.

Jack thought a minute about how he should defend himself. He decided on two things. *First, I'll stay focused on the business. As long as I deliver, it'll be harder for Pieter to axe me. Second, since I burned my credibility with the board on the Pieter topic at Sea Island, I can't go to them.* Jack would have to hope Pieter blew himself up somehow.

Jack held his monthly business review with his staff, the best team he ever had. They were different from each other and brought a variety of views on every topic. This made staff meetings challenging, like trying to herd tigers but the product of those meetings never disappointed.

BioNeura was doing well; very well, in fact. Under Jack and Meg's leadership, revenues and profits were growing ahead of what Wall Street expected. And the pipeline, under Jean-Luc's guidance, likewise progressed ahead of targets. The work his legal and scientific teams did on the patents covering the Alzheimer's program made them stronger. After his staff left, Jack allowed himself a moment of thankfulness. *At least the business is moving well and I like my team,* he thought. *Otherwise, with Pieter and Bill slinking around laying land-mines, this place would be pure hell.*

Amoxicillin (Amoxil®)

90

A few months after the Sea Island Board meeting, Meg Wilson exploded into Jack's office, her face flushed with anger. "It's him or me, Jack! This is the last straw!"

Jack leaped to his feet and closed the door. "What's the last straw, Meg?" He motioned her to sit down, but she remained standing.

"Pieter forced himself on our sales rep from LA. He invited her to his room and she agreed. On the elevator, she changed her mind and Pieter got ugly. He forced himself on her in the elevator but she got out when the elevator doors opened for another guest – another female rep who's had her own problems with Pieter."

"Is this LA rep going to press charges or do anything about it?"

"She wasn't planning to, but when word spread of the elevator incident another rep decided to come forward about something that happened to her a few months ago. She is ready to go on record, having seen how her previous silence perpetuated the problem. And I'm told there are others thinking of complaining. But my reps are demanding action on this or they're going to take it to the Board or the press. So far, no lawyers are involved."

After Jack's shipwreck at Sea Island and fearing anything he said would look like he had a vendetta against Pieter, he decided to take the issue directly to Pieter. To Jack's surprise, Pieter appeared calm and seemed genuinely concerned. He immediately agreed to meet with the two women and arranged for them to fly to San Francisco the very next day.

In that meeting, Pieter performed at the top of his game. He projected charm, concern, contrition and confidence. Looking directly at the two women, Pieter said, "I apologize for any misunderstanding and for any embarrassment I might have caused you both. I admit I'm too flirtatious and this often sends unintended signals. I feel terrible about all of this." Before either of the women could respond, he continued. "I've been thinking for some time that we needed a new approach to women's issues at BioNeura. Your visit crystallized for me what we should do, but I want your valuable input. I have in mind a panel, co-chaired by the two of you to help me set policy in this area. What do you think?" *The snake*, thought Jack. *At least he's consistent. He's using the same approach he used on Bill – the old fame-and-fortune tactic. They won't fall for it.*

What happened next blew Jack away. The women became visibly relaxed and seemed pleased that they had been heard and that their CEO was apologetic and willing to do something about it. They also obviously felt that they would be excellent co-chairs of this important new panel. "Can we think about it for a few minutes?"

"Of course," said Pieter. "You can use my conference room down the hall."

Jack couldn't even look at Pieter, so he excused himself to go to his office until they made their decision on Pieter's idea. *Meg and I should resign,* he thought. *Such a waste, and just when the business is running so well.*

After about an hour, Jack saw the two reps leave their meeting room and make their way to Pieter's office. As he stood up to join them, he saw Clara leave the same meeting room that the two reps just left. It registered to him that something was weird about that but he had too much on his mind right now to give it a second thought.

When they were all back in Pieter's office, Jack closed the door. Before he had even taken his chair one of the women spoke up, aiming her comments directly at Pieter. "We think the creation of the panel is a good idea," she said.

Adios, BioNeura. I am toast," thought Jack.

"Despite that," she continued, "we find your response inadequate. We were expecting far more serious action."

"My head on a plate?" Pieter asked, flashing a broad and charming smile.

"Something like that, yes," she coolly replied. "Your idea of a panel gave us our own idea. We've decided to consult others with whom you have *flirted* . . . " saying the word flirted with mocking emphasis, " . . . to see what we want done."

"Surely we don't need to make a mountain of a mole hill," Pieter said. "We can work it out right here, right now." He was clearly nervous now, which he attempted to cover with another forced smile, this one looked creepily like the melding of a smile and a grimace. The women were resolute. After fifteen minutes of more and more desperate but failed attempts to dissuade them, Pieter thanked them for their visit. They coldly shook his hand and left his office.

Jack left Pieter's office without saying a word to him. *This is going to be interesting,* he thought – *and dangerous.*

91

"An unmarried mother, a Dalit or "untouchable," the lowest caste in India, abandoned the premature baby on a filthy street in Mumbai on the day it was born." The priest continued, "Someone found it bawling and near death and delivered it to an orphanage that was little more than a human junk yard. I ministered at the orphanage and learned that the infant was sold to a wealthy, long-childless Indian couple in London, days after it was born. With the help of many well-placed bribes, Indian officials told the couple that the baby was the son of a high-caste rural couple who died in an accident and left no living relatives. In a carefully executed plan, the couple took an unexpected and extended vacation in Asia ostensibly to help with her frazzled nerves and as if by miracle, they returned to London with a child they passed off as their own." The priest smiled and explained. "This was before internet and cell-phones, when such a thing could be done." He continued, "The couple loved him and they raised him in the community of their high social station."

"Why are you telling us this story?" asked the man of the house.

"Well sir, I am that priest. You are the childless couple and your son is that untouchable."

The ten-year-old boy hidden from view had listened in horror to the priest tell this story – a story that the boy just deduced was his own. After the priest finished, the boy saw his father write a check and hand it to him.

"You understand that you are to never return and never breathe a word of this fantasy to anyone. If you do, despite the crucifix you wear around your neck, I will personally hang you with it. Do you understand?" The priest nodded, bowed and departed.

The boy never told his parents what he had heard and they never told the boy what they had learned. But things changed in his family after the priest's visit. He spent his next and every school year thereafter at a boarding school and his entire summers in various camps around the world. This knowledge about himself caused his self-image and personality to abruptly change. He developed a pervasive suspicion of everyone and never allowed himself to get close to anyone. He feared that they might learn his horrendous secret – that he was the spawn of an untouchable and not the son of high-born, Anglo-Indian aristocracy.

Ten years later, the boy looked at his university diploma. "Nathaniel S. Shah," it read. He was now an educated, refined and articulate man – a man forged and hardened by the heat of the secret he carried and driven to prove that both his biological and adoptive parents made a horrible mistake by throwing him away. He was a walking contradiction – externally confident and proud while internally terrified and ashamed.

92

After the sale reps' visit to BioNeura headquarters, things developed in an unexpected way and with breathtaking speed. Despite Pieter's elaborate efforts to keep the matter quiet, the Board somehow got wind of their visit and the growing wave among several victims to push for legal action.

Jack wondered who informed the Board. Given how poorly he was perceived for having brought this topic to their attention months ago at the Board meeting in Sea Island, it certainly wasn't him. It had to be someone in the office. As he thought more, a smile appeared and then slowly broadened and he let out a laugh, shaking his head in disbelief. *It had to be Clara. While meeting with the two women sales reps in that conference room, she must have convinced them to inform one or more members of the board.*

The Board called an emergency meeting that excluded Pieter but included an external expert labor lawyer and BioNeura's head of human resources. The local Directors, including Greg were in BioNeura's Board room and the rest were present by phone. Once all the directors were on the line, Greg called the meeting to order. They listened to the complaints as reported by the head of human resources. Greg recalled that one of the complaints sounded exactly like what Jack had reported to him in his downtown San Francisco office some time ago. The board of directors asked the HR head many questions. When they were satisfied, Greg thanked her for her help and excused her.

Bill Copley looked up from the Board table, struck by a cold stare from Greg. Greg's demeanor carried no ambiguity – he was furious.

"Do you have anything to add, Bill?" Greg asked.

Bill's mind raced. Fearing that Greg had his and Pieter's collusion all figured out, Bill panicked and began yammering. "You don't know how charming and persuasive Pieter could be. Oh, this situation is so unfortunate. I have always been loyal to a fault to my bosses, always gave them the benefit of the doubt." He paused as if struck by an idea. "Knowing what we know now," Bill said, "if it were put to a Board vote, I would vote to remove Pieter from his CEO position."

So much for loyalty to a fault, Greg thought. "Now we need a closed session of the Board. Bill, as you are now personally involved in this situation, you are conflicted so you will need to step outside."

93

Wen had never been happier. His experiments were going very well and with the support of the Board he had launched a new program in the area of Parkinson's disease. But all of that paled in comparison to his pride in his son, Gabriel. Gabriel loved the laboratory and performed remarkably sophisticated experiments in his science class at school. Wen had always been careful not to push Gabriel into science but the boy seemed naturally drawn to it, which pleased Wen to no end.

He loved the days Gabriel would come to the lab with him. On one such day Wen watched his son tinkering on the lab bench and reflected on his good fortune. *I have it all*, Wen thought, *a wonderful wife, a healthy and capable son and a rewarding career with people who support me . . .*

Just then a darkness passed over Wen's face. *It's all fragile. Everything could change without notice.* He physically shook it off, shaking his head fast like he was trying to remove water from his ear.

"What's the matter, Dad?" Gabriel asked.

"Nothing, son," Wen said. "Just a little chill."

Gabriel shrugged and continued with his work.

94

It had taken the Board no more than five minutes to decide on its action. By a unanimous vote, Pieter was fired as CEO. "Now we have to select Pieter's replacement," said Greg. "Any thoughts on internal candidates versus going outside?"

A lengthy discussion ensued and the Board decided to nominate an internal candidate given the circumstances of the recent merger and the fragility of the organization, especially with the CEO departure. Two names came up, Jack Callahan and Greg Jimko, the current Board Chairman and previous BioNeura CEO.

Greg remained uncharacteristically quiet during the discussion. In his mind he was stitching together all the unsettling moments of the past few months – the private conversation with Jack in his office about Pieter's antics . . . Pieter and Bill's behavior in Sea Island . . . Bill's unusual attack on Jack during his presentation there . . . Pieter's nomination of Bill as a director . . . Bill's rapid backpedaling at this meeting. After a few minutes, Greg had an epiphany. *Only one thing could explain this chain of events*, he thought. *Bill Copley must've promised not to disclose what he had uncovered about Pieter in exchange for a seat on the Board and maybe the CEO role later on.* Greg recalled how Pieter's nomination of Bill had surprised him at the time, but he'd felt he had to support it.

Now he thought of sharing with the other Directors his deduction about the likely deal between Pieter and Bill – but on second thought he decided against it. Even though he knew it in his bones to be true, he had no proof except his 35 years of business experience during which he had seen his fair share of weasels and rats.

Jack Callahan certainly doesn't fall into that category, Greg thought, consciously deciding to support Jack for CEO. In an aggressive move, he withdrew his name for consideration citing workload and delivered his strong support of Jack as CEO. Given Bill's poor behavior and the confirmation of Jack's veracity, the Board immediately gave Jack Callahan its unanimous support. Greg called Jack into the board meeting. "Jack, this has been a hell of a ride for us over the last few months – for you, especially, but I hope you will see it as worthwhile." Jack didn't understand what could make it worthwhile. "We have voted to name you CEO. Congratulations, Jack."

Now all of them – Jack as CEO and the Nominating Committee of the Board – were tasked with recommending how to deal with Bill Copley. That he would step down from the board was obvious. Jack reviewed for the Directors his, and the company's, history with Bill.

Trying his best to do the best thing for the company, despite Bill's mistakes and behavior, Jack described his skills and strengths as well as his shortcomings. The biggest issue for the Board was the fact that there was no internal successor; they worried about the unsettling message it would send to the investment community and the employees if the CFO were fired shortly after the previous CEO abruptly "retired."

This was a major consideration. On the other hand, Bill made a massive error in judgment which had to be weighed. After a half hour of discussion, Greg stopped the debate. "Jack, you've heard all the advice and views. You're the CEO and the CFO works for you. What's your recommendation?"

Jack took a deep breath and let it out slowly and audibly. "I want to fire Bill," he said. Jack heard several murmurs in agreement. "But," Jack continued, "Bill Copley is a very talented CFO. I need a strong CFO and there's no one at BioNeura ready to replace him. Bill made a stupid mistake, but it's the only big one I've seen him make in the years I've known him. I'll give Bill a 90-day period during which we'll see if we can rebuild the trust that must exist between us. If after 90 days we do, he stays. If not, he goes. In the meantime, we'll start a quiet process with a recruiter to see if there is a strong CFO out there who might be available to quickly replace Bill if needed." The Board was unanimous in its approval of Jack's plan.

Prednisone (Deltasone®)

95

Within a week of the press release announcing Pieter's "retirement" and Jack's appointment, Jack began a cross-country tour starting in Boston. With the unexpected departure of Pieter and the arrival of Jack, the Board recommended that Jack hit the road to meet current and prospective investors, financial analysts and investment bankers.

He spent two weeks working his way from Boston to New York to Philadelphia. Before leaving the east coast he made a brief stop in Baltimore to visit a major mutual fund that's very important in shaping views of biotech companies and a current large shareholder of BioNeura. He stopped briefly in Chicago, dropped into Denver on his way to LA and then spent the last two days making the rounds in San Francisco. It exhausted him but he felt the time had been well spent. Within two weeks he had met all the major investors in BioNeura and most of the serious biotech investors and influencers. The best indication of the success of his trip was that BioNeura shares regained all of what they lost when Pieter resigned and added an additional five percent to that.

When the news of Pieter's demise became public, Nathaniel Shah was in Paris to accept the prestigious Prix Galien, the award given to the company that had made an unusually important pharmaceutical innovation during the previous year. At the dinner table with various guests, the President of the Galien Committee mentioned to Shah in small talk about Pieter's departure and Jack's promotion. When a colleague told Shah at dinner about Pieter's "resignation," he leaned over to Gloria and whispered with pure schadenfreude, "I just learned that Pieter blew himself up at BioNeura. The bastard who screwed us on Cogitate just got screwed at BioNeura . . . Delicious!"

A week later, Shah was in London accepting a second prize on behalf of SNS. The *Financial Times* named SNS the number one European Growth Company, an award that was especially validating for Shah. After leaving his former employer BPL, the second largest Pharma Company in the world, Shah was being celebrated with a high-profile award in the headquarters city of BPL. He asked his communication department to make sure that all the BPL brass got invitations to the event. None attended. That didn't surprise Shah, but it hurt him nonetheless.

96

On the day that BioNeura was scheduled to learn the results of the Phase II trial on BIO230, Jack couldn't sit still. He kept getting up from his desk every couple of minutes to putter around the office and look out the window. Checked his email, checked his stock quotes; did whatever he could to distract himself.

At 9:30 a.m., Jean-Luc came to Jack's office to report the results. Jean-Luc wore his best poker face and showed nothing despite Jack's attempts to see it – but lost his composure after only a few seconds. He hurriedly closed Jack's office door and then burst into joy. "It works! It works, Jack! The results are clear!" Jack and Jean-Luc studied the data and stared at the charts and graphs. "It's unmistakable, Jack. BIO230 cleared amyloid plaque from the brain and patients stopped their slide into worsening Alzheimer's disease symptoms. Look at this table! Some patients may have even regained *some cognitive function*. BIO230 works!"

At times like this, Jack felt lucky to work in this industry. Developers of new medicines were something special, he thought. They were hopeless optimists who worked like plow horses for a decade or two against terrible odds and with enormous financial costs and *occasionally* won. Cynics say it's the money that makes them do it; the generous returns for the risks taken. The cynics were partially right, Jack knew. Without the chance for large rewards, none of the angel and venture investors would be there. Without those investors there would be no biotech company start-ups and as a result far fewer new medicines. The financial rewards also drove the big Pharma and big Biotech firms of course, but they create fewer innovative new medicines.

The system is one that rewards risk-taking and while imperfect, it's the best system yet devised to discover and develop medicines that changed how well and how long humans lived. Jack knew from his experience that while the financial rewards enabled the system, the vast majority of those searching for new medicines and dedicating their lives to this work were motivated *first* by the patients that needed them to find a new medicine.

Jack smiled at Jean-Luc as they enjoyed the success and he thought to himself that as excited as they were, having spent a half-billion bucks and well over a decade, successfully passing Phase II made the chances for success only a little better. Based on industry history, they now had about a 40 percent chance to get this med to the market. He kept that statistic to himself – his team cleared yet another hurdle and they needed to cherish the accomplishment. "Get the gang together. We need to celebrate!"

97

Jean-Luc and his team worked around the clock to prepare the summary of the Phase II results for presentation to the scientific community. The ideal venue they knew, would be to present at the upcoming ANA, the American Neurological Association convention. The most important clinical trials debut at this meeting, and to be featured here confers a stamp of credibility on the trial and all those associated with it. While they had already missed the regular submission deadline, they felt that given the break-through nature of these data they would qualify for the "late-breaking clinical trials" session of the convention. This session is like the Oscars of neurology.

After four days of non-stop work they concluded their analyses and sent the abstract to the ANA. Now it would be several weeks before they'd hear if their presentation had been accepted. *Hurry up and wait*, thought Jack. It wasn't as if Jack didn't have enough to distract him as he waited for the ANA news. The time had come for him to make his biggest decision yet as CEO – a "bet-the-company" decision.

The decision concerned the manufacture of BIO230. Since a manufacturing plant for a biological drug is enormously complex, it takes years to design, permit and build so they would have to start now. Each facility costs hundreds of millions of dollars and if BIO230 were successful, the demand for the medicine would be huge, requiring more than one factory.

The inconvenient fact was that these plants took years to build which meant that they needed to commit to manufacturing now, before the critical Phase III results could conclusively confirm in a larger group of patients with Alzheimer's disease that BIO230 was truly safe and effective. Since the Phase III studies required for FDA approval had not even begun, this decision was like walking up to the blackjack table and making a multi-hundred million dollar bet before seeing neither the dealer's up card nor your own second card. It was a bet of educated hope, nearly-blind faith.

Jack knew that if the Phase III studies failed, BioNeura would've built a manufacturing plant for nothing. At best, he might sell the plant for 20 cents on the dollar. Then again, if BIO230 failed the whole company would be in crisis; an empty manufacturing plant would be only one of many existential problems for the company.

After getting the advice of several experts, Jack worked out a creative sequential approach to building the facilities. As the Phase III clinical trial enrolled patients an independent board of physicians and statisticians would take quarterly interim safety analyses of the data to make sure the patients in the trial were not being harmed in any way. Jack timed the incremental manufacturing investments to these interim analyses of the data in the two planned Phase III studies. In this way, if BIO230 showed signs of trouble in Phase III he could slow the construction or even stop it completely. If the plant wasn't too far along, he could still sell it to one of the many companies manufacturing or planning to manufacture in Ireland because of the attractive tax structure offered to high-tech companies there.

The Board strongly supported Jack's risk-management approach and gave the plant a green light. Coincidently, shortly after the Board approved the plant construction Jean-Luc and his team received a green light from the ANA – they accepted their abstract for the high profile Late-Breaking Clinical Trials session at the conference. BioNeura was going to the big time!

98

"Hello, Dr. Rostov. How are you today?"

"I'm pretty good, Dr. Bonner."

His clinical objective for the day was to judge her cognitive abilities so he pulled out his stethoscope to make her think she was getting a physical check-up rather than a mental exam. "So, how's your son, Ben?"

"It's Alex, Dr. Bonner, not Ben. Have *you* been to a doctor lately? Maybe you're getting this disease!"

He liked that she still had a keen sense of humor and knew her son's name. But as they chatted more he noticed an unmistakable pattern. Dr. Rostov struggled naming items and finding words. She was clever in her attempt to hide it.

"I am feeling OK, doc. I noticed though, when I am in the kitchen using the . . . the uh . . . you know . . . the um . . . "Did you see the moon the other night? Wasn't it spectacular?" He noticed this twice; after desperately searching for the name of a familiar object she changed the subject as if she just remembered an exciting bit of news. Dr. Bonner noted in his file that Darya was exhibiting a coping mechanism to hide her loss of memory for words, names or events; a typical behavior of AD patients.

Bonner noticed she became anxious and agitated whenever this happened. The disease was terrifying her because she was losing her greatest strength – her brain. It was as if Darya Rostov were watching herself fall in slow motion from a cliff of unknown height. That she would hit bottom was certain; she knew that. Only the duration of the fall was unknown.

As usual, Alex was waiting for her. *How lucky she was to have such a devoted son,* Bonner thought. He noted that Alex looked a little worse for wear than last time. The huge boulder that every AD caregiver carries had bowed but not yet broken him, but Bonner knew it may happen. The progression of his mother's disease would slowly increase the fatigue, stress and strain on Alex and he would start to weaken. Eventually he would reach the inevitable point of surrender, unable to care for her anymore.

99

The ANA presentation of the BIO230 results stole the convention. In the meeting room, the largest of the convention there was standing room only. The principal investigator of the Phase II study, a renowned physician-scientist made the presentation on behalf of the doctors and nurses at more than one hundred medical centers in the U.S. and Europe that had enrolled patients in the trial. The key executives of BioNeura were there, plus a special guest, Wen's son Gabriel. Now in the eighth grade, Gabriel was mature enough to appreciate what an accomplishment this was for his dad. After the presentation Gabriel gave his dad a double thumbs up and an enormous grin. Wen smiled back and had to look away to hide a tear of joy.

There were two immediate results from the presentation of the BIO230 data at the ANA conference. First, the BioNeura share price soared by over 20 percent in the hour after the presentation, and this was on top of 30 percent when they announced the top-line data a couple of months ago. Second, in the days thereafter Jack's office got inundated with calls from companies wanting to collaborate with BioNeura on the development and marketing of BIO230. Jack had been waiting for these data to be made public before implementing a major part of his Strategic Plan, finding a major company partner who could help BioNeura take BIO230 to the next stage of development. The right partner would bring four things to the table: capital, expertise, world-wide scale and risk-sharing.

For this, Jack would have to go on the road again in the spring, to Europe and Asia. He was glad Diana was feeling better. Maybe she could join him in Japan at the end of the trip. Jack started in Europe with a list of companies that had expressed interest in BIO230 and had a credible story for how they could help BioNeura. To that list he added companies that *should* be interested in BIO230. The first stop was at BPL, the London-based giant and then took the TGV to Paris to visit the single remaining French force in pharmaceuticals, Paneq Pharmaceuticals. Then on to Basel to meet with the two Swiss pharmaceutical giants.

Everywhere, the routine was the same. Each side did their show-and-tell and there was an agreement of next steps. Jack's mission was to see how interested each company was. Most telling on that score was who each company sent to the meeting with him and his team. If a very senior executive showed up, it demonstrated a strong and serious interest. To Jack's pleasure, he met with the number one or two executive of nearly every company.

Asia was less complicated. The only country in that part of the world doing any serious pharmaceutical R&D is Japan. Although China is developing, Japan is the only country with the patent protection, infrastructure and economy to support an innovative pharmaceutical industry. Jack's Asian tour involved only two cities, Tokyo and Osaka and as with the Europeans a key aspect of what he was after from the Japanese was a "quid," a product that Jack could develop in the U.S. and possibly Europe in exchange for letting the partner company develop BIO230 in Japan.

While the Japanese don't have a lot of cardiovascular disease when compared to Americans, they're facing a huge aging population that suffers from Alzheimer's. A product such as BIO230 could have huge healthcare implications for the country, which explained why the reception for Jack in Japan bordered on regal. He not only met the CEOs of each company for intimate meetings before the formal meetings, he also sat beside them at elaborate dinners.

The trip wrapped up in Tokyo and Diana flew over so they could spend some time together in a city that neither had ever visited as tourists. It was springtime and the cherry blossoms were blooming in a riot of color and fragrance. Diana felt better but still wasn't up for a lot of running around which suited Jack just fine. He had endured enough running over the previous weeks so all he only wanted was to enjoy Diana at a very slow pace and to show her extra-special treatment.

One of the Japanese CEOs that he particularly liked told him about an exclusive Japanese spa that specialized in helping people recover from harrowing life events and worked with executives to prevent "karoshi," death by over-work. Jack thought it would be a great place for Diana and Jack and arranged a stay there. They were picked up at their hotel by private limousine and they arrived at the spa in the late afternoon. What unfolded over the next few days was an unending series of sensual, physical, culinary and spiritual pleasures. When their visit finished, they were driven back to their hotel to a magnificent meal served by Geisha in a private dining room at their hotel.

After the dinner, feeling very content but not over-fed, they fell into each other's arms on the bed. "I don't know what the spa people put in their aroma steams and oils," mumbled Diana as she drifted off to sleep, "but whatever it was it relaxed every muscle, tendon and synapse in my body." Jack followed shortly after her and they both enjoyed the deepest, most restful sleep of their lives.

The day before their return to San Francisco, Jack sent the CEO a thank-you note. He had it written in Japanese, as translated by the excellent translator he used in Japan and had it hand-delivered that day. Along with his thanks he extended an invitation for the CEO to come to San Francisco so Jack could return the favor.

Sertraline (Zoloft®)

100

While in Japan, Jack and Diana had talked and laughed like they hadn't in years. But the return trip seemed to physically tax Diana much more than it should have.

When she got to their apartment in San Francisco, she looked pale and drawn. "It's just jet lag, Jack," she said with a weak smile. "I'm fine. I just need some rest." And she shuffled off to take a bath before going to bed.

At breakfast the next morning, Jack suggested that she see a doctor. To his surprise and alarm, Diana agreed. Usually he had to work on her for days before she would agree to see a doctor. This time she had agreed immediately.

Jack set her up to see his internist early that afternoon. He was an excellent doctor and a friend of Jack's from the golf club they belonged to. He trained at the Mayo Clinic and was now on the teaching faculty at Pacific University medical school and head of their internal medicine department. He would oversee Diana's care.

101

In the midst of Wen's elation, he had also started feeling something else. His "baby," BIO230 was beginning to grow up and to show great potential, but in truth he had been relatively uninvolved in the development of BIO230 for several years now. The development team rarely even asked his opinion on BIO230 topics anymore. Wen felt like a father watching his child being raised by another family.

But that was only part of the problem. Much more troubling was the fact that since he had conceived the concept of BIO230 well over a decade before, he hadn't made a single additional important contribution to science. He had published some follow-up results of his experiments but these were minor, essentially inconsequential contributions to the literature.

In his darkest moments the words of Dr. Schwartz, his former boss at the Pacific University lab so many years before, haunted him. If BIO230 ended up working in the definitive Phase III studies, Wen will have made a huge contribution. But if it failed, he likewise would have failed. He will not have found another piece of the massive human jig-saw puzzle, had not wrested even one more tiny secret from that notoriously stingy Mother Nature.

Wen had worked on many exciting projects and spent several years and tens of millions of dollars on each of them, but every single one since BIO230 had ended the same way – in complete failure. A fear had started growing in Wen's gut that in fact he wasn't a great scientist, maybe he's just a lucky one – if BIO230 worked. This shook his self-confidence to its foundation. Intellectually, he knew that making even one major discovery would be more than the vast majority of hard-working and brilliant scientists could ever claim.

But what role was played by good science and what role by good fortune? Those questions ate away at Wen like the rust that had consumed his old Honda Civic in the parking lot.

102

When Jack and Diana were called in to meet Diana's doctor, he got right to the point. "Diana, I'm very sorry to tell you that the results of all of the tests that you have endured these past few weeks confirm that you have cancer of the pancreas. I wish I could say it was something we had a good success rate with. Unfortunately, the prognosis is poor."

Jack saw Diana wobble slightly, and he could feel his own heart sink. She fired off. "What are we talking about? What kind of success rate? What do we do to fix this?"

"Pancreatic cancer is a very bad cancer. We give patients like you much less than a fifty-percent chance that we can change the outcome of her disease."

"And the outcome is what, exactly?" asked Jack. Jack knew the answer but he was in denial, hoping his deduction was wrong. The doc paused a moment, knowing the gravity of what he would deliver.

"Diana and Jack, the outcome is almost always fatal; usually the best we can do is buy time."

"How much time?"

"About six months, plus or minus. We'll do everything we can. Sometimes we win and cure the damn disease, but you have to know that this is rare. You both need to have realistic expectations so you can make your plans. I wish I had something better to tell you."

"Make your plans" hit Jack like a dagger to his heart, he imagined how it hit Diana. *This isn't happening, it isn't real. Not Diana!*

Looking into Diana's eyes, Jack fought the urge to break down. He returned a smile – one as forced as her own.

"We'll be OK," she said, touching his check. "We'll beat the odds and we'll make it." Jack instantly deciphered the false confidence and experienced a wave of helplessness.

Hand in hand they walked from the doctor's office and back to the car. Sometime later they found themselves in their apartment with no recollection of having driven home. No one had wept yet. They were too stunned to cry – shaken to the core by this news that had just upended their world.

Diana looked at Jack, "I'm so scared!" Then the tears flowed, followed by body-wrenching sobs and a fall into a desperation, the depths of which words couldn't begin to describe.

103

The next couple of months were a nightmare. Jack called on all of his contacts in the industry to get the best care, the best doctors and even access to promising experimental medicines. This cancer allowed no time to be wasted. With the help of her doctor, Diana began her treatment within a week and after six weeks the first cycle of treatments were done.

Jack always appreciated his excellent team at work but never so much as now. In this time of his personal need they kept him informed of only the most important things and worked well together within the objectives and parameters that he set before his leave of absence.

Three months after getting the life-changing news, Diana began to flag. Her optimism, which had always been her defining character trait, began to fail her as she started to accept the cruel hand she'd been dealt. For Jack, this slow but steady raising of her white flag frightened him more than anything he had experienced in his life. Diana was always the rock in their relationship. Jack was master of his business world; Diana was the anchor of his *life*. She kept Jack balanced and tethered and he was terrified that if he lost her he would drift out of control.

These days were like the violent thunder storms he recalled from his childhood in Chicago. Right after a fierce and close lightning flash, a deafening roar always followed. Jack felt that the news of Diana's cancer was the flash – since then he awaited what he knew must come. There was no stopping it; he could only brace himself for it. The pressure of the waiting had mass; it weighed him down, made it difficult to breathe. He wanted the crash to come to stop the pressure but he knew the crash would end it all for Diana, and himself. He focused now on making Diana as comfortable as possible before the final deafening thunder clap.

He could see Diana fade very fast now. The medication helped, but it was a taker. It took away the crushing pain that contorted her body but also took her awareness, her personality, the brightness from her eyes and her connection to him during their last precious hours.

Her family and friends began the heavy and sad process of saying good-bye. Diana asked for Clara to come to her side. After this, she asked everyone to give the two of them a private moment.

"Clara, you're my dearest friend. I am worried about Jack. He will have a very rough ride after I go. He and I were everything to each other and we didn't need to build a huge network of very close friends. So he doesn't really have anyone to watch over him." Taking Clara's hand, Diana looked deep into her eyes. "I am going to ask a terrible thing of you, a thing I never wanted to ask of anyone."

Before Diana could say another word, Clara put her finger to Diana's parched and cracked lips. "Diana, sweetheart, of course I'll watch over Jack." Clara joined Diana in the bed, wrapped Diana's spindly arms around her and pulled her close. Trying to cut the heaviness of the moment, Clara added, "Hell, it's no big deal, Diana. I already keep Jack out of trouble now – it's in my job description already!" They both laughed through drenching tears, their chests heaved with sobs and sad laughs as they rocked each other in their last embrace.

After a few moments, Diana ended their moment. "Thank you, my beautiful ballerina. Keep dancing for both of us, OK?" Clara nodded and smiled, biting her lower lip to hold back the tears. "Could you get Jack, please?"

Clara gently kissed Diana's forehead. "Good-bye, Diana," she whispered through her trembling lips.

When Jack saw Diana, his heart broke into pieces. The mascara she vainly applied to look decent for her visitors had run dark lines from her swollen, red eyes toward her neck, making a black connection between eyes and heart. He feared Diana was going fast. Rushing to her side, he took her hand. "Jack, I think it's time . . ."

The thunderclap arrived. It roared and vibrated through him; it rattled and shook him to his knees. Jack climbed into bed with Diana and entwined his body with hers, now so thin and frail. He stroked her cheek, kissed her eyes and lips, ran his fingertips over her strong chin and long slender neck. He gazed into her beautiful eyes, now more serene and rested his head next to hers for several minutes. When he pulled back and looked again at Diana's face Jack saw that it was no longer contorted but was at peace and carried a very slight but definite smile on her lips. With his warm tears dropping onto to her checks, Jack kissed those lips for the last time.

104

After the funeral, Jack felt he needed to take some time off. Against the advice of both Meg and Clara, he named Bill Copley as his temporary stand-in. Bill hadn't failed him since Sea Island, and in fact had been a huge support to him when Jack cared for Diana over the past several months. With Bill in place as interim leader and an understanding Chairman looking in on things, Jack was able to get away for a while. He decided to start hiking the Appalachian Trail, beginning at one end in Georgia. It would be a long-term mission. Each summer he would hike another section as a celebration of Diana and their life together. It would be his way of keeping her with him.

In Geneva, Nathaniel Shah heard of Jack's loss and his planned leave of absence. *Poor guy*, thought Shah. In a nanosecond, his mind quickly shifted to the next thought. *I wonder what opportunity his absence might present for us.* He decided to have someone poke around at BioNeura to see if he could steal some scientists or unsettle the team at the company that he feared would someday be his archrival. But after discreetly trying through headhunters who told the BioNeura employees they were being recruited for a new company, Shah came up empty. Nobody wanted to leave BioNeura, at least not now.

Tamsulosin (Flomax®)

105

Bill Copley threw himself into the role of interim CEO. No one gave him that title; he just informally assumed it. Jack's team was intensely loyal to him and Bill's actions at Sea Island were more widely known than either Jack or Bill knew. This made for an uneasy chemistry in the leadership team.

As Bill took on his new role, a subtle but unmistakable transformation took place. With each passing week, the power in his hands outweighed a little more, the reason in his head. He became addicted to the CEO's power. Clara noticed it first because she watched Bill like a hawk. She had the skill of a master spy when it came to observing without being observed and she didn't like what she was seeing.

Clara noticed that Bill had a lot of contact with the Board. She distinctly remembered that Jack had made it clear to his own staff and to Bill how he wished contact with the Board to take place in his absence. Jack's staff would take an issue to Bill, who would speak with Greg, the Chairman. Greg would decide if contact with additional Board members would be appropriate.

Now Clara noticed that more and more, Bill operated outside of these rules and had direct and regular contact with all of the Board directors, not just Greg. Clara's concern was intensified because she hadn't heard from Jack in several weeks. She held as sacred her promise to Diana and she imagined the worst of catastrophes that could have happened, from desperate and hopeless leaps off craggy ridges to more mundane accidents or mischief on The Trail.

106

Jack surveyed his progress on the Trail. He had hiked nearly 500 miles in 35 days, an amazing pace for an amateur. He found that when he wasn't moving, his mind quickly fixated on Diana and he sank into an empty, lonely place. So, he kept moving until he became completely exhausted at the end of the day and he collapsed into sleep right after he ate.

After having his breakfast one morning, Jack was surprised by the face that reflected in the bottom of his metal coffee cup. To get a better look, he pulled out his camping mirror. It was the first time he had seen himself since beginning his trek. A now heavily bearded man with hardened eyes and gaunt features stared back at him. Putting the mirror back in its assigned place, he noticed his legs were thinner now but much more muscular and as he rose he noticed that his hiking shorts were hanging from him. "I've lost some serious weight," he said to himself, surprised that he had only now noticed it. He realized that he had been in some sort of zone; a protective cocoon in which he operated without thinking of himself or others. He knew this wasn't healthy but it kept the pain away.

He decided to descend from the trail on the following morning to buy some provisions, get a hot shower and check in with Clara. After hiking a full day, he made camp in a designated campsite. As night fell, he walked a hundred yards to a ledge overlooking the high ridge that he followed that day. The stars were coming out now. The night was clear without a moon and the air was sweet and still.

One star caught his eye and inexplicably, he started weeping, sobbing. For the past month, he had done his best to keep Diana and her memory in an emotional box, closed up and locked tight. He hadn't had the strength to open that box because he feared he would fall into it and never come out. Now the box had broken open on its own. He started talking to Diana through his tears. At first, he couldn't complete full sentences, as great waves of emotion rolled over him. Gradually the words flowed more smoothly.

After several minutes, he lay on his back and got more comfortable. He told Diana how he missed her so much and how his heart ached for her. He told her about his progress on the Trail and how he would continue until he finished it for her one day. He told her about his favorite memories of her and of them. He sighed, cursed and cried into the dark night. But he also smiled for the first time since she left him. The conversation was good and as it went on Jack grew more and more tired. Finally, he fell into a deep and peaceful sleep.

The sun on his eyelids woke him. He looked up to the sky where Diana had been and she was gone. But Jack knew she was there even though the sun hid her from him. That thought made him happy; like the stars during the day, he *knew* Diana was there even though he couldn't see her. At that moment and for the first time in months, Jack felt a hint of warmth in his soul, a stirring of life within him, less numb. In fact, as he stood, he noticed that his legs ached and his feet were sore. His back, having carried 40 pounds of gear for over a month, now complained. Jack welcomed the pain. It was a sign of life, like a blade of grass poking through snow in early spring, hopeful.

He walked back to his campsite, ate breakfast and after packing up he began his hike to the next village about nine miles away. He got there just after noon and found a motel room to rent. After weeks of blocking out everything except the reality beneath his hiking boots, he was suddenly very curious about the company and his team. He looked forward to the call he planned to make to Clara. The work day was just getting started in San Francisco. He imagined Clara sitting at her desk with the morning sun slanting across her desk.

"Clara," he said, "this is Jack."

There was a brief pause at the other end, then a rush of words. "Jack! Where are you? How are you? We've been worried sick . . ." She stopped herself. She knew Jack wouldn't like knowing that people were worried about him. "We've been anxious to hear from you," she continued. During their conversation, Clara heard a different Jack than from a few weeks ago. He sounded more alive now; less monotoned.

"So, has Bill moved into my office yet?"

She was pleased that Jack offered a joke, but uncomfortable with how close it came to the reality of the situation. "No, of course not Jack. What are your plans?"

"I'm thinking of coming home soon."

"I'm so happy to hear that, Jack. We can't wait to see you but only come when you're ready."

"I think I'm at the beginning of some kind of recovery, Clara. I'm starting to feel like...well, I'm starting to *feel* and that's a good start at least." She heaved a sigh of relief. "Yes, Jack. That *is* a good thing."

When Jack spoke briefly to Bill, who gave him a brief update on the business, Clara overheard Bill's end of the conversation. "You take all the time you need, Jack. Don't come back before you're ready. That wouldn't do you or us any good." *Yeah*, Clara mocked Bill in her mind. *Stay away so I can have more time to show the Board I can do your job and the first time you stumble I'll be there to take it...*

The next morning Jack joined the trail again. As he walked, he became more certain that it was time to return to life. For whatever reason, he no longer feared of thinking about his life after Diana. It helped that her star would be in the sky every night. He could still talk to her. She could still watch over him. He realized that here on the trail he made the first step in his true journey – from blocking out the pain of losing her to something like the beginning of acceptance.

A few days later, Jack found himself at a small country store outside of a no-name village just off the Trail. He saw a pay phone and made a decision.

"Clara, it's Jack. I want to come home now." He looked across the street and saw a small bed and breakfast called The Pine Tree Inn. A sign said they had a vacancy.

"Call me at the Pine Tree Inn," he said, and he read her the phone number from the Inn's sign. "When you've figured out how to get me home, call me there."

"You got it, boss. We can't wait to see you!"

"I'll see you soon," Jack said, and he hung up the phone, walked across the street and checked into the inn.

107

Bill overheard Clara talking to Jack and realized he had to work fast. Over the next few days, he spoke with each Board member to tell them of Jack's return and how he thought they all should help him with what would surely be a difficult re-entry. Bill applied all of his dramatic skills over the phone to show how happy he was that Jack was coming back... but very concerned that it might be too soon. He wove his concern subtly throughout his conversations, nothing too heavy. In this way, he laid the groundwork in case Jack screwed up soon after his return. Bill could then reference the concern that he had shared with the Board.

Bill's other agenda was to make sure the Board members understood the many great things he had done while Jack was away and how he had kept the business afloat during this very difficult time.

108

Four days after talking with Clara from the Pine Tree Inn, Jack was back in his office at BioNeura. His return was none too soon. Bill had been riding Jack's team roughly and several were near mutiny.

"Jack, we're *so glad* you're back," said Jean-Luc, giving Jack a big French-Canadian hug and kissing him on both cheeks. Jean-Luc had a tear in his eye.

"If you didn't come back when you did, there would have been some dead bodies stuffed in lockers here." Jack looked at him, puzzled.

"It's okay," Jean-Luc said. "I'm exaggerating a little, Jack. Bill's ego got a little out of control. The Napoleon in him rose up – but thankfully you returned just before he marched us to Waterloo."

Jack heard similar reports from others – everyone except Meg. "He was fine with me, Jack," she said. "Early on, I told him to stay out of my business until I screwed up." She smiled. "And I wasn't going to let *that* happen, now was I?"

Jack was conflicted. He was deeply grateful to Bill for covering for him, but also disappointed that Bill had overstepped the rules they agreed on when he left. He decided that that was exactly what had to be said to Bill.

Bill was the last of his staff to come see Jack, blaming a minor emergency. Clara was skeptical. Bill had drunk from the chalice of power and was still intoxicated by the elixir it carried. Jack closed the door after Bill entered; they shook hands in a cold and formal way and chatted about Jack's trek. Then Jack opened the subject. "First, I want to thank you, sincerely, for covering for me, Bill. I spoke with Greg this morning and he said you did a great job and things are running smoothly."

Bill smiled and thanked Jack, saying it was his duty and pleasure. "That said, I gotta say I am disappointed at how you overstepped the rules we agreed to before I left." At this, Bill recoiled. His head snapped back and he crossed his arms tightly. "Jack, those were *guidelines* and you trusted me to adapt them to the circumstances."

Jack took a couple of steps to his desk and pulled a piece of paper from his top drawer. "This is what we agreed on before I left, Bill. If you needed to change them, we agreed you'd get Greg's approval beforehand."

"Greg's a busy guy, Jack. I really thought you and he would trust me to use my judgment when you were out of it."

Jack suddenly felt a fire rise in his chest. Bill's choice of the phrase "out of it" struck him as totally disrespectful to him and Diana, and he couldn't forgive it. Bill was now furious, too. Not only had he abruptly lost his interim role, now he was being scolded by someone Bill thought wasn't his equal.

"Bill, again," said Jack, struggling to get both himself and the situation under control, "I'm grateful for the job you did. While I have a crystal-clear recollection of the rules we agreed to before I left, I'll accept your view that there was a misunderstanding, but you'll have to do some fence mending with my staff. They felt you were a little too...enthusiastic."

"I didn't realize they were so fragile, Jack. We're in the big league now; we can't coddle them."

"Bill, I'm on the edge of losing my patience with you." He stood up. "Let's pick up where we left off. I'm anxious to dig in."

Bill reluctantly accepted Jack's extended hand, but he stung mightily at the phrase "where we left off." It reminded him that he had been returned to his old role as number two. He had to remove his lips from the chalice and return it to the altar.

109

Before he began his leave of absence, he began a project on the potential acquisition of a company called APT, American Pharmaceutical Technologies. The acquisition would put BioNeura firmly in the mid-league. The BioNeura share price was very strong and Jack wanted to strike while their "currency" was highly valued. APT had good products on the market, a strong sales force but no pipeline. They also had a lot of cash and generated a good cash flow but they were being criticized because they had no pipeline of new products, which BioNeura had.

To his credit, Bill had done an excellent job quietly studying APT and evaluating the fit with BioNeura. The fit was as good as Jack thought it could be. And with the Board's approval, Bill had approached the CEO of APT a few weeks before Jack returned so a discussion was already underway.

Jack was thankful for the project because it consumed every bit of his free time. And he was enjoying it. He was developing a rapport with Ken Carlisle, the CEO of APT and it was exciting to watch the project develop the momentum so necessary for the consummation of a deal. These days flew by for Jack, but the nights were painfully long. He arrived at the office early and left late to decrease the time he'd be alone in his empty apartment.

One night when Jack was working late at the office he decided to take a walk outside to get some air. As he rounded the corner to the back of the BioNeura building he heard a noise from the area where the company's trash was set out for collection the next day. He approached slowly and quietly, staying in the shadows. To his amazement, he saw a man in the dumpster wearing a lamp device on his head. He wasn't rummaging for food, he was reading papers and putting some in a satchel that hung from his neck.

Jack called 911. The dumpster diver evidently heard Jack's call – the man's head popped up, he leapt from the dumpster and bolted to a waiting car. It screeched away and was gone in seconds. When the police arrived, they couldn't do more than take a report. After that, Jack decided he would call it a night. But he knew it would not be a restful one. What he had seen troubled him deeply. *Who was that guy? What was he looking for? Who sent him?*

Fluticasone (Flonase®)

110

Nearly 6,000 miles away Nathaniel Shah was also anxious but for a reason he couldn't put his finger on. He too had been working late at the office and thought a little exercise in the crisp air before going home would burn off the nerves. So, he grabbed his briefcase and began walking.

As he neared the end of his thirty-minute walk, he turned the corner and saw his limo driver leaning inelegantly against the door of the car in front of the SNS offices. The driver snapped to attention as soon as he spotted Shah but he knew it was too late. He knew he would catch hell for looking unprofessional.

Shah walked more briskly now, so focused on the limo driver that he didn't see her coming. As he fell to the ground he heard a grunt and smelled an awful odor. He was startled at finding himself sprawled on the street and revolted by what he saw as he lay there. Within a foot of his face was an old, filthy and toothless woman. She bent over him, staring at his face. Recoiling from her stench, Shah quickly got to his feet and dusted off his clothes.

She kept staring at him, her strange eyes inspecting him. "Do you have a franc or two for an old woman, sir?" She disgusted him and he shouted to his driver, "Give this wretch a few francs and call the police about her. I don't want her fouling our streets or our building."

He picked up his briefcase and walked to the car. The driver was fishing in his pocket for some money as the old woman stood with outstretched hand. "Could you be any slower?" Shah seethed, drumming his fingers on his briefcase as he waited for his driver to return to open his door. Once in the safety and comfort of the limo, Shah angrily opened the newspaper and tried to read the news of the day. But he couldn't concentrate. He kept seeing the old woman's eyes in his mind. "What a pathetic thing," he said aloud.

"What sir?"

"Nothing...just mind the bloody road."

111

"I'm a hundred percent convinced that the dumpster diver was involved in corporate espionage, Mr. Callahan," said the security expert Jack called to look into the dumpster episode. His security guy was retired from the CIA and was former military. His bearing was stiff, formal and precise.

"The likely sponsors of the theft," he continued, "are plaintiffs' lawyers trying to collect evidence to use against you in a potential legal case. Or a company that wants to buy you and would like some inside information before launching a hostile takeover bid. Or a competitor wanting your scientific secrets. I'll let you decide which is most likely for your company, Mr. Callahan." *It could be any of those*, Jack thought.

"What's most important, right now, Mr. Callahan is that you have a security threat and I suggest you take it very seriously. I can assess your procedures and make some recommendations."

"Give me a proposal on what you'd do in the assessment and a cost estimate of that, as a first step."

"Yes sir. You'll have it ASAP."

When his security expert had gone, Jack reviewed the possibilities. With BIO230 potentially a multi-billion-dollar product, any number of competitors, investors or acquirers might want to know about its progress in development and many other secrets. *Which threat is most likely?,* he asked himself.

112

By now, Jack and Ken Carlisle of APT were past the early, tenuous phase of their business relationship. Trusting each other enough to peel away the veneers of their companies and talk candidly about a merger, they had agreed to take it to the next level.

Each man approached his Board for approval to begin negotiations toward a definitive agreement to merge and the respective Boards quickly gave the go-ahead. They gave Jack a target price, above which he could not go. Ken likewise got a target price, below which he would not go. After some conversations testing on price, they both agreed that they were in the neighborhood of where a deal could be done so each company called its favorite investment banker and law firm to support its team in the negotiations.

Things were proceeding well. The teams of lawyers, accountants and bankers were behaving themselves with no signs yet of testosterone flares or grandstanding. Jack and Ken had set the tone early in the negotiations by appearing together and projecting mutual respect and a will to try to do a deal that made sense to both parties.

Almost all the tough issues had been framed up, leaving just a couple of difficult but solvable issues to deal with. Creative and flexible minds would find a way to get it done if they wanted a deal. Jack now spent more time planning the post-merger aspects of a BioNeura/APT combination than managing the details of the negotiation process.

Clara stuck her head into his office. "Jack, Ken Carlisle's office just called. He needs to cancel your meeting with him today."

"Thanks, Clara. We'll just do it tomorrow." It was no big deal. Jack hardly looked up from his emails.

"His secretary said it wouldn't be until late next week. Some sort of personal issue, she said."

That got Jack's attention. Now he worked it over in his mind. *This train is hurtling down the track. Ken and I are talking a dozen times a day...* They both had been concerned that word of their discussions would leak, sending APT's price skyward and making the merger too expensive for BioNeura. *Ken knows he has to sell his company because he has no new product pipeline,* Jack thought. *The longer he waits, the sooner the market will penalize his share price for his lack of products in development. If he loses my offer, he's hammered. So, he has no incentive to delay.*

After tumbling all these points around in his head, Jack could come to only one conclusion: "He has another suitor." He picked up the phone and called Ken.

"Mr. Carlisle's office, how may I help you?"

"Hi, it's Jack. May I speak with Ken please?"

Based on the pattern of recent weeks, she answered from habit. "I'll get him on the line."

Jack waited for 30 seconds and his assistant came back on. "I'm sorry, Jack. I thought he was in his office but I was mistaken. Can he call you back?"

Jack remembered Ken's office set-up. His assistant faced Ken's glass-framed office. There was no way she could miss him.

"Yes, please have him call me back today."

"I will," she replied. Though her tone was full of commitment, Jack guessed he wouldn't hear from Ken today. He was right. At the end of the day, Clara popped her head into Jack's office.

"That was Ken's assistant. She apologized that Ken couldn't get back to you today."

"Did she say when he'd call?"

"No, she didn't say. Should I call her back?" Jack didn't want Ken to think he was anxious.

"No thanks," he said, and he had a bad feeling that he wouldn't be hearing from Ken until he returned from his "personal" trip late next week.

113

"What I have for you Mr. Carlisle is a very attractive offer and a draft contract endorsed by the Board of my company to acquire APT for twenty dollars per share."

Shah's quick and competitive offer impressed Ken. He flipped through the contract and it wasn't window-dressing but a very detailed and thoughtful draft. *The contract terms are remarkably close to where Jack and I were coming out*, Ken thought. The price was very attractive. While he and Jack had traded numbers, this offer touched the very high end of that range.

"I know I've hit you with a lot, Mr. Carlisle. Please sleep on it and let's talk tomorrow."

Ken was excited, jet-lagged, and intrigued all at once. Immediately upon entering his room in the Hotel des Bergues, a grand Geneva hotel in the European style, he downloaded the contract from the flash drive Shah gave him and emailed it to his staff and his lawyers for their analysis of this deal versus the one he and Jack had hammered out. He demanded a detailed response within four hours.

Standing to get blood pumping to his fatigued brain, he walked to the window and looked out at the amazing view. Ken had seen pictures of this place – beautiful marina, amazing private yachts, remarkable fountain. The pictures didn't do it justice. *Geneva is even lovelier than they say it is,* he thought.

The phone rang in Ken's room exactly at noon. "So, what do you think, Mr. Carlisle?"

"My staff and I think this is a reasonable offer," Ken said. "I'll recommend to my Board that we begin negotiations immediately. Since we may be spending a lot of time together, let's dispense with the formalities. You can call me Ken. Should I call you Nate or Nathaniel?"

Shah's head jerked back from the phone before a contorted smile formed on his face. "Nathaniel. Nathaniel is fine, Ken," Shah said, forcing each word.

Ken sat down at the desk in his room and phoned his Chairman, who agreed that an urgent telephonic Board meeting was indicated. At midnight Geneva time and 2 p.m. in San Francisco, the teleconference took place. As he expected, the APT Board felt compelled to entertain such a serious offer.

His Chairman summed up the meeting. "A little competition won't hurt and we owe it to our shareholders to try to get the best deal possible. Ken, stay in Geneva a few days and see how much better you can do than what we've got from Callahan at BioNeura."

Then Ken called the private number that Shah had given him.

"Dr. Shah speaking," came the crisp and elegant answer.

"Nathaniel, as I expected, my Board authorized me to work with you to try to do a deal. However, you should know that time is of the essence. We have to start right away."

"Is tomorrow morning soon enough?"

"Let's make it noon. That'll give my bankers and lawyers time to get here from New York."

"Noon it is, Ken."

Ken's lawyer and banker responded to his summons with a mixture of intrigue and anticipatory fatigue.

"You'll both have an electronic copy of the draft contract in your email within thirty minutes," promised Ken.

"Once you get it, have your staff work on it while you're in the air."

"Will do," replied Ken's lawyer.

"Ditto," replied his banker. *Such compliance*, thought Ken. *Big fees buy such good attitudes.*

Ken didn't look forward to this negotiation. He expected a long, hard slog like he'd had with BioNeura. It was the way these things were done. He hadn't slept well, and when he awoke the next morning he was pleased to see that his law firm had sent him an email with an attachment. *Very good, I've got a great team behind me,* he thought.

He scrolled through the hundred-page primary agreement from SNS and read the comments underlined in black that noted the key differences between Shah's proposal and Callahan's. At first, Ken was pleased but then became inexplicably troubled by what he read. The SNS terms and conditions were remarkably close to those of the BioNeura deal he had already hammered out with Jack. Ken mentally scanned the rosters of his team and Jack's. *No*, he thought, *these are trustworthy professionals.* He couldn't believe anyone on his *or* Jack's side would have struck some kind of deal to share the details of their draft agreement with Shah.

He shrugged off the remarkable similarities in the drafts, attributing them to the small world of M&A lawyers applying well-worn solutions to similar challenges on different deals. After reviewing the relatively few major issues, Ken realized it might be possible to reach an agreement in principle in a few days of hard work.

He stopped reading and got up to take in the panoramic view of the lake. His thoughts drifted to Jack. They had developed a good relationship and were almost finished doing their deal.

"Oh well, that's business," Ken said aloud to himself. "If he wants my company, Jack will have to beat Shah's offer now."

He sat down and called room service. Then, after a wonderful breakfast of pain au chocolat, yogurt and café américain he snapped open his *Financial Times* and scanned it for other news of the day.

114

"Any word from Ken Carlisle?"

"No Jack, not a word," Clara said. "Should I call?"

"No, no. Let's wait till Tuesday morning. I really don't want Ken to think I'm too anxious."

"That security expert you hired called," added Clara.

"Great," said Jack. "Would you get him on the line, please?" In a couple of minutes, Clara had them connected.

"Have you seen my proposal, Mr. Callahan?"

"Yes, I have. It's a little pricey."

"Security is always more expensive when you don't have it, Mr. Callahan."

"Let's start on the security assessment and the forensic study," said Jack.

"OK, I can do that. One team can study your security process and I'll show you where and how to harden it. At the same time, I'll do the forensic myself. I'm sure you'll want me to sign a confidentiality agreement since I'll be exposed to a lot of confidential material."

"Of course. Can you start today?"

"I'll be there before noon."

Jack slowly returned the phone to its holder and shook his head. All of this felt so dirty. *It's business,* he thought, but he couldn't help feeling personally violated by the knowledge that someone was apparently stealing or trying to steal information from his company and shareholders.

Pravastatin (Pravachol®)

115

"Hello, Ken. I hope you slept well," said Shah warmly. "And I hope you're hungry." He swept his arm gracefully toward a waiting table set in the most elegant style imaginable.

Ken's team had arrived with a list of twenty issues that they recommended Ken and Shah work on in a one-on-one meeting before the full teams faced off in the big boardroom. This was that meeting. The server bowed ever so slightly at Ken and touched the back of the chair. Ken took the invitation and made his way to Shah and the chair.

"Yes, I slept well. Thanks Nathaniel, I am really hungry. Who could resist such an elegant table and host!"

The wine flowed as they took their seats. Shah swept up his glass and raised it to Ken. "A votre santé!"

"A la vôtre!" replied Ken, raising his glass and thankful for having brushed up on his rudimentary French before he came to see SNS.

After lunch, they got down to business. One by one, Ken presented his view on the critical points in the proposed contract and how he would like to see them. Shah, an artful negotiator didn't attempt to reach agreement on any of these points, not knowing the totality of the points Ken was going to discuss.

Shah listened very carefully and asked many questions to understand not only what Ken wanted, but also – and more importantly – why he wanted it. Shah knew from experience that this knowledge would become very useful later on when horses were traded and deadlocks needed breaking.

Shah's assistant tapped on the door of his office. "Monsieur, tout le monde vous attend." Shah looked at his Patek Philippe watch. "My, my. We've been keeping our expensive bankers and lawyers waiting for three hours. We'd better go in there soon and at least have them work for their fees. I have an idea, Ken. Why don't we assemble everyone in the big conference room and I'll review my understanding of your eleven key points? That way, I can get everyone up to speed and also make sure I've heard you correctly."

"Good idea, Nathaniel. But there's a twelfth point."

"Oh?" Shah leaned forward toward Ken, his mouth frozen in the shape of the word he just said.

"Price, Nathaniel. I want it understood that the price you've offered is attractive enough to let you do the due diligence you need but my board expects that after having completed your diligence, you will improve your offer to one that would be attractive enough for us to sell the company. I am prepared to continue working only if you are prepared to meaningfully raise the price."

Knowing that his answer and body language would be carefully scrutinized, Shah paused for a millisecond and looked directly at Ken. "Ken, I'm assuming you viewed our price as attractive enough to drag your team to see us. I am likewise assuming that you believe we have some upward room in our price, but only a certain amount."

"Understood," replied Ken.

"My flexibility on price will be somewhat influenced by your flexibility on your other eleven key points," Shah said.

Ken couldn't push for more than that. "Yeah, they are certainly linked, Nathaniel."

"Right, so let's gather the gang together in the Boardroom and go through your points."

A massive rectangular antique dining table that originally stood in a chateau in the Burgundy region of France dominated the room. An eclectic collection of chairs from various eras and countries surrounded the magnificent table. Shah delighted in having an audience to which he could display his refined taste. "The chair at the head of the table is a Louis XIV which caressed the buttocks of the Sun King himself. At the other end, the desk chair of Kaiser Wilhelm." Shah walked around the room and placing his immaculately manicured hands on the top of each chair, he described it. "This one was General Eisenhower's from his headquarters in Hampshire, England while he prepared for D-Day...this one from Eva Peron's last apartment in Buenos Aires...this one... "

After the antique show was finished, Shah opened his arms in a regal gesture motioning all to take their seats. More than one hesitated, unsure if they were worthy of parking their behinds where such famous posteriors had been planted.

Once everyone was seated and settled, Shah opened the meeting. "Mesdames et Messieurs, Bienvenue à Genève. We are delighted to have you here and we are looking forward to concluding a deal to merge APT and SNS, two fine companies."

He introduced his staff, his bankers and his lawyers and Ken did the same. After the pleasantries were over, Shah jumped right in. "I apologize for keeping you all waiting for so long but Ken and I were making such good progress, the time slipped away. I am happy to report that we made very good use of the time and this should help us make more productive progress while we are together. Ken described to me the twelve key points that if satisfactorily resolved, would make the SNS draft proposal acceptable to the board of APT." Shah turned to Ken to see if he had anything to add.

"I'm very pleased with the progress Nathaniel and I made this morning," Ken said. He didn't notice the effect his words had on Shah's staff, who, to a person, felt buffeted as though by a sudden strong gust of wind. None of them had ever heard Dr. Shah referred to with such familiarity. Ken continued, oblivious. "I am convinced that he understands the concerns of APT on the twelve points and we both hope that our teams can quickly reach a workable position on each one."

Shah clapped his hands once and with a broad smile said, "So what are we waiting for? Let's get to work." After Shah's team of bankers and lawyers clarified the position of APT on each point, they asked to be left alone to think about them and to prepare a counter-proposal. Ken of course agreed and he took his APT team into a separate conference room at the other end of the building. There they waited, and waited and waited.

It was now almost 7:00 p.m. Shah and Ken had engaged in short one-on-one conversations while Shah's team caucused and now Shah came by once again. To the group, he said, "I apologize for the time we've taken. I am sure you are growing most annoyed and you must be hungry." Some acknowledgment rumbled from the APT staff. "I have reserved a private dining room at my favorite restaurant in Geneva, Le Lion d'Or. They are expecting you and your cars are waiting outside now."

Ken was a little disappointed at the slow progress made that day. The first draft was remarkably close to what he could agree to and Ken had thought he and Shah had nailed down the points of concern. He at least expected a counter-proposal before dinner on some of the points. Shah, always a keen observer of men, noted Ken's disappointment and gently pulled him aside. "Ken, lest you think we are wasting your time, I assure you that my staff will work while you are having dinner. We will then work with the time zones and send our comments to our colleagues in New York by e-mail. They will rework the draft document during our night. By 8:00 a.m. tomorrow local time, I will hand you a new draft agreement that incorporates our counter-proposal on your twelve points." Ken nodded, thinking that Shah was obviously serious about his interest and was putting everything into it.

"OK, Nathaniel. We'll have a nice dinner and meet you at eight tomorrow morning to review the new draft contract."

"Splendid. Trust me, Ken. I think you'll be pleased with our draft. If not, I'll have some lawyers to kick around."

"Can I help?" said Ken, laughing.

"Two boots are better than one," said Shah with smile.

"Thanks, Nathaniel. See you tomorrow."

Ken and his staff were driven in three sleek black Mercedes sedans to the restaurant. *The Europeans do have a sense of style*, Ken thought. The owner welcomed Ken. "Bienvenue dans mon petit restaurant, Monsieur Carlisle."

"Merci beaucoup, Monsieur," replied Ken as he began one of the most memorable gastronomic evenings of his life.

He enjoyed watching the young lawyers and bankers not yet spoiled by life in the fast lane, their eyes bugging out of their sockets at the unfolding pageant of wine, food and culinary savoir-faire. Ken missed those days when he got so totally blown away by his first haute cuisine experiences. He knew the young lawyers and bankers around him would likewise one day miss *these* days, the days before they were spoiled.

116

It was spring. Alex thought it would be good for his mother to get some fresh air, so he took her out for a cup of coffee. At a small neighborhood café near Dr. Rostov's home they settled into a booth near the back and placed their order.

A few minutes later, a young woman sat at the table next to them. She smiled in their direction and then pulled a huge textbook from her bag and placed it on the table. The title caught Dr. Rostov's eye: *Space and Responsibility*. With some trepidation, Alex heard his mother strike up a conversation with the young woman, who – it was quickly apparent to Alex – was greatly impressed by Dr. Rostov's knowledge of space, space junk and efforts being made to manage it.

"If you look in your index, you might find my name there...Rostov."

The young woman's eyes widened twice their size. "Wow, there you are...are you *THE* Dr. Rostov?"

Darya only smiled. Suddenly the conversation took a bad turn. "The problem has . . ." Dr. Rostov paused for several seconds, losing her train of thought. "I was in the space program from the very beginning...did I tell you that? Space junk...it's...it's." But she lost herself again and stared through the young woman. The young woman smiled politely at Alex. Dr. Rostov looked at Alex too and then back at the young woman. Alex saw his mother frown, frustrated at her inability to express herself.

"Sorry we disturbed you," Alex said to the young woman.

"No problem at all. It was an honor meeting you Dr. Rostov," she replied. "Have a nice day."

"Who is that woman Alex?"

117

"Still no word from Ken?" Clara noticed a little anxiety in Jack's voice.

"Nothing," she said. "Is it time to call them?"

"Not yet, let me get some input from our Chairman, Greg. Would you..."

"I'll get him on the line," Clara said, anticipating his request.

When Greg answered, Jack laid it all out for him. "Something's up with APT," he said. "We had agreed on the essential terms and were reviewing a draft of a final contract, when all of a sudden Ken Carlisle and his staff went silent. There was an excuse about a sick European relative, but I don't think it's true. In fact, I know in my gut it's not."

"What's your concern, Jack?"

"I think that we aren't the only company after APT."

"Exactly when did he go silent?"

Jack thought a moment. *Ken went silent a day or two after I surprised that dumpster diver.* After a few more questions, Greg agreed that Jack was probably right that something was up.

"What do you recommend?" Jack said.

"Let's smoke him out. Send a confidential letter by courier to Ken's office telling him that your Board has begun to get cold feet on the deal. Tell him that unless he contacts you immediately and gets things going again, the momentum would be lost and the deal would likely crater."

"I like it," Jack said. "Consider it done."

Jack typed up the letter himself, made a copy, and put the original in an envelope. "Have this delivered to Ken Carlisle's office within an hour," he said to Clara. "If Ken isn't there, insist that his assistant accepts it and immediately reads it to him over the phone."

"Will do," said Clara, a little hurt that he hadn't trusted her with the contents of the envelope.

Well, thought Jack, *the bait's in the water.... let's see if Ken rises for it.*

118

As promised, Shah had a new draft contract on the conference table when Ken's team arrived at 8 o'clock the next morning. Ken asked Shah for an hour or so to read the black-lined changes and then Ken's team retreated to their conference room to study the new draft. Ken, however, left the assessment to his people while he took a walk along the marina.

The reality of what he might do started to sink in. He was likely going to sell his company soon, either to Shah or to Jack. And while Ken was intellectually ready to do it – he knew it was the right time to sell – he had to admit that he wasn't yet emotionally ready.

As he walked, he thought about the team he had built. From the receptionist back home to the group he had just left in the conference room, they were consummate professionals. They had given their all to help him build the company. Those people back there at Shah's office were working their tails off, even as they prepared to sell their company and in the process very possibly lose their jobs. That thought made Ken feel very sad and very guilty, which stifled some of the excitement he'd been feeling about cashing out and taking some well-deserved down time.

On the other hand, Ken could take consolation in the fact that he had made the proper treatment of APT employees one of the "twelve points" to be dealt with in this negotiation with Shah. Nobody could say he had not fought for his people. That thought only marginally lightened his step as he began making his way back to the SNS office and his loyal team.

"So, how does it look?" Ken asked as he entered the conference room. "Some pluses, some neutrals, some minuses," replied Ken's General Counsel.

"OK, take me through each one," Ken said.

After nearly an hour reviewing his team's assessment, he agreed with them; it was a mixed bag. He was most disappointed on the topic of the provisions for APT employees. On this point, SNS was vague and very noncommittal. No numbers.

A knock on the conference room door sounded like a cannon to the team that was intensely focused on the documents. Soon a small, elegant envelope was discreetly placed in Ken's hand. Ken opened it. Several things struck Ken as strange. The envelope had the markings of his hotel and was sealed. The notepaper inside had a message written in an exquisite hand that simply said, "Please call your assistant immediately."

Ken excused himself and was shown to a private office where he placed the call to his assistant. He used his cell phone, trusting that more than the SNS line.

"It's past midnight in San Francisco. What's so important? Why didn't you just call me at SNS?"

She then read to Ken the note from Jack.

"Oh.... I see why you didn't have Jack's letter sent to me here. Well done." "What can I do to help?" she asked.

Ken thought a moment. "Well, first thing is–don't breathe a word of this to anyone as it's incredibly sensitive information."

"Of course, Ken"

"Call Jack's office late afternoon your time tomorrow. Tell him you got his message to me shortly before you called him and that given the time zones, I'll contact him first thing the *next* morning." Ken figured that with the nine-hour time difference, this would buy more time to see if he could squeeze a better deal out of SNS than Jack's deal.

"OK, Ken," she replied. And then, as an afterthought, she said, "How is Geneva?"

"It's very beautiful here," Ken said, thinking with regret that she would likely not survive the acquisition with SNS. After promising to call later in the day to check in, Ken hung up the phone. But he couldn't get his loyal assistant out of his mind. She'd been his first hire at APT more than twelve years before. *Damn*, he said under his breath and then he returned to his team in their conference room.

SNS and APT spent the day in non-stop negotiations; give, take, push and pull. More than a couple of times, Shah and Ken had to pull their teams away from the table to extinguish a flame-up between them, ignited by the combination of emotional intensity, deadlines and close quarters. During these time-outs, Ken and Shah would listen carefully, excuse themselves for a few or many minutes and return with a Solomon-like decree. Then the teams would go back to the fray to hammer out the language in the contract and negotiate the next point.

At the end of that day, substantial progress had been made. Shah and his team again worked through the night and had their New York staff apply the spit and polish during *their* night, returning a pristine document where once existed a riot of edits and corrections.

Ken and Shah decided to meet at noon the next day, after APT's team had reviewed the reworked draft and debriefed Ken. At 11:00 in the morning, Ken's staff went over the draft contract with him. "It's slightly better than what we got from BioNeura," began his General Counsel. When they got to point nine, the treatment of APT employees, Ken hoped the language would be more precise than when he had seen it last.

He was disappointed. The section amounted to a very oblique and lawyerly collection of words that seemed to say that APT employees would be treated fairly and be given every opportunity in the new combined company. After reading this section several times, Ken felt like he had been eating lettuce – lots of chewing but little flavor and no satisfying fill of the stomach.

As he listened to the team's view of points ten and eleven, he was still distracted by the previous section. He got most of what they said and sensed that his team was reasonably happy with the proposed draft.

Ken and Shah began what they both expected to be their final meeting on key terms and they made good progress. When they finished with point eight, Shah suggested they move on to items ten and eleven.

"I know that item nine, the people point, is important to both of us, Ken, so let's treat it last," said Shah, successfully deferring the point for the moment. Ken agreed, but his antennae were vibrating.

After about an hour ironing out the wrinkles on the other points, Ken and Shah finally returned to item nine. When they did, Ken pounced. "Nathaniel," he said, "I am totally unhappy with the lack of clarity in this section of the agreement. I read a lot of words, but I'm not seeing what we had agreed in principle several days ago."

Shah studied Ken's eyes before responding, measuring his emotion and gauging his response as he did. "Ken, you know I am committed to those principles. You can trust me to follow them faithfully. However, you know that we can't promise continued employment to APT employees – or SNS employees, for that matter. And I really don't know if the U.S. headquarters for the combined company will be in San Francisco where you are or in New York where we are."

They then spent an hour searching for language that would satisfy Ken and Shah. As the conversation continued and Shah made more concessions, he noted that Ken was getting more demanding. *Time to shift the momentum,* he thought.

Shah took a deep breath and removed his glasses for dramatic effect. "Ken, let's table this point about employees for a moment and move to point twelve, the price. Since we have satisfactorily reached agreement on all of the main points, save the employee issue, my Board has authorized me to offer twenty-two dollars per share of APT stock, a ten percent increase over our initial offer. Seventy-five percent cash and twenty-five percent in SNS stock."

Ken looked closely at Shah's eyes, which were as black as oil and full of self-satisfaction. *Check,* thought Shah. Shah and Ken both knew that the ten percent sweetener on the offer price was very valuable to shareholders and couldn't be ignored for any reason, especially for what shareholders considered "soft" reasons like employees, for whom they had no concern in the context of a sale of the company.

"I'll share the revised offer with my Board," Ken finally replied after a few moments of contemplation. Ken then excused himself and privately updated the team on the progress, leaving out the price topic. He then needed to get ready for the pre-arranged status report to his Board. He looked at his watch. It was eight o'clock in the morning in San Francisco.

As Ken well expected, his Board was pleased with the terms of the SNS deal to acquire APT, especially the ten percent sweetener in price. Then Ken presented the downside of the employee issue, explaining how a demoralized APT staff could make integration of the two companies difficult and negatively impact the share price of SNS, which would be a concern of current APT shareholders, at least until they sold those shares.

The Board listened carefully to his argument, but after all, what Ken said was purely theoretical; and besides, as CEO they knew he *had* to stand up for his employees. In addition, most APT shareholders would have dumped any SNS shares they had long before any integration issues affected the share price.

The Chairman wrapped up the meeting. "Gentlemen, I say we have a deal here."

There was no disagreement from the other directors. But the lead independent director, a seasoned corporate lawyer, interrupted. "That may be so," he said, "but before we rush into this deal, it would be prudent to see if BioNeura would beat the SNS offer."

"Right," the Chairman said. "Ken, you're authorized to approach BioNeura with the goal of securing a higher value offer."

Ken nodded. "Understood. I'll do it right away."

119

Clara had almost made it to her desk with her first cup of coffee when the phone rang. "Jack Callahan's office," she answered, nearly knocking over her cup.

"Hello, Clara. Ken Carlisle here. Is Jack around?"

Clara placed Ken on hold and sprinted to the conference room where Jack was meeting with his team. "That analyst you've been playing telephone tag with is on the line," Clara told Jack in their agreed-upon code for Ken Carlisle.

Jack immediately feigned a "duty calls" look to his team and excused himself in as cool a manner as possible. But inside, he felt anything but cool. He prepared himself for what might be bad news from Ken Carlisle at APT.

"Jack, I'm sorry I haven't gotten back to you sooner. Something came up that I had to take care of and it's kept me totally consumed for days."

I'm right, thought Jack. *Merger discussions.* He glanced at the caller ID number and saw Ken's cell phone. *Damn, no clue there.* "That's all worked out now, Jack," continued Ken, deepening the necessary mendacity. "I want to pick up where we left off."

"That's great, Ken," said Jack. "I was beginning to think you were working on a deal with someone else."

Ken laughed but said nothing, ignoring the bait. "Let me get right to the point, Jack. Your price isn't good enough." Then, adding his own agenda item to the call, he added, "And I need more clarity on what you intend to do with our employees."

Even though he wasn't specifically authorized by his board to negotiate on the outcome of Ken's employees, Ken figured there was no harm in opening this second line of inquiry. *Hey, if BioNeura could meet or beat the price and take care of APT's staff, everyone would win.* Before responding, Jack wanted to look Ken in the eye to gauge the strength of his position. He also wanted to find out if Ken were in town. "I think this is better discussed in person, Ken," Jack said. "Can we get together this morning?"

"I can't do that Jack, sorry." Jack knew better than to press for details. He also knew he had to assume that Ken was with the company trying to buy APT.

Jack tried for a videoconference.

"No, Jack," Ken said sharply, knowing full well that the location of Ken's up-link would be too revealing. "The phone will have to do, my friend."

My friend, thought Jack. *Could he take that as a hopeful sign? And what, beyond price, would clinch the deal? It has to be the employee issue Ken mentioned. That's his balance tipper.*

"Okay, Ken," he said. "Call me back near the end of the day here and I'll have a response for you."

Tramadol (Ultram®)

120

It was now Shah's turn to be kept waiting. He left several messages at Ken's hotel and got no direct replies, only messages from Ken's staffers that Ken's discussions with the Board were taking longer than he'd expected. This made Shah extremely nervous. He had given all he could on price and his Board wouldn't pay a dime more for APT.

Shah invited Ken to dinner, figuring that he would have to respond to this invitation. And he did, after making Shah phone him several times. "Nathaniel," Ken finally said, "thanks so much for the invitation. Unfortunately, I have to decline. I've got to give my Board a complete briefing of your final offer and contract terms. They insist." His deception was a necessary tactic to buy time.

A long pause preceded Shah's reply. "Yes, of course, please thank your Directors for taking my offer so seriously." He then wished Ken luck with his Board and arranged for a breakfast meeting the next morning. Ken hesitated for a moment, and then agreed so as not to spook Shah. But Shah, taking note of Ken's confident tone and his brief hesitation, was indeed spooked.

After hanging up, Shah reached into his desk drawer and pulled out one of many cheap disposable cell phones he kept at hand and dialed a number. When the person answered, Shah stated flatly and without a hello. "Put the specimen under the microscope. I fear a bacterium has infected it." He hung up the cell phone and tossed it into the bin marked "incinerate."

Shah then called Gloria from his desk phone. They discussed the state of the negotiations and agreed that they had taken it as far as they could. "I have an idea," said Gloria. "Let's push Ken over the edge with a platinum parachute for him when he leaves the combined SNS/APT after the merger. Say, two million dollars a year for five years to consult with us, plus a pile of stock options in the new company." Shah thought a moment. "No, Gloria, Ken isn't the type to be moved by that. A platinum parachute offer might totally backfire on us."

Gloria saw his point. "Yeah. He is a goody-guy, isn't he?"

Before hanging up, they agreed that once the deal was done they would celebrate it with a lovely dinner and discuss how to integrate SNS and ATP.

"I see a bigger role for you in the integrated company, Gloria."

*I'll believe it when I see it...*she thought.

121

During the pause in negotiations, Jack and his team had been working for days on how they would integrate the ATP and BioNeura teams. It gave Jack something to focus on as he fretted about losing the deal.

The BioNeura/APT Integration Plan was a polished document outlining in detail how the two San Francisco companies would merge and what would happen in terms of overall employment. Since BioNeura's plans expected a lot of growth in employment, and their acquisition of APT was not a merger based on cost-cutting, the reduction in force or "RIF" would be modest. Jack was pleased that he could respond well to Ken on the employee side, what he suspected was Ken's hot-button issue.

The price would be tougher. Jack had five percent more to offer, maybe seven or eight percent, but he didn't know if that would do it for Ken. The first hurdle was getting the BioNeura Board to approve a higher offer and Jack wasn't sure he could pull them all into the boat in such a short period of time, a matter of hours. Urgency made many boards members nervous, so the mettle of his board would be severely tested today.

The hastily called Board meeting began on time. After declaring a quorum and confirming that all directors could hear well, the Chairman, Greg, teed it up for Jack. "We need to make a sweeter offer for APT and we have to decide within a few hours. Jack, the floor is yours."

Though Jack would've preferred a less brusque intro, he had to admit that this one was apt, given the timing. Jack recounted his conversation with Ken, explained his reasons for thinking there was a better competing offer on the table and asked Bill Copley to present the rationale for why BioNeura could pay eight percent more than the Board had authorized, but not more than that. Then Jack walked the Board members through the tables and charts he had emailed to them only two hours earlier. A full discussion ensued, with questions coming at Jack as if from a machine gun.

When the Board was ready for a vote, Greg led the way. "Noting that the discussion was full and all questions answered, does anyone wish to offer a motion?" A motion was made: "I move that we increase our offer to twenty-one dollars and sixty cents per share for the acquisition of APT." The motion was seconded.

"All those in favor?" asked Greg. "Aye," came the unanimous vote to the affirmative.

"Jack," said Greg, "you have your sweetened offer. Close the deal with APT."

Tingles ran down Jack's spine as he heard this approbation from Greg.

122

Jack's elation at the results of the Board meeting was soon spoiled by a phone call from his security consultant. "Mr. Callahan, it seems you just had a security breach."

"Another dumpster dive?"

"No, there's nothing to see in there anymore. Our new 100% shredding policy makes sure of that. This was a far more sophisticated breach. Your IT network was just hacked. It seems that multiple attempts were made to breach a common file that your executive team has been working on – Project Ramses, whatever that is."

Jack's mind raced: *That's our plan for the APT acquisition and for integrating employees in the APT/BioNeura merger.*

"Did the new software keep them out?"

"We believe so, but there were earlier versions of the Ramses document that were not in the new secure file, and those could have been breached."

"Could have been?" asked Jack.

"Likely were," he replied.

"A week or so ago I told your executive staff to keep all confidential files in our file server dedicated to such information, but some of the execs are less sophisticated or less disciplined in managing confidential information. So, some files were in easily accessible areas. We've already closed that door, Mr. Callahan, but I suggest that you assume that at least some horses have left the barn. I assume you know by now who's looking into your shop and why."

"Not really." But Jack could guess. Whoever was competing with them was doing so by looking at BioNeura's play book and Jack thought of a competitor who was ruthless enough to operate like that. An idea leapt into his brain.

"Can the hacker determine if we know he's trying to hack us?"

"No sir. But we could do some things to our IT defenses that a sophisticated hacker would see and deduce that we are expecting him. Do you want us to let him know that we know he is out there?"

"No," Jack said. "Don't alert him. Let's let him think we're unaware."

123

Gloria Segovia stared out at a moonlit Lake Geneva and assessed her situation. Besides being SNS's Chief Operating Officer, she was Nathaniel Shah's lover, advisor and muse. But what did all that really add up to? *It was a good move coming here with Nathaniel,* she thought. *I've broken out of the M&A mold and have proven myself as a successful business person. I love Europe and now feel more at home here than I do in New York.*

Her forehead wrinkled a little as she turned the next thought in her agile mind. *Most of Shah's recent successes are from seeds that I sowed years ago – yet he gets all the credit. He gets the* Financial Times *and* Wall Street Journal *stories and I get a random line in the occasional industry rag.* She took a sip of champagne. *Okay, that's fine. Shah's much older than I am, and there is nobody in the organization to challenge me for his seat when he steps down – or gets fired – and he did promise me he would step down in the relatively near future.*

With her gaze focused on a light far across the lake, Gloria wondered how sincere Shah's promises really were. *Had Shah spoken to the Board as he promised about succession planning – and if so, had they decided that I would take over if Shah died, got fired or became incapable of leading?* The more Gloria thought about this, the more uneasy she became. After all, he had never mentioned actually having that conversation with the Board.

She had two choices. She could decide Shah had lied to her and take appropriate actions or she could decide he hadn't. As she thought this over, she slowly finished the bottle, surprised at herself how angry she was becoming as she did. *Maybe I need to hedge my bets here,* she thought.

124

As Jack put his plan in motion, he felt like he was in a spy movie. His hands trembled. Despite the tension, he couldn't help smiling as he wrote out an email memo entitled "Project Ramses." The memo was short and direct: "After reviewing all of the alternatives, we have concluded that we cannot justify paying more than our original price of $20.00 per share for APT. We also cannot absorb many APT employees so we would have to lay off most of them, incurring additional costs and disruption to our business. The board and I have concluded that our plan to acquire APT is no longer viable. Consequently, I am closing Project Ramses. Thanks for all of your hard work. We didn't win this time – we'll bag the next one."

He clicked "send" and his computer immediately flashed a big, bold red message telling him to encrypt the message for confidentiality before it could be sent. Jack typed in the commands his IT security consultant told him to enter and after responding to the warning message once more to confirm his intentions, he sent the ghost e-mail message addressed to his leadership team. The instructions his IT guy gave him would put his email message in the Project Ramses file. None of the internal addressees would actually receive it – but it would be seen by hackers as if it were sent.

"There," he said under his breath, "the trap is set. Let's see if the snake goes for it."

Montelukast (Singulair ®)

125

Shah was drifting in and out of his fitful sleep when he heard a chirping coming from his briefcase. He shot his hand into his custom-made Prada attaché case by the bed and retrieved the throw-away cell phone.

"Yes?" he said, turning on the light.

The voice on the other end was deep and gravelly.

"The bacterium has removed itself. There is no more threat to the host." Shah asked him to repeat the message to be sure he heard it correctly.

"The bacterium we were worried about is no longer a threat to the host."

"I want to see the proof," Shah demanded. Two minutes later, Shah's disposable phone chirped once more. On its tiny screen Shah read a copy of the ghost email from Jack Callahan to the Project Ramses file calling off BioNeura's attempt to acquire APT.

Yes! Thought Shah, and he gleefully tossed the cell phone into a bedside bin for incineration. For the first night in many, Shah slept soundly.

126

Ken called Jack at 5 o'clock p.m. on the dot. "Ok, what do you have, Jack?"

"Ken I'm authorized to offer you $21.60 per share for your company. I also have a detailed plan on how we would absorb the vast majority of your APT employees into the new company. Can I walk you through it?"

"Yeah, send it to me by email and then walk me through it."

"If you don't mind, Ken, I'll fax it to your office and your assistant can fax it to you where you are. And could you return any correspondence the same way? I know faxes are old school, but we're having a little maintenance done on our email network and I don't want my documents to you to get delayed for any reason." Jack didn't dare to use his email with the hackers lurking.

Within an hour, Jack had explained his integration plan to Ken. "The employee integration plan is excellent, Jack and that means a lot to me," Ken said. "But can you get me a little more on the price? I need more."

"I've given you all I've got, Ken." After some back and forth in which Jack failed to convince Ken, Ken stopped the conversation.

"Jack, if you want APT, you gotta give me more."

Ken was sitting on an offer from SNS for $22.00. "I'll call you back within a couple hours," said Jack, without a clue in his head as to how he might find a way to offer more on the price and unaware that it was now 4 o'clock in the morning where Ken was.

Convening his team, Jack led them through a renewed dissection of the deal. After an hour of struggle, they found one percentage more from various areas, getting the price to $21.80. Bill then banged a little harder on his calculator.

He summarized. "The new integration plan we just finished today forecasts far less expense for employee terminations than we originally forecast and the acquisition allows us to forgo the expenses in recruiting and training new employees that we planned on incurring over the next few years. We also can be a little more aggressive on the other synergies we expect to capture from the integration since we had taken such a very conservative view in our first projections. So we can get the additional juice to get to 22 bucks even, Jack."

With great trepidation at the thought of going back to the Board, Jack called Greg and explained the situation. Greg quickly agreed to convene the Board and had them on the line within an hour. After minimal debate, they agreed to improve the offer to $22.00 but not a penny more. Jack assured them he had no more to give. At this price, it was a great strategic deal but he couldn't justify paying more. For each deal, a "walk-away" price had to be set and held. Twenty-two was it.

He immediately called Ken's assistant and asked her to have Ken call him right away. The phone rang in less than five minutes.

"Ken," Jack said, "I can go to twenty-two even. That drains the well."

"OK. No changes on your proposal regarding the integration of employees or any other terms or conditions that we had agreed and no other changes?"

"None," replied Jack.

"OK," Ken said, "I'll call you tomorrow with my answer."

127

In a meeting with his lawyer prior to his breakfast with Shah, Ken knew that he had a fiduciary responsibility to his shareholders to try to maximize the value of a deal by pushing Shah's last terms to try to get a deal better than Jack's latest offer.

Now, assessing Shah across the breakfast table, Ken was surprised by Shah's tone. Something had changed. Yesterday, Shah had been so accommodating but today he was acting like he thought he held all the cards. Shah responded in a surprisingly firm, bordering on rude way to Ken's attempt to get a better offer. "Ken, I assure you that you have my best offer on the table," he said.

Ken leaned back in his chair and stroked his chin. "And what more can you do for the employee transition?"

"Ken, I'm doing more for them than what any other company would do." Ken was surprised by Shah's stance, a new confidence, a new edge. "Nathaniel," he said, "your offer needs to be sweetened to convince our board."

Shah's black eyes burned into Ken's for what seemed like an eternity while not a word was exchanged between them. *I know he is bluffing*, thought Shah, *and badly at that.*

"I'll take my chances, Ken," Shah finally said, his eyes continuing to study Ken's for clues. But all Shah saw was a coldness that reflected his own.

"OK, Nathaniel, I think we've done all we can do here. I'm taking my team home." *Another bluff*, thought Shah.

"Well, Ken, I'm sorry you're leaving us. I hope you and your Board will see that my offer is the best you'll get. I'm sure you will."

Ken thanked his host for an enjoyable and comfortable stay and left on the noon flight to the U.S. Shah was surprised that Ken and his team actually left, but he was confident that his next move would be Shah-mat, Persian for checkmate.

128

The Press Release two days later took Shah's breath away. "BioNeura and APT to merge." He gasped as he read aloud these words to Gloria from the headline.

He looked at Gloria, who eyed him in a way he didn't like. "This is not my fault!" Shah said, his voice rising to a shout. "I am a victim of incompetence! Why do I surround myself with fools?"

Gloria turned red with anger for being implicitly included in his list of fools and shot back. "I'm not the fool who just got out-played, am I?"

Shah delivered his hottest black-eyed stare in his arsenal and Gloria engaged him with equal intensity, defiantly. Shah blinked, then looked away and collapsed into his chair.

He brooded, replaying in his computer-like mind the conversations, timing of events and processes he had gone through with Ken Carlisle. "I wanted APT so badly," he seethed. "APT was a critical step in my...our... plan to build the world's dominant neurological company."

Retrieving a throw-away cell phone from his desk drawer, Shah dialed the familiar number. When the party answered he nearly jumped into the phone, his hand trembling with rage. "Read the news wire! You're fired. And don't think about asking for fees on this job. You are finished doing business with me, and I'll make sure that you are finished with every other firm of consequence on the continent!" He threw the phone at the incinerator bin, missing it, and it shattered against the wall.

Gloria, familiar with such outbursts, hardly took notice of the projectile and its obliteration. Instead she walked to Shah, held his hands, kissed his forehead and left his office. She knew from experience that he was not one to be around at a time like this.

Shah stayed in his office for the rest of that day. He fumed, cursed and simmered and as he did he slowly started to realize that he was somehow played. Night fell and daylight broke...and night fell again. Shah hadn't eaten, had taken no calls and had refused to answer knocks at his door. His now heavy and dark beard projected externally the dark and rough place his mind was in now. He was back there again, trapped deep in his black pit of self-loathing. Memories of the visit by the priest at his home when he was a boy flooded his mind...when he learned that he was the lowest of the low...a Dalit, an Untouchable. That's how he felt; unworthy.

129

"Welcome to BioNeura-APT," Jack announced to the assembled employees of the two companies assembled in the grand ballroom of the Fairmont Hotel in San Francisco. "I want to share with you my vision for our exciting new company, an enterprise that will enrich the lives of our patients, the employees who work here and the shareholders who support us. A company that will stand among the leaders in our chosen field of neurological disease. A company that will make a difference."

The stingy applause disappointed Jack. He thought they should see this as an exciting new chapter. After a second, he knew the reason for their reticence. These people were in the post-news, pre-integration phase of this chapter of their lives. Their worlds and how they defined them had just been abruptly and brutally shaken, as by a killer earthquake. They were struggling with basic fears and questions.

"Will I get fired?"
"How will I pay my mortgage?"
"Can I still send my kids to college?"
"Will I have to move?"
"If I get a new boss will I like him or her?"
"Will they like me?"
"Will my work change?"
"Will my project, the one I've dedicated ten years of my life to, be killed?"

Jack knew that he was attempting to break through this real and tangible noise with a speech about intangibles, such as vision and mission. He also knew he was failing.

"So, in conclusion," he said, "I foresee minimal reductions in staff or projects as we grow into an exciting, new, and powerful force in neurological science."

After the polite applause, Ken Carlisle took the podium to a strong welcome from his APT employees. The applause for Ken was likewise meager. As Ken handed the microphone to Jean-Luc Dumas, the VP of R&D for the new, combined company, he whispered, "It's a tough audience, Jean-Luc. Good luck."

But Jean-Luc took a different approach, one that Jack immediately saw resonated much better with this audience. Jean-Luc first described in great detail, patients suffering from various neurological diseases. He then told about the R&D programs in progress that could make a difference in these lives. Assuring the audience that the major programs would continue, he then announced his new team, a group with strong representation from both companies. This went far to convince the APT staff that they could have an important role in the new company. Jean-Luc reminded the sales and marketing staff of their role in all of this – they were the ones who generated the revenues required to fund the massively expensive R&D programs. The audience gave Jean-Luc a strong and sustained applause.

"When their minds are cluttered appeal to their hearts," said Jean-Luc, winking as he handed the microphone back to Jack.

Jack announced the timeline for the integration of the rest of the company. He knew the staff could handle ambiguity and lack of clarity as long as they had a firm idea about when the clarity would come. No decisions on staff reductions would be made for several months, he said, and he could feel the collective shoulders of the audience relax a little.

"At least I'll have time to see what the new company looks like."

"I'll have time to look for a new job."

"At least I'll have a job at Christmas."

In making his various promises to this audience, Jack knew that he had to deliver on every single one or lose forever his credibility with the new employee base. In closing, he borrowed from Jean-Luc's theme, focusing on the patient and how BioNeura would make a difference. *That was better received*, he thought, as he thanked the employees for coming and wished them a good afternoon.

Escitalopram (Lexapro ®)

130

Returning to his apartment was always the worst part of his day. When Diana was alive, opening that apartment door was like opening the door to a sensual smorgasbord. There were aromas of delicious food, perfume, flowers and sometimes the faint scents of Diana's oil paintings. There was always a buzz of telephones ringing, music playing and Diana singing or whistling, which Jack found so delightful in its care-free way. The apartment always offered something new to see; a new book, the latest magazine, a poster of a new gallery, or an interesting new floral arrangement. And, of course, there was always Diana, greeting him with her warm, full and lovely smile.

Jack fumbled with his keys and the bag of Chinese take-out, stepped inside and flipped on the light. It was so different now. Instead of a place that filled up his senses and charged his spiritual and emotional batteries, his apartment was now a vacuum that sucked the air from his lungs and held him down until he could escape in the morning. The smells, textures and sounds were all gone. The plants had long since faded and died. There was no evidence of current affairs, no signs of a life being actively or meaningfully lived. The place was outwardly tidy but sterile – much like Jack's existence.

He immediately turned on the TV to drown out the deafening silence. He used to hate TV, seeing it as an intrusion on his life but now it had become his best friend, his savior from complete isolation, the companion he spent his evenings with. Jack opened the Chinese food boxes and began eating.

He ate without tasting, without joy or appreciation – he ate for survival. As often happened during these lonely evenings, salty tears rolled down his face and into the corners of his mouth. He didn't bother to wipe them away. He just kept chewing. He had begun going to bed early to limit the time he had to spend in the pit of this dark beast. After dinner, he downed a couple of cognacs and prayed for sleep to rescue him.

Jack rose the next morning before sun-rise. He had so much work to do. Jack welcomed the 24/7 demands of the acquisition and integration of the two companies because while he worked he didn't fixate on the hole in his life left by Diana. On an intellectual level, he knew that his excessive work pace was a bandage for his oozing wound. On an emotional level, he wasn't yet prepared to deal with the wound. *I'll face that after the integration is done*, he told himself.

131

The next few months flew by. BIO 230 was well along in its Phase III trials, the last phase of development before a company can ask the government for approval to make a medicine available to the public. The two trials included more than 3,000 patients and were being conducted at sites all over the world.

The integration of APT into BioNeura was a success on every level, but Jack had to make some very difficult decisions concerning his staff. He'd decided to keep Jean-Luc as head of R&D and Meg Wilson as head of sales and marketing. The rest of his staff would be filled equally with APT and BioNeura executives, not by design, but by merit and fit. Jack felt lucky and pleased to have such a fine team to lead during the exciting next stage of BioNeura's future.

The toughest call was in choosing the new CFO. "Bill, have a seat," Jack said. Bill Copley, BioNeura's CFO for the past several years looked Jack in the eye for some clue to what was on his mind. "Bill, after a great deal of thought, I've decided that our SVP of Finance will become the interim CFO for BioNeura while we look outside the companies for the new permanent CFO."

Bill didn't blink or speak. His face gave no indication that he had heard or understood what Jack had said.

Jack broke the awkward silence. "Bill, I'm sorry it worked out this way. We'll be as generous and as supportive as we can." Bill continued his expressionless stare, seemingly looking right through Jack. Jack was starting to get uncomfortable with Bill's stony countenance and began to think Bill was in some kind of emotional shock.

Then Bill blinked, showing the first sign of life since they started their conversation. He folded his arms and sat back in his chair.

"So, this is payback time, eh, Jacky?"

"What?"

"You've been waiting to nail me since that Board meeting in Sea Island. You just waited until I did all the heavy lifting on the APT acquisition and the integration and then you flush me."

He leaned forward to Jack. "You bastard. I've dedicated all these years of my life to this company. I was here before you were, Jack and you have the nerve to cut *me*? I am BioNeura, Jack. You're here *only because I allowed it!*"

Jack unloaded on Bill with years of accumulated anger. "You arrogant little prick!" he shouted. "*You're* only here because I gave you a second chance after you tried to crucify me at Sea Island. You're here because *I* allowed it!" That last point he punctuated by banging his fist on his desk. Then he paused a moment and collected himself.

"Bill, take this envelope we've prepared for you and read about your severance package. You'll see that it's generous and fair. After you've had a few days, let's talk again."

"No need for that, Jack. We've said all that needs to be said." Bill looked at Jack with seething contempt and snatched his envelope from the table. He started to say something more and then stopped himself, turned on his heel and stormed out of Jack's office.

After the meeting, Jack replayed the conversation in his mind. Bill was right in one respect. Jack hadn't forgiven or forgotten Sea Island and Bill's role in that sinister affair. Now, after firing Bill, Jack realized he felt guilty. Not for the firing or for anything he said to Bill – he felt a little guilty for feeling so damn *good* about it.

He also felt ashamed at how he had lost his temper and shouted Bill down. Jack always felt that control under fire was a defining characteristic of a first-class, professional executive. He had failed today.

132

That night, as Jack was flipping the television channels in his apartment he came across a new documentary about animal testing by the cosmetics and healthcare industries. He turned up the volume as he ate his take-out dinner from its box.

"PFA, People for Animals, an animal rights group is one of the many critics of the pharmaceutical industry," began the announcer. "PFA was the earliest and best known of the animal rights groups. Michael McPherson, Ph.D. in zoology from the University of Massachusetts, rose through the ranks of PFA and made important gains for the cause. A few years ago, he decided to focus his full attention on the use of animals in healthcare research.

"He quickly showed a talent for aggressively exposing the abuses of animals. McPherson's colleagues at PFA supported his zealous and strident criticisms of the industry's use of animals in its testing. While a few complaints were registered from the more conservative quarters of the PFA organization – a faction that cringed at McPherson's high-profile tactics – the mainstream members fueled his passion to go even further for the effort."

The reporter continued, "But after a while, even the mainstream began to back away from his more sensational tactics. The straw that broke the camel's back was when McPherson had more than a dozen surgical staples stapled to his own body and walked nearly naked into the lobby of the largest surgical staple company in America. He arranged for the media to be there to record every staple, dripping with blood."

Jack finished his dinner as he listened to the show.

"The criticism McPherson received from the PFA board, including a formal censure, led him to decide that he had to move past PFA to accomplish his ultimate goal, the cessation of all medical research using animals. With his more radical followers, he created SPOT, for Save our Pets from Outrageous Torture. This acronym captured the essence and brilliance of Michael McPherson. He moved the focus from rats and mice to our pets–cute rabbits and most importantly, lovable dogs. The logo for the SPOT organization was 'Spot,' an adorable Labrador retriever. It captured the emotional tie everyday Americans had with their pets."

Jack cringed at the publicity for SPOT. He knew it was brilliant. He knew the media would eat it up. He also knew it would be trouble.

Jack respected what McPherson had accomplished in raising sensitivity to the humane use of animals in medical research at university and corporate labs throughout the country. McPherson was widely recognized as the driving force behind new laws that ensure humane and respectful use of animals in research, and Jack – and as far as he knew, everyone in the industry – supported the laws.

But he loathed McPherson's fanaticism, his complete disregard for the value of ethical and humane experimentation on animals to extend and save human lives.

Americans spent billions of dollars per year on their pets and the organizations to protect animals were well funded. They recruited the highest-profile, most-motivated celebrities to their causes.

But Jack felt that something was out of balance when pets in the so-called developed countries ate better and received better health care than the majority of humans on earth. He supported what PFA and SPOT were doing; he just thought that humans across the globe should be taken care of at least as well as pets in America.

The show's narrator continued. "In an effort to address the pressures of the animal rights groups and cut costs, industry has developed ways to test some medicines without subjecting animals or humans to experimentation. The beauty and cosmetic industry now test most of their products on harvested human tissue and computer-aided simulations. The pharmaceutical and medical device industries have made similar progress."

Jack shuddered. As much as he challenged his thinking and that of his research scientists on the topic, he was convinced that there was unfortunately no substitute for animal testing when the alternative was human testing. Life-saving surgical techniques and devices that were now standard practice were first tested on animals. Jack couldn't possibly imagine asking parents to grant permission to test an experimental device, surgical procedure or medicine on their child without having first gained experience from animal testing. The vast majority of parents wouldn't allow it. The FDA in fact *required* that medicines and certain devices be well tested in animals before testing in humans.

The TV host continued…"After cutting his teeth criticizing the cosmetics, medical-device and surgical-instrument industries," McPherson has focused his new organization, SPOT, on his intended final target, the pharmaceutical industry. McPherson will become every pharmaceutical

CEO's nightmare. Extremely intelligent, militant and outspoken he is a maestro at manipulating the media. In his mind, a religious zeal drives him to protect God's creatures." That was enough for Jack. He clicked off the TV and went to bed.

133

BioNeura had released its first post-APT acquisition quarterly earnings report at 4:30 a.m. San Francisco time and 7:30 a.m. New York time. Jack and his team were ready to begin their pre-arranged teleconference call with the Wall Street analysts and investors who tracked BioNeura. Once the operator told Jack that the pace of new registrants for the call had begun to wane, Jack asked the operator to open the line to him. It was 8 o'clock a.m. on the dot.

"Good morning, and welcome to the BioNeura quarterly conference call," Jack began, reading the prepared script carefully while still trying to make it sound as unscripted as possible. He was well aware that everyone listening knew that every word of these presentations was reviewed and scrutinized for legal reasons before the CEO uttered a single word. Making such a script sound natural was therefore an unnatural task, but Jack tried anyway.

He moved through the script in fifteen minutes and then asked the operator to open the lines for questions. Jack and his team had prepared for a couple dozen questions that they expected; more importantly, they agreed on the answers they would give, and who would give them. He now braced himself for the flow.

"Congratulations on an excellent quarter," began the first questioner, raising Jack's hopes that the other analysts would see it as she did. "I'm pleased to see that you beat our estimates for cost synergies and your revenues didn't seem to suffer in the disruption of the APT integration. Do you expect your costs to remain at this level for future quarters, or was this a one-time savings in this quarter?"

Jack loved answering questions like that. "Thanks," he said, "we're likewise pleased with the results. We expect the new levels of spending to be roughly the same in future quarters."

The next analyst identified himself and launched his comment followed by a question. "Great quarter, Jack. What was your turnover of key employees and sales reps in the integration period?"

"Nice to see you beat our projections," started the next analyst. "Are you going to raise your earnings guidance for the rest of this year?"

Jack knew from the tone and tenor of the first few questions that the audience was happy and upbeat. As was his custom, he let his staff handle questions in their areas, both to give them a sense of accountability and to show "The Street" that BioNeura had a strong and deep management team.

The conference call flew to its scheduled time limit and Jack announced that they would take no more questions; anyone who had more could call his Investor Relations Director for answers. He closed the call and thanked the listeners for their interest in BioNeura.

Now they waited and watched. The pre-market action on the stock was positive. It looked like BioNeura would open strongly higher. At 9:30 a.m. eastern time, BioNeura burst out of the blocks. In the first 30 minutes, BioNeura popped up 15 percent. The market hungered for a growth company with good products, strong pipeline, and capable management. The early integration success removed some of the remaining questions and now many investors were willing to make big bets on BioNeura. BioNeura was on its way to become the new darling of its sector.

As Jack and Jean-Luc saw the Street's positive reaction, Jack remarked, "The shorts are helping us today."

Jean-Luc replied. "I've heard about them. Who or what are shorts?"

"Shorts find companies that they think are over-valued and headed for a fall in their share price. They borrow shares from a shareholder of that company and pay them a small borrowing fee, along with a promise to return the borrowed shares later. They immediately sell the borrowed shares on the open market at the current market price that they believe is high. Since they have sold shares they didn't own, they are 'short' those shares. If the shorts are right and the company's share price decreases, they buy the now cheaper shares of the company on the open market and return the borrowed shares at the higher price at which they borrowed them, pocketing the difference" After some clarification, Jean-Luc got it.

"So how are the shorts helping us today?"

"Well, we knew before our deal that we had a lot of shorts playing our stock. When our strong quarterly financial results came out today and the Street liked the news, our share price rose...and the shorts had to quickly *buy* shares on the open market to return their borrowed shares before the share price ran even higher. On top of that, those that like our future, "the longs," are also buying our shares."

Jean-Luc jumped in, "So the combination of both shorts and longs buying our shares boosted our share price?"

"You got it Jean-Luc. Nothing pleases us more than seeing shorts get fried, like we are seeing now.

Mmmmmm, thought Jack. *Such a delicious aroma, fried shorts!*

134

Shah listened to the BioNeura teleconference call from Geneva, having registered as Bill Himmel, a private investor. His teeth grinded as he heard the ebullient tone of the analysts. He well knew how the market would respond to BioNeura's impressive financial news.

When the call was finished, Shah placed his phone gently into its cradle, the calmness of his actions in stark contrast to the raging storm inside his head. *"That company, APT was mine,"* he seethed. He then flipped to his financial website and watched the reaction to the news – and watched BioNeura gain value by the minute.

Shah had always taken pride in the valuation of his company compared to that of his rivals. In its market segment, SNS was number one in almost every metric and this had been Shah's yardstick to measure his self-worth, his great pride derived from knowing he had created more value than all of his competitors. Now, as he watched BioNeura's share price climb steadily, Shah felt very unsettled. He made some rough calculations based on BioNeura's current market capitalization and concluded that BioNeura was now his number-one rival for the throne in this segment. And as the BioNeura stock climbed, they were closing in on SNS fast.

After a full two hours of pacing his office and neglecting all phone calls and appointments, Shah settled down. As was his response to past disappointments, he simply increased the pressure on himself and his staff to win the next one. The fire of the moment lost its blaze but settled into a solid, white-hot engine of motivation. He gazed out his window but saw nothing outside.

"I will not lose again," Shah said under his breath. "I will win the next round, whatever it costs. It's time to turn up the heat at SNS." And with that he headed for the conference room to meet the staff he had just summoned. For them, it would be a very, very unpleasant meeting indeed.

Carvedilol (Coreg®)

135

"I'll be right back, Mom. Just stay here until I park the car." Alex settled his mother on the bench in front of the department store and drove to the mall parking lot a few hundred yards away.

A few moments later, Dr. Rostov's eye caught sight of an item in one of the store's big front windows. It was a telescope display and she couldn't resist. She walked over for a closer look. In the window were images from space that she easily recognized. She was so excited to see old friends – the moon, the constellations, the galaxies, red giants and nebulae.

Wanting to see more, she pulled open the heavy door of the department store and began walking to the window where the telescopes and images lay waiting for her. She thought. *Let's see, they were to the left of the door and about fifty feet away, so I should...*She paused. *I should go...this way.* She went the wrong way. Sensing that she was off track, she started walking faster as though she would find her way better by doing so.

Wait, where am I? How did I get here? She was getting scared now.

She was alone and terrified. She screamed out loud, "Help! Help me!" and she fell to the floor, sobbing.

Alex had a hard time finding a parking place and was gone much longer than he'd expected. He ran all the way back to the bench where his mother was waiting, but when he got there she was gone. His heart jumped from his chest. Her handbag was still there, but she was nowhere to be seen. He grabbed her bag and shot into the store, scanning it as he ran at full speed.

After a few minutes of frantic searching and calling out for his mother he heard his name over the shopping mall's public address system.

"Would the relative of Dr. Darya Rostov please go to the main information desk immediately?" He asked a sales clerk how to get to the desk, then continued his sprint to find her. He felt terribly guilty. What had he been thinking? He should never have left her. As he raced up to the information desk, he saw her. She was sitting in a chair with a security guard standing beside her. She looked fine. She was chatting up the gentleman behind the desk.

The security guard deduced that the frantic, sweat-soaked man running toward him was who he was waiting for. "Are you a relative of Dr. Rostov?" the guard said, looking at the identification bracelet that Alex had placed on his mother some weeks ago and glad of it now.

"Yes, yes, I am," said Alex, between gasps of air. He knelt down beside his mother and put his arms around her.

This confused Dr. Rostov immensely: *Why is Alex being so emotional and dramatic?*

"Really," she said to the guard, "Alex is acting a little strange today."

136

The next several quarters rolled along with the power and momentum of a freight train. Nothing seemed capable of stopping the BioNeura momentum. With each quarter, Jack announced a little more good news. He had not given all of the good news at the beginning for two reasons. First, he was unsure that his new team could hit the numbers they said they could. Second, he wanted to continue the pattern of meeting or beating expectations.

He couldn't keep this up too long before the analysts would start raising their expectations for BioNeura too high. Managing information and the expectations of very smart analysts was a high-wire act without a net. If you got it right, it was a crowd-pleaser. If you slipped, you were punished – very painfully and very publicly.

On the other side of the Atlantic, since the loss of APT, Shah focused his team on finding another company to buy and he drove them even harder to grow SNS. The compounds in his pipeline progressed well and hit their milestones. His legendary talent for picking winning molecules in the lab served him well at SNS and he had advanced five novel compounds for neurological diseases into Phase II and Phase III clinical studies.

He was building a world-class neurology pipeline. Gloria, as COO, was doing a fantastic job building the SNS presence in the U.S. while shuttling back and forth to the SNS headquarters in Geneva. They were hitting on all cylinders. While Shah still grinded his teeth whenever he thought about losing APT, he soothed his pain by thinking about the huge gains SNS had made since he took over as CEO.

137

Clara's agenda for the day started with a school tour, part of Jack's campaign to educate the local community on the exciting contributions to healthcare that were being developed in their communities. Several other companies also participated, and the program had been a great success so far. Clara led the greeting of visitors and made sure the tours were escorted properly. Jack was scheduled to talk to them later in the day.

Clara was perfect for this role – articulate and professional, conveying an excellent first impression of the company.

"Welcome to BioNeura," she said.

"We're very pleased that you're here and we hope to make your visit as informative and interesting as possible. Please stay with your BioNeura guide. As I am sure you'll understand, some areas are not accessible to non-employees. This is for your safety and for our company's security. I'll see you all at the end of your tour when you will have a chance to meet our CEO, Mr. Jack Callahan. Save all of your hard questions for him."

The group politely laughed and eagerly followed their tour guide through the door. The tours were growing in popularity and this group was the largest yet. As Clara went back to her office, she made a mental note to work with the tour guide to limit the size of the groups in the future.

About thirty minutes later, Jack's phone rang. "Mr. Callahan, we've got a situation!" It was Jack's security consultant, and Jack could tell from his tone that this was serious.

"Our security in the animal lab has been breached, sir."

"What do you mean breached?"

"At least two unauthorized individuals have gained access to these labs. They've got masks on and are taking pictures, roughing up our employees and trashing the place. What do you want me to do, Mr. Callahan? We have only one guard here and he's not exactly trained for this type of situation. We don't know if the intruders are armed."

"No guns, for Christ's sake. I'm on my way."

Jack dropped his phone and rushed toward the animal labs. Before he got there, he heard a huge crash of breaking glass and felt the building shudder under his feet. He increased his speed to a full run, dodging employees in the corridors along the way. He arrived at the door of the animal labs with his chest heaving and gasping for air. As he reached for his security badge to open the door he heard a sound that was totally out of place – the unmistakable roar of a car engine and screeching wheels coming from the normally quiet animal lab on the other side of the door. He couldn't believe his ears.

But as he skimmed his access badge through the security slot to open the door he peered through the small window in the door and his eyes clarified what his incredulous ears had just told him. There in the animal lab was a black van with black tinted windows, covered with shattered glass and debris. It was backing out of the lab, its wheels spinning on the tile flooring, its engine roaring trying to make traction for its quick getaway, through the opening it had made a minute ago.

When the blinking red light on the touchpad indicated access to the lab, Jack flung open the door and found his senses under attack. The acrid smell of burned tires and the oily stench of car exhaust mixed obnoxiously with the lab chemicals released into the air by the crash.

His ears rung with the screams, moans and howls of animals and humans and his eyes took in what could only be described as mayhem. Lab benches pushed aside by the crashing van, equipment strewn as if hit by a tornado and smoke, dust and burning tires fogged the whole scene.

Unable to see through the smoke, Jack worked by sound. He knew there were usually twelve or so employees in here at any time and he had to make sure all of them were OK.

Jack shouted to his security guy. "Are you here?"

"Yeah, Mr. Callahan!"

"Is everyone OK?"

"I don't know yet. I'll have an employee list in a minute. It'll tell me who was in the lab before the crash."

Jack dropped to his hands and knees to get better visibility. Breathing through his handkerchief, he crawled over broken glass toward voices. He found six employees, thankfully all in pretty good shape. He helped them into the hall to relative safety and took their badges to compare them to the list the security team would have.

"I have six accounted for. How many do you have?"

"Five. We should have twelve all together."

Jack's heart flipped in his chest. "Someone's buried under this stuff. We've got to find them – now! Who is it again?"

"It's Roy Fong."

"Oh, thank god," said Jack. "I saw him in the hall before I came in here. He was running from the lab right after the crash."

A few minutes later, after the smoke had cleared and their nerves had settled a bit, his expert pulled Jack aside so nobody could hear them.

"You have a decision to make."

"What's that?"

"You can do a quick assessment of the situation and call the police after you've figured out what happened...or you can call them now. Do you have anything here that you're not proud of?"

"No. There's nothing here that isn't in fifty companies in the Bay area and we are 100 per-cent compliant with all of the laws and regs. Call the police."

"OK, but call your PR people. This will make the news."

138

"What's the damage, Wen?"

"It's bad, Jack. We've lost several animals and several experiments are ruined. We have to start again from scratch on many of the pre-clinical experiments we had underway."

"How much time did we lose?"

"Hard to say. A year or so."

"Damn it Wen – that's a disaster!"

"I know, Jack, but at least they didn't take any data or equipment – they just shot their photos and left as far as I can tell."

His security expert stepped into the conversation. "If I were a corporate spy, I'd want lab notebooks and the hard-drives from PCs. They didn't take any of those so I agree with Wen, the objective was the pictures."

"Maybe," said Jack, "but if I were a competitor, delaying BIO230 would be a worthy objective."

Jack and Jean-Luc spent the next several days in a firestorm of PFA, SPOT, the government and the media.

139

On the same afternoon as the attack on the lab, Michael McPherson received an envelope on his desk at SPOT. He didn't see anyone deliver it. It was plain, white and with no return address or postage stamp. McPherson had no idea how it got to his desk.

The standard operating procedure for mail entering his office through unknown channels was to run it through a security scan. While some of his more radical disciples had made spectacular statements using explosives aimed at companies or their CEOs, McPherson deplored their use. And he feared these radicals – what if one of them believed McPherson wasn't "aggressive" enough? He placed the envelope through a security device down the hall. After a few seconds, the device told him there was a low risk of suspicious contents. He then pressed a button on the machine and it immediately agitated the envelope and searched for traces of biologics or chemicals. After 15 seconds, the machine flashed a green light.

McPherson removed the envelope from the machine and returned to his office. He opened the envelope very carefully. Inside was a single sheet of folded white paper and a smaller envelope. As he unfolded the paper, a small envelope tumbled from it and gave him a scare that made him shriek like a little girl. He looked around to see if anyone had heard his unmanly reaction. *Nobody there, thank God.* He placed the small envelope on his desk and looked at the unfolded paper. Printed on the paper in large red block letters was a one-sentence message: THE ANIMALS ARE CRYING AND DYING AT BioNeura – HELP THEM!

Michael McPherson received many such tips. Most were the ruminations of well-meaning but ill-informed animal activists. Others were spiteful attacks by disgruntled or former employees against their onetime employers and still others were the work of certifiable lunatics. McPherson opened the small envelope, pulling from it a small memory card used in digital cameras. This was a first, he thought. He inserted the memory card into his PC and called up the computer's photo software. As he worked his way through it, he felt his excitement growing. It was as if he was on a scavenger hunt and nearing his prize.

At last he saw six small images appear on his laptop monitor. He took a deep breath and clicked on the first, then the next and the next until he had seen all six. McPherson had seen enough animal labs to know that what he was seeing was a clear violation of the recent laws on the proper care of laboratory animals. Whoever took these pictures knew it too. He noticed that in several pictures there was a logo that he couldn't make out. Clicking on one image of the logo, McPherson zoomed in closer.

He had seen this logo before. He knew the company. McPherson closed the file and slipped the memory card into the safe in his office. Then he grabbed his phone and dialed a number. But before he could tell the person he called about the photos, McPherson was asked, "Did you hear about the break-in over at BioNeura a few hours ago? Pretty wild."

"No...." McPherson said, starting to wonder how that envelope had arrived on his desk, so soon after the break-in. "But I've got something interesting for you," replied McPherson.

Alprazolam (Xanax®)

140

The buzzer at Jack's apartment startled him. He hadn't heard it in months. After Diana died, his friends tried to see him but most were ignored so often that they had given up. The few who had gotten over or around his self-constructed wall had found his presence painful or awkward and eventually they too had stopped calling.

The buzzer sounded again and Jack pressed the intercom.

"Who is it?"

"Jack, it's me, Clara." Jack looked at his watch – seven o'clock on a Saturday morning. Puzzled but pleased by this unexpected surprise, he buzzed her in. In a minute, there was a knock on the door. As Jack went to open it, he thought how nice it was to have someone knocking on his door again.

"Hi, Clara," he said. "What brings you here at this hour?"

"Jack, you didn't answer anyone's texts or calls so I was asked to make sure you saw this. She showed him her smart phone. Read this," she replied, the news headline read: "THE BioNeura TORTURE CHAMBER." Jack's jaw dropped and he slowly sank onto the sofa to read the article. As he did, Clara looked around the apartment. It was pathetic to see how much life had drained from it. It felt sterile and bloodless. She noticed the photos of Diana filling the place, reminding him of his painful loss. As Clara recalled the newspaper headline, it occurred to her that Jack was living in a torture chamber of his own.

Jack focused on the last picture in the article, beneath which was a caption identifying Michael McPherson, President of SPOT. "I was given these photos by an unknown source," McPherson was quoted as saying. "It's sad to see these conditions and the torture of these animals. BioNeura has some explaining to do."

Confused and angry, he let the phone fall to the floor. Clara felt so bad for him. She sat down beside him and put her arms around him. After a moment of being frozen, he slowly returned the friendly embrace. The human contact, the feminine contact felt *so* good to Jack. The rush of exquisite feelings from her form, her fragrance and the warmth of her embrace overcame him. *I'm getting too much pleasure from this*, Jack thought uncomfortably, but he also didn't want it to stop. It had been so long since anyone had touched him.

Clara also found herself with feelings that she hadn't anticipated. What had started as a friendly, supportive hug now felt different, way different. She began to panic as she recognized this feeling – and just then Jack broke the embrace. They looked at each other awkwardly, then down at the more comfortable floor. Jack stammered a comment about the article and she made a similarly feeble reply. *This is awkward*, he thought. They looked at each other for a moment. "Well, thanks for bringing this by, Clara. I need to get to work on damage control."

She took her cue and got up to leave. "Good luck, Jack. Let me know how I can help." As the door closed behind her, that familiar vacuum once again sucked the air from Jack's lungs.

141

On the following Monday morning, Wall Street reacted negatively to the news. "If BioNeura plays loose with its labs, what else is going on?" seemed to be the overall sentiment from the Street. There was selling pressure on the stock which lost nearly ten percent in the first hour of trading.

The BioNeura Board agreed that they had to immediately disclose the fact that the BIO230 program would be delayed about a year, which they did by filing an 8-K document with the SEC. This sent the stock into free-fall, pleasing and enriching the shorts.

A few days later after the damage to the stock and their reputation was done, Jean-Luc came into Jack's office. "Jack, I feel terrible."

"We all do, my friend."

"No, it's something I should have immediately caught."

Damn, thought Jack. *We can't take another torpedo – not now!* "I was looking at the pictures of the lab break-in from the newspaper when something jumped out at me." He spread the paper out on Jack's desk. "Look at the wall, Jack."

"It's a wall, Jean-Luc – what's the point?"

"These are pictures of our *old* lab, Jack. The walls of our new lab are white – not that urine yellow we always joked about."

Jack leaned back in his chair, trying to integrate this new information. "But the break-in was in the new lab, Jean-Luc. They took pictures and sent them to that maniac McPherson."

Jean-Luc took a deep breath and then gave the worst news of all. "Jack, these pictures are our own pictures. We had them on file for various internal presentations. They are many years old, taken before the new animal management regulations were enacted."

The events of the last days exhausted and frustrated Jack. "Please, Jean-Luc, connect the dots for me. I'm not following you."

Jean-Luc tapped the pictures with his index figure. "The break-in was a diversion. Getting these pictures in the hands of the press was the real goal. The break-in made us – and the rest of the world – assume that the pictures were of our current lab. In all the commotion and the subsequent media and investor frenzy yesterday, we didn't notice that they were pictures of our old lab – taken before the new regs for animal tests. The intruders succeeded in making it look to the world that we were torturing animals – right here and now."

Jack understood – it was a perfect sabotage operation. It painted BioNeura as a cruel and heartless company that tortures poor creatures. On top of that, the break-in delayed BIO230. The damage was done. The general public didn't have the training to know what practices were or weren't in compliance with the ethical standards in animal testing. The public tends to react viscerally to a mental image of their pet dog on the laboratory table.

To them, pictures of animals being tested in even the most humane manner possible are upsetting. Therefore, telling the public that BioNeura's current practices were in complete compliance to the new regulations would be of little help when the images in the mind of the public were so graphic. Besides, it would require divulging that BioNeura was likely the target of sabotage. This was something no one wanted to do.

"How did they get these old pictures?" asked Jack.

"Has to be a current or former employee. Security is looking into that one right now," Jean-Luc said.

Meanwhile, the bleeding of the stock price continued. The shorts sustained their relentless attack and longs bailed out, driving the BioNeura share prices to levels not seen in two years. With big drops in share prices and angry shareholders a different kind of corporate trouble often comes – and Jack would soon find out about that.

142

Shah was loving life. SNS was booming and he was the darling of the investment community. He had made them tons of money by growing the value of SNS. He decided on the spur of the moment to take Gloria on a surprise long weekend in the Alps. Shah directed his assistant to quickly make the arrangements while he went to buy Gloria some flowers. The assistant never did this to Shah's satisfaction, so he did it himself.

As he made the short walk to the florist, the thought registered to him that he was seeing more homeless people on the streets of Geneva lately. One appeared to be following him. Shah changed directions twice and was now sure of it – she *was* following him. He might have been scared if she wasn't so obviously old and frail, struggling to keep up with him. Finally, she sat down on the curb, exhausted, some fifty feet behind him. Shah had had enough. He looked for a police officer but couldn't find one.

"Damn it," he grumbled under his breath, "I'll deal with this myself." He began walking towards her, his hands and teeth tightly clenched. When he got within an arm's length from her, he stopped.

"Old woman," he said, "stop following me or I will have you arrested."

She lifted her head and looked him straight in the eye. Shah was struck by her eyes – huge and as black as ebony, penetrating but also warm and peaceful. He had seen her somewhere before. *It's that wretched woman I knocked over some time ago.* Although he was repelled by her stench and filth, her eyes held his. They slowly softened him.

"What do you want, old woman?" he asked, much less harshly now, almost gently. He reached into his pocket.

"No sir, no money. I only want see you." She said in a thick accent. This stunned Shah and he took a half-step away from her. *Why would this street woman want to see me?*

"We met long time ago. I only want say hello and good luck." He heard in her voice a heavy accent that was familiar. He searched her creased and filthy face for clues, his face screwed tight with curiosity. Her eyes were disturbing but familiar.

After a few moments of searching her face and eyes his face suddenly slackened and his mouth hung open; he shook his head slowly and the word "No" formed silently on his trembling lips. He took a full step back, and then another and then turned and walked quickly away, looking back every few steps. He was relieved that she was not following him.

143

"Well, Jack, we expected this," said Barbara Siegel as she dropped a document on his desk. Jack was glad he had convinced Barbara to join BioNeura as General Counsel for times like these. "With the big drop in BioNeura's share price and alleged poor practices in the animal lab, the lawyers smell money here. Kennedy, Clive and Posner, the big plaintiff's law firm, filed this suit an hour ago. It's already on the web."

"So, what do we do, Barbara?"

"Nothing now. We'll issue a press release saying all the right things and then we'll let it run its course."

"And what is that?"

"Like sharks, once they smell blood in the water, the lawyers will swarm. Within a week we'll see many more filings and they'll all compete with one another to sign up shareholders who want to be compensated for lost share value. What we'll see next is lawyers fighting with each other."

"What a nice thought," said Jack.

"After the lead law firm is established, we'll hear from that firm. And after years, and millions of dollars in legal fees, we'll probably settle for pennies on the dollar. The lawyers will get their fees and the investors will get next to nothing. It's a lousy game, but that's how it's played." *Things just get better and better*, thought Jack.

144

In a hollow victory, the government's investigation into the practices of BioNeura was resolved favorably. In fact, they found BioNeura to be a model of good animal management practices.

Regarding the photos, BioNeura's security expert thought it might be a competitor. Jack didn't disagree but he had his own theory on the photos.

He was convinced that someone from inside BioNeura was the culprit. While he couldn't prove it, he strongly suspected that Bill Copley had slipped the photos to McPherson at SPOT.

Bill had cashed out all of his stock options a week before the break-in at the animal labs, so the recent plunge in the share price didn't hurt Bill. Bill also had access to photos from various presentations he had seen over the years. He also had motive – revenge for Jack's firing him. Jack shared this idea with the FBI. After a brief flourish of investigative activity, the FBI came up with nothing. Bill couldn't be implicated. The FBI soon concluded their investigation.

But Wall Street was nowhere near finished with BioNeura. "There are many, many rungs on the ladder going up," a college professor of Jack's had once told him, "but there's often only one rung on the way down – all the way down."

Jack thought of that line quite often these days. Both he and BioNeura had gone from being heroes to being pariahs. And while Jack knew that the analysts and bankers were never really his friends, just business associates, he nonetheless felt betrayed by them as they now criticized him and his company, often brutally and personally.

"The analysts can't tell their clients and investors they were wrong, Jack," his old college buddy consoled him. "They have to make you look like you misled them or that you were less than forthcoming or incompetent. It's a dirty game of CYA – cover your ass."

With the share price cratering, the class-action lawsuit looming and the credibility of the company eroding some analysts and large investors were quietly talking about "making a leadership change" at BioNeura; a euphemism for canning Jack Callahan. Jack felt he still had the confidence of the Board – at least as far as he knew. *Now don't get paranoid*, Jack thought. *You've got to stay cool.*

"Jack, Greg's on the line," Clara said. "Should I put him through?"

"Sure, Clara. Put him through."

After the customary small talk, Greg dropped an ominous message. "Jack, I've received a few calls from big investors in BioNeura and friends on the Street. In light of our long association, I am going to be totally straight with you."

"I appreciate that, Greg. What's going on?"

"The general message is that some in the financial community are losing faith in you. I assured them that I still had confidence in you and the Board was behind you."

"Thank you, Greg. In times like these, I appreciate . . ."

Greg cut him off. "While I do have faith in you, Jack, we're all unsettled by the share price. It's in free-fall. The bankers are telling me that the planned fund-raising will be impossible now, or in the near future. If we can't raise the funds to complete the Phase III trials of BIO230, I don't have to tell you how screwed we'll be. We could find ourselves taken over by another company."

A chill ran down Jack' spine. *Does he want my resignation? Has the Board turned against me?* Before Jack could respond, Greg added. "You need to turn this thing around, Jack. You have some time, but not much time. I'm calling you as a friend and as your Chairman. I want you to succeed, and I'm here to help. Just call me if you need me."

Jack's head felt like he was in a barrel rolling downhill. He managed to bleat a decent response to Greg. "Thanks for the call, Greg. I've heard your message loud and clear. I'll make it happen."

"I know you will, Jack."

But Jack wasn't comforted by this vote of confidence. He knew Greg had a job to do, and friendship or history had nothing to do with anything. Jack had to deliver or *he* would be history.

Later that day, the VP of Human Resources dropped in to see him.

"Jack, we need to address the stock option issue."

"What issue?"

"Since the stock price collapse, the options granted to our employees are deeply underwater."

Jack understood. BioNeura, like all small companies, offered generous quantities of stock options in place of the greater salary and bonus packages of larger companies. The idea was that if the company became successful, the price of the stock would exceed the option price, allowing the employee to exercise their options to buy shares at their low option prices and then sell those shares at the market price, banking the difference.

When the share price increased, as it had over the last few years, employees became "paper rich." When times were good and the share price was increasing, the options were "in the money." That tended to keep employees loyal, since the options only became usable over a period of years, when they "vested" and became sellable.

But when the company's share price declined below the employees' option price, their options became worthless, or "under water." They lost their retention factor and a morale issue often ensued.

"We're starting to have some significant turnover of employees, Jack," the Human Resources VP said. Jack knew he shouldn't, but he took the employee departures as a personal betrayal. He felt that defections were like a vote of no-confidence in his leadership.

These were very dark days – the darkest in Jack's career. He kept waiting for things to bottom out, but each week seemed to plumb the depths for another new bottom. For the first time in his career, he felt like his hands weren't on the steering wheel, like his car hurtled out of control as he watched it career and swerve, unable to affect its path. It was a scary and very unwelcome feeling.

Warfarin (Coumadin®)

145

America, Shah's Harris hawk rode the thermals high above the SNS headquarters in Geneva as Shah tracked him with his binoculars. *This creature has adapted well to the local environment,* Shah thought. *He hunts as well as he did in Central Park. Better even. He's stronger now and far more patient.* Shah smiled as the predator glided on the drafts below his wings, like a skilled archer with his bow at full extension, poised to strike at any second.

After some time surveying the landscape, America suddenly folded in his wings and dove at lightning speed. *Knowing when to strike is his greatest instinct, thought Shah.* After disappearing for several minutes behind the ground cover, America emerged carrying a squirrel, pumping his powerful wings to return home. With a flourish of wings and feathers, he landed on Shah's outstretched arm.

"Timing and speed are the essence of a successful predator," Shah said, stroking his impressive beast. Then he watched America rip the little creature to edible shreds. Shah made a notation in his feed book not to feed America for a few days. A satiated predator wouldn't be hungry enough to hunt.

146

Jack got to the office a little late, at 9:15 a.m., and when he pulled into the parking lot he noticed a unique automobile in the visitor's area, an antique Mercedes convertible, a fine machine. Jack knew it belonged to Greg. Greg often stopped by at random when he was in the area, so Jack refused to allow paranoia to dominate his thoughts. *He's just in the neighborhood*, he thought.

Hurrying to his office, Jack found Greg sitting there reading the morning newspaper. "I'm sorry to keep you waiting, Greg."

"Not at all, Jack. I never get to read the local news anymore." Greg rose and shook Jack's hand. Then he reached behind Jack and closed the door. Jack couldn't help reading something ominous into that. "Jack, let me get right to it," Greg began, looking Jack right in the eye.

Jack was surprised. He had thought he had more time to turn things around before he got the axe. It hadn't been all that long since Greg gave him that friendly warning.

"Jack, we received an overture from SNS, you know, Nathaniel Shah."

"An overture?"

"Well, to be precise, it's an offer to buy the company at a healthy premium to today's price. If we refuse, he'll go hostile and make a public tender offer for all outstanding shares of the company. We have a telephonic Board meeting in an hour to discuss it."

"How are you leaning, Greg?"

"If we can get him to sweeten his offer by 20 or 30 percent I'll recommend selling the company. We're in tough shape. And we'll have difficulty raising the money needed to survive. If we were to sell the company at a decent price, we could get out with some dignity. Shah might be our life boat."

Jack reeled at the thought. *Sell the company? I'm in a bad dream that won't quit.* But he did his best to be objective. "I know we're in tough shape, but we've been in far tougher shape."

Greg slowly rotated his head from side to side. It was as if he were saying, "I'm not so sure."

The Board of Directors call was intense. After weighing all of the alternatives, they agreed to fight the takeover in an effort to raise the price to an acceptable level while they also tried to turn the company around. If all worked right, the share price would rise to a level that made the acquisition too expensive for SNS. If it didn't, they'd be no worse off than they were today.

147

Shah wasted no time. When the deadline he had set for a friendly negotiation expired, he ran a press release and directed his legal team in New York to launch a tender offer for all outstanding shares of BioNeura.

The BioNeura Board issued its own press release stating that the offer was inadequate and urged the shareholders to not tender their shares to SNS but to hold on to them as they would be worth far more in the near future. The war of words and will had begun.

The battle was very public, with missiles launched at the other party in the form of open letters to shareholders and press releases issued from Geneva and San Francisco. In the middle was the shareholder, watching with interest as the share price rose quickly to the price that SNS offered and then some. The share price advance above that of the SNS offer indicated that there was an expectation or a reasonable hope that another suitor would enter the fray with a still higher price -the so-called "white knight" scenario or BioNeura would sell itself to SNS but at a higher price.

The language in the press releases followed the usual script. BioNeura: "The SNS offer vastly undervalues the tremendous potential of BioNeura and its assets and the combination would be anti-competitive due to the overlap of product lines of the two companies." SNS: "The recent events at BioNeura and the destruction of value by the current management team compel the shareholders to change control of BioNeura to realize its full potential. SNS has demonstrated consistent shareholder value creation and can be trusted to continue this uninterrupted track record." The campaign unfolded over several weeks, with each side fighting hard.

Then the plot thickened. It became known in financial circles that SNS had recruited Bill Copley, the former CFO of BioNeura to advise them. Non-compete clauses in California being virtually useless and enough time having passed since Bill's departure would make this on the margin of ethical behavior, but probably not illegal. Jack said he would not be surprised if this news of Bill advising SNS were true. It reinforced his suspicion that Bill was somehow involved in the lab attack, the photos and the subsequent crash of BioNeura stock. Another rumor circulated that SNS was working with Pieter Verplanken, the former BioNeura CEO that the Board had fired a couple years before. Verplanken was said to be helping Shah assess the BioNeura business in order to make the smartest offer. Jack thought. *The wolves smell wounded prey and the pack is gathering.*

In fact, it was true that Pieter was involved. Several weeks earlier, a meeting had taken place in Shah's office in Geneva.

"Pieter," Shah had said, "I always thought what happened to you at BioNeura was a scandal, a downright outrage. You were the man to run BioNeura, not Callahan. Everyone knows that."

"I can't disagree, Dr. Shah," said Pieter, warming to the compliments.

"I'd like to work with you on a project, Pieter. A project that should appeal to you on many levels."

"I'm all ears."

"I remind you that you have signed a confidentiality agreement with me – and that you have been given a handsome consulting fee for doing so."

"No need to remind me, Dr. Shah," Pieter said. "Please tell me how I can help you."

"I'm going to make a hostile bid for BioNeura." Pieter broke into a huge smile.

"Yes, I thought that would amuse you. In any case, since this is not a friendly offer, BioNeura won't give us access to their inside information. So, I need someone knowledgeable about BioNeura to help me assess the true value of the company. Are you interested?"

"Perhaps, what terms did you have in mind?"

"A handsome consultation fee and a princely success fee when I buy BioNeura." Shah was already moving on to the next point.

And so was Pieter, who knew he had leverage in the situation. "Money is always nice, but I would expect a senior role in the company."

Shah was entirely prepared for that. "Pieter," he said, "I'm looking ahead a couple of years. I want to slow down a little. I've decided I'll need a CEO to run the combined SNS/BioNeura organization, but not right away. My thinking is that once we've bought BioNeura you would start as

President and COO and I would move up to Executive Chairman.

"Over a short period, I would transition out of the Executive Chairman role to a non-Executive Chairman role and make you the CEO in charge of the whole thing. How does that sound?" Despite his excitement, Pieter tried to appear cool. "Under the right terms and circumstances, it could be interesting."

Shah looked him straight in the eye. "I am *sure* we can work out the 'terms and circumstances' as you call them, Pieter." Then Shah smiled and reached across the table to shake Pieter's hand. Pieter returned the handshake with gusto, and they toasted the acquisition with a bottle that Shah had chilled for the occasion.

Along with the wine, Pieter liked the sweet taste of revenge in this scenario. Even if he didn't care much for Shah, he respected his business acumen and drive to win. *Being continental, he doesn't have those Puritanical views on things that don't mean a damn if they don't interfere with business*, Pieter thought.

"Until the deal is done," Shah said, "let's keep this between us, shall we? We wouldn't want to upset the apple cart."

"Of course, I understand."

"Great," replied Shah with a forced smile – a smile that he had become much better at representing as genuine.

And so, began a several weeks process that led Shah to make the hostile offer at a very attractive price, with the vital insights supplied by at least Pieter Verplanken.

Meanwhile, the date for the expiration of the tender offer rapidly approached. Jack and his team spent all of their time urging shareholders not to tender their shares. Their anxiety grew, knowing that the few days before the expiration date would be when their future got decided. Jack and his group pitched the big institutional investors, telling them why they shouldn't tender their shares to SNS. More than once, they ran into the SNS team pitching the same shareholders. The looks exchanged by the two teams would make lasers seem benign.

After several weeks of public skirmishes and minor battles, the decisive battle of the war was at hand. The shareholders would either tender their shares or not. From the bankers advising him, Jack was told that it would be very, very close. SNS would prevail only if a majority of the BioNeura shares were tendered.

A few days before the tender deadline, SNS sweetened their offer by ten percent. "We're dead, Jack," said Jack's banker. "We may have had a slight edge before the new offer, but I'm afraid SNS just struck the fatal blow. I have to hand it to them."

Jack was less generous. "Damn vultures," was all he could say as he collapsed into his chair and stared blankly out the window.

The longest three days in Jack's life was the period just before the expiration date of the tender offer when the majority of the BioNeura shareholders decided to tender their shares or not. He could only wait and hope. He and his team had done their best to win the wallets of their shareholders. The fate of his company was in their hands now.

148

Alex Rostov was having a bad time. He had been under a lot of pressure at work, writing a major piece for the newspaper and the pace was crushing him. Having just turned 55, Alex was no longer the young, strapping reporter he once had been.

But it wasn't the work or the fatigue that was really bothering him. While taking two weeks off to rest after his big piece was done, Alex noticed even more his subtle but unavoidable symptom. He was having occasional trouble remembering things – little things. At first, he ignored his forgetfulness, attributing it to fatigue or stress, both of which can cause the brain to process slowly or inefficiently.

But when he finally began to accept that he might have a problem, a wave of fear washed over him. He had visions of his mother morphing into himself. He knew he should see Dr. Bonner, but he couldn't bring himself to do it. His terror of finding out that he had Alzheimer's disease was more powerful than his anxiety of not knowing.

149

The wait was now over and the votes now counted. The BioNeura shareholders had voted to accept the offer of SNS. Control of BioNeura would be passed to SNS, subject to Federal Trade Commission approval.

"Now that we've officially bagged BioNeura, I thought we'd finalize the press release on my appointment to President and COO of the combined company," said Pieter.

He had his feet up on his desk and was using his speakerphone. "Yes, I've been thinking a lot about that lately, Pieter," replied Shah.

"We seem to have a bit of a problem."

"What sort of problem?" said Pieter, leaning forward, his feet now firmly on the floor.

"Well, in preparing for this announcement, we came across some embarrassing information about you, Pieter."

Shah paused for a second or two. "In light of the high profile of the position and the fact that our company is publicly traded, I'm afraid it's impossible to follow through on our plan for you to become President and COO. I wish you had been more forthcoming about your work history."

"What kind of 'embarrassing information'...what the hell are you talking about?" asked Pieter. Shah could hear the stress in his voice and he became aroused – like he did when he saw prey trembling uncontrollably in his hawk's talons before its imminent decapitation.

After confirming that Pieter was on-line at that moment, Shah pressed the send button on the e-mail he had queued up to send. "Open the file I just e-mailed to you, Pieter."

Shah heard the ring of Pieter's e-mail in-box bell. Pieter clicked on the e-mail's attachment, fearing that he knew its contents. As he began scrolling through the file, he saw a virtual diary of his misadventures and dalliances, including strikingly accurate details of settlements made out of court with various sweet young things in his past businesses. Pieter's blood boiled up to his lips as he read the file. When he had finished, he simply said, "I understand," in a detached, robotic tone. Then he hung up the phone.

Shah smiled, as pleased as he could be at how he had used Pieter – and others – to build the information on BioNeura that he needed to make the hostile offer and then shut him out of the new company. Silently Shah thanked Gloria, his able General Counsel for her foresight in collecting this information on Pieter long ago and for patiently keeping it on file to use at the right time.

Clopidogrel (Plavix®)

150

Jack stared out of his apartment window watching a heavy gray fog roll over the city. The fog quickly consumed what had been visible only moments before, leaving no hint of the beautiful and impressive structures now shrouded in gray. *Huh....this scene is a fitting metaphor for my circumstances at BioNeura.* But after some brooding, he collected himself. *I can't sit here pouting. I gotta get to the office and start working on my plans for my future – whatever that might be.*

As he turned the corner in the office park where BioNeura's building was located, he recalled the first time he had seen the little office. It was so many years ago. From that humble start had come years of accomplishments paid with blood, sweat and tears. Each person who had entered the humble BioNeura doorway, every member of the team, had carried the same dream. They took it home with them every night and awoke with it each day.

That dream, which slowly but surely turned into reality, was now dead. Jack sat in his car for a few minutes watching his people walk into the office. He saw an unmistakable change in their gait. What had once been the purposeful and crisp stride of winners was now the walk of losers – a slow and distracted shuffle, eyes fixed on the ground.

Jack collected his thoughts and then got out of his car. He did his best to set an example by walking strongly with his head held high. His head seemed to weigh a thousand pounds as he made his way to the front door of BioNeura. He dreaded looking the BioNeura team in the eyes. He believed that he had let them down. He had been entrusted with the dream, and he had squandered it. He had no idea what would become of them all at the hands of SNS.

As he walked from the front door to his office, he noticed that the usual buzz of activity was gone. The place felt like a morgue. When he reached his office, he just wanted to sit there and vegetate, but he knew he had to walk around the office to give the employees courage and hope. This walk made his trek on the Appalachian Trail seem like nothing at all. As he saw each face from a distance, he confronted a vertical climb. Speaking with each old friend was like a painful slog through deep snow.

He walked around the office every day. As painful as it was, he saw it as his penance. He owed it to his team to be present and to be visible, as hard as it was for him. He owed them so much more.

151

Shah couldn't shake the memory of her eyes from his mind. Each day, while being driven to and from work, he looked for her on the street. Then one day, about a week since he last saw her, he caught a glimpse of her.

"Stop!" he shouted to his driver, recognizing the shabbily patched coat that she wore. Shah sprung from his car before his driver could help him out and in a moment, he was in a full run toward her. She heard him coming and began running with a pathetic, disjointed hobble, her body bent nearly in half at the waist. In no time, Shah caught up to her and grabbed her arm, turning her to him.

Shah was breathless as he looked into her eyes. But he quickly realized that it wasn't her. The old woman tried to wrest her arm from his grip and kicked him in the shin. Shah winced from the pain and from her awful odor.

"How did you get this coat?" he demanded. "What have you done to her?"

"She gave it to me sir," the woman replied. "She said she didn't need it anymore."

She jerked her arm and he let her go. As he watched her limp away, he reached into his pocket for his handkerchief and tried to wipe his hands of her odor.

When he returned to his car, his driver said, "Anything I can do sir?" "Just take me home," Shah replied. As the car sliced through the thick, humid evening air, his black eyes anxiously scanned the streets for her.

152

"Mr. Callahan, so nice to see you again," beamed Shah, striding briskly toward him. Jack slowly rose from his office chair to shake Shah's outstretched hand. "Dr. Shah. Thank you. I wish we were seeing each other under different circumstances."

"Oh well, that's understandable, Jack. This must be very difficult for you." Shah loved the moment – the vanquished, impotent before the magnanimous victor. Jack felt close to vomiting – his presence, his over-done tone, his devilishly black eyes – everything about him made him sick.

Jack closed the door and they began a long discussion about Shah's plans to integrate BioNeura and SNS. As Shah laid out his plans, Jack became increasingly uneasy. It was clear that Shah's plan was to rape and pillage BioNeura – fire staff, kill programs, delay others – to make his financials work given the high price he paid for BioNeura.

After another hour of presenting his plans, Shah abruptly stopped. He took a sip of his tea and slowly set it down, as he planned out his next words very carefully.

"Jack," Shah began, his black eyes smiling, "I would like you to stay on at the new company. You, and what you've done here have always impressed me. It would be a great comfort to your employees if you stayed."

Before Shah's visit that day, Jack had decided to resign from BioNeura. His letter of resignation sat already signed in the top drawer of his office desk, ready for the day the acquisition was finalized and his "change of control" severance package kicked in. But halfway through Shah's presentation, Jack decided that he had to stay, at least for a while. He had to make sure his employees were respectfully treated in the transition.

"I'd like to stay, Dr. Shah…" Shah beamed with delight, "…for a short transitional period during which I would help with the integration."

Shah now frowned and stroked his chin for a few moments. "Agreed," he said. "And Jack, it will be my challenge to convince you to stay on with SNS much longer than that." *Keep hoping all you want, Shah...that'll never happen,* thought Jack.

Later, alone in his office, Jack sat at his desk and looked out the window for a very long time. He had known that his still-open wound after Diana had to be closed eventually; now it seemed that the loss of his company was a good time to step up the process. He needed a fresh start, just as soon as he could get it. Where he would go and what he would do, he had no idea. All he knew was that there were too many memories here. He needed to be in new surroundings – not to forget Diana but to finally allow himself to heal.

One thing he had been thinking about was continuing on the Appalachian Trail, picking up where he left off. By the time he had returned to work after Diana's death he had completed a substantial piece of the Trail, and his time there had been very therapeutic. Once the stress and strain of the SNS takeover was over, he would be ready for another dose of Appalachian therapy.

153

They were in the pregnant stage of the deal; the market was expecting. Only a few routine government hurdles had to be cleared before the new SNS was born.

The SNS lawyers swarmed over BioNeura to expedite the mountains of paperwork required by the various governmental agencies. This was mostly routine form-filling, but was necessary: the faster it was done, the faster Shah would have his prize.

One of the agencies, the Federal Trade Commission had to review the deal to make sure the combination of SNS and BioNeura wouldn't create a monopoly or prevent strong and healthy competition in any segment of their business. The piece of legislation that governed this area was called the Hart-Scott-Rodino Act and carried the acronym "HSR."

While Jack thought the HSR review of the merger might run into some challenges he and most observers also expected the FTC to eventually approve it, perhaps with SNS agreeing to divest or license a small asset or two in a specific market segment. The acquirer, SNS, led the process, but the FTC contacted both companies independently for information. As with the SEC filings, the SNS lawyers wasted no time with the HSR Review, filing their document to the FTC shortly after the shareholder vote was done. In their document, they presented their view that the combination of BioNeura and SNS would not in any way decrease competition or create a monopoly.

After a couple of weeks, Shah was told that the FTC lawyers were taking more time with Shah's lawyers and his managers than Shah's lawyers expected. This kind of attention wasn't surprising as the FTC often takes its time and interviews doctors and others to make sure they get it right. Jack had felt that the HSR review was largely a rubber stamp, given that the world's largest pharmaceutical company had only three or four percent of the entire pharmaceutical market; a monopoly in such a circumstance was hard to imagine.

And yet, the FTC lawyers were taking it all very, very seriously. Their questions showed that they had an impressive grasp of the scientific, commercial and patent aspects of the R&D compounds and the many marketed products of the two companies. Besides that, they could've been superb poker players as they gave no clues about their thinking, despite probing by BioNeura and SNS lawyers.

"Jack," Clara said, "Dr. Shah is on the line. Do you want to take it?"

"I think you know the answer to that one, Clara," he said. "But I have to, I'm afraid."

The call was even more unpleasant than he had anticipated.

"Mr. Callahan," said an icy Nathaniel Shah, "if you think you are clever, if you think you can scuttle this merger, I am calling you to dissuade you of such a brainless notion."

Before Jack could answer, Shah continued. "I have crushed far more formidable foes than you, Callahan. Listen very carefully. If you continue to complicate the HSR review at the FTC, I will sue you personally for the lost value to SNS shareholders. I will have you in court for years. I might not win, but I will ruin you financially. I will also see to it that your character and reputation will be sullied so completely that you will be forever unemployable in this or any other industry." Shah paused. "Have I made myself clear Mr. Callahan?"

By now, Jack had recovered from the initial ambush. Unable to fight back the urge, he responded with dripping sarcasm.

"Nate, Nate" he began, knowing this familiar tone would send Shah into orbit, "does this mean that you no longer want to woo me into staying at SNS post-merger? Regarding your allegation, it's baseless. Your paranoia has reached clinical proportions, doc. I suggest some counseling and some medicine."

The line went silent. Jack could only imagine what Shah was thinking. Jack continued. "For the record, neither my staff nor I am doing anything that you allege. If the FTC has some issues, I suggest your lawyers call them. But I recommend you adjust your tone before you do."

Shah was seething. "I'll forgive you for being a pompous Yank," he said. "You can't help your upbringing. But remember what I told you, Jack. Stop the bullshit or I'll bury you alive."

Before Jack could respond, Shah hung up. Back in his Geneva office, Shah dropped his throw-away cell phone in the bin marked for incineration. He wanted no trace of that particular phone call leading to him.

154

Weeks passed without any news from the FTC. Jack continued his walk-arounds at the office, trying to keep the staff focused and as positive as possible. Then Barbara Siegel, Jack's General Counsel, burst into his office.

"Jack, this is interesting," she said. "My counterpart at SNS used to call me ten times a day since we announced the deal. Two days ago, he stopped calling – zip, nada. And he's not returning my calls."

Jack was baffled at Barbara's take on the situation. He worried that the stress had finally cracked her. "Maybe they're at an off-site planning meeting for the integration," he said, in his most comforting voice, "or overwhelmed with the details of the merger."

"I don't know, Jack. Something tells me there's more."

"Well, I really don't think there's anything here. In a day or two, you'll be moaning that he is driving you crazy again."

As they moved on to other matters, Jack couldn't help feeling a little worried about Barbara – taking such minor things as "signs." She needed a rest, he thought.

Pirfenidone (Esbriet®)

155

"The issue is manageable. We anticipated this potential challenge when we approved the acquisition months ago, so there is no reason to panic or make any rash moves."

Despite his inner anxiety, Shah was making a Herculean effort to project calm and confidence in front of his Board of Directors. His Chairman led the discussion.

"Well, Dr. Shah, exactly how do you propose to manage the current view of the FTC? Despite doing a very fine job with them, your team has so far failed to persuade them that the merger has absolutely no HSR issues – as you assured us – and the Street."

"That's true, We've negotiated a solution with the FTC," Shah said. "The FTC has stated a concern about our Parkinson's disease product Parkote and a promising new BioNeura product for Parkinson's. They claim that the merged company would have a dominant position in this market, suppressing competition. I am confident that all we have to do is commit to divesting either Parkote or the BioNeura products after we merge and the FTC will approve the deal."

An intense discussion ensued. Shah did his best to make the divestiture of Parkote appear to be inconsequential. This was a lie considering the fact that Parkote was a meaningful contributor of profits to SNS. Parkote was essentially a "cash-cow," a brand that required little investment anymore and because of its market dominance this translated into very important cash flow for SNS.

Divesting the BioNeura product would be likewise problematic, as it represented a significant part of the value that SNS had placed on BioNeura when they offered to buy the company, and would compete with Parkote.

The debate ran for three hours. Financial projections had been re-crunched, showing that the deal could still be positive for SNS even after they divested themselves of certain of their own or BioNeura products. To make the numbers work however, the new forecasts put more value on BIO230, the new drug of BioNeura for Alzheimer's disease now in Phase III clinical trials and also assumed a higher probability that BIO230 would be approved by the FDA for the U.S. market and by the EMA for the European market.

Sensing that the Board was about evenly split, Shah decided to press his hand. "Gentlemen, this is no time for faint hearts. If we want to do great things, we must make bold moves. Napoleon, Alexander the Great and Sun Tsen would be unknown today if they had they not seized opportunities and made courageous decisions." He paused. "I also think the FTC's position is rubbish."

The Chairman looked over his reading glasses at Shah. "Thank you for your speech, Dr. Shah," he said, with unmistakable sarcasm. "We all admire your sense of history and your passion. But as for the FTC and their rubbish, since they make the rules, their rubbish is haute cuisine as far as this merger is concerned."

Surveying the room, the Chairman asked if anyone had any questions that had not already been answered. He got no response. "Very well. Using Dr. Shah's term for the FTC opinion, we need to figure out if we are willing to swallow the rubbish or spit it out. Gentlemen, it is time to cast your vote on the revised proposal by Dr. Shah to purchase BioNeura and divest either Parkote or the BioNeura asset as he outlined."

After giving the directors thirty minutes to re-read Shah's proposal and pose any last questions to management and its bankers, the board reconvened. The Chairman returned to the conference room and took his chair. "Gentlemen, are we ready for a vote?"

All nodded affirmatively.

"Very well. All those in favor of the proposal to move ahead based on the new financials?"

He counted the hands. "All those opposed?"

He again counted the hands.

"The Board is deadlocked. He frowned. "According to the by-laws of our incorporation, in this circumstance as Board Chairman I am called upon to break the deadlock."

Shah leaned forward, hardly breathing and attempted to project a cool demeanor. The Chairman spoke, "Dr. Shah presents a very compelling argument. BioNeura represents a rare opportunity to transform our company into a major player in our segment and if BIO230 is successful, one of the major companies in the world. As Dr. Shah so eloquently put it, we must be prepared to make bold moves." *Absolutely*, thought Shah.

"Bold moves must be made after weighing all aspects and must be made with a full appreciation of the probabilities of success and consequences of failure. Dr. Shah has also pointed this out for us very well."

Get on with it, you old fool, thought Shah. He wanted to choke him dead.

"As is typical in most decisions, the gray area is navigated with judgment. Dr. Shah has presented his judgments, which I respect. His track record speaks to his sound judgment."

Come on, come on...give me my vote and let me build my company. "I have focused my attention on one important assumption. When we agreed to make a hostile bid for BioNeura we assumed that BIO230 was only 30 percent of the risk-adjusted value of BioNeura. The new figures now assume over 40 percent of the BioNeura value is ascribed to the BIO230 product. I am correct about this, right?" he asked looking at the bankers. They nodded affirmatively.

The Chairman then stacked his papers, closed his elegant ebony Mont Blanc fountain pen and removed his reading glasses. "The solution proposed by management to the FTC's concerns about us creating a potentially monopolistic franchise was to dump one Parkinson's product. But this would create a hole in our valuation of the merger.

As we know, management has proposed that since we made our bid for BioNeura they are comfortable increasing the estimate of the probability of the eventual FDA approval of BIO230 and assuming an approval one-year earlier than our previous forecast. These adjustments would cover the lost value from divesting the Parkinson's product. Since we made our original bid for BioNeura no news has emerged on BIO230 that would convince me that these adjustments to the FDA approval assumptions can be so significantly changed, despite the assertions that our prior estimates were very conservative."

Shah's heart was in his throat and the entire Board leaned in as they waited for the final verdict. "In conclusion, my vote is negative. So, based on the tally but more importantly, the lack of unanimity among us, we will withdraw our bid for BioNeura."

The Chairman looked at Shah. He was ashen which made his black eyes show an even deeper black. "I am sorry I had to take this position, Dr. Shah. I know I speak for the entire Board in saying that we hold you in the highest regard and respect your views on this subject. This vote is in no way one of no confidence in you or in your management team."

Shah stared at his Chairman; actually, stared through him. He felt disconnected from space and time. He was in a nightmare. He was that scared little boy again, listening to the visiting priest tell his parents exactly what kind of boy he was. Somehow, he managed a respectful bow of his head and a few appropriate words. "Thank you, Mr. Chairman, and my colleagues on the board for considering my views."

156

BioNeura was running as usual, assuming they were going to be "integrated" into SNS in the coming weeks and months. The thought had become somewhat accepted – the BioNeura staff were moving their collective feelings of grief towards acceptance, though some were at much different stages of the spectrum.

"I can't stand the suspense, Dad," complained Gabriel.

"I can't either," replied his father, Wen.

Gabriel pleaded, "When are we going to know the results of the two Phase III studies on BIO230?" He decided this was a teaching moment for his son was very interested in the business.

"Now let's see, it's been two years since the start of our two huge Phase III studies, Study 101 and Study 102. The results to those studies should be known in about 18 to 24 months – you remember that Study 102 is about nine months ahead of Study 101, since it enrolled much faster."

"Yup, 102 is the lead horse," replied Gabe.

"The two studies are nearly identical but have some small differences in what they are measuring. In both Phase III studies, half of the patients receive a commonly prescribed product for treatment of the symptoms of Alzheimer's disease plus BIO230 and the other group also gets that product but instead of BIO230, they get a placebo."

Gabe interjected, "I've read about some companies getting a drug approved with only one Phase III study – how does that work?"

"Good question, Gabe. The FDA has a process to approve a new medicine with positive data from only one Phase III study instead of the more usual two Phase IIIs, but there are strict conditions. The disease has to be very serious, the current therapy inadequate and the data in the one study have to be impressive and unambiguously positive. And depending on the strength of the data in the one study and some other technical details, the FDA may require the company to show supportive results in an additional so-called confirmatory study to maintain their FDA approval."

"Makes sense, dad. Given the severity of Alzheimer's disease and the lack of a disease modifying medicine for patients with Alzheimer's disease, BIO230 certainly qualifies for a one-study approval, right?"

"Absolutely correct, Gabriel."

"So, we could get BIO230 approved with one study?"

"Yeah, but this one-study approval route is rare and really too much to hope for."

"OK" said Gabriel, "but aren't there interim analyses that could end the two studies sooner?" Gabriel's insight impressed Wen.

"Yes, there are. At pre-specified points in the two trials, a group of very experienced experts looks at the interim results of the trial. The experts in our case are mostly world-class neurologists but also include internists, gerontologists and statisticians. And they're all independent of the company sponsoring the trial. Collectively, the group comprises what is called the independent DSMB, or Data Safety Monitoring Board. You understand so far?"

"Uh-huh."

"Gabriel, the DSMB has the important job of protecting the patients in a clinical study from side effects from experimental medicines. On a quarterly basis, they do safety analyses of our studies to see if patients treated with BIO230 are having significantly more side effects or worse, more deaths than the placebo patients. You with me?"

"Yep. Keep rolling, Dad."

"OK, if an unambiguous difference in serious side effects or deaths is observed and the DSMB believes the new drug is the culprit, they will blow the whistle and call the study to a halt. Sadly, the industry is littered with the bones of experimental drugs that died in Phase III for this very reason."

"That sucks," replied Gabe, "but they gotta protect the patients."

"Exactly."

"Okay, to finish answering your question about interim analyses, the DSMB also conducts regular *efficacy* interim analyses. In our case, when a pre-defined number of patients in each of our two studies reaches several pre-defined durations of treatment, the DSMB will do an interim analysis of efficacy. They look at "blinded data" meaning that no one knows which group got the experimental medicine and which group got placebo. This blinding is done to eliminate the chance of anyone's bias being injected in any decision-making. If the DSMB see one group doing statistically much better or worse than the other, they can have the data "un-blinded" to see if the patients doing better or worse are on the experimental medicine or placebo. They could stop the trial if after un-blinding the data, the patients on the experimental therapy are the ones doing better – or doing worse – than the placebo patient. A lot of Phase III studies get stopped when the study is deemed futile – meaning the results at a certain point in time in the study have met the pre-determined criteria that would make expecting a good outcome futile."

Gabe summarized perfectly. "So, when the DSMB has something important to say to the company about safety *or* efficacy before a trail is completed, odds are it isn't good news." "Exactly, Gabriel."

157

"The next time I tell you I'm feeling something, Jack, you'd damn well better believe me."

Barbara Siegel appeared in his doorway with her hands on her hips. In one hand she clutched a piece of paper. "Look at this," she said, handing it to him.

"I know!" said Jack, jumping up and giving her a big hug. The press release she had handed him was timed at 4:00 p.m. eastern time and said: "Societe' Nationale de la Suisse (SNS) withdraws tender offer for BioNeura shares, cites HSR issues."

"I was about to come see you," Jack said. "I just this minute got off the phone with my buddy, Dr. Nathaniel Shah" – Jack pronounced Shah's name in an exaggerated and haughty British accent. "The right honorable doctor told me that he decided that BioNeura wasn't worth the price and that they were issuing a press release as we spoke. I told him I thought he could have done his homework better and saved everyone a lot of aggravation."

Jack smiled. "He didn't appreciate that."

"I wouldn't think so, old boy," said Barbara, having her own fun with the British accent. They were giddy with the news.

Jack announced an all-employee meeting for 25 minutes from then. When he entered the dining room/auditorium to address the troops, he saw that everyone had heard the news. The employees were singing and dancing to "I Will Survive," Gloria Gainer's disco-era anthem that someone had piped into the public address system. The troops were in a party mood. Jack wanted to go with the emotion of the moment and dance along with them – but he wanted more to get to business.

He took the podium in the big meeting area. The music stopped and the crowd, with still smiling faces remained standing anxious to hear what Jack had to say. Looking at the familiar faces in the audience, he was glad he had continued his walkabouts during the buy-out process. All through this excruciating process he had kept telling everyone that it wasn't over until it was over. And even if the merger were done, their future could be interesting in the new company. Now Jack was rewarded heartily for his leadership. The employees cheered him as soon as he opened with "Good morning." They applauded for a long time before he got them to take their seats.

"Welcome back to BioNeura!" he shouted, and the roar of the happy audience returned. "By now, you have heard the news. SNS has withdrawn their offer to buy us." The staff erupted in more applause. "While this is wonderful news for those who wanted to stay independent, I have to prepare you that we will have very, very tough times ahead."

The crowd suddenly grew more quiet and attentive. "If any of you were thinking that today's news meant that we can now return to the 'good old days,' I have to remind you that the days before the SNS bid were rough ones for us. And I have to prepare you that we are returning to those tough days and we will all need to work together to get through them."

The crowd grew even more still. Jack saw in their faces the effects of being whip-sawed by the events of the last few months – flying high, crashing to earth, almost being bought out and then returning back to independence. Jack knew he had to be careful managing his fragile workforce and he was doing his best to alleviate the highs and lows of their collective emotions.

When he was finished addressing the crowd and taking their questions, the mood was now somber and anxious; a far-cry from the disco-beat that filled the room a half an hour before. *Damn, this business is tough,* Jack thought. He wondered how his team would handle this latest turn in their roller-coaster ride.

158

Since the SNS announcement was made after the stock market closed on Friday, the impact of the news on the BioNeura share price wouldn't be seen until Monday. Jack called his VP of Investor Relations at 6:00 a.m. local time on Monday morning.

"The pre-market trading this morning is pretty grim, Jack."

"Yeah, I looked it up a few minutes ago. Where do you think our share price settles?"

She paused for a couple of seconds. "I figure we'll drop back to where we were before SNS made its offer to buy us. Maybe lower if the Street feels we're damaged goods now."

Jack knew she was probably right in her prediction.

BioNeura opened the following Monday down 25 percent, and lower than the pre-SNS-bid price. For thirty minutes, Jack was thinking it could stabilize there. But by 10:05 New York time, BioNeura had lost another 10 percent.

It was now down 35 percent, well below the original pre-SNS offer price. A weak rally of support began near the end of trading and BioNeura finished the day down 30 percent.

Jack phoned Greg to discuss the carnage of the day. "Well, you still have a Chairman's job, Greg."

"And you, a CEO job, Jack – as long as you get the business quickly back on its feet."

Greg felt he had to let Jack know exactly where he stood and what was expected.

Jack faced the biggest leadership challenge of his career. He had to lead a demoralized, weakened company with weak investor support and tons of short-seller interest out of troubled waters.

"Jack, everyone out there knows that BioNeura needs cash," said his banker. "You'll need 150 million dollars or more to finish the Phase III trials you've already started for the approval of BIO230 and you only a hundred million or so on hand – and you're burning through it fast. Since that laboratory animal fiasco, your company's reputation ain't the greatest, so raising capital on decent terms in your condition will be nearly impossible."

"Ever the optimist," said Jack.

"Jack, you don't need optimism. You need realism."

"Yeah, I know." He also knew that knowing he needed cash and getting it on terms he could live with were two different things.

Wall Street was well aware that BioNeura was running out of money. That meant they had to raise more cash by issuing new stock. Since the price of the company's shares was so depressed, BioNeura would have to issue a massive amount of stock. This in turn would make current shareholders even unhappier because their ownership of BioNeura would become diluted. With current investors unhappy and future investors not buying, BioNeura shares continued to slowly, but very surely slide.

As the share price eroded, BioNeura became vulnerable to being a target of a takeover attempt by another company. Jack worked feverishly to strengthen the confidence of the Street in the company and the shares but at the same time he also prepared himself for The Phone Call. It would likely be from a "big Pharma" company, one of the top 20 companies and it would probably be their Chief Financial Officer on the line, not their CEO – the latter wouldn't want to stoop to the level of a small company CEO. The message would be something vague, like "We'd like to meet you to discuss potential common interests." The objective would be understood as "We think we may want to buy you."

Jack wondered how he could summon the strength to lead his team through yet-another merger maelstrom. He began consciously working to steel his own mind – hardening himself to this inevitable phone call and preparing for the exhausting swing of emotions that he and his team would go through in the weeks and months thereafter.

Sure enough, "The Call" came. "Jack, I have the assistant to a Mr. Dennis Bower on the line. She says Mr. Bower is the CEO of Kinney-Harbor." Kinney-Harbor was one of the biggest of the so-called "big-Pharma" companies created a couple of years earlier from a mega-merger between number five ranked Kinney Labs and number nine, Harbor Pharmaceuticals.

Jack was pleasantly surprised that the CEO himself had made the call.

"Hello, Dennis. I don't know if you remember that we met years ago in Paris when I was at Covington Labs."

"I remember very well, Jack," answered Dennis.

"I met your wife, Diana, and I was so sorry to hear about her passing."

Jack was always impressed at the staff work that the big Pharmas could have at their disposal. Dennis probably had in front of him Jack's picture, bio, comments from peers, hobbies, favorite sports teams, family info etcetera. "Thanks for that, Dennis," he said, feeling a little inadequate at not being able to remember the name of Bower's wife, whom Jack had met at the same event. "Jack," continued Bower, "we've noticed that you're in a challenging situation these days and we have an idea that might be beneficial for both of our companies. We'd like to run it past you to see what you think."

Pretty much according to script, thought Jack, but more respectful than he had expected. "Well, Dennis," he said, "I happen to be in New York later this week. I could drive down to New Jersey to see you."

"Great, let's put our assistants back on to take care of the details. I'm looking forward to seeing you again, Jack."

159

Jack and a small circle of his staff, including his banker, prepared for Jack's meeting with Bower. Before Jack left for New York, they had put together an impressive overview of Kinney-Harbor and Jack's banker supplied the background on Bower. Jack knew that his banker would love to land Kinney-Harbor as a client, but in this potential transaction he focused totally on his current client, BioNeura. Having cleared the conversation with his Board, Jack left for the airport looking forward to meeting Dennis Bower.

After landing at Kennedy, he saw that he had a voice mail message. It was from Bower. *The meeting's off,* Jack thought, but that wasn't it at all. "Jack," began Bower's message, "I was wondering if you'd consider having our meeting in my private box at the hockey arena instead of at my office. They'll serve us an edible dinner there, we can discuss our business and we can see the New Jersey Devils play." Pleasantly surprised, Jack returned the call. "Dennis, that sounds great."

"OK," said Bower. "I'll get the tickets to your hotel today. Let's arrive and depart separately. There's a private entrance. We don't want to start any rumors."

"Of course."

"See you there at 6:30, Jack."

"Looking forward to it."

Jack's meetings in New York went as expected. He met with various bankers. They all chirped the same song in different notes:

"It's iffy, Jack."

"Not the best time to be raising capital."

"When you get your Phase III data in, we'll be there for you."

"We can raise the capital for you, but you'll need to give a big discount on the share price to get it done."

Oh, what a difference a few months make, Jack thought. Back then, BioNeura was the cock of the walk and these guys were falling over themselves to do business with BioNeura. But in fairness to the bankers, the company had really fallen from grace since then.

That evening Jack found the private entrance to the corporate boxes at the arena and presented his ticket. The security officer studied Jack's driver's license and entered it into his PC. "Mr. Callahan, please enter door C to your left and continue until you meet the next security point." Jack did as he was told and repeated the drill at the next level. He was then personally escorted to the door outside the Kinney-Harbor box and his escort pressed the doorbell.

Bowers answered the door himself. "Jack, so glad you could come," Bowers said, ushering him into a suite that was remarkable in its understated décor. Jack had expected this one to be like most of the other corporate sports suites he had been in – an over-the-top suite to rival any hotel suite in Vegas. Instead, here was a family feeling with comfortable chairs and functional furniture. The flat screen was the most impressive feature in the room.

"I know," said Bowers, noticing Jack's double take on the TV. "It kind of defeats the purpose of being here, but it's great for instant replays."

They ordered their meal and got themselves a drink. Then Bowers raised his eyebrow to the waiter, who got the message and immediately disappeared. They spent a half-hour chatting and getting to know each other. Jack liked Dennis more and more.

"Jack, our dinner will arrive in a half hour. Can I propose my idea to you?" "Sure, let's hear it."

"Well, I don't need to summarize your situation. You know it far better than I do. I want to do a deal with you, but I don't want to buy your company."

Jack was knocked off balance. He had fully expected to hear Dennis's offer to buy BioNeura for a certain price per share so he wasn't prepared to hear this angle. "What do you have in mind?" was the best Jack could offer in his momentary state of disequilibrium. "I'm sure you noticed that our last acquisition, the GentaBio deal wasn't a big success, Jack. In truth, it was a friggin' disaster."

Jack liked Dennis's humble honesty. "Well, Dennis, maybe it didn't work out like you hoped, but the rest of your business is doing very well."

"That's true, Jack. Thanks for mentioning it. But as much as I'd like to buy BioNeura, mainly for BIO230 if I bought your company and BIO230 were never approved, I'd have my head handed to me – and it would be fully justified. So, here's my thinking... You need a lot of capital but you don't want to or can't raise the capital at your current share price right now. I want to participate in BIO230. I propose we make an alliance to develop and commercialize BIO230 together."

It was a *very* appealing idea, and Jack had to concentrate to keep from appearing overly eager. "It could work under the right circumstances. Tell me more. How do you envision its structure?"

"Essentially, we'd give you a substantial up-front payment to compensate BioNeura for a significant share of the investment you have made in the program to date. We would provide a substantial milestone payment to BioNeura when your regulatory submissions to the FDA and EMA are filed and another set of payments upon regulatory approvals."

"What's the rough size of the payments, in total?"

"All-in, the milestone payments would be more than large enough to cover your cash needs for the two Phase IIIs on BIO230 and build a manufacturing plant. We have enough biologics manufacturing capacity in our various plants around the world to obviate your need to pay for and build a second plant – we'd agree on industry standard contract manufacturing terms to get paid for making half of the BIO230 demand. We'd split the operating profits 50/50."

Jack was trying not to jump out of his chair for joy – *He's offering us a life raft that doesn't involve selling the company!*

In spite of the danger of moving too fast, Jack decided to strike now for fear that another company would swoop in and buy BioNeura at the company's currently depressed price. Leaning forward and looking

Bowers in the eyes, he said, "How serious are you about this, Dennis? If you are, you'll have to move fast." It was a little ploy aimed at conveying the impression that there were – or could soon be – other interested suitors. Jack was honest about the latter.

Dennis's eyes showed the smallest hint of anxiety at Jack's comment, but it faded in an instant. Then he leaned in to Jack. "I'm dead serious, Jack. It's my idea and I can make this elephant of a company dance much faster than you'd think."

"OK," Jack said, "let's see how far we can take this tonight. Let's craft out the skeleton of an agreement."

"OK, let's do it," Dennis said.

Immediately they started hammering out the high-level concepts, many of which Dennis had already thought through with his team. After an hour of intense discussion, interrupted only by the serving of dinner, they had a high-level outline of a deal.

After confirming and polishing the key points with Jack, Dennis pressed a speed dial on his cell phone. "Come up here right away. And bring one of those lawyers that are entertaining you."

When he hung up, Dennis said, "That's my Corporate Development guy. He's below us in the arena and he'll be right up to meet you."

Within five minutes, they heard a knock at the door. Dennis excused himself and answered it. Jack heard some whispered talk and then Dennis reappeared with his colleagues and introduced them. "Jack and I just agreed on a deal structure to collaborate on BIO230 subject to all of the usual conditions, some diligence of course and don't worry, we still have to agree on the exact numbers. Here it is. Please have a proper term sheet drafted by the end of the game tonight." Dennis' colleagues looked at the hen-scratch notes, each other, Dennis and then Jack – the look on their faces said they were searching for hints that this was a gag. But instead of seeing Dennis or Jack crack a smile to reveal the joke, they got only a stern look from Dennis when he saw them hesitate. This, they now understood, was dead serious.

"Right away, Dennis," they said. "Can we use the office equipment here?"

"Of course, help yourself." Whereupon they retreated into the small but complete office in the back of the suite.

Once again Jack found himself impressed by the machine of big Pharma. Within 15 minutes, the notes had been scanned into documents and e-mailed to the homes of company and external lawyers who had already been called to expect them. By the end of the hockey game, Dennis' team had printed off the draft. "Here's the draft, Dennis," one said. "And one for Jack, please" said Dennis, visibly annoyed that Jack had been slighted.

"Of course. It'll be printed in just one minute." Before the arena was empty, Jack and Dennis had reviewed the draft. Dennis's lawyers were extremely nervous about going so fast and having their CEO doing the negotiation, so they had plastered the first page with a list of disclaimers and a declaration that no agreement was reached, nor could be reached, unless a host of conditions and approvals were met, etcetera. Dennis and Jack breezed beyond that, compared notes and gave their comments to the lawyers standing by.

More scanning, more e-mailing and more word-smithing. Dennis convinced the security guards to let them stay another hour. By the end of that time, Dennis and Jack had signed a Heads of Agreement, which would be shared with their respective Boards. Jack feared that he may have gone too far in negotiating the outline of the deal before first getting his Board's approval, but he had sensed that he couldn't chance squandering the precious chemistry and momentum that he and Dennis had developed. *And besides, the heads of agreement have some TBDs in it and it's ultimately subject to board approvals,* he said to himself.

They agreed to reach agreement on the exact size and definitions of the milestone payments within a week and if they agreed on those, have the due diligence done simultaneously with finalizing a transaction agreement. They targeted a public announcement within four weeks. What made this agreement in principle possible was that both Jack and Dennis had the same goal – to share risk and reward, address BioNeura's immediate cash needs and to not have the company change hands before the potentially value-driving Phase III results of BIO230 were known. Since SNS had withdrawn its offer, the clock was ticking. BioNeura's price per share was staying at a level that was temptingly low for a rapacious acquirer. Jack was sure that many bankers were actively "pitching" BioNeura to many companies as an acquisition idea.

"It's a shame we missed the game, Jack," Dennis said, as they packed up to go. "I'll invite you and your executive team to another game to celebrate the closing of our deal."

"It would be our pleasure," replied Jack. He was really impressed at how Dennis could move this large organization with such agility and speed. *He's one of the few who's got the big Pharma game figured out,* thought Jack as he shook Dennis's hand and walked out into the cold night air. He spotted the limo that would take him back to Manhattan, about thirty minutes away. In the car, Jack could hardly contain his excitement.

Emtricitabine (Emtriva®)

160

Within four weeks of the hockey game, the deal was done. The Kinney-Harbor lawyers were beside themselves with worry over the many sections of the agreement that were essentially "agreements to agree" at a later date. But Jack and Dennis had quickly developed an unusually strong mutual trust that allowed them to be comfortable with the few areas of looseness in the agreement. They announced their Agreement in the trade and financial press.

Wall Street loved the news for BioNeura as they got a cash life-line, validation of their technology and a global manufacturing and commercial powerhouse as a partner. The Kinney-Harbor shareholders liked the idea of getting a collaboration on what could be a huge new product without doing a risky acquisition, given that the last one they saw turned out to be a disaster.

BioNeura got $400 million at signing of the deal so they could afford to finish the ongoing Phase III trials on BIO230 and keep building the manufacturing plant – without issuing more BioNeura stock. They would also get up to $600 million if BIO230 got registered in the US and $300 million for an approval in the EU.

BioNeura shares surged almost 25 percent on the news of the collaboration. Seeing the share price of BioNeura surge, Jean-Luc called Jack on his cell phone. "Hey Jack, I'm loving that aroma of fried shorts, you?" asked Jean-Luc.

Jack was breathing easier now. The share price was higher, he had a strong partner and he had solved his cash crisis. A bid for the company was possible, but much less likely now. With the survival of the company seeming somewhat more secure, Jack could allow himself to focus on normal business of BioNeura for the first time in many, many months.

161

Six months later it was time for the data and safety monitoring board or "DSMB" review of the two Phase III BIO230 trials. This would be the sixth such review, the trials having been enrolling patients for over three years. The Chairwoman of the DSMB and the chief of Neurology at Harvard, ran a very efficient process. She was a dead ringer for Margaret Thatcher – matronly, tough, and serious. Under her leadership, they had established a quick and productive work rhythm.

"Let's have the safety and adverse experience analysis, please," the Chairwoman said immediately after calling the meeting to order. "Nothing remarkable here from a statistical point of view," summarized the statistician on the DSMB. "We need to look over the results all the same," she ordered. She took her responsibility seriously and led the team to share her conscientious approach. So, they reviewed every metric. Indeed, after reviewing the summaries, there was nothing remarkable. "All right, no apparent safety or side effect signals. Good" the Chairwoman said. "Let's move on to the interim efficacy analyses."

The neurologist on the DSMB then led the larger group through "blinded" efficacy data in Study 101. "As you recall, both groups in this study receive the standard medicine for symptomatic care. One group receives that plus BIO230 and the other group gets the standard medicine plus placebo. In summary, at this interim analysis, there are no statistical differences between the two groups on the primary endpoint or any secondary endpoints. However, a nominal difference between the groups is apparent on several study endpoints including the primary endpoint and the difference is approaching statistical significance. This is possibly very encouraging given the consistency of the signal across all endpoints and the relatively early stage of the study, but these differences could possibly reverse themselves by the next time we look."

"Okay, indeed this is very encouraging but we're not there yet," said the Chairwoman as she peered over her bifocals. "Now let's see Study 102." The neurologist continued, "I remind us that this study is about nine months ahead of Study 101 so patients in this study had a much longer time on treatment. The neurologist paused and glanced at the statistician. "I asked the DSMB's statistician to check and re-check the statistics before we shared them with you. They are correct." Several members glanced at their peers as they anticipated an interesting time ahead.

The neurologist continued. "There are highly statistically significant differences and I am sure you will agree, clinically important differences between the two treatment groups in three out of five metrics of efficacy, including the primary endpoint metric, the ADAS-Cog score which measures cognition. The differences on the remaining two endpoints is approaching statistical significance."

A lively and very excited discussion ensued as all committee members realized they were part of an historic moment in medicine. "According to our pre-specified protocol for this situation, we un-blinded the data to see which therapies each group is receiving." Now everyone leaned in. "The group showing the positive effects is the group whose patients were given BIO230. Ladies and gentlemen, we have a drug that modifies the outcome of patients with Alzheimer's disease. This is a ground-breaking finding!"

After this sunk in, the Chairwoman spoke. "So, we must talk to the BioNeura people who will likely want to immediately consult with the FDA and the European regulatory authorities. Before they started the two studies, they agreed with the regulatory authorities that a positive result from an interim analysis with the strength of the statistical difference that we now see, would be acceptable to them for purposes of marketing approval. This result will require the company to stop both studies as it would be unethical to deprive the placebo patients of BIO230."

Jean-Luc Dumas had been waiting outside the room in case the DSMB needed him. In the six previous DSMB meetings, they never needed him so he expected it would be the same this time. He was surprised when the door opened and the DSMB Chairwoman crooked her finger and summoned him into the meeting. *Oh shit,* he thought. *This must be bad.*

"Jean-Luc, we have a finding in the Phase III program," she said once he had taken his seat.

His heart flipped in his chest as he scanned the faces in the room for a hint of whether the finding was good or bad.

"You have a winner, Jean-Luc!" she said. Jean-Luc couldn't believe it. He looked down at his trembling hands. He was breathing shallowly and quickly; his chest was tight and his head was feeling light. Had he not known better, he would say he was having a heart attack.

Must be an anxiety attack, he thought. He had played this moment in his mind hundreds of times, but now he had forgotten the script. *Du calme, doucement,* he said to himself. Concentrating mightily on getting a grip of himself, he slowly felt his self-control returning to him. Finally, he was able to listen to the results and prepare himself to tell the news to his team.

162

Jean-Luc and the DSMB Chairwoman together contacted the review teams at the EMA in London and the FDA in Bethesda to request an emergency meeting. They gave them just enough background to get the regulators to understand the urgency involved.

Before the end of the London day, the conference call with the appropriate divisions of the FDA and the EMA was happening. After an hour of questions and discussion, the heads of the two regulatory agencies agreed that the very strong results of Study 102, combined with the supportive emerging data of Study 101 would be sufficient for approval. The question of whether or not BioNeura had to do a confirmatory trial after marketing approval – or even could do a placebo-controlled trial given the results was discussed. Both the FDA and EMA agreed that it would be impossible to convince patients to enter a placebo-controlled trial once the news of the Phase III studies was out so they acknowledged that a confirmatory trial wouldn't be required for approval. They did express a strong interest in having the company do a study in patients with earlier disease than those studied in Studies 101 and 102.

Now Jean-Luc reflected. *C'est un rêve*, he thought. *It's a lovely dream from which I don't want to wake!*

163

Shah was taking a rare walk back to his office after a business lunch not far away when his eyes suddenly flashed wide open and he gasped. He saw her standing not fifty feet from him and not far from where they last spoke.

He approached her with his usual brisk step. When he neared her, she recognized him and cowered, remembering her unpleasant last encounter with him.

"Hello, old woman," he said softly, continuing, "I have been searching for you for quite some time. I think I may know who you are. Please look at me."

She slowly turned to him and after a moment's pause, her eyes slowly ascended to meet his. He studied her eyes. He was sure now. Her eyes were his own eyes. Looking at them was like looking into a mirror.

164

The release of ground-breaking data that BioNeura and their partner, Kinney-Harbor were about to share with the world carried an immense responsibility. There were so many constituencies with which to communicate – patients, care givers, physicians who did the clinical studies, employees, investors, the media, medical publications and of course the regulatory agencies.

In light of the care and planning that had to be exercised in such an announcement, and the confidentiality that had to be maintained, a very small team of executives at the two companies were told the news. Before they were told, each had to sign a non-disclosure agreement which made them promise that they wouldn't tell anyone before the news was made public and outlined the retributions that would be exacted if they did. The punishments went well beyond simple dismissal, if someone bought BioNeura shares on their leaked information they could go to jail.

Once they signed the agreement, they were shown the data. Jack enjoyed watching their faces as the BioNeura team soaked it in. He knew this was a once-in-a-lifetime occasion and he was getting to see it played out on the faces of people with whom he had sweated, struggled and scrapped to get to this day – some for well over a decade.

While his team was on their feet, hugging and congratulating one another, Wen sat perfectly still. Tears were running down his smiling face as he thought about the role he had played in finding a piece of the human jig-saw puzzle that Dr. Schwartz told him about all those years ago in the Pacific University lab. He had finally caught her...

Irbesartan (Avapro®)

165

After a non-stop schedule over 48 hours the team completed their preparation for the news conference. Jack's Investor Relations VP gave him the schedule, down to the minute. "Jack," he said, "the press event is all set for the Westin hotel at Grand Central Station, scheduled for 5 p.m. on Monday. The press release will go out at 4:01 that same afternoon, immediately after the close of trading on the stock exchanges. The media won't be happy with the short fuse, but it can't be helped. They'll be pleased with the story. At 4:02 we'll blitz the phones to make sure they've seen the press release and will attend the five o'clock press conference."

"What about interviews?" asked Jack.

"You, Jean-Luc, and Dennis Bowers will lead the way. The Questions and Answers document and the key messages are agreed with Kinney-Harbor. Your media training will happen at two o'clock this afternoon and we shoot the video after that." Jack loathed media training. He knew it was a necessary step to increase the consistency and quality of the message, but he loathed it nonetheless. He also grudgingly acknowledged that he could use a little tune-up on how to manage the media and make it work for the company.

166

"Wow!" exclaimed Jack's VP of Investor Relations "We got 'em all!" It was 4:30 on the day of the press release. "All the major networks want the video backgrounder that we prepared, and they want to interview you and Dennis."

Finally, it was beginning to become real for Jack. Thirty minutes ago, he had announced to the world in his press release the exciting results of the Phase III studies. Now, the world's media was falling over themselves to talk to him, Dennis, and Jean-Luc. In 30 minutes, he would hold his press conference and then a conference call with the financial analysts. For the remainder of the afternoon, into the evening, and then for days, he would be interviewed about this story. Jack mentally braced himself for the physical and mental challenge that lay in front of him.

As his day unfolded, he thought several times how much he wished Diana were here to see this. She was with him from the beginning. She was the one who encouraged Jack to take the job with BioNeura when it was just a bud of a flower a decade ago. She was the one who encouraged him to stay at BioNeura after the merger with Cogitate even though he didn't get the top job. Now this moment, like all his moments of intense professional joy for Jack since Diana died, was wrapped in a wet, heavy blanket of personal emptiness.

In 48 hours it was over, and the word was out. The world knew there was a ray of hope on the horizon for patients with AD – Abetatide®, the new trade name for BIO230.

Now that the Phase III study was unambiguously positive, the odds of getting Abetatide approved and marketed had risen to between 70 and 80 percent, according to industry averages. Since the initial discovery of the BIO230 concept by Wen more than fifteen years earlier, well over one billion dollars had been invested, not including the manufacturing plants, putting the price tag for this drug at somewhere around 1.5 billion dollars.

Jack knew what the vast majority of the public doesn't know that many, many companies have invested that much only to have their entire investments vaporized when they were turned down by the FDA for one of a host of technical reasons. Even though the Phase III studies looked strong, the FDA has a huge responsibility to assess the benefit-risk ratio of a medicine and the agency often rejects new drugs on this basis. "It's not won yet," was the mantra Jack kept repeating to his team.

167

Jack and Dennis sat in Dennis's office outside Summit, New Jersey reviewing the results of their media event. Dennis handed Jack a printout from Bloomberg, the financial service, showing the share price of BioNeura climbing almost vertically since the Phase III data had been announced.

"I now wish I bought your company, Jack. I'd be praised as the biggest friggin' genius in the pharmaceutical industry."

Jack smiled at the odd twists of fate and fortune. "You'll just have to settle for being viewed as the brilliant guy who got a nice piece of Abetatide for what is now viewed as a great price."

"I know, Jack. The human beast is never satisfied, is it?"

"Besides, just think how much worse it could be. You could be Nathaniel Shah at SNS right now!"

"That's cold, Jack."

"Yes, Dennis, *he* is!"

It had only been a week since the positive news on Abetatide, and Shah couldn't take his mind off his disappointment. Despite his efforts to distract himself with his own business, he watched with horror as BioNeura rocketed past SNS in terms of market value, Shah's metric of his self-worth; the metric that compensated for his feelings of genetic inadequacy.

Unlike other disappointments in his career that faded with time, this one was impossible for him to digest. Each day a hard mass of disappointment in his stomach refused to be digested and grew larger. The hard mass was the knowledge that he had the chance to buy BioNeura only a year before the Phase III data showed what they did. It was the realization that with

Abetatide, SNS would now be the largest company in its niche and on its way to becoming one of the major companies in the industry. It was the certainty that Shah, had he landed BioNeura and Abetatide, would be enjoying his rightful recognition as one of the captains of the industry.

How close I was, he obsessed. *How foolish those cowardly Board directors were to go against me. That half-witted American, Callahan doesn't deserve his good fortune. BioNeura was supposed to be mine...I deserve it!*

168

After Jack and Dennis finished their meeting, Jack was whisked back to Manhattan for more meetings with financial analysts and bankers. He couldn't help smiling. Only some months before, Jack was a persona non grata on Wall Street. He couldn't squeeze a nickel out of any of the bankers, and the analysts had downgraded their ratings of BioNeura stock. But since the news about Abetatide, bankers were falling over themselves to raise capital through equity, convertible notes; whatever they could sell. The analysts had all up-graded their ratings to "Strong Buy" or "Out-perform."

As Jack's car made the big sweeping arc onto the access ramp to the Holland Tunnel from New Jersey, the Manhattan skyline came into view across the Hudson. The view never failed to capture Jack's attention and his imagination. In mere minutes, he would be entering the gates of the currency kingdom. Last year he was shunned; now he was returning as the conquering hero.

Jack held no contempt for the bankers. Everyone had a job to do and everything moved fast, especially in this town. You had to enjoy the good times, because they could turn bad in a heartbeat. Recalling a quote from William Butler Yeats that spoke of perseverance, Jack recited it aloud as he admired the Manhattan skyline: "Being Irish, he had an abiding sense of tragedy which sustained him through temporary periods of joy." Jack reflected, *Huh...what a fitting quote for a biotech CEO...*

169

"Wen, how you been? I haven't seen you for a while."

"Hi, Jack. I'm doing great. Wow, *you've* been going like a crazy man for months. So, what's next for my baby, BIO230?"

Jack pulled Wen into his office and shut the door. "Okay, now that the Phase III data are in we need to focus on completing the Biologics License Application or BLA and its European counterpart, the marketing authorization application or MAA. Europe is especially complicated. The first step there is to get experts from two of the member EU countries to serve as 'rapporteur' and 'co-rapporteur.' The job of the rapporteur is to lead the medical and technical review of the MAA and coordinate input from various countries' representatives. The rapporteur typically comes from a country with a long experience in reviewing pharmaceutical files and the co-rapporteur is from one that's less experienced."

"Who do you think will be our rapporteur?"

"Well, we requested Sweden as our first choice and the U.K. as our backup. But after a six-week wait, we were just informed that Germany will be the rapporteur country and Portugal will be co-rapporteur."

"What about for the US?"

"For the FDA, it's more straightforward. Jean-Luc and his team just visited the FDA for a pre-BLA meeting. The purpose of that review was to go over in a summary fashion our latest data and our plans to submit the BLA."

"How'd it go?"

"It went terrific. We've got a great relationship with the FDA, and they agreed to our plan for submitting the BLA to them."

"Can you believe this, Jack? We're actually talking about a BLA! It's been such a long and hard road."

Recalling the Yeats quote, Jack advised Wen. "Let's not count this done until it's done, OK Wen?" Jack continued, "With the news of the Phase III success of Abetatide I expect an avalanche of requests from the families, friends and doctors of patients around the world who will want to get their hands on it. This'll be a public relations nightmare for us."

"Why not let anyone get access to it?"

"Fair question. If we allowed uncontrolled use of the medicine for some patients, it might result in the reporting of unexpected or inexplicable data that could delay the approval of BIO230 for *all* AD patients. Our challenge Wen, is that we have to say 'no' in the most compassionate, consistent and objective way possible, while at the same time working as hard as we possibly can to get the medicine approved as fast as possible."

"You know I'll do all I can to help, Jack."

Oxaliplatin (Eloxatin®)

170

Helmut Schulz dialed the number. He dreaded this call. He and Jack had worked together at Covington Laboratories, and later Jack had recruited him to BioNeura to oversee the manufacturing of BIO230, now Abetatide.

"Jack Callahan's office," answered Clara in her usual pleasant, professional voice. "Oh, Helmut, how are you today? Thanks again for the Belgian chocolates you sent me. They were sinfully delicious."

"You're welcome. I'm happy to contribute to your debauchery. At my age, chocolate is the only way I can impress the ladies." He laughed, and then quickly became serious. "Is Jack available?"

"He is, Helmut. He just got back from New York and is buried with work. He'll be a little impatient to get to it, so I suggest you be your usual efficient self."

"Thanks, I will." As she transferred the call, Helmut became even more nervous.

"Hello, my friend!" said Jack.

"How's my favorite Belgian doing?"

"I'm pretty good, Jack. And you?"

Jack instantly heard the tension in Helmut's voice. And when Helmut was nervous, Jack became very nervous too. "I'm fine, Helmut. What's up?"

"Well Jack, your good news with the clinical study came earlier than any of us expected. While this is great for patients, it presents a massive problem for the manufacturing side of things."

"Wait a minute, Helmut – before we gave Wall Street our estimates of launch timing, we checked with your team and you told us you were confident with our ability to accelerate the production side of things."

"I was, Jack, until I learned of a new problem."

This sounded ominous. Over the years, Jack had learned to read Schulz's business vocabulary. For Helmut, complicated issues were "technical challenges." Only very serious matters he described as "problems."

"When we decided to accelerate the new Swiss manufacturing plant in order to be ready for an earlier launch of Abetatide, we expected no issues. We had done smaller batches many times before without problems."

"Helmut, you're killing me. Tell me, *what's the problem?*"

"Unfortunately, the result from our Swiss plant wasn't as good. I can't sugar coat it – it was a bust."

"What exactly is the problem, Helmut?"

"We're not sure. We know the process is exactly as it is in Dublin. But the finished product from the Swiss plant isn't conforming to the specifications we set for its release."

"So, what do you think is going on?"

"I wish I knew, Jack. We're working on it."

Jack sighed. "So that essentially takes the Swiss plant out of the equation for supplying the launch."

"I'm afraid you're right, Jack. "When will you know the impact on our launch timing?"

"Probably in six weeks or so."

171

The old woman sat in her apartment trying to adjust to her strange new surroundings. The apartment was clean and beautifully furnished. She had lived her entire life on the streets and had slept wherever she could find shelter. This place was as foreign to her as another planet. She was afraid to sit on any of the furniture as it was clean and mostly white. So, she sat on the floor in the middle of the living room and surveyed it from there.

The kitchen had appliances and electronic gadgets that she feared to touch – they looked dangerous and she feared breaking them or hurting herself. She looked down at her feet again. Her shoes were clean and new; the first in her whole long life. She couldn't stop looking at them.

The closet next to her bedroom was a room in itself. It was full of clothing – dresses, blouses, belts, bags, shoes, slacks, and some things she had never seen before. She had only seen such beautiful clothing behind the windows of the elegant shops by which she walked and near which she often slept.

She didn't know for whom all of this clothing was – she couldn't begin to imagine it was all for one woman and certainly not her. She was excited to be surrounded by all of this luxury but also felt very uncomfortable and knew that she didn't belong here. She wanted to leave. She stood up and walked to the window to look upon the streets that she roamed for many months. As she surveyed the city and recalled her time on those streets, she was startled by a knock at the door. She cautiously shuffled across the room and stepped up on a stool in order to peer through the peep hole. Once she focused her sight a wide, toothless grin appeared on her face and her black eyes shined like wet polished onyx.

172

Six weeks had passed while Jack waited for Helmut to see if they could come up with an explanation – and a plan to rapidly fix the manufacturing problem in the Swiss plant or see if a Kinney-Harbor facility could bail them out. At the same time, thoughts of the implications of not fixing it began to crowd Jack's mind. He was exhausted by the stress. It was Friday night at 7:30 and he needed to go home.

When he got to his apartment, he flopped into bed only partially undressed. He was deep asleep in minutes, and before long he had drifted into a dream. He and Diana were walking hand in hand along the beach in Maui. The wind blew warm and fragrant, tousling her hair into a wild, beautiful mess. The golden sun hung large on the horizon, just about to drop into the ocean. The sand sifted through his toes as they walked along a long open beach, alone. She put her arm around his waist as they walked together. Jack was enjoying her closeness again. A phone invaded their lovely moment. Jack was angry and looked around the beach for it, but couldn't find it. Again, the phone rang, more loudly now. Again and again it rang. Pulled rudely from his dream, he rolled over and picked up his phone.

"Hello?" Jack looked at his alarm clock. It was 2:30 A.M.

"Jack, Helmut here. I'm sure I woke you, but you asked me to call you the moment I heard any news."

"Yeah...of course...Helmut." Jack's mind was slow from sleep and it was still on the beach with Diana.

"We've now run a new lot in our Swiss plant that fixed a mistake we made earlier. The Swiss plant is going to be fine, Jack!"

Helmut got no response. "Jack? Are you there?"

"Yeah, Helmut, that's great news," he said flatly, trying to burn into his mind the feeling of Diana's hand in his before he lost it. "It's fantastic news," he added, this time with a little more emotion.

"OK, Jack, you sound tired. We'll let you go back to sleep."

"Helmut, great job...and thank you."

Helmut hung up the phone. *I expected he'd be screaming for joy,* he thought. *Maybe he has a lady friend with him. That would be a good thing....*

Jack quickly rolled back to the same spot in the bed where he'd had his sweet dream. He tried to return back to sleep and Diana on that beach before the sun set. He tried so hard, but his sleep didn't come fast enough. When it did, she was gone.

173

They were ready to submit the Biologics License Application, or BLA, to the FDA. "If we were submitting this same BLA not so long ago, two semi-trailers would pull up to the building and we'd load boxes upon boxes filled with binders of documents," said Jack, reminiscing to Clara. "Usually, the employees surrounded the truck for a picture – the submission of the BLA was a very visible and tangible event. The truck would leave our parking lot and be driven to the FDA in Bethesda, Maryland, and would be met by one of our employees who made sure the BLA was delivered to the FDA."

Jack laughed at the memory.

"Today, it's very different, and in many ways a less real affair. In one key-stroke of a computer, a gigantic electronic file is sent to the FDA. I really miss the sense of teamwork and accomplishment that a company got from rallying around the truck full of BLA papers and watching it drive to the FDA. But we'll make the most of it."

And they did. The entire company was assembled in the parking lot. There was music playing, people were dancing and having a great time.

Then Jack took the microphone and asked that the music be stopped. "Today is the day," he announced proudly, "that we promised delivery of our BLA," he said, "and today is the day it will be delivered!" The BioNeura employees responded with loud whoops and cheers. "To recognize the extra effort you've put in and the weariness you feel, I officially declare this work week over! After the party is over, go home and enjoy a very long weekend. You've earned it!"

As the crowd cheered and clapped, Jack looked at them proudly. It was a great team. Their faces beamed, and as tired as they were, they were revved up and ready for the next phase of the long journey -getting the Abetatide BLA approved.

On Monday, the press release went out: "BioNeura Submits BLA on Schedule" read the headline. Quoting Jack, the release went on to say that he and the rest of the company's management "now await the FDA's determination that the BLA is acceptable for review. The FDA makes that determination within sixty days. If it is accepted for review, they will tell us at that time the status of the review. Given the disease, we expect that the FDA will grant the file 'Priority Review' status, which means a six-month review rather than the normal ten. We have also been granted 'Breakthrough Therapy Designation,' a special designation for compounds that have strong promise to treat a disease for which there is no therapy or current therapy is inadequate."

174

This was a heavy day for Alex Rostov. He was meeting with Dr. Bonner to have the discussion about his mom that he had dreaded for the last several years. Alex's mother had deteriorated to the point that in-home care with a visiting nurse was no longer enough help for her. She had lost all interest in eating, dressing and personal hygiene. Incontinence was a daily event in her life and she was becoming increasingly agitated and verbally aggressive toward everyone. The decision was clear and sadly, unavoidable.

One week later, Dr. Darya Rostov, Nobel Prize winner, mathematician, Medal of Freedom winner, and national treasure was institutionalized.

The home was very nice as rest homes were concerned. The staff seemed genuinely caring and patient. *They are Angels*, Alex thought. He was grateful that there were people to care for those so hopelessly incapacitated. Alex got his mother settled in her room and a wave of guilt crashed over him. On one level, he was relieved that she was here. The burden over the past seven years had been so heavy. On the other hand, he felt the guilt that all sons and daughters feel when a parent enters a home. *Is it pure guilt, or is it that plus a recognition of mortality – hers or mine?* he asked himself.

Alex looked at his mother, who was oblivious to her surroundings. She was beside a window in her wheelchair and gazed out the window with a ten-mile stare, a faint smile on her now gaunt face. From behind her, Alex bent over and kissed her on the top of her head. As he raised his head after kissing her, he suddenly caught his own reflection in the window. The reflection made it appear that his face was on the body of his mother. This vision of what might well be his future chilled him to the bone. When Alex said good-bye to his mother and left the nursing home, he was fully cognizant of the fact that she never would leave this place.

Bretylium Tosylate (Bretylol®)

175

It was 10 p.m. when Jack checked into the hotel in Bethesda. It was far from luxurious, but convenient; only five miles from the FDA building at which they'd be making their fateful presentation to the FDA Advisory Committee in less than a week. The BioNeura team and their consultants had arrived the day before to set up. After unpacking his suitcase, Jack went downstairs to the "Boiler Room," as his team called it, the core of the effort to make the presentation to get BIO230 approved. In this room, they would work to polish up the presentation that they had already polished dozens of times before. They would rehearse the choreography of the presentation, go over expected questions and their answers, and perfect the necessary slide support. Jack surveyed the room, which to his mind resembled a mini NASA control room.

"This is very impressive, Jean-Luc. It's all working?"

"Of course, Jack. Otherwise, I'd be screaming like a crazy Quebecois right now. You see how serene I am?"

Jack knew that inside, Jean-Luc was as serene as a hurricane. "We start at eight o'clock tomorrow morning," Jean-Luc said. "Will you join us?"

"I wouldn't miss it for the world."

Over the next few days, Jack learned firsthand why they called this the "Boiler Room." From all of the PC's, projectors, and people gathered in there, the space was as hot as hell. The hotel's poor ventilation didn't help. As the hours and days clicked by the emotional temperature increased and tempers boiled over from time to time. The room was a pressure cooker.

By the third day, he had seen the presentation more than a dozen times. Each time it got sharper, more concise and more effective. Jean-Luc pulled Jack aside saying, "Jack, we've got less than two days before show time. If you're happy with the core presentation, we should lock it now and have the key presenters rehearse it until they know it backwards and forwards. That'll get us to one day before the actual presentation. We'll use that day to rehearse the question and answer session using slides that we've prepared."

"Sounds good, Jean-Luc. Let's do it."

Jean-Luc looked relieved. He pulled his three team leaders together and explained the game plan.

With 24 hours to go, the Boiler Room had been transformed. The room had been arranged to resemble, as much as possible, the set up for the actual Advisory Committee meeting. It would be their last "mock panel" session – the last in a series of four mock panels conducted over the last few months, each with the goal of preparing the BioNeura team members to give the performance of their lives.

In the room, a series of nine tables were arranged together in the shape of a letter U. Behind each table were two chairs. At the open space of the U next to the Chairman's chair, the podium stood. To the left of that a large projection screen waited. Also in the room were rows of chairs without tables. This was the audience. Seated at the U-shaped table were several consultants hired by BioNeura to play the roles of the FDA Advisory Committee members. Beside the table was a collection of computers on a table with a few chairs, an area called "the bullpen" where company personnel and consultants would wait to be called into the game to answer a question from the FDA or the Committee. A prominent neurologist played the role of Chairman, and performed it as tough as the actual Chairman they would face for real the next day.

The consultants playing the roles of the Committee members had been briefed on the questions the FDA had released to the public the day before. They had also reviewed the sections of the BLA that were relevant to the role they would play. This mock panel meeting, like the other mock-panel meetings they did in the past weeks, took most of the day. After it, everyone had dinner together. Then they all went to their individual rooms, looked over their notes one last time, and tried to get some sleep on what would likely be the biggest day of their professional lives.

The radio alarm clock shocked Jack. Although he had slept poorly, he jumped from his bed, his adrenaline already jolting him into action. By eight o'clock he was at the hotel meeting room at which the real Advisory Committee would soon be convened. The excitement was palpable; nervous chatter buzzed in the room and anxious smiles and thumbs-up gestures were exchanged among BioNeura staff. The meeting room was basic, even austere – plain and functional and very much inconsistent with the magnitude of the decisions made within its walls in its regularly scheduled sessions. In this room, the fate of the lives of millions of Americans are regularly decided.

Surveying the meeting room, Jack spotted a familiar face; Wen Lin's son, Gabriel, who was now in his first year at Johns Hopkins in pre-med. Jack remembered when he first met Gabriel's dad. He recalled that Wen had told him that Gabriel was conceived about the same time Wen conceived the idea for BIO230, that they now called Abetatide. *Amazing,* thought Jack. *Eighteen years later, Gabriel's here cheering on his dad's project – a project as old as Gabriel himself.*

176

The Chairman of the Advisory Committee called the room to order and made his opening remarks almost exactly as they had been spoken in the BioNeura rehearsal the day before. He asked the FDA's advisory committee coordinator to explain how it handled any conflicts of interest. The FDA was advised that there were none.

After the FDA reviewers finished with the administrative items, the Chairman introduced Jean-Luc and invited him to present an overview of the company's presentation. Everything went as planned for Jean-Luc's presentation – no glitches, no dead laptops, no gaffes. The company's principal investigator, an eminent neurologist, added his views on the clinical data on Abetatide.

Jack felt a sense of déjà vu: The actual meeting unfolded precisely as they had rehearsed it. It was as if he were watching a movie that he had seen several times before. He also felt a more powerful and uncomfortable feeling as he sat in the audience, separated from his team–a lack of control over what was unfolding, while being completely accountable for the outcome.

Then the FDA medical reviewer and the biostatistician presented their view of the data, which was somewhat harsher than the mock panelists had presented it–and they dwelled on a side effect in the kidney. Jack hoped his team wouldn't get discouraged or thrown off track by this bit of criticism.

The Chairman retook control. "It is now time for the Committee to pose general questions to the sponsor and the FDA." Dr. Kelleher, the FDA pharmacologist, posed the first one. "I don't quite believe the sponsor has adequately explored the dose-response relationship. Please explain why you believe that you have determined the dose that maximizes the benefit-risk ratio of this drug."

Jean-Luc took the two-part question, which his team had anticipated and the slide to answer the question was already visible on the monitor before him. "Slide twelve, please." Instantly, up popped the slide for all to see and Jean-Luc fielded the question as rehearsed. Dr. Kelleher asked a clarifying question and Jean-Luc advanced two slides and answered it crisply – exactly as planned.

Dr. Jackie Kowalski, the FDA statistician, came next, posing a series of three related questions about the statistical analyses around the key clinical trial, study 102. The BioNeura statistician walked to the podium. By the time she arrived at the podium, the bullpen had several slides on the PC screen on the podium. She quickly scanned them and said "Slide twenty-two, please." The slide emerged within a second…the company's team was doing a great job. The biostatistician delivered a strong answer to Dr. Kowalski's questions, and Jack felt pretty good about this section. The tough questions had not come yet, but he knew they would.

Dr. Bill Hoyers, head of the FDA's Chemistry, Manufacturing, and Controls department, weighed in. "I have a question about the manufacturing process change that you informed us about around the time of your BLA submission. Besides the fact that the modest modification to the process in the Swiss plant was so late in the game, I am unconvinced by the sponsor's claim that the process is stable and under control. I ask the sponsor to please explain again the steps taken and the documentation to confirm that the drug that is now manufactured is indeed the same drug that was studied over the past let me see, eight or nine years or so."

Helmut Schulz took the podium. He had been rehearsing this cameo appearance for weeks. At the mock panel meeting he was flawless. "I will use slides twenty-eight through thirty-three, please," he said in his German-accented baritone voice. He marched through the history, the data, the analyses, the documentation, the independent laboratory analyses, the new controls and procedures, and the on-going studies to prove that the material manufactured in the Swiss factory had the exact same characteristics of the material that was manufactured in Ireland and used in the studies over the past eight years.

Bill Hoyers asked a few more follow-up questions and leaned back in his chair. Jack studied him for a sign. Hoyers must've played some poker in his day, Jack thought. His face gave no hint whatsoever if Helmut had convinced him or not.

"Please explain again the kidney toxicity issue," asked Dr. Williams, the FDA's clinical pharmacologist. "Specifically, what is your explanation for this and what plans do you have for monitoring this going forward should this drug get approved by the FDA?"

As rehearsed, Dr. Scott of BioNeura delivered a very logical and reasoned response. The pressure of the moment caused him to slightly stumble over his material – unlike during the dozen rehearsals before – but he was still very effective. Dr. Williams asked a couple of follow-up questions. Jack studied his face, which revealed a trace of discomfort. Dr. Williams started to ask another question, but then stopped himself. Jack didn't know if that was good or bad.

The questions and answers continued for almost an hour. It was like a tennis match, the crowd's head moving from questioner to responder in a steady volley. At a given moment, it looked bad. Fifteen minutes later, it looked good. Most of the time it was impossible to know *how* it looked. During this review, the financial analysts were reporting to their offices and clients via their mobile devices right up to the moment when the Chairman called for a one-hour lunch break.

After the lunch break, the Chairman reconvened the meeting. "The FDA serves to protect and foster the health of the American public," he said. "Accordingly, before we begin the vote on the formal questions that the FDA has posed to the Committee, it is our custom to open the floor to the public in order to benefit from the insights and points of view from interested citizens. We now invite our first speaker to address the FDA's advisory panel and the FDA itself. As you do, please identify yourself and disclose if you have received any financial support or assistance from any entity to be here today."

At this point, a woman in her early seventies stepped forward. She was attractive, fit and confident. "Thank you, Mr. Chairman," she said into the microphone. "My name is Rita Caruso. I have received no financial incentives to be here or to say what I plan to say. My husband was diagnosed with Alzheimer's disease nine years ago. I represent the tens of millions of wives, husbands, sons and daughters who are the caregivers of the more than five million Americans stricken with Alzheimer's disease."

Her delivery was strong and self-assured, and she had the attention of everyone in the room. "The cost of this disease to society can be measured in dollars and cents. The Alzheimer's Association estimates that our nation spends approximately 300 billion dollars per year on the care of patients with Alzheimer's disease. This is a staggering economic metric but it's only getting worse as some estimates say we will spend one trillion dollars per year by 2050." She paused a moment, jutted forward her chin and readied herself for her next point. "How does one value the slow, grinding destruction of a husband, wife or lover? How does one value the loss of missed milestones of the human existence – weddings, births, graduations? Just as tragic, how does one value the literally countless lost memories, special souvenirs of one's accumulated experience on earth – the very essence that binds members of a family? The patient stricken with Alzheimer's disease is the shell of the person he once was, lingering long after his mind had melted away. Like the rusted hull of a freighter still stranded on a reef, it is a constant reminder of tragedy and loss."

Mrs. Caruso went on to tell the story of her and her husband, Joe – how they met and the wonderful family they'd made together. She described his long, slow forced march to limbo. "He recognizes no one in his world now. He is that wreck on the reef. When we consider that over five million Americans are stricken with Alzheimer's disease, the annual human cost in terms of the toll exacted by this evil disease is incalculable." She looked at the Committee members. "We need your help!" she said through quivering lips.

The audience fidgeted in their chairs, deeply affected by the human tragedy of the Carusos and millions like them. Mrs. Caruso slowly scanned the panel, spending a moment to connect her soft but strong blue eyes with theirs. "The estimated twenty million caregivers and the over five million patients they care for need help. We hope this learned and wise Committee finds Abetatide acceptable and approves it as soon as possible. Thank you."

"Thank you, Mrs. Caruso," said the Chairman. "We appreciate the pain and suffering you have endured, and our hearts go out to those you represented so well today." Mrs. Caruso nodded slightly to acknowledge his remarks, turned and walked confidently toward her seat – but she remained standing, determined to make her presence, and that of those she represented felt during the Committee's voting. The Chairman invited her to sit. She nodded her acknowledgement of his invitation – and remained standing.

Several more advocates for patients took the floor and shared similar stories. By the time they were done, over an hour had passed and there wasn't a dry eye in the room. When they were finished, the meeting room hung with a heavy silence.

Finally, the Chairman cleared his throat and called his panel to order. "As is our established routine," he said, "we will now refer to the five questions that we publicly published two days ago and the panel members will vote on each one. With each vote, we give the panel member the opportunity to comment for the public record."

177

The funeral for Dr. Darya Rostov was a beautiful and respectful homage to her life and her contributions to mathematics, astrophysics and to her country. As a testimony to her stature and contributions, representatives from the Nobel Prize organization, NASA, and the ranking U.S. Senator on the Defense Committee attended the memorial services.

Alex Rostov, her son, provided the eulogy. It was a warm and tender recollection of Dr. Rostov as a mother, scientist, Russian and American. But even as he spoke, Alex could not banish from his thoughts the feeling, or maybe the fear, that his mother's fate would also be his own – a "long goodbye" followed by a demise of which he would have no awareness. He felt guilty thinking so much about himself while everyone was celebrating his mother. But despite his guilt, he couldn't shake his growing fear.

178

The vote would unfold before their very eyes in less than an hour. The outcome of 15 years, 1.5 billion dollars and countless man-hours of work would be known in 60 minutes. The weight of the moment was crushing.

Jack looked at his team, some on the floor with the Committee and some in the audience. They were watching him. He gave a confident smile and nod. They returned nervous nods, but their hands betrayed their worry – wringing fingers, fidgeting with pens or shuffling papers.

Each member of the BioNeura team was re-playing his own performance: *Did I make that point clearly enough? Was my analysis convincing? Did I finally answer his question or did he just get tired of asking it? Did I blow it for the whole company...for all those poor patients... and their families?*

The meeting room rustled audibly as they made themselves comfortable for the last act in the drama that would now unfold. Jack's mind went to a metaphor he found odd at this moment, but it seemed to fit. *We're like the crowd outside St. Peter's Church awaiting the vote of the College of Cardinals*, he thought. *The difference is that we'll see the voters.* He fastened on thoughts of the white smoke released when a new Pope was elected. *The white smoke they were now awaiting would be just a blur of emails, cell phone calls, texts, tweets and other modern-day smoke signals. And if Abetatide is rejected, the white smoke will be from the burned dreams of the families of Alzheimer's patients waiting for help. Not to mention the enormous amount of invested capital, over a million hours of work, and many, many billions of dollars in lost market value reflected in the crushed BioNeura and Kinney-Harbor stock prices.*

The Chairman of the Committee began. "On question one, did the sponsor demonstrate that Abetatide can be reliably manufactured and that the manufacturing process is under control? Please enter your vote on the device in front of you. Enter Yes, No, or Abstain. The computer will project the results of the voting on the screen as soon as you have all entered your vote." All eyes went to the blank blue screen and were locked there. No one dared look away.

"Ten yes, two no, and one abstained. The FDA needs to know why we voted this way to help them decide what to do with the sponsor's BLA. So, let's now explain our votes for the record."

The Chairman then asked the external panel member brought in to consult on the manufacturing question. "I believe the process is under control." However, I have one thought. Wouldn't it be a tragedy if Abetatide were approved and after a year or so, the adjustment needed in the Swiss plant needed to be done in the Dublin manufacturing plant and some patients couldn't get any Abetatide? The question is more a clinical question, but I offer it for the panel's discussion. Perhaps the Agency could require the sponsor to prove they can manufacture the drug consistently over a longer period than the three lots required by our regulations."

Jack winced. This would mean, at a minimum a significant delay of the approval. If it bothered the physicians on the panel enough, it could postpone the approval even longer. "Thank you," said the Chairman. Then he turned to Hoyers. "Please clarify for the record why you answered the question as you did."

Jack held his breath as Hoyers cleared his throat and squirmed in his chair. "I answer affirmatively," he said. "The process is under control according to our definition of having successfully manufacturing three lots in succession. The sponsor accomplished this in their Dublin plant." Jack exhaled. That meant the two manufacturing experts, one from FDA and one external, both voted with BioNeura.

"OK," said the Chairman. *Man, that was a lot more of a cliff-hanger than I thought it would be*, thought Jack. But they had won that question.

Jack kept track of the votes of each member on each vote. It reminded him of when he was a boy in Chicago, keeping the box score at Wrigley Field when he watched the Cubs. *First inning,* he thought. *Home team is up one to nothing. No errors.* He readied himself for the next inning.

Without pause, the Chairman moved on to the question about the adequacy of the data regarding Abetatide's safety. Based on the excellent presentation made by BioNeura's experts, Jack felt this would go smoothly. The clinical expert of the FDA, summarizing his thoughts and concerns said, "I am reasonably comfortable that there is likely no obvious major safety issue with Abetatide, but I am concerned that the number of patients exposed to BIO230 may be too small to be certain. I would recommend that the sponsor perform a registry of patients to track the safety of the drug in a larger number of patients and over a longer period of time." Then the rest of the Committee members asked questions, made their points, and voted.

"Nine votes in favor, four no votes," announced the Chairman. Jack was suddenly unsure of how things were going as they headed to some difficult questions.

"Now we wade into the black art of statistics," began the Chairman with a smile. "Question three involves the validity of the statistical methods and analyses used by the sponsor to demonstrate that Abetatide plus standard therapy was more effective than those receiving standard therapy alone."

The chairman asked if there were any final comments before voting on the statistical question. The FDA statistician raised his hand and was invited to speak. He didn't at all fit the stereotype of his profession. Dr. Frank Ellington was cool. He was casually but smartly dressed, wore trendy eyeglasses, and was tall, fit and tan. He looked more like a professional tennis player than a number jockey. He spoke in crisp and clear bursts.

"I would have posed the question a little differently," he said. "No matter. A couple of considerations. First, BioNeura chose to stop Study 102 before it was meant to be stopped. Second, they made a modification of statistical analysis plan before the data were un-blinded, which is not necessarily a bad thing as this is often done, but I just want the committee to be aware of this before I make a couple of comments."

Ellington then launched into what sounded like a foreign language to most, talking about sample size, randomization schedules, various forms of bias, subset analyses, statistical methods and a host of similarly technical comments. The rest of the Committee appeared to follow him but

Dr. Ellington's dissertation went well beyond Jack's training in business school and his on-the-job training in the industry.

While this performance was going on, Jack watched BioNeura's biostatistician for any signs of worry. As flashing neon lights replaced her usually calm eyes, Jack became worried. She leaned over and whispered in Jack's ear, "I can't figure him out. This guy may be back-tracking on what he told us when we asked him over a year ago about the statistical conditions under which we'd stop either of our studies at an interim efficacy analysis."

Jack nodded and leaned back into his seat. He recalled the FDA agreed with their plan but with the usual qualifiers, which went something like, "If the data were clean and the statistics unambiguously met the agreed thresholds for stopping the study, they would support stopping early one or both of our studies." Now the statistician seemed to be advising his fellow committee members to consider various esoteric considerations when they voted on this topic.

Finally, the chairman glanced at his watch and then asked Ellington to summarize. Ellington seemed a little disappointed, having his soapbox kicked out from under him but he recovered quickly.

"All things considered, in my opinion, the statistics clearly prove that there is a treatment effect of Abetatide."

Jack's heart leapt…and then sank with Ellington's next comment. "However, if one used the statistical methods that the sponsor originally proposed before they started their Phase III program, the magnitude of the treatment effect would be somewhat diminished and the strength of the statistical difference would be decreased."

Ellington paused, too long for anyone's comfort. He was savoring the power he was holding over the Committee and the audience.

Step up, Ellington! Screamed Jack in his mind. *Step up to the agreement we made over a year ago!*

"In summary," intoned Ellington, "while it is not *exactly* what I would have done, the sponsor's statistical approach was reasonable and appropriate."

Again, Ellington played a long pause for dramatic effect.

Now the chairman lost the last shred of his patience.

"Dr. Ellington?" he asked, exasperatedly, wanting to know if he had yet another comment.

"I am done, Mr. Chairman."

The chairman continued collecting comments from the remaining committee members.

When this process was done, he asked for a vote and when seeing the results, announced, "Let the record show that on question three, we have ten yes votes, two no votes and one vote to abstain."

Jack hadn't noticed it before, but he was sweating heavily and his hands were cramped from strangling his armrests. He forced himself to breathe regularly and deeply and after a few minutes he calmed down...a little.

"Now on to question four," began the Chairman. Jack knew this one was considered by most experts to be the crucial one.

"The FDA usually requires two positive adequate and well-controlled trials, in an appropriate group of patients with the disease to approve a new medicine. In certain circumstances, such as serious diseases for which no therapy is available or if studies would be very difficult to perform the FDA is often asked to make a judgment call: is *one* adequate and well-controlled study sufficient considering all issues, or must the sponsor conduct a second trial?"

It helped that the FDA had confirmed to BioNeura that a single large, well-run trial with strong and unambiguous results would likely be enough. But given the gravity of the decision, the Committee itself would have to be convinced that the data from this one study were compelling enough for FDA approval.

As the committee clinicians prepared to weigh in, Jack began the waterworks again as beads of sweat popped from his brow and upper lip and his heart thumped in his chest.

The chairman invited final questions and discussion before the vote. Based on the intel that his team had collected of the four clinicians, one was likely neutral – as far as BioNeura could tell – one was likely positive, one was vocally very negative and for one they had no idea. The negative one, Dr. Cox, was purported to be closely but unofficially aligned with Upton-Phipps, the pharmaceutical powerhouse that was developing a future potential competitor to Abetatide. Jack hoped Cox would neither start nor finish the neurologists' commentary. The fourth expert neurologist, Dr. Winningham gave no clues on his views.

"Dr. Cox," said the Chairman, "as you are the newest member of the panel, I invite you to make the first comment or pose the first question from the neurologist's point of view."

"Damn it," said Jack under his breath.

"I wish I were more convinced by the data," Dr. Cox began, "A diagnosis of Alzheimer's is a death sentence followed by interminable solitary confinement for the patient and hard labor for his caregiver before the sentence is carried out. My colleagues and I pray for the day that we can offer our patients a cure. Despite our prayers and hope for a treatment or cure, I must force myself to not allow the desperation of our patients to cloud my judgment on this matter. The first rule of medicine we are taught is that of Hippocrates: 'First, do no harm.' Taking that axiom to mind, I am bothered by the kidney side effects seen in some patients in both studies."

Cox launched into a detailed summary of the side-effect profile of BIO230. He offset that with a repetition of some of the statistics questions raised earlier by the FDA statistician:

"I want to congratulate the sponsor for having cast some encouraging rays of sunshine on an otherwise gloomy landscape of Alzheimer's disease therapies, and I encourage them to continue the development of Abetatide.....However, I wish their results were more conclusive."

This got the audience humming.

Many observers in the room began furiously drumming their thumbs over their mobile devices, sending messages from their seats directly to the in-boxes of their clients: investors, hedge funds, publishers, and companies.

"Your comments are noted, Dr. Cox. Now to our next external expert, Dr. Wilma Hechter."

"Thank you, Mr. Chairman," she said, "While I share some of Dr. Cox's concerns on the risk-benefit ratio of Abetatide, I find myself much more on the positive side of that ratio. The drug clearly arrests the disease and in light of the devastating nature of the disease, the kidney side effects are acceptable, especially as they are easily monitored with standard blood tests and they are reversible with decreasing or discontinuing BIO230. If the panel wants more details of my rationale, I would be happy to give it. In the interest of time, I'll stop there."

Emotions in the room swung once again.

"Dr. Gupta, any comments or questions on question four?" asked the Chairman.

A shy, quiet, and brilliant man Dr. Gupta was barely audible, despite his microphone. The audience became still in an attempt to hear his soft-spoken words.

"I understand the views of my colleagues and unfortunately find myself in between them," said Dr. Gupta. "I ask myself; shouldn't the bar be lowered for a disease like Alzheimer's? On the other hand, if we lower the bar here, how can we objectively do so in a way that medicines that we review in the future get equal consideration? I struggled and ultimately failed to identify objective criteria for lowering this 'bar,' as we call it. Having failed, I fall back upon the regulations, which we are told by the FDA are relatively clear, with room for judgment. Two trials are *usually* needed but exceptions are made in certain circumstances. As a neurologist, I find the results in Study 102 exciting and compelling. Patients on Abetatide in Study 101 were treated for about nine fewer months than those in Study 102. The graphs that the FDA presented to us today show that patients in both studies were on the same trajectory at a given duration of therapy. This tells me that if Study 101 continued, it would have likely shown the same strong results of Study 102 and this is supported by the strong favorable trends on multiple endpoints we saw in Study 101. So, I leave to the FDA, the question of whether or not the company met the guidelines they were given by the FDA regarding what it would take to approve Abetatide with one Phase III study."

The audience hummed again, and so did Jack's mind, wondering, *If the FDA required us to do another Phase III study, this would mean a five-year delay and at least another half billion dollars. We don't have the cash, precious patent life would be wasted and Kinney-Harbor may not want to take the chance. This could sink the company and kill this new medicine.*

"Dr. Winningham, the floor is yours," announced the Chairman.

Dr. Peter Winningham was without doubt the world's premier neurologist. When he was only in his late thirties he had already established his brilliance by publishing breakthrough data on the role of the dopamine receptor in Parkinson's disease.

This breakthrough led to the use of a new class of medicines that delayed the development of this destructive disease. That contribution was more than thirty years ago, and since then Winningham's reputation had only grown. His name was always at the forefront of new breakthroughs in neurology.

As Dr. Winningham began, the audience became silent out of respect for this éminence grise of neurology.

"As you know, I have an interest in Alzheimer's disease," said Winningham.

That's the understatement of the decade, thought Jack. Winningham had literally written the book on Alzheimer's disease, his textbook *Contemporary Principles of the Diagnosis and Treatment of Alzheimer's Disease* being used by medical students throughout the world.

RACE FOR THE MIND

"I have already disclosed my previous association with BioNeura," said Dr. Winningham for the record, "having consulted for the company about eight years ago on the very first clinical trial of Abetatide. The FDA has decided that this prior association presents no conflict of interest. And now, having dealt with the preliminaries, I have a few points to make on this question...The theory around amyloid plaque as the main cause of Alzheimer's disease, while interesting and with scientific merit, has not been categorically proven, at least to this interested observer..." Jack loved Winningham's old-fashioned and eloquent delivery.

"However," Winningham continued, "we are not asked to comment on the cause of this pernicious disease, but rather on whether or not an experimental drug arrests the disease in a way that causes less harm than the benefit it delivers. I suggest that we consider the current therapy for the disease. In a word, it is poor. At best, current therapy delays the symptoms a little and gives caregivers and physicians a positive but fleeting period in which they are helping their stricken loved one or patient. A few months or maybe a year of symptomatic delay is worth something meaningful, considering the hard road ahead for the caregiver and his patient. Despite the treatment, the disease marches on in complete defiance of this therapeutic intervention."

Dr. Winningham took a drink of water and moved his comments into another gear. "Having shared my dim view of current therapies, I turn my attention to the side-effect question. My esteemed colleague Dr. Cox correctly pointed out that Abetatide increases the side effects when added to current therapies. While this is true, I prefer to focus on the burden of these additional side effects versus the benefit of the additional medicine." Jack held his breath once more. This meeting was more taxing than his usual workouts; his heart rate was elevated and he was sweating profusely now.

Dr. Winningham continued. "It is my view that the effectiveness of Abetatide is *underestimated* in study 102. I believe that had this trial run to its originally intended completion date, given the progressively destructive nature of the disease, the treatment effect would have been significantly greater. Based on the side-effect data I've reviewed, I am not bothered by it. And we did not see it increasing over time in study 102. Therefore, while I wish we had more data to evaluate, my judgment of the data provided by the sponsor proves to my satisfaction that Abetatide adds far more benefit than it costs in terms of side effects and it appears to be the first disease-modifying therapy we have ever seen."

"Thank you, Dr. Winningham," said the Chairman. Getting no more comments, he asked the panelists to vote. Within a minute, the results were on the screen, "Eight yes votes and three no votes," announced the Chairman. "And one vote to abstain…"

He let out a long sigh and furrowed his brow as he looked at the serial abstainer before announcing the next question. The stress and fatigue from the last seven hours were showing. The Chairman was visibly angry at the one Committee member who continued to abstain and wondered…*Why had he bothered participating if he hadn't an opinion or the courage to share it? Wasted space.*

Jean-Luc looked around at his colleagues, now his good friends. He thought back to when he had joined this company, even before it was called BioNeura, before a single one of the others had come aboard. There was Wen Lin, whom Jean-Luc had coaxed out of Pacific University to join him and take his idea to fruition. And, of course, Jack – how they had instantly hit it off in Las Vegas all those many years ago.

Next to Jean-Luc was Helmut, breathing heavily under his ample girth. He had overcome huge challenges at the eleventh hour to successfully manufacture Abetatide. Jean-Luc's eyes moved from face to face as he felt a wave of emotion well up inside of him. He was so proud to be part of this team. Whatever the outcome, they, together, had given everything they had to the effort. Jean-Luc pretended to scratch his nose so he could catch a tear before it fell.

The chairman began again, "Ladies and gentlemen, we are ready for the last of our five questions. The question is: Considering all aspects, do the data presented provide substantial and compelling evidence that support the approval of Abetatide for the treatment of patients with Alzheimer's disease? You have all had ample opportunity to express your views as you voted on your previous questions. Are there any remaining comments or questions before the final vote?" he peered over his glasses and scanned the panel, "Seeing that there are none, please cast your votes."

179

It was late in the evening in Geneva. In his darkened office, Nathaniel Shah was watching the webcast of the Advisory Committee proceedings. He had almost finished the bottle of scotch that he had opened at the beginning of the meeting more than seven hours earlier.

Shah was deeply conflicted about all this, and he tried to quiet his conflict with the liquor. He wanted his nemesis, BioNeura, to fail...of course he did. They were his principal competitor for the top company in the field of neurology. And he detested that Callahan, who was just lucky, not good.

But if BioNeura failed, Shah's Board would be proven right in their decision to overrule Shah and not acquire BioNeura due to the risk involved. Shah couldn't begin to face *that* humiliation. Finally, Shah wanted a new medicine approved for Alzheimer's patients and the data supporting its approval were compelling to him. After all, he was a physician himself. He recognized the suffering those patients and their caregivers had to endure.

He just wanted to be the one to provide that new medicine for them. He poured himself another glass.

Esmolol (Brevibloc®)

180

It happened very fast, as if the previous few hours had been just a wind-up for this vote. Within ten minutes it was all over. The votes were now on the screen.

"The Committee has spoken," said the Chairman, "Ten yes votes, two no votes and one vote to abstain. Before I give my concluding remarks, let me remind everyone that an advisory committee *recommendation* is exactly that. While the FDA generally accepts the recommendations of an expert advisory committee, it is not bound to accept the recommendations and has on several occasions decided to overrule them. That said, let the record show that the vote was strongly in favor of Abetatide's approval, and that many of the votes against approval or to abstain had to do with a request for more supportive data, which could be collected after an FDA approval. In light of this, we will recommend to the FDA that if they approve Abetatide, the FDA should gain a commitment from the sponsor to complete an appropriate post-approval study or studies to confirm and extend the efficacy and/or safety data that we have seen to date. In so doing, we can get Abetatide approved as soon as possible while the sponsor collects more data to ensure us that drug is indeed as effective and safe as the available data show. Our meeting is adjourned, thank you."

The Committee members gathered their notes and shook one another's hands as the room became a buzz of controlled, excited chaos.

"Mom, the FDA's advisory panel said yes!" a young woman sitting near Jack shouted into her cell phone over the din. "Dad should be able to get on this new medicine before he gets much worse! We'll have him longer!"

Tears ran down her face and she nodded as she listened to what her mother was saying in reply. Jack smiled as he walked past her. Then he heard a stock analyst talking into her mobile:

"Yeah, Abetatide will almost certainly be approved within a couple of months. We made the right call to invest in BioNeura! It's going to soar tomorrow morning when trading resumes."

BioNeura's PR agent forced her way to Jack and began guiding him to a nearby media room, where CNN, Bloomberg, CNBC, ABC, Fox – all the networks and media outlets wanted to interview him. As he was pushed along, Jack spotted Dennis from Kinney-Harbor. Their eyes met and with a big smile and fists pumping, Dennis showed Jack how he felt. Dennis himself was being pulled by his own PR staff to meet the media. The two men had rehearsed the key messages for every possible outcome. While they would be separate for most of the interviews, their messages would be virtually identical, different only in style.

As he entered the media room filled with bright lights and cameras, Jack heard the CNN reporter speaking into his camera:

"*In medical news, this is the event of the decade. The first medicine proven to arrest the advance of Alzheimer's disease, Abetatide, was recommended for approval just moments ago by an Advisory Committee to the Food and Drug Administration or FDA. Most experts believe that the FDA will soon approve Abetatide and that the medicine's approval in Europe would likely follow within a few months as the Abetatide file has been under active regulatory review there for several months....*"

The media frenzy didn't end until around midnight, when the West Coast news reporters had filed their evening stories. Back at the hotel, Jack spotted Clara tipping a bellman.

"Clara, I thought you'd be on the town celebrating with the team," Jack said. "Oh, I'm going there now," she said. "I just had to take care of something for a friend."

As she spoke, Jack noticed she had a strangely sad smile on her face. He wondered, fleetingly, *why wasn't she looking happy after such a great day?*

"OK, I'll be there soon," Jack nodded, "I just want to change clothes and catch my breath."

"See you there, Jack," said Clara, and she turned and walked away.

As Jack entered his room, he tossed his key on the table and clicked on the television and saw his face on the TV, from an earlier interview. In the light of the TV he noticed something on the table. When he switched on the light above it, he saw that it was a bottle of champagne in an ice bucket. There was an envelope propped up against it. Jack walked over to the table and opened the envelope.

"*Dear Jack,*" began the letter.

He instantly recognized the handwriting. He slowly sank into the chair by the table, one hand on the letter and the other hand clutching his forehead. "I knew you would do it!" the letter continued,

"I am so proud of you and so happy for you! You remember that night at the Chateau in Normandy all those years ago when we decided that you'd take the job with BioNeura? You remember that you ordered Dom Perignon Enothèque 1973 to toast to our decision?"

Jack looked through his rising tears to see the same brand and vintage in front of him in the ice bucket.

"Drink from this bottle, Jack, and toast to the times we had together. Toast to the life we lived. Toast to the lives you will improve and extend with your new medicine, Jack. One more thing, my love. If I know you, you may have remained alone since I've gone. I hope not, but if you have, it's time now for a new beginning. Toast to your new beginning. Give yourself a life. You have just given millions theirs!"

Jack could hardly read now through his tears. At the end of the letter, she had written, "*I love you from far away, Diana.*" Below her name was an imprint of her lips made from her favorite lipstick. Jack brought the lips to his. As he did, he smelled her perfume, a drop of which she had placed on the letter long ago. It was a sensual and emotional experience that overcame him. He collapsed into a chair and sobbed.

After a while he regained himself. As he reflected on her words, he realized she was right – he *had* died with her.

He read the letter again and again, kissing her lipstick lips each time and trying to recall the softness of her lips. He opened the champagne and poured himself a glass. "To Diana," he said, raising his glass, "My lover. My champion. My best friend. My only love."

In the background, the TV droned on about the "historic" approval of Abetatide. But Jack was somewhere else now. Lost in memories of Diana. Each memory brought a smile, and he raised the glass over and over in her memory. Finally, the champagne, the stress of the committee meeting, and finding Diana's letter began to take over. He reached for the letter and kissed her lips goodnight. Then threw himself into sleep, hoping to meet her there.

181

Alex Rostov waited in the waiting room he had come to know so well when he had accompanied his mother Darya to this office. Now it was his turn. When Alex had first noticed signs in himself that were reminiscent of those he saw in his mother, he had come to this very room to wait for a consultation with Dr. Bonner. After several tests, Bonner had confirmed that Alex had early-onset AD.

This time, Alex wasn't quite sure why he was here. It was a just a few months after he had received confirmation of his disease, and Bonner had called and asked if Alex could come in to see him. Alex feared the worst... *was his AD more advanced than Bonner had thought?*

After twenty minutes in the waiting room, Alex saw Dr. Bonner's head appear around the door. "Alex, come on in." They shook hands and Alex followed Bonner to the same large leather sofa where his mother had sat on her first visit to his office.

"How are you?" asked Dr. Bonner.

"Physically, I'm fine, Doc. Mentally, I'm a wreck. I saw how this disease ravaged my mother...."

"I understand your anxiety, Alex," said Bonner, "It's *very* common and perfectly understandable in your circumstance, having witnessed it firsthand. You'd be surprised how many people I've seen though, in your *exact position*... which is why I'm hoping what I share with you brings hope.... So, let me get to why I wanted to see you." He saw Alex go a bit pale and start to squirm and added, "No, Alex – please don't panic – it's nothing bad. . . I'm participating in a new clinical study on Abetatide, formerly known as BIO230. Abetatide has already been proven effective in patients with more advanced Alzheimer's disease than you have. This new study is in patients like you who are showing very early symptoms of the disease. The hope is that arresting the disease early will give the brain a chance to stop the advance of the disease. Are you interested?...Wait... before you answer, you should know that it's a placebo-controlled trial, which means you'll have a 50-50 chance of getting a sugar pill instead of Abetatide. I'm pretty sure your mom would have done it – and would want you to do it too."

"Well then, *I'll* do it...Yes, I'll do it...Sign me up," Alex stated, nodding firmly, deciding as he spoke.

His race for his mind had just begun.

> *This space is reserved for the structure of*
> *the first medicine to cure Alzheimer's disease.*
> *We hope to be able to fill it in as soon as possible.*

ACKNOWLEDGMENTS

It takes on average, fifteen years and one to two billion dollars to transform an idea from the scientist's laboratory into a medicine on the shelf of your local pharmacy. While I didn't spend billions developing this book, I did take about fifteen years from the first draft to publish the book – including several multi-year periods of dormancy and countless re-drafts. I am deeply grateful to my friends who from time-to-time patiently reviewed one or more drafts of *Race for the Mind* and gave me honest and helpful advice: Joe and Paula Boudreau: Phil and Judy Clifford; Lynda Durso, Lars Ekman, MD, PhD; Sander and Mechele Flaum; Dick and Barb Haiduck; Bill Hunter; Mike Powell, PhD; David Redlick; Bill and Sue Ringo; Mark Robinson; Clay Siegall, PhD and of course my hardest-working advisor, my wife Marie Welch.

During my long journey while writing this book, I learned what real writers already know – that writing is *hard work* and it's a craft with important methods, tricks of the trade, conventions and proven formulae. Along the way, I turned to some experts who gave me important guidance on and suggestions for character development, character arcs and developing tension in the story. These lessons led to one major reconstruction of the book and several significant re-models for which I cursed them at the time as it required a lot of work on my part. However, their guidance was invaluable and now that the work is behind me, I can thank the following individuals for the value they added to the final product: Rhonda Cawthorn, Jane Harrigan and James Morgan.

AUTHOR'S NOTES

I wrote *Race for the Mind* for several reasons. First, I minored in English Literature in college and always enjoyed reading fine prose. While I would never dream of counting *Race for the Mind* among those works, I wanted to attempt to write a competent novel of which I could be sufficiently proud to publish. Second, I have spent 40 years in the business of making medicines and during this time, I was often frustrated by how poorly and one-sidedly the pharmaceutical industry was treated by the media. I thought – perhaps naively hoped – that I could tell an engaging story and while telling it, stealthily educate the general public about another way the industry could be portrayed. That other side of the story would be the one of terrible odds, horrendous sums of money and the stunningly long drug development process and also, of the courageous and dedicated men and women who devote their entire lives to helping people they have never met live a longer and better quality life. Last but not least, my family like so many other families has been visited several times by Alzheimer's disease.

All of the characters in *Race for the Mind* are entirely fictitious and creations of my imagination. Therefore, any conclusions that are drawn about the real identities of the characters would be those of the reader. *Race for the Mind* isn't autobiographical. Since an author is often advised to "write what you know," inevitably some parallels may be found between my personal story and those of one or more characters in this book but this is coincidental and a product of writing what I know.

The chemical structures that appear every fifth chapter are those of some of the most widely consumed or prescribed medicines today. Several of them are medicines in which the author played a role.

ABOUT THE AUTHOR

Dan has spent his entire career in the pharmaceutical business – decades – in multi-national pharmaceutical companies and smaller, US-based biotech companies. He has had a leadership role in the development and launch of several "block-buster" medicines; some of the most prescribed in the world and in break-through medicines for life-threatening diseases. Dan also worked in venture capital and private equity firms; essential sources of capital for developing new companies and medicines. His experience leading over a dozen successful biotech companies include roles as CEO, Chairman of the Board, Board Director and Advisor. Dan travels the world, loves his wife of 40 years, his two adult sons, fly fishing, ice hockey and everything about wine. He makes his home in California and Colorado.

Made in the USA
Columbia, SC
26 September 2018